# Praise for
## *The Second Chan*

"A charming novel of breathing life into things (and people!), *The Second Chance Store* tells the story of a floundering woman who needs a purpose. She finds one in a story line about love and loss, one that will both capture your heart and warm it, with a satisfying ending that will leave you searching for other books by Lauren Bravo."

—Courtney Cole, *New York Times* bestselling author

"If you've ever wandered into a thrift store and wondered what the story was behind all that stuff, Lauren Bravo's moving and touching novel answers that question. *The Second Chance Store* is a charming tale of why people (and things) deserve a second (or third, or fourth) chance to get it right when it comes to loss, love, and life. I loved this book filled with humor, humanity, and hope." —Lian Dolan, author of *Lost and Found in Paris*

"I think I've been waiting for a novel like *The Second Chance Store* for my whole reading life. This is a luscious, shimmering book of depth and delicacy. It's sad, hilarious, tender, brutal, brilliantly observed—there is a sense of magic on every page."
—Daisy Buchanan, author of *Careering* and *Insatiable*

"Lauren Bravo is one of my very favorite writers."
—Dolly Alderton, author of *Ghosts*

"Laugh-out-loud funny but also poignant and tender. . . . An absorbingly special debut novel. I devoured in equal measure the delicious descriptions of food and the moving vignettes of preloved treasures peppered throughout the book, while the nineties and noughties nostalgia had me gasping with pleasure."
—Laura Price, author of *Single Bald Female*

"An absolute triumph. It's so rare to find a book that you feel so invested in . . . So ruddy good. And clever. And funny . . . It was like *High Fidelity* for charity shops . . . The writing is so natural, and there's a sense of wonder on every page . . . Honestly, it's just a brilliant book. I loved it so much."

—Eva Rice, author of *The Lost Art of Keeping Secrets*

"Just like that once-in-a-lifetime charity shop find, this is a gleaming prize to be treasured. Lauren Bravo is witty and thoughtful in her exploration of our relationship with objects and trends, believing that just as a pair of shoes can have many, many lives, so can the people that wear them."

—Caroline O'Donoghue, author of *Promising Young Women*, *Scenes of a Graphic Nature*, and the Gifts series

"My goodness how I loved this book! Lauren Bravo's characters are so beautifully formed they instantly felt like friends—especially Gwen, whose accomplished and authentic voice captured me so effortlessly I missed her when our conversation was over. *The Second Chance Store* is full of sharp observations on life, loss, regret, and self-preservation, but it's also spilling over with wit and hope. Cleverly interwoven with stories of the myriad reasons items find their way into charity shops, the joy, friendship, and ultimate enlightenment Gwen discovers offers a quirky and poignant reminder that one person's trash is always somebody else's treasure."

—Julietta Henderson, author of *The Funny Thing About Norman Foreman*

"Full of relatable anecdotes, lively, funny, and modern, *The Second Chance Store* is a moving tale of emancipation and friendship. I loved it!"

—Margaux Vialleron, author of *The Yellow Kitchen*

# The
# Second
# Chance
# Store

## Also by Lauren Bravo

*What Would the Spice Girls Do?*
*How to Break Up with Fast Fashion*

# The Second Chance Store

A NOVEL

# LAUREN BRAVO

AVON

*An Imprint of* HarperCollins*Publishers*

"Love to Love You Baby." Words and music by Donna Summer, Giorgio Moroder, and Pete Bellotte. Copyright © 1976 Rick's Music Inc. (BMI), Sweet Summer Night Music (ASCAP), and Warner-Tamerlane Publishing Corp. (BMI).

All rights on behalf of Sweet Summer Night Music administered by Warner Chappell Artemis Music Ltd.

All rights on behalf of Rick's Music Inc. and Warner-Tamerlane Publishing Corp. administered by Warner Chappell North America Ltd.

Permission to reprint lyrics to "Love to Love You Baby" is granted by Estate of Donna Summer Sudano and Sweet Summer Night Music (ASCAP).

*Some Tame Gazelle* by Barbara Pym. Copyright © 1983 by Barbara Pym. Reprinted by permission of Georges Borchardt, Inc., on behalf of the Estate of Barbara Pym.

This is a work of fiction. Names, characters, places, and incidents are products of the author's imagination or are used fictitiously and are not to be construed as real. Any resemblance to actual events, locales, organizations, or persons, living or dead, is entirely coincidental.

THE SECOND CHANCE STORE. Copyright © 2023 by Lauren Bravo. All rights reserved. Printed in the United States of America. No part of this book may be used or reproduced in any manner whatsoever without written permission except in the case of brief quotations embodied in critical articles and reviews. For information, address HarperCollins Publishers, 195 Broadway, New York, NY 10007.

HarperCollins books may be purchased for educational, business, or sales promotional use. For information, please email the Special Markets Department at SPsales@harpercollins.com.

Originally published as *Preloved* in the United Kingdom in 2023 by Simon & Schuster UK.

FIRST U.S. EDITION

*Designed by Diahann Sturge*

*Illustrations throughout © Ekaraksasa Studio; picher design; Designifty; Theraphosath; Kyle Cr80n; Vectoressa; paspas; luimonts; ALX1618; ksenya Savva; Lesya Mashtakova; ideyweb; saba vector; RNk07; Ukki Studio; kazki / Shutterstock and Oleksandr Panasovskyi; Vectors Point; Danil Polshin; Amethyst Studio; ibrandify; Tatyana; Hey Rabbit; Adriano Gazzellini; A'lvavo Romis; oleksandr; Edvin PM; Chiara Rossi; Alexander Skowalsky; Juan Pablo Bravo; Lance Knadie; Olena Panasovska; Oksana Latysheva; Ben Biondo / noun project*

Library of Congress Cataloging-in-Publication Data has been applied for.

ISBN 978-0-06-327778-6

23 24 25 26 27 LBC 7 6 5 4 3

*For Matt,*
*my very favorite old thing*

If only one could clear out one's mind and heart
as ruthlessly as one did one's wardrobe.

BARBARA PYM,
*Some Tame Gazelle*

# Gift

---

It sits outside the shop, self-conscious in its splendor.

An odd sight among the usual split bin bags and supermarket carriers, spilling old sweatshirts and balled-up T-shirts like soft guts across the pavement. A gold holographic gift bag—pristine, not a reuse—with a foil rosette stuck to the side and carefully curled ribbons around the handle.

The bag stands proudly upright despite the wind. Something heavy inside weighs it down, from within a crinkling nest of polka-dot tissue paper. There is a tag on the side—inscribed, so now it can't be reused—with a message in black ink, slightly smudged.

*Suzy Q, saw this and thought of you. Hope you like it. Lots of love.*

# 1

It was the dinner that did it.

Gwen sat, chewing. She rolled the braised ox cheek with buttery Parmesan polenta around her mouth, and as she did so the thought popped into her head. It arrived in two beats, *ba-dum*, like coins dropping into a slot machine.

*This might be one of the nicest meals I've ever eaten*, it went, *and there is nobody here to tell.*

It wasn't self-pitying, exactly, the thought. She didn't bat it away, the way she might have done—*had* done—so many times in recent years. She merely took the thought out as if from some mental filing cabinet, held it up and considered it as fact.

It *was* fact. There was nobody else here to share it with, except the waiter. The nice waiter, who had discreetly turned the sleeve of her coat the right way out again and picked up her hat in one clean, deft motion when she had dropped it on the floor with an apologetic "oof." Did the waiter count? Not really.

She would tell him it was nice, but it wouldn't be news to him. The waiter probably ate braised ox cheek with buttery Parmesan polenta for his dinner three nights a week, whenever he wasn't eating leftover razor clams or picking at the blackened ends of rolled loin of pork. No, the waiter wouldn't care that this meal set a kind of high watermark in the oral history of Gwen's stomach. He would smile, because she would smile. He would smile, because she would tip.

She hadn't even had dessert yet. What would happen when dessert came? Sticky toffee pudding with bourbon ice cream *and*—because Gwen liked to believe she had given up living within other people's limitations, at least when it came to sweet condiments—a jug of custard. Both, not either/or.

Perhaps dessert would be disappointing, she thought. She half hoped it would be, for by now she was swept up in the idea of this dinner, this surprisingly good dinner in a near-empty sub-urban gastropub, as both pivotal and fateful. Perhaps the pudding would be dry and claggy with not enough sauce, and she'd snap out of it and remember all the reasons she was alone here with nobody to tell. Good reasons! Multiple reasons! Reasons she had recited once, over and over, in gulping half-sentences on the top of the 43 bus.

Or would she take one bite of the best sticky toffee pudding she'd ever had in her life, and cry in front of the smiling waiter?

The pudding came. It was dark, sticky and dense with dates, swimming in a generous lake of treacle. It wasn't the best she'd ever eaten, but undeniably top five.

Gwen didn't cry. Instead, she made a list.

*1. Find something to do*

This was too vague, she knew even as she was halfway through writing the sentence. The TED Talk she'd watched several months ago on Better Goal-Setting to Harness Your Untapped Productivity Superpower had made it clear: be specific. Or at least she thought that was the gist.

But if Gwen had specifics then she wouldn't be writing the list, or surreptitiously licking a dribble of toffee off the paper with a smeary finger. Vagaries were the best she could manage right now. The weak, fridge-magnet platitudes of the suddenly unemployed.

*Unemployed.* She repeated the word a few times under her breath, plodding and ominous. Three dumpy syllables that felt too heavy for someone who hadn't even left yet. Not technically. Not for another four days.

Officially, it was company cutbacks. The economic climate, necessary restructuring and streamlining in the face of a fast-evolving market, yada yada, blah blah.

Unofficially, it felt like no small coincidence that Gwen had lost her job a week after pointing out, in a client meeting, that the agency was overcharging a small not-for-profit with inflated rate cards and several billable services they weren't providing at all. Gwen didn't usually cause scenes. A tense silence had fallen over the sandwich platter.

Her redundancy package—her boss had insisted on calling it a "package," as though the money might come wrapped up with a complimentary tote bag and a selection of snacks—was generous, enough to live on for a few months at least. It was a token of appreciation for her loyalty to the company, he'd said, though this felt spiked with irony. Besides, Gwen knew the amount was stipulated by contract on the basis of how many years she'd been either too lazy or too underwhelming to get hired elsewhere. HR were probably kicking themselves for making her too comfortable. She was kicking herself for not dumping them before they could dump her.

Still, it turned out mediocrity had a price tag, and it was enough to cover her rent and bills and food while she found something new. Gwen should feel lucky, really—and perhaps she would, once she had stopped putting herself into the recovery position to ease the breathless panic that choked her sleep every night. Once she'd stopped sitting down in the shower.

For now the future was hazy, a distant shape at the end of a long corridor that could be squinted at more closely in time. It was tomorrow and the next day that worried her. She could see their form clearly: an arse-shaped indent in an already sagging sofa, strewn with hairs and crisp crumbs.

So: find something to do. She muttered it under her breath. *Anything. Do a thing! Next.*

*2. Instigate social occasions*

Gwen regretted this one before the ink was dry, because nobody wanted to come to social occasions instigated by a person who called it "instigating social occasions." But she supposed it did the job. She would, she vowed, make more effort. She would take a pair of jumper cables to the friendships that had begun stalling over the years, and get them . . . ah, back on the road. (Gwen couldn't drive).

But how did anyone do that? How did a person in their thirties round up their friends without the three-line whip of either a wedding, baby, or significant birthday as their weapon?

How did you text someone and say "Hey! Fancy going to the cinema tomorrow?" without making it sound like you were going to look deep into their eyes and tell them you were secretly in love with them, or had cancer?

If she knew the answer to that then she wouldn't be here, slurping at what had been gin but was now a glass of lukewarm molten ice, resisting the urge to chew the lemon slice in case the nice waiter saw her.

Losing her job, was that anything? Enough to warrant coos and a sympathetic head tilt, yes—but enough to summon people to dinner on a weekday night at will? Unclear.

She had long fantasized about something she liked to call "the rally round." Friends dropping everything to race across town and appear on each other's doorsteps, the way they did so frequently and easily on TV. In recent years, in darker moments, she'd caught herself cooking up elaborate daydreams about divorces, bereavements, broken hearts, broken limbs. Any tragedy in which distance and practicality might go out of the window and people would simply turn up, diaries cleared and arms outstretched.

But even in her daydreams she was never the object of the rally round, just a willing participant with a bag full of wine and frozen pizza, briskly running baths and tucking her friends into bed with the kind of intimacy and affection they hadn't seriously enjoyed since about 2008. She watched the shows and the films and read the books about intense female friendships and wondered if it was bad that nobody had ever wanted to share a bath with her. Gwen had never held anyone's skirt while they peed on a pregnancy test, and sometimes this felt like a fundamental failing.

Still, it hadn't always been this way. At one time it had been easier: back when her social life simply happened around her like a fast-moving river, and it was actually more effort to resist than to give in and let it carry her off to another pub quiz, another semi-ironic dinner party, another round of leaving drinks for the friend of a friend's boyfriend who was going backpacking in Acton. (The drinks were in Acton, not the backpacking.)

Once upon a time, Gwen and her friends had done things for the sake of anecdote and little else. And thank god they had, because without being able to say "Remember the time . . . ?" whenever the conversation flagged, their sporadic meetups now would be painful. Perhaps friendship in your twenties was like storing nuts for winter. You spend as much time as you can frantically filling the pantry, so you have enough to live on in your thirties once stocks start to dwindle.

She scooped up the last bite of pudding, making an effort to sluice every remaining bit of sauce from the bowl with it— and then, carefully, poured the last of the custard directly onto the spoon. Gwen looked at it for a second: the final, glistening mouthful. Forced herself to stop and savor a moment's delayed gratification before shoveling it in. She'd always been sentimental about endings.

*3. Call Mum and Dad*

This one was not so much from a desire to be a better daughter, but because it had now been five weeks, three days and Gwen was forced to admit that her latest game of emotional chicken had failed. Again. What had started as an experiment, to see how long it would take them to worry and check in on her, had only high-lighted their ongoing lack of concern while exacerbating her own.

Things had been heading this way in the Grundle family for years. At first, it was a forceful jollying-on; a refusal to go all touchy-feely in the face of tragic events that, by most people's es-timation, would warrant it. Not wanting to drag each other down, or rile each other up, or puncture the thin skin that had begun to grow again over the open wound, like clingfilm on a too-full jug of gravy. Better not to ask than to get an honest answer. She understood, even as she resented it.

But more recently she'd started these games: leaving longer and longer between her phone calls, waiting with curiosity to see when her silence might jolt them into making contact. It hadn't yet. And what if something terrible had happened to them in the meantime? What if she was forced to explain to the authorities that she was a grown woman playing hard-to-get with her own parents?

She decided to call tomorrow, to check they were alive. Then get off the phone before she was dragged into a lecture on herba-ceous borders.

### 4. *Go to the dentist*

At some point over the past decade, going to the dentist had qui-etly evolved from something nobody actually did, to something everyone did but never talked about. And so Gwen had been merrily ignoring the regular text reminders for years, assuming everyone else was too, until Sonja at work had taken a morning off for a dentist appointment that turned out to genuinely *be* a dentist appointment—not, as Gwen assumed, a covert job interview or leisurely bikini wax—and the question had come up.

It turned out that nobody over twenty-five on her team had gone longer than eight months without a checkup. Some of them even owned floss, and used it. Gwen was, as the interns said, shook.

She wasn't even afraid of the dentist. In fact she had a respectable threshold for pain, and a secret fondness for any activity that involved being intimately cared for by a stranger. Having her hair vigorously washed by a salon junior, for example, or her pulse checked by a soft-handed GP. She had once spent hundreds of pounds on six months of appointments with an osteopath above a chicken shop, who failed to fix her bad knee but would cup it, tenderly, while they both talked about *Masterchef*. She never examined this memory too closely in case it made her a pervert.

Gwen even quite liked the idea of taking an afternoon off for the dentist, and sitting in a coffee shop afterward. A treat.

Really there was no reason at all for never going, except that the dentist tended to fall into that unreachable void in her head, along with the texts and emails left unanswered until it was too embarrassing to reply, the birthday check from an aunt she still hadn't deposited and the yogurt that had moldered at the back of the fridge for going on eight months now. Seemingly easy, straightforward tasks slipped into this void, sometimes without warning, and leaning in to retrieve them took more effort than Gwen could muster. So she didn't. But now she would.

### 5. Get rid of it

To anyone else reading her list this one would be confusing, she realized, then felt briefly embarrassed for even thinking the thought. *When would anyone read this, Gwen? As your estate sorts through your personal effects, perhaps, looking for things to publish after you've died? Is that likely to happen, to a senior account manager from Dorking?*

A *former* senior account manager.

Gwen blushed and scrunched up her face as hard as she could, a form of outward grimace that doubled as an inward sneer. *Don't be ridiculous.*

"It" meant the piles of relationship detritus she had bagged up, methodically, ritualistically, all those years ago. "Your emotional baggage," Suze had called it at the time, as she tripped over the black plastic sack every time she went to get the Hoover out of the landing cupboard. After a month it had been gently suggested that the emotional baggage needed to go somewhere—a bin, ideally, but if not the bin then perhaps back into Gwen's room, where she could trip over it herself?

She'd relented, and so the bag had taken up residence behind her bedroom door, where it could be forgotten in the presence of others but would taunt her each time she was alone.

Over time, the bag had become buried. In an old towel, a fallen-down dressing gown, a sheet of bubble wrap saved for a hypothetical future padding emergency. The grain at the center of a shitty emotional pearl. Before long, the bag had slipped further into The Void than perhaps anything else ever had, until the very idea of unpicking the dusty layer cake and extracting that black sack of memories felt so beyond her it was almost hilarious. When she'd moved out, she'd simply scooped up the whole heap in her arms, dressing gown and all, dumped it into a blue Ikea bag and carried it calmly into the next place. Then the next. In this way she managed to almost neutralize the bag; it became a piece of admin, something to be shunted aside while looking for a lost sneaker. It caused her physical pain roughly twice a year, when it fell on her head from a top cupboard, and emotional pain only slightly more often than that.

But not anymore. She was going to get rid of it. The list had spoken.

Gwen might have continued into further specifics, but at this point the nice waiter appeared in her peripheral vision, doing the polite hover that signaled it was time to pay up and let him get back to . . . what? Wife and kids? Husband and schnauzer? Comrades in a warehouse squat? Hot bath and tin foil package of three-day-old vanilla cheesecake with sea buckthorn coulis? Gwen forced herself to look up as though she'd only just noticed him, caught his eye and mimed the universal "bill please" mime. Unfortunately the nice waiter had moved closer in the last few seconds, so that she was now silently mouthing the word "please" at an audible distance, to a man standing five feet away in an empty restaurant.

Flushing from neckline to hairline, she folded the list three times into a neat square and slipped it into her pocket, then made a show of rummaging in her bag for lip balm to fill the silence while her card payment went through. Eventually it did. The nice waiter bid her goodnight and disappeared into the kitchen. She watched his retreating back, then put on her scarf and left, issuing a small-voiced "thank you" over her shoulder.

Gwen stepped out into the biting April wind and began to make her way along the street toward the hotel room where her laptop and a whisky miniature were waiting.

It wasn't actually the worst birthday she'd had, she concluded.

Not the worst, but undeniably bottom five.

## 2

The worst birthday Gwen had ever had was six years earlier. Her thirty-second, which had been spent at a crematorium, a B&M Homestore, and an out-of-hours walk-in clinic, in that order.

This one was fractionally better than her thirty-fourth, which had come to an abrupt end at 9:42 p.m. as her three companions all waved away the dessert menu and started pulling their coats on, muttering things about last trains and yoga in the morning. She knew the exact time the dinner had ended because she remembered looking at her phone, having decided that anything after 10 p.m. was acceptable. Gwen often entered into these private contests with herself. She usually lost.

It definitely wasn't as good as her thirtieth ("Thirty, hurty, and thriving!" she had bellowed into various ears on the dancefloor at the Old Grey Bugle, which had a DJ until midnight on Fridays outside wedding season) but better than her thirty-fifth, when a minor terrorist attack at the other end of the Northern line had given everyone slightly-too-convenient reasons to cry off. Since then she'd stopped planning anything, always in the faint hope that someone—Suze, she supposed, maybe one of the interchangeable Claires and Gemmas at work—might organize something for her, the way people did for their friends in TV shows. She would protest, of course, because the whole thing would be agonizing and people would only come because Suze or whichever of the

Gemmas would have guilted them into it. But she never had to protest, because it had never happened.

The circumstances in which Gwen found herself alone on her thirty-eighth birthday in a gastropub somewhere vaguely south of Leicester were too pathetic to go into. Not a long story, just one that began with her manager asking her to "make nice" in his place at a two-day client immersion session, and ended with Gwen being too adept at making nice to say, "It's my birthday that day, so no."

Or, "You've just sacked me, so no."

Or indeed, "What's an immersion session?"

She could have left the company immediately. They'd offered pay in lieu of notice, for a swift and painless exit. But a strange mix of fear and obstinance had led her to dig her heels in and hang on for one final, awkward week.

"I'd prefer to wrap things up myself," she'd sniffed, trying to sound gracious. "It feels only fair to the clients."

The idea that this trip might constitute any sort of treat, a final taste of the executive high life before she was booted out into the corporate snow, was a stretch. Even for Chris, the sort of boss who was perpetually one weeping intern away from a mandatory HR course. He had looked shocked when Gwen had agreed she would still go; had asked Gemma Three to book her "the penthouse suite" as a thank-you-slash-bribe not to shame the company in retaliation. This ended up meaning a family room on the fourth floor of Lutterworth Travelodge, but still. It was a moral high ground of sorts.

More importantly, the real reason: it had gotten her out of London. It meant she could roll her eyes and adopt a "what a martyr, me!" face if anyone asked what her birthday plans were. She could say something self-deprecating about enjoying the bright lights of Lutterworth. And now she could climb into the starchy-clean void of her budget hotel bedsheets with her swollen belly and watch Netflix, farting freely, until she fell asleep. All without having to question what she would have been doing at home on her birthday instead.

Plus, she now had a plan of action. A five-step program for life recovery. Tomorrow there would be tiny toiletries, warm butter pats spread on cold toast, and the mercifully early confirmation that the immersion session would not require a swimsuit. It was a good decision.

Gwen murmured this to herself, the time-honored old mantra she'd used many years before, as she kicked at the tucked-in sheets until her feet were finally freed. Trying to believe it.

As she listened to the whirr of the hotel air conditioning, a baseline under the orchestral gurgling of her stomach. And as she set her phone alarm, ignoring the messages on the locked screen—a text from Suze, brief but laden with emoji balloons, and a happy birthday email from a tapas restaurant she'd visited once in 2014.

*It was a good decision.*

## 3

Her next good decision came a week later, when Gwen carried her emotional baggage into a local charity shop and deposited it triumphantly in front of the counter.

"Hiiiii!" trilled the man behind the till, without looking up from his crossword. He was slim, shrewlike, anywhere between forty and sixty, with a tanned, sheeny complexion that gave him the air of a recently retired waxwork at Madame Tussauds.

"I've brought you some donations," Gwen replied in the same bright tone, trying to sound as though she hadn't rehearsed it.

"Lovely! What are they?" asked the man, licking a finger to turn a page. He had a soft, melodious Birmingham accent. He still didn't look up.

"They're—it's—well . . . Aha," Gwen stalled, thrown off script by his friendly voice and entirely indifferent body language. "It's men's . . . ah, *wear*? Menswear," she repeated, firmly. "Some jumpers, a couple of shirts. Some T-shirts. A hat. A terrible hat, actually, I'm sorry for . . . um, what else. CDs! Do you take CDs? I wasn't sure, seems so archaic . . . but that's insensitive isn't it, there must be lots of people who still . . . ah . . . books, too, a few paperbacks. I can't vouch for quality but one of them won the Pulitzer so I suppose my opinion is . . . um . . . there's some flip-flops, I think, not very seasonal but I thought you could keep them for the summer, or . . . well, those people who wear flip-flops in the rain. Shin pads! I think they're shin pads, not to protect anything . . . else. Um. Two sets of whisky stones. An unopened tin of something called beard butter."

She paused, cleared her throat. Took an emotional run-up.

"And this."

Gwen took the small leather box out of her pocket and placed it on the counter. She opened it, in a moment of painful parody, to reveal the emerald-cut diamond glinting inside.

"That is, if you take rings too?"

A week, it had been, of incremental progress. First taking the blue bag down from the top cupboard and leaving it in the middle of the carpet for a couple of days. Then, slashing the bin bag with a pair of kitchen scissors, in a way that felt to Gwen vaguely reminiscent of a TV crime drama, to rifle through the stuff inside and check it hadn't morphed at some point over the past six years, into counterfeit handbags or several hundred wraps of cocaine.

This took a while, because every time she caught a whiff of the clothes—their curious signature blend of laundry detergent, Mitchum for Men, and Fishermen's Friend cherry lozenges taken for chronic sinusitis—she had to steel herself against the urge to climb into bed with her laptop and cruise his locked Instagram account via the fake profile she'd created for the purpose.

She had tried the ring on again, because of course she had. She'd briefly considered keeping it, wearing it on another finger, as . . . what? An empowering reclamation? A comedy prop to unsettle people with at parties? She'd thought about selling it many times over the years, whenever a council tax bill landed or a hen weekend threatened to bankrupt her. But profiting from it, even now, made her feel itchy all over. Giving it to charity might not shake her conscience clear like an Etch A Sketch, but it was the best solution she could come up with.

Seeing the ring there on the counter, Gwen fantasized about picking up a golf club, taking a huge swing and, with an almighty *thwack,* hitting it far, far into the distance. She could almost feel the impact of it reverberating through her arms.

Finally, the wax man glanced up from his paper. He looked at the ring, then at Gwen, and blinked, his expression unchanging.

"I do!" he replied.

# **Dust**

To the ignorant, all charity shops are the same.

The particular smell of softening biscuits, yellowing paperbacks and aged storage heaters turned up slightly too high. The distant sound of *Steve Wright in the Afternoon* crackling through a portable stereo. The racks, a little too close together for comfortable browsing, laden with items at once both too old and too new to be fashionable. A bookshelf of indeterminate filing system that will reliably contain several copies of *Shantaram*, *The Dukan Diet,* and *Bridget Jones's Diary.* A glimpse through an open door into a stockroom beyond, filled with bin bags, half-drunk cups of tea, and the theatrical hiss of a steaming machine.

And behind the counter, a kindly soul whose job is to scrutinize you. A generous person who has given up their time for the benefit of those less fortunate, who will probably rifle through your donations after you've gone and laugh at how gross they all are. An angel on earth, who will nonetheless hold up your ill-judged holiday shorts from 2009 while shrieking, "Cor, Brenda, get a load of these!"

And they're allowed to, because after all, what have *you* sacrificed to help others recently? The shorts? Is that it?

To the uninitiated, all charity shops have the same air. A potent blend of the depressive, the nostalgic, and the worthy. The lingering essence of a grandparent, distilled into boxes of clumsy bric-a-brac.

The unbearable sadness of unwanted gifts, never taken out of their plastic packaging. A childhood memory too far gone for conscious recollection, which now exists only as an occasional twang in the pit of the stomach, triggered by a waft of a certain perfume or the feel of bobbled cotton between two fingertips.

And death. The thing that squats like a fat elephant in the corner of every charity shop in the land. The reason half this stuff is here, and often the reason it's being sold. Dead people's clothes, in aid of dead people diseases, sold by people closer to death than you are. It's a lot to take on for a cheap T-shirt.

But the truth is, there are as many flavors of charity shop as there are charities to run them. There are posh charity shops and hip charity shops and hippie charity shops and minimalist charity shops and obsessively neat charity "boutiques" and muddled, must-addled junk emporiums. There are charity shops for every neighborhood, for every purpose, metabolizing all that waste and using it to generate a new kind of energy. Each shop becomes different each day, as more new-old bundles are unpacked into its belly. Continually reconfiguring to reflect the world around it. Or, the world that was around it five to ten years earlier.

And if you can learn a lot about people from peering into their trolleys at the supermarket, you can learn even more from the things they give away. They're a telling inventory of hobbies that never caught on and relationships that never bedded in. Every castoff has a story, from "For sale: baby shoes, never worn" to "For sale: Nutribullet, never opened." It's a story that's only half-written at point of sale; off to live another life and inspire another volume with some new owner.

"Second chance saloons," Michael liked to call them, in reference to himself as much as the stock. It's ironic, he thought privately, that the people who are squeamish about buying secondhand are often the same people who like to pretend everything was better in the past.

The volunteers referred to him as "St. Michael," named more for his ability to identify a piece of old Marks and Spencer at twenty paces than for his heavenly customer service. In fact, in the grand tradition of the virtuous, he often came across as a raving misanthrope. St. Michael was fine with this. He had learned the hard way in life that there's usually more to be gained from watching people than there is from charming them.

"Charity shops make people uncomfortable because they do so much good," Michael was fond of saying at parties, at bars, or to people he met in queues. "They raise money, they reduce waste, they help poor people, they help mad people [here, he would gesture to his own face and wait for a small laugh], they give rich people a place to offload their crap and feel better about it. But all the ways they're good just serve to remind people of all the ways they, personally, are shitty. That's why people turn their noses up. Nothing to do with the smell."

He would leave a pause here, but not such a long one that people would think he had finished speaking and move on.

"Personally, I lean into it," he would add, with a conspiratorial smirk. "It started as therapy for me, but now I'm the therapist. The counter is my couch. And honey [here, he would affect an American accent with Joan Rivers-esque hand gestures], let me tell you—sometimes everybody needs charity."

If anyone asked for examples, which they rarely did, he would tell them. About the stories he filled in between the gaps, the way he did with the *Evening Standard* crossword. About the elderly widower, handing over faded floral blouses from the drawer he finds another man's letters in. Or the woman who needs clothes to wear to the interview she needs for the job she needs to earn the money she needs to come back to buy the clothes her children need. The millennials who buy vintage to offset the guilt of their coke habit. The boomers who donate cashmere to offset the guilt of voting Leave.

The teenager patching together a new identity from pieces of other people's wardrobes. The couple who buy latex and masks "for Halloween" in April. The millionaire who can't make peace with spending more than £4 on a shirt. Or the woman who walks in one afternoon with a bin bag, and hands over an engagement ring.

If charity shops remind you of death then that's only because they're so full of life.

# 4

Gwen had seen the sign in the window as she walked in, though she was preoccupied in the moment. She noticed it again as she left, walking slowly this time, stroking an idle finger along the sleeve of a nearby sweatshirt and pausing to have a cursory flick through a box of thick magazines marked ARTY, £2.

She lingered, because it felt strange to walk out again so soon after such a monumental task. Gwen half-expected someone to run out of the back room shouting, "Wait! Stop! Would you like to talk about it?"

But once she had reached the door, moving so slowly she stumbled over her own feet at one point, nobody had and there was nothing left to do but walk through it and into her baggage-free future.

Unless! There it was again, written in Sharpie and stuck to the window with masking tape at the corners. VOLUNTEERS UR-GENTLY NEEDED.

"It would be nice to be urgently needed" was the first thought that occurred to her, which was bleak. That wasn't supposed to be the main reason you volunteered for something. But Gwen reassured herself that if anyone asked, she could always lie. She could say she wanted to give something back. That she had decided to diversify her hobbies and reconnect with her local community. This wasn't entirely untrue, after all; it was point number one on the action plan, or thereabouts. *Find something to do.* And now here was something to do, right in front of her, conveniently piggy-backing on point number five.

It was the day after her redundancy payout had landed in her bank account, giving her a buzz of illusory wealth in the same way Student Loan Day used to. She'd need to find a proper, paying job again soon—sure. Within five months and two weeks, if her most wildly optimistic sums proved true. But didn't she deserve a bit of a break? And yet didn't the idea of more downtime fill her chest with thick terror? And anyway, wouldn't volunteering look good on her CV? Yes. Yes to all three.

It was important to follow through on this now, she knew, while she was still giddy from the rush of admin successfully completed. Before it fell into The Void. So Gwen performed an exaggerated double take in case anyone was watching, turned around and walked back up to the counter, where Wax Man had just reached the property section.

"Hi again!" she half-sung at him.

"Hiyaaa," he replied, eyes fixed firmly on a feature about why Bognor is the new Bexhill which was once the new Balham.

"I was wondering about volunteering," she continued, smiling broadly at the top of his head.

Without looking up, Wax Man reached beneath the counter and smoothly produced a form, SO YOU WANT TO VOLUNTEER? printed along the top in Word Art. He slid it across the counter with a single, assertive finger. Gwen took it, awaiting further instructions, but it seemed their interaction was over. He yawned and turned a page of his paper. She left.

In a coffee shop up the road, she dunked chunks of banana bread into a flat white with a spoon and thought about the qualities that would make her a good candidate for volunteering. It was quite hard to look beyond the most obvious: being willing to volunteer. She couldn't see how a charity shop would be so overwhelmed with offers that they would need further criteria.

*I have a strong interest in old things*, she wrote, then worried this sounded as though she was referring to the patrons. Or the staff. Although from her limited interactions with the shop so far it didn't look like it was run by shuffling retirees, so much as what her mother would call "characters." People with blue hair and red-rimmed glasses and the kind of flexible schedules that allowed them to spend Tuesday afternoons pricing DVD copies of *Dude, Where's My Car?*

She tore off another piece of cake. Loaded it onto the spoon; allowed it to sit in the foam, soaking up the coffee until it threatened to disintegrate, before maneuvering it into her mouth.

*I believe passionately in the work that*—shit, what charity was it? Children? Cancer? Cats?—*your organization does, and would love to play a part in supporting it.*

Gwen paused and looked at her handwriting: the inconsistent scrawl of the elder millennial. It always started off confident and elegant for a couple of sentences, then went off the boil as her hand started to seize up at the shock of holding a pen. Once upon a time, she had practiced her handwriting throughout the school holidays, taking pains to reinvent it as part of her annual personality upgrade. Curly tails on her *g*'s and *y*'s. Circles instead of dots over her *i*'s. Now it looked like the writing of somebody who had suddenly felt a gun at their temple halfway through the sentence, sloping off into scratchy despair.

*I am keen to diversify my hobbies and reconnect with my local community*, she added.

Like many Londoners, Gwen was passionately defensive of her local community without actually being able to name anyone in it. She had lived in broadly the same area for the past sixteen years, ever since luck and a friend of a friend of Suze's cousin had deposited them both in that first grotty houseshare in the backwoods between Kentish Town and Holloway Road, where the kitchen cupboards were padlocked, the number of official residents was forever in flux and Gwen had to scrape mildew off her trainers in the morning. "It's near the flat from *Spaced*!" had seemed, back then, a more important selling point than double glazing.

In the following years they had zigzagged their way across the north of the city, through a series of increasingly smaller, warmer, more expensive places with quieter, cleaner, less criminal housemates. Their final spot together had been just the two of them, in a sweetly shabby two-bedroom off the top of the Harringay Ladder. Now, Gwen lived alone. In a one-bedroom flat within a vast, badly converted late-Victorian mansion house, with original windows, a tiled fire surround and stripped floorboards peppered with woodworm holes. These architectural curiosities were her reward for enduring an avocado bathroom suite, orange mold between the tiles, and a collection of mousetraps that caught mice rarely enough to sit and gather dust on their lumps of Cathedral City Cheddar, but not quite rarely enough to be put away. She supposed she loved her flat. It was, emotionally if not legally, hers.

The sensible thing would have been to go back to sharing and save up to buy somewhere. An ex-council "with potential" on the fringes of zone five, or a part-ownership deal in a development next to the north circular called something like "Elderberry Grove Lawns," where she'd have to walk for twenty minutes to reach a corner shop. But she refused to. Staying in her drafty, decadent rented shoebox felt like a tiny rebellion.

*I am currently taking a short career break.*

Anyway, Gwen knew she'd been lucky. Location was everything with London, and by pure chance she'd ended up in a good one. A place with just enough charm to garner loyalty and affection, but not so much that it ever attracted tourists or hordes of pouting teenagers. Where she could have a favorite café, a backup favorite café, and a café she never used on point of principle because of some small misdemeanor she'd long since forgotten (stale scone? Disgusting toilet?) but never quite forgiven them for. The pace of gentrification was slow here, relatively speaking, and for every hip new business there were at least three with pleather furniture and Papyrus font on the laminated menus. Estate agents called it "vibrant." Her parents called it "cosmopolitan." She could access several wild, open green spaces and a popular dogging spot within half an hour's walk of her front door, and easily pass whole weekends without ever setting foot on public transport.

None of this was guaranteed. Back in the early years, she'd watched her friends and acquaintances take the requisite deep breath and move to the city, full of hope and excitement—only to end up in a bleak, charmless pocket off a main road, chosen because it had some frippery like an en suite bathroom, without consulting anyone who knew the ropes and could steer them in a better direction. They would quickly end up jaded and lonely, their life one big long commute from the arse end of the District line—and after a year or two they would leave London again, claiming it simply wasn't for them. Too big, too hard. Too lonely. Too expensive.

Gwen always felt privately furious when this happened. Furious and partly responsible, as though maybe she could have saved them herself with better brunches and more demonstrative flat-hunting advice. If they'd had more fun, if she'd *been* more fun, maybe they'd have stayed longer. She smiled blithely through the leaving drinks and goodbye toasts, promised to come and visit them in Berkshire and Bristol and Welwyn Garden City. And beneath it all she'd be wailing: *You quitter! You traitor! You wimp.*

But she also knew the truth: that London really wasn't for everyone. Not back then, when the gradually hardening shell of people's personalities was still so fragile, and a few months being jostled and ignored in the armpit of the metropolis could be enough to shatter their confidence for years. And certainly not now, when everyone was spawning like salmon and swimming upstream toward the affordable semi-detacheds in good catchment areas. Toward the places where you could stretch out and inhabit life fully, without your fists bumping off your bedroom walls. Staying in London in your late thirties was only for fantasists and millionaires, everyone knew that.

Besides, even the people who stayed still left you, in other ways, in the end.

SPECIAL SKILLS? asked the form.

Gwen frowned. After some time, she wrote down *MS Word, MS Excel, Keynote*. Was that enough? Did they want to know about her GCSE German or her bronze Duke of Edinburgh?

She paused, chewed her pen, then added, *Stamina*.

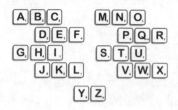

# Scrabble

They had bought it twenty-five years ago, to take to Wales.

Maureen, who had a superstitious streak that she had learned to keep quiet around her husband, believed that the more wet-weather activities and diversions they piled into the boot of the Ford Escort, the less it would rain when they got there.

Ellen was struggling at school and Mark, as his grandmother had mentioned through pursed lips the last time she'd babysat, could do with widening his vocabulary. Scrabble had won out against Mousetrap (too many bits, which would end up strewn across the caravan carpet to be trodden on by unsuspecting bare feet), Operation (same, with unpleasant medical subtext), and Frustration (Len couldn't abide the popping dice and Maureen couldn't abide Len not abiding the popping dice; the name was altogether too accurate). So, Scrabble.

The journey had been hell, as it always was. Ellen had been sick, as she always was, in an old Gino Ginelli tub somewhere just beyond Chieveley Services, and had sobbed for another forty-five miles as Maureen endeavored to wash it out of her hair with weak lemon barley water. Mark had complained loudly about the smell and taunted his sister by demanding an enormous burger with extra gherkins from a roadside van, which he then puked up theatrically as they went across the toll bridge.

Len had refused to consult the road atlas, as he always did, and as a result they had arrived at the holiday park several hours later than planned, the atmosphere inside the car thick with queasy resentment.

Rain lashed the caravan on that first night, as it always did. While the kids took turns holding the TV aerial out of the window and Len hoovered the crumbs out of the car with his portable Dustbuster, Maureen produced the dark green box and waved it hopefully at her family.

"Scrabble? Who's for a nice game of Scrabble?"

Nothing. Mark yelped as an image briefly manifested on the TV screen, then roared as the blizzard of static returned. He began hitting his sister with the aerial instead, who bit his leg in retaliation. A swift, confident bite, like a Tudor king tearing into a drumstick.

"Scrabble?" she tried again, her voice firmer this time. "Winner gets first go on the flume tomorrow!"

The tussling continued, as Len returned from the car to announce that one of the tires had gone, and so had his back, and they'd forgotten to pack the pump for the airbed. His tone implied, as it always did, that this was Maureen's fault. The missing pump, the flat tire, the holiday, the weather, the children. The eggshells she was continually breaking, all day, every day, despite her most careful steps.

Her steps had become smaller over the years, as she endeavored to move through life minimally, quietly, without triggering the Mousetrap chain reaction of his mood. But not tonight. Tonight, she was Buckaroo. She flipped.

"EVERYBODY SHUT UP, WE ARE PLAYING BLOODY SCRABBLE!" Maureen bellowed. Stunned, everybody did shut up. The distant *doof-doof* throb of the campsite disco leaked into the momentary silence. Three berths down, a dog whined.

They played Scrabble. Maureen didn't remember who had won, but she remembered laughing a lot. The breathless release of it. Proper fits of giggles, clutching at the fold-out table and wiping away tears with the sleeve of her fleece. Which was odd, because who *laughs* at Scrabble? Scrabble isn't funny.

For an hour or two the storm had broken and there had been ceasefire. Her family were united in mutual absurdity, their tempers rerouted into bickering over juvenile expletives ("git" [4], "bumhole" [14]) and what constituted proper nouns. The laughter continued as they made attempts to puff up the airbed with their own lungs, before giving up to sleep on a pile of musty sofa cushions. Afterward her stomach ached like the spine of an old book, newly cracked.

The next morning, the sun had made an appearance. Not for long, but long enough to keep them gazing hopefully skyward for the rest of the week. It was the last holiday they'd all take together, although of course nobody knew that, and if you'd asked her children they'd probably have believed that holidays would continue in this style, gray and fractious and disappointing, until the end of time.

When they got home, the Scrabble was shoved to the back of a cupboard behind some other crap. It stayed there, untouched, for more than two decades. Until Maureen's sister started clearing the house, ready to be sold.

"Scrabble?" she'd asked, turning to the corner where Ellen sat thumbing through an old photo album, stroking an affectionate finger over her mother's bygone perm and looking for hints of how bad things would become. No reply.

Her aunt didn't care to interrupt; better they completed the process quickly anyway. Maureen was never one for fuss.

So for a moment she paused with the dusty game in her hands, scanning it for value—sentimental or financial—before making the call and placing it into the cardboard box marked CHARITY SHOP.

# 5

Gwen had always assumed that carrying a cardboard box of possessions out of an office was something that only happened on TV, until she found herself doing it.

Maybe she'd only done it *because* it was what they did on TV? In hindsight, one of the office's eight thousand promotional tote bags would have done the job just as well and been far less mortifying on the Tube. But she had carried the box, and now her seven (*Christ, was it really seven?*) years of service to strategic marketing and synergetic branding solutions were reduced to the world's shittest hamper: a foam wrist rest, an individually sized cafetiere, a promotional stress toy shaped like an avocado, a bag of roasted almonds with a best before date of 2017, her framed First Aider certificate and five orange-tinted Tupperwares in varying states of fermentation.

She had left the box on her kitchen table for several days, edging around it like it was an unexploded bomb. Gwen stroked a hand along the box now, as she listened to the nervous chirp of her parents' landline, her phone already hot against her ear. First, something else needed unpacking.

Her father answered today, which meant that Gwen enjoyed a whole thirty seconds of silence-filling noises "dum de dum," "boop-ba-do," "where's the buggering wotsit then") while he went, automatically, to fetch her mother. No mention was made of the fact that six weeks, now, had passed since they'd last spoken to their only daughter. Her mother picked up the conversation as though halfway through the sentence she'd last left her on.

"I was just saying to Yvonne the other day, I don't know how Gwendoline can stick it" was the opener.

"Stick what?"

"The noise!"

On their last, and in fact only, visit to her current flat, during a May bank holiday heat wave several years earlier, there had been a barbecue in the tiny garden below. They had sat, the three of them, drinking tea and perspiring quietly, while her neighbors' laughter drifted in through the open windows and the thumping bass of a subwoofer rattled the rotting sash frames.

"It isn't noisy. That was one time," she protested. "It's actually a very peaceful street."

"Well, you don't want it too quiet," retorted her mother. Even after thirty-eight years, Gwen was never braced for these U-turns. To agree with her mother was to risk conversational whiplash. "It's the quiet ones that are most dangerous! When you're coming home all hours of the night, all on your own. I worry."

Gwen was faintly touched by this, although more by the idea that she might still go out until "all hours of the night" than by any hint at her parents' concern. When her mother said "I worry," it tended to come across as an unwelcome physical complaint. *I have a headache. That sandwich gave me indigestion. I worry.*

"Mum. It's fine. I'm fine. It's quiet, but there's, ah, a lovely sense of community."

Was this true? Perhaps it was true. Certainly she stood behind people in shops who seemed to know each other, and eavesdropped on surprise meetings on the bus. The lampposts were plastered with missing cats, and the estate agent signs adorned with children's drawings advertising school summer fairs. Somebody had put a leaflet through her door once about a street party for the Jubilee. Or was it the Olympics?

Gwen had smiled at the barbecuing family a few times, imagined an alternative reality in which they lent each other tools and gossiped in the hallway. But being in a third-floor flat put her at a disadvantage, she felt. She couldn't strike up a chat over the fence the way other people could. What was she supposed to do, yell pleasantries at them from an upstairs window? Drop a basket on a wire with a note that said *Be my friend?*

"Are you still there?" asked her mother, slightly muffled. She was balancing the phone on her shoulder while wielding pruning shears again, Gwen could tell. A metallic slicing and rustling was audible in the background. "I was asking if they'd said anything else about the promotion?"

She wondered if all parents did this: referring to a vague, omnipotent "they" as a source of all order and justice in the world. "*Surely they can't expect you to work on a Sunday?*"; "*Have they said anything else about your rash?*"; "*I thought they'd stopped saying 'disabled' now?*" Whoever "they" were, her parents had more faith in them than they ever seemed to in her.

"No, nothing yet." She gripped hard at the squeezy avocado stress toy and forced a smile for the phone. "But hopefully soon!"

"Hopefully soon" was enough rope for her mother to grasp onto, but not enough for Gwen to hang herself with. She'd tell them eventually. She'd tell them once she had something new lined up and could frame it as a dynamic career change.

"Ah well," said her mother, a touch robotically. "Hopefully soon."

Gwen had often marveled at her career, and not in a good way. "Honestly, even *I* barely know what I do all day!" she would quip at the blank politeness that invariably met her answer.

Other women tended to greet anything along these lines with a spluttering noise and instant diagnosis of impostor syndrome—but she would shrug this off. She didn't believe she was underqualified for her job, so much as she believed the job itself was stupid. She didn't worry about being exposed as a fraud, so much as she worried that one day she would come to the office and find that Invigorate Media Inc. had disappeared overnight—nothing there to show for it except a toothless old man in a tin foil hat, and a vape shop where the breakout space used to be.

With each passing year she had become more embarrassed to have the kind of job that sitcom writers made up as satire, complete with air hockey table and fridges of isotonic sports drinks. She envied the friends who had one-word Happy Families–style job titles, easy to explain at family functions. Teacher. Doctor. Butcher. Baker. When Melody from Accounts had genuinely left to become a candlestick-maker, Gwen had almost signed up for the same beginners' ceramics course. She liked the idea that when people asked her what she did, she could say "This!" and whip a small rustic bowl from her backpack.

Still, it had been more comfortable to inhabit her job than to scrutinize it from the outside. On the good days, it had been like speaking a shared, made-up language with seventy-four other people. On those days, the pomp and swagger of a pitch win or a brainstorming breakthrough felt like the kind of elaborate fantasy game she'd loved as a child, becoming so absorbed by the rules and texture of an imaginary world that it was hard to shake it off and go in for dinner.

But the promotion had never existed. She had made it up six months ago to reassure her parents that she wasn't simply treading water, professionally or otherwise. For years she had been content, mostly, with the unspoken agreement in which she stayed competent but just lazy enough for her bosses not to feel bad about her stagnating position. She was content, until acquaintances asked what she was "doing now" and tilted their head in sympathy when she had no small, polished nugget of progress to offer them. Until she watched people frown when they realized they had to recategorize her from "career woman putting personal life on the backburner" to "drifter/loner/possible cause for concern." Until her mother started asking questions.

After she'd returned from the Lutterworth make-nice with her pockets full of free shortbread, Chris had sat on her desk (Chris was a rampant desk-sitter) and asked if she'd "sounded them out for the Churchill project." Gwen had never heard of the Churchill project.

"Winston or nodding dog?" she'd asked.

Chris had laughed as though she was hilarious, drummed decisively on the desk between his legs, asked her to "pop it all in an email, cheers G" and sauntered out to lunch. Gwen had sent him nothing. Chris hadn't mentioned it again.

Three days later, after a sedate lunch with her team, clutching a leaving card of her head Photoshopped onto an image of Dame Maggie Smith (why?) by an overworked junior designer who didn't know her name, Gwen had left Invigorate Media for good.

She'd looked back at the office as she walked away, half-expecting it to flicker like a faulty hologram. But it had never looked more solid. A steely, dropped anchor of a building that would now tether this part of the city to another past failure. The map was littered with them by this point. Emotional no-go zones, more plentiful than Pret a Mangers.

"Anyway, the bastard greenfly have virtually destroyed the lupins," Marjorie was saying now. Any lull in conversation tended to lead them back to the garden. "Your father tried blasting them off with the pressure washer but he didn't warn me and it ended up like that film with the wet woman. You know!"

Gwen didn't know.

"You *know*," she clucked, impatient. "The wet dancing woman, in her pants. Jazz Spray."

"*Flashdance?*"

"Exactly. Half-chewed to pieces, honestly I could weep."

There was a pause, a respectful silence for the lupins. Then: "Your father had his results back. He's quite upset."

"Results? Results for what?" Gwen's mind rattled through the possibilities like a morbid slot machine. Tumors? Blockages? STIs? Had this been mentioned when they last spoke? Wouldn't she have rung them sooner, if she'd known there were capital-R *Results* on the cards?

"His genetic test, the spitty tube thing. Everything Nana Marlowe always told him about being an eighth Māori wasn't true at all; he's ninety-seven percent Welsh. Such a waste of money."

Gwen opened her mouth to respond to this bombshell, but her mother had already moved on to developments in the council wheelie bin timetable, seemingly without pausing for breath.

Marjorie Grundle was a talker. Though not always outwardly confident—she tended to become nervous and fluttery around authority, and authority could include anybody from neighbors with detached houses to waiters who wanted to "explain the menu"—in her own domain she was so energetically verbal that often the only way to end an exchange with her was to simply walk out of the room. Even that didn't always work; more than once, Gwen had found herself making affirmative noises from the other side of a toilet door.

In recent years her mother's chat had become increasingly one-sided, like being fired at by one of those tennis ball training machines. While you scrabbled to catch one topic, she was immediately on to the next, usually with little interest in your return. It was as though she stored up every idle thought and opinion and meager scrap of domestic news for weeks on end, just waiting for someone to tell them all to. Which, Gwen realized now with a sad lurch in the pit of her stomach, she probably did.

A couple of years ago Marjorie had mentioned that several of her friends had family WhatsApp groups ("It's called a Who's Up chat") where they exchanged updates on their grandchildren and conservatories and multi-level marketing schemes. Gwen had offered to set one up for the three of them, but her mother had resisted.

"I wouldn't know how to use it."

"I'd show you."

"No no, I don't think so. Buzzing away all hours of the day! No thank you." She had been quiet for an uncharacteristic moment, fiddling with the lid on the mustard pot. "Besides"—a slow, pointed exhale—"we wouldn't have anything to send."

The unspoken words had curdled the air. *Not anymore.*

"Anyway, I'd better go!" Gwen cut across the latest update from a distant cousin's bitter custody battle. She found she was suddenly exhausted, and there was guilt creeping in around the edges.

"Of course, of course, I'll let you get on," replied her mother. Chastened, as though it was she who had phoned and interrupted Gwen's busy schedule. "Nice to speak to you."

The clipped formality only made it worse.

"You too," Gwen replied, trying to sound upbeat. "Lots of love to the lupins!"

There was a faint harrumph at this, then the click of her hanging up the phone. Golden late afternoon sunshine streamed in from beneath the blinds that Gwen hadn't bothered to open today.

Beyond the window, everything on the street was silent. One less lie, at least.

# Shoes

---

They hurt, but that wasn't the point. Or it *was* the point, even—a sacrifice to the party gods in exchange for a better night out.

The next day Nish and her friends would hobble heroically, compare blisters with pride. They were still several years away from understanding that feet weren't dispensable. Once, her friend Rana had trodden on a broken glass bottle, barefoot, outside McDonald's and had to be rushed to A&E with a wad of napkins to stem the blood that flowed thick as poster paint. Nobody had wanted ketchup for a while after that.

When they'd arrived at the hospital, no amount of explaining to staff that Rana wasn't drunk, *she didn't even drink*, would stop them putting her in with the Saturday-night booze hounds and their unpredictable fluids, until eventually she fainted. Nish had stayed with her until 4 a.m., when they had finally stitched up her foot and sent her home in borrowed flip-flops. The flip-flops, Rana felt, were the greater injury.

Nish had saved up for them, these shoes. They weren't top-tier designer, only mid-level, but they came with their own dust bag and that was prestige enough. Five weeks of the tutoring money that topped up her student loan, plus swapping her lunchtime sushi boxes for miserable chicken wraps that she got up early to make each morning before lectures—but they were worth it.

High, but not stupid-high. White leather, which probably *was* stupid, considering the city grime they'd have to navigate on a regular basis, but Nish was a firm believer in dressing for the life you wanted, not the one you had. The life she wanted had taxis and smooth, clean Chelsea pavements.

Spike heels, pointed toes, with slim, buckled straps that criss-crossed over her arches like architectural latticework. They reminded her of the roof in King's Cross station, a pie-crust dome of lines and curves that she loved to stare up at, especially late at night, twirling slowly in a circle before her eyes started to swim and she began to topple over backward, had to grab on to a ticket machine for support while her friends cackled and jeered from across the concourse. Unlike Rana, Nish did drink.

There was no occasion for the shoes. "The shoes ARE the occasion," she'd announced in the group chat, insisted that plans were canceled and new plans made to herald their arrival and justify their price tag. She'd told her mother that they were from the sale at Peacocks. She wouldn't know the difference anyway.

That first outing, she winced her way around two bars and then on to a club Millie had suggested—some dingy basement full of beery thirty-somethings rapping along to UK garage. Not the scene the shoes deserved, but better than traipsing the streets for hours with their noses pressed to Google Maps.

It was usually at this point in the night that the group began to splinter. The sensible ones would start making noises about chips and bed and early lectures. The coupled ones would take to calling their boyfriends from the street outside for twenty minutes at a time: conversations that consisted only of narrating the whole of the evening's fun so far while preventing the fun from continuing. And one or two would go missing in action, only to resurface at hometime with a new best friend, an incomprehensible story or an estate agent from Pinner attached to their neck. Often there'd be cross-pollination; other groups containing friends of friends and brothers of friends would merge with theirs, familiar faces from school and uni might loom up on the dance floor. It wasn't uncommon to end up hugging an exuberant goodbye at the bus stop, only to ask, "Who actually was that?" as you walked away and discover that nobody knew.

But tonight, Nish was the only splinter. She'd felt his hand on her waist before she'd seen him, had stepped aside to let him pass. Except he'd kept it there, pulled her gently into him as they danced. Rana would have slapped it away if she'd seen, screamed at him until the dance floor parted and the bouncers started mobilizing. But she hadn't seen, and Nish had kept on dancing. It was usually easier to keep dancing.

After a few beats she had allowed herself to look back at him. Brown hair, blue shirt, gray eyes, unwavering grin. Wholly generic, but there was something puppyish about the smile—like a schoolboy conducting a prank he couldn't quite believe he was getting away with. A wet paper towel on the ceiling. A hand in the Bunsen burner flame. Nish didn't smile back, but she didn't move either.

He was a bad dancer. Shuffling from one foot to the other, sporadically trying to mimic the popping hips and syncopated arms around him, then stumbling and going back to his flat-footed sway. She half-wondered if he was keeping his hand on her for balance. As one track merged into the next and he clearly considered enough time to have passed, he bent down and breathed into her hair. "Cannagetyouadrink?" Nish shook her head. She might have liked a drink, but yelling awkward conversation at the bar was a prospect she found she didn't have the energy for. "Shhhh, mmagetyouadrink," he replied, giving her waist a squeeze.

"Honestly, nah thanks," she replied, holding her hands up and twitching her hips in an attempt to flick his hand off. It stayed firm.

"Gooooon," he tried again, the smile slipping. It was as though he was playing a computer game and believed buying her a drink was the only way to unlock the next level. Nish smirked at this thought, and kept dancing.

For a few beats he did too, while she scanned the room for her friends—half exit strategy, half to see if they were watching. As she strained her neck in an attempt to see through the throng of bodies, the man moved his hand down to her hipbone. He pulled her into his pelvis, with an exaggerated grinding motion that made her faintly embarrassed for him. Any kindling desire she might have had was extinguished there, just as she felt his own become more viscerally apparent against her hip. Nish reached down and took his hand off her, holding it in a mock-ballroom pose as she twirled around to face him. "Maybe see you later, yeah," she shouted, a deliberate lack of question mark.

Over his shoulder she spotted Millie's blue hair and Rana's be-jeweled phone case in the queue for the toilets, and started toward them just as the boy—even in later recollections, she couldn't bring herself to think of him as a *man*—stepped sideways to block her path. One of her spike heels landed square in the middle of his toes (brown loafers, what else had she expected?) and he howled, a guttural howl, pain laced with something else. Fury.

"BITCH!" he roared at Nish, killing the "sorry" dead on her lips. Instead she turned on the same heel and began pushing her way through the crowd towards her friends. *'Scuse me. Whoops. Sorry. Watch out.* Something bitter rose in her throat but she swallowed it down and swung her hair over her shoulder. Fixed a wry smile to her face. She was already polishing up the anecdote, in her mind, for their entertainment.

An hour later they were leaving, clattering up the stairs, pulling on jackets and bickering about bus routes, when she saw him up ahead in the stairwell. Nish looked down at her phone to avoid his gaze. As she approached she saw, with a tingle of satisfaction, the black mark her heel tip had left in the middle of his tan suede.

He was silent as she passed, though she felt his eyes on her. *Up, down, up again.* Then, a second before she stepped out of his reach, she felt it—warm, alien fingers beneath her dress, grasping hard at the flesh between her buttock and thigh. Nish threw her arm back to slap his away, but in the same second he retracted it and instead her phone flew out of her hand, bouncing on several steps before landing on the polished concrete at the bottom of the staircase with a sickening crunch. Her turn to howl.

His cold, machine-gun laugh smarted in her ears as she pushed past him and raced down to retrieve her phone, the screen shattered in a way that reminded Nish, abstracted in the moment, of her mother's best cut-glass dessert bowls. She could feel his eyes on her, still, as her cheeks burned and her skin crawled with the fresh memory of his touch, but she willed herself not to look up.

"Nishaaaaaaaa," came Rana's screech from the top of the stairs, followed by the thunder of her cavalry arriving at the scene. By the time they'd fussed and commiserated and lamented her clumsiness, he'd disappeared. She didn't tell her friends; didn't have the energy this time. She never explained why she was shaking.

Nish only wore the shoes twice after that. Once to somebody's birthday drinks (a waste, everyone else was in Doc Martens) and once on her cousin's hen weekend, where the bride had decreed that the whole party dress entirely in white. Each time, Nish had taken them off at the end of the night and wiped them down carefully, checking the leather for nicks and marks. She stroked a finger up the heel, lovingly buckled the crisscross straps, and slipped them back into their dust bag.

A pang would hit her, when she saw their box under her bed—not guilt, but something with a similar flavor. Eventually her mother sent them to the charity shop without asking. Why should she be so angry, came the argument afterward. They were only cheap rubbish from Peacocks, and she never wore them anyway.

"Let somebody else ruin their feet," her mother had called over her shoulder. It was harder to argue with that.

6

When she went back to the shop for her first shift, Gwen couldn't see the ring anywhere and she was relieved.

It made her hot-cheeked with embarrassment, the idea of spotting it priced up in the valuables cabinet alongside watches, digital cameras, and celebrity perfumes still in their wrapping. The idea of seeing a stranger appraise it, try it on, discuss it with a friend, was unbearable—and she wasn't sure which would be worse, watching them buy it or reject it.

"Have you steamed before?" asked the young deputy manager, who had been assigned to train her. She was flame-haired, ink-eyed, and quietly self-possessed, with intricate floral tattoos peeping out through a loose crochet sweater and a lilting Scandinavian accent that made everything sound like a trick question.

"No. I mean, not, um, clothes," Gwen replied, as though perhaps she steamed her vagina instead. The woman, Lise, nodded as though she suspected as much.

"Everything is steamed before it goes on the shop floor," she continued.

"Even books?" asked Gwen, who was working so hard to sound engaged and attentive that she was neither engaged nor paying attention.

"No," replied Lise, eyes narrowing. Was she mentally barring her from keyholder privileges? "We clean the books with an antibacterial wipe."

Gwen wrote this down on her induction form. *Books = wipe*.

She was nervous, which was ridiculous. It was volunteer work! She couldn't get fired, she wasn't even being paid! Surely the main joy of this entire exercise was the chance to feel good about a job without actually having to *be* good at the job. But nobody had told this to her lower abdomen, which was swirling, cramping, and gurgling with the same volcanic fervor it usually reserved for first dates and client presentations. Her bowels didn't understand the volunteering loophole. They regarded this as just another chance to mess up.

While Gwen clenched discreetly, Lise walked her through the basics of steaming clothes. How to hang them, how to refill the machine, how not to scald herself and sue the charity for negligence. She showed her how to tag clothes using a pricing gun, which brought to mind the piercing gun a twelve-year-old Gwen had begged for months to be allowed to mutilate her in the window of Dream Cutz on the high street.

"Cap on at all times," Lise said solemnly. Gwen imagined the various ways she could accidentally impale herself, or other people, on its spike.

Finally, Lise explained how to sort the donations into the filing system that regimented the chaos of the back office.

Unlike the main shop, which displayed some half-hearted attempts to modernize—pale gray paint, a single velvet footstool, Aldi reed diffusers on several surfaces—the back office was a brown-carpeted portal to an earlier world. Not much larger than Gwen's own bedroom, it was lined on three sides with a forest of clothes, hung on sturdy industrial rails and delineated by various laminated signs saying things like MEN'S COATS, WOMEN'S JEANS, and KEEP ME FOR HALLOWEEN. The remaining side had a small beige kitchenette, a dusty window, a computer desk, a shelving unit piled high with boxes, till rolls, balls of rubber bands, jars of bulldog clips, rolls of sellotape and other detritus, and a pinboard on the wall plastered with rotation schedules, calendars, campaign posters with curling edges (it was a mental health charity, it turned out), oversized greetings cards saying "Thank You!" and "You're a Star!" in foil writing, and a painted metal sign bearing the legend MORE COFFEE, LESS MONDAY.

Gwen immediately liked it in here. She liked the coziness of it, the honest, industrious shabbiness of it, which all felt so far removed from the ironic pop art and aggressive clear-desk policy at Invigorate Media Inc. She liked the general sense that she would never be more than three feet away from a cup of tea in a chipped Forever Friends mug.

She didn't like the fact that the toilet was within audible earshot of the back room and most of the customers. But at least there was a hand dryer she could blast for the duration.

At break time Gwen made stilted conversation with Lise, feeling the way she had used to when encountering one of the junior designers in the office kitchen. Both painfully aged, and somehow also too ignorant for the world.

"Do you live nearby?" she asked, as they waited for the kettle to boil.

"Yes, over there," Lise replied, jerking an arm toward the window. A cluster of mid-rise tower blocks was visible, edging the park.

"Ah. Lovely," said Gwen. Then, as silence descended and the kettle was still holding out on them, "How long have you been there?"

"About four years," answered Lise. "I moved there after I left . . . what's the word . . ."

"University?" supplied Gwen, helpfully.

". . . rehab," finished Lise, at the same time. The kettle clicked off as more steam filled the hot little room. "Would you like milk?"

Next, Lise taught Gwen to use the till and she discovered she liked that too. There was a pleasing rhythm to it. Tapping in the numbers, folding the clothes, the mechanical *scoosh* of the cash drawer into her abdomen and the solid *ker-plunk* as she slammed it shut. She enjoyed having a script, of sorts. "Hi theeere thank you six pounds please cash or card would you like a bag there's your receipt thanks again, byeee." It was a framework around which she found she could be charming and cheerful without trying too hard. Nobody was expecting her to dazzle them with witty badinage; they simply wanted to pay for their new backpack or set of five Ikea dinner plates (£3.50, sold as seen) and be on their way.

Of course, Gwen reminded herself, it was easy to be charming and cheerful because she was doing this for a few hours, not days or months or years on end. She was just playing at shop on a Wednesday afternoon, while her bank balance still reflected a job in which she was never required to use an antibacterial wipe on anything.

Still, it felt nice. It felt nice to lean her hip on the counter, a mug of tea in her hands, whistling along to the radio with the calm authority of One Who Is Supposed to Be There.

And in fact, not every customer did want to pay and be on their way. Many were keen to linger and chat, some greeting her with familiar "hello darling!"s and "how are you today?"s despite never having seen her before. Women her own age came in pairs, wearing yoga pants, exchanging a steady, unbroken stream of personal news and gossip as they combed methodically through each rail. A gaggle of teenagers stayed for ages, preening in unlikely outfits, getting in everyone's way, and yelling cryptic jokes across the shop floor.

More people seemed to buy something than not. A few seemed to be buying any old junk just to prolong the activity, as though leaving the shop without spending a quid on a Velcro wallet or an Otters of the World desk calendar simply wasn't an option.

One elderly woman with a walker-cum-stool parked herself cheerfully beside the counter for forty minutes, requesting a parade of items from around the shop be brought to her for inspection. These included a pair of football boots, a sequinned miniskirt, and a set of ceramic salt and pepper shakers shaped like frogs. At each one she would peer with great concentration, slowly turning it over in her hands, then suck her teeth at the price tag and hand it back to Gwen, dismissing her with a regal hand wave. Eventually the woman stood up and began her slow shuffle out, bidding a gracious farewell with the air of a minor royal having opened a leisure center.

Before long it was 5 p.m., which was closing time. Even the idea of a shop closing at 5 p.m. felt comforting to Gwen. When she visited her parents in their Surrey market town ("the suburbs of the suburbs" was the pithy descriptor she'd hit on while she was at uni, back when taking a verbal dump on your hometown felt as obligatory as Toulouse-Lautrec posters or boycotting Nestlé), she used to despair at the way everything except pubs and takeaways shut its doors so early. It seemed pigheadedly provincial. This was the internet age! Time was a superficial construct! Did businesses not *want* extra income from the aspirational evening shop-popper?

But these days it was soothing, to think about a world where the working day concluded before dusk and you could be home by the end of *Pointless*. It tapped into a yearning that crept up on her sometimes from nowhere, for a kind of peacefully analog, butter-dish-and-toast-rack pace of life that maybe didn't exist anywhere anymore, not even in the suburbs of the suburbs.

This wasn't a desire she'd ever articulate to anyone. It seemed patronizing, vaguely problematic. Probably ignorant. Possibly Tory? But she felt it all the same.

Gwen flapped about uselessly now, straightening the paperbacks and cradling her third mug of tea, as Lise and the other staff closed up. The other staff today were a silent teenager in a hoodie named Harvey, a wiry septuagenarian in neon trainers called Brenda, and the Wax Man, the store manager, whose name was Michael and whose only interaction with Gwen so far had been to greet her with "Ah, the runaway bride!" and hand her a volunteer liability waiver.

Now, he appeared in the doorway to the back room, looked her slowly up and down and said: "You're losing your biscuit." He said it in such a dour, Eeyoreish tone that it took her a few seconds to realize this wasn't a critique of her first day's performance, merely a heads-up that her Hobnob was about to fall into her tea. She didn't know what to make of Michael.

But the others seemed nice, or at least benign, and Gwen's insides had settled and solidified themselves at some point during the afternoon. When Lise waved a schedule at her and asked if she'd be back, Gwen said yes and signed up for another shift on Sunday, and another the following Tuesday.

"Good," Lise nodded, smiling as though she had won a private bet. "I think you show potential."

Leaving the shop, Gwen saw her bus pulling into the bus stop about fifty meters up the road. She didn't run for it, because Gwen didn't run for buses. Or trains. Or anything, anymore. That was her rule.

"If you run, you might miss it anyway. But if you don't run, you still have your dignity," she had explained once to an exasperated Suze, in the times long before taxi apps. And now, she watched as the last passenger ahead of her boarded the 341 and the bus chugged into motion, leaving her alone on the pavement with her dignity.

This was fine, she decided. She could use the walk.

# Hat

It was a stupid amount of money to spend on a hat. It was a stupid amount of money to spend on anything you couldn't sit in or drive or live in. And yet it was a form of contract; a tacit agreement upon even setting foot over the threshold of this shop—this tiny, archaic boutique tucked away down a side street between Soho and Piccadilly Circus, with its towers of tweed deerstalkers and felt fedoras all stacked up in the window—that one was prepared to spend a mad amount of money on a hat. The moment the bell tinkled your arrival and you accepted the eager greetings of the man in the horn-rimmed glasses behind the counter, your fate was sealed.

Toby found this oddly freeing. Once he'd stroked a finger along a few brims, once he'd tried on several, once he'd asked for a certain style to be fetched down from an awkward shelf and been duly reassured that yes, it was a perfect shape for sir's face and no, it didn't make sir's features look like a *Spitting Image* puppet, the matter was already out of his hands. The money was as good as spent. All he had to do now was hand his card over, take receipt of the stiff, cardboard carrier bag and leave the shop in a dignified manner without turning and rushing back to shout "THERE'S BEEN A TERRIBLE MISTAKE."

Toby wasn't a hat guy. Statistically, who was? One in ten? One in fifty? They're a rare beast, a person who can put a hat on in complete seriousness, without everyone they see greeting them with a too-cheerful ". . . hat!"—and Toby would never before have presumed to have been one, despite a hairline that might have encouraged it. But today he had woken up and thought, *Fuck it, why can't I be a hat guy? Why not me?*

He had a head, didn't he? He knew he did, because Deborah had thrown a plate at it last week before she moved out. She'd wanted it to smash with dramatic effect on the wall behind him, he knew. But because Toby wasn't even capable of being dumped in a passionate manner, it had twanged against his left ear and landed with a lame thud on the carpet.

And now she was gone, moved in with some man from her book group with a gold tooth who kept pythons. And now Toby was a hat guy, or at least he was according to his bank statement.

The law of the eye-watering impulse purchase, he knew, is that it only goes one of two ways: either you wear the thing incessantly, out of guilt and determination to get your money's worth, or you never wear the thing at all, out of guilt and desire to pretend the whole thing never happened. Toby was curious, as he stepped out of the shop and seemingly forward in time by about three decades, to see which this would be.

**7**

> Hey! We're having a bit of a thing next month,
> on the tenth. Come round? Feel free to bring
> someone! X

This was incredibly Suze. "A bit of a thing" could mean anything from a Domino's eaten standing up at the kitchen island, to professional catering and a string quartet tucked discreetly under the stairs.

Once, a few years ago, Gwen had turned up with wet hair and a corner shop bottle of Barefoot to find everyone wearing backless dresses and drinking negronis made by a man in a waistcoat.

"Why didn't you *tell* me it was going to be fancy?" Gwen had demanded, clutching her parka closed as though she was accidentally naked beneath it.

"It wasn't supposed to be!" Suze had wailed back. "It's his friends, they think everything's the Serpentine sodding summer party." She later admitted to having hired the bartender herself, but insisted the waistcoat wasn't part of the contract.

Although Gwen's heart had leaped pathetically at the message as it lit up her phone, the "feel free to bring someone" part pinched a little. It was hard to say why. Maybe because it hinted that Gwen was an awkward presence, one Suze didn't want to feel obliged to babysit all night. Or perhaps it was because Suze should, by rights, know that there was no "someone" to bring.

*

Since Ryan there had been, on average, one and a quarter men per year. Gwen often worked it out this way in her head, spreading her romantic history thinly across the years to make it go further. One and a bit men per year, or 0.09 men per month, or 0.023 per week. A meager ration, but for the most part, she accepted it. Modern dating was a barren landscape, everybody said so, and anyway vibrator design was so advanced nowadays.

At first it had felt like penance. A voluntary vow of celibacy. Wasn't that the least she could do, after what she'd done to Ryan? To prove to onlookers (Gwen's actions were often accompanied by an imaginary Greek chorus of "people" with "opinions') that she was remorseful and "going through something" and definitely not breaking up with him because she had shagged anyone else.

It took nearly a year of abstinence, refusing to install dating apps and shrinking away from the workmates who leaned too close at the bar, refusing even to meet men's eyes on the Tube, for god's sake, for her to start to wonder if this approach might actually be worse. Would it have looked better if she'd left Ryan for a *purpose*? To let rip, sow some wild oats, live her life more fully? The more she thought about it, the more she worried that to have smashed apart a perfectly decent relationship and canceled a perfectly nice wedding to stay home with her misery and the Satisfizer 3000 was actually a greater crime.

It took a while longer for Gwen to realize that in fact, nobody was watching. Not really. Not even Ryan.

After that, there had been Theo, the flop-haired Belle and Sebastian fan in a cardigan, who had taken her for flowering jasmine tea on their first date and proposed an ayahuasca retreat for their second. Lawrence, a "semi-professional DJ" in his early fifties who she'd met on a broken-down train just outside Woking, and who had cooked her stroganoff and stroked her hair in a fatherly way that she enjoyed so much she decided she could never see him again. Matthias, one of the monosyllabic tech guys from work, who had taken her back to his after the Christmas party and forced her to join in several rounds of Never Have I Ever with his housemates before sticking his hand up her top in the kitchen.

Rav, a kind-eyed social worker who she had met during the final weeks before Guardian Soulmates shut down, when the whole site had had the frenzied feel of the last ten minutes of a school disco before the lights come back on. She had dated Rav enthusiastically for a month, before he ended things due to her lack of interest in the Marvel Cinematic Universe and reluctance around sending nudes. Kyle, who had seemed promising until he told her she "walked with a heavy tread" and then ghosted her. Ben, Beige Ben, Big Beige Ben, who was so dull that she didn't ghost him so much as forget he existed until she found his text on her phone a fortnight later. And Marcus. An actor who occasionally cropped up as a bit part on ITV legal dramas and adverts for car insurance, who had taken her on one lavish date to the restaurant at the top of the Heron Tower, and then invited her over to his on precisely three occasions to have sex and watch him play Assassin's Creed. The last time, a pizza delivery had arrived just as she was pulling her tights back on, and he hadn't offered her any. Marcus was the one that still hurt.

That had been over a year ago, and since then Gwen had retreated back to her old vow of celibacy. Not for Ryan, but for her own dignity. The well was empty. What was she supposed to use to lure in potential dates? How perfectly she'd mastered the art of scrambling a single egg in the microwave? The eight-strong split end she'd found on a strand of her hair last week and kept in her pocket for posterity?

It was all too hard, so she'd granted herself a few months off. As a treat. Time to recharge and regroup. Plan a new strategy. Get a new haircut. But the few months turned into more months, as they always did, and then into winter, and then . . . Lent? And before she knew it her love life had slipped into The Void along with her overdue gas bill.

*

Gwen didn't open Suze's text for three days, to avoid the read receipts she was terrified of but also too lazy to locate and switch off.
    Finally, she drafted a reply.

> Sounds lovely, thanks! Probably just me though x

She paused, deleted it, and wrote another.

> Sounds lovely, wish I could! But I have another thing that night :(

She deleted this second part, unconvinced even by her own lie.

> But I have to have a root canal that night.

This felt too much like tempting fate.

> But I have to unpack a cardboard box that night.

> But I have to leave the country on classified maneuvers with MI6.

> But I don't want to.

> But I want to too badly.

Gwen deleted the text altogether, and turned off her phone. The Greek chorus sighed in frustration.

# Tie

---

It was the tie he'd bought with the tenner his mum had given him from her purse. As a congratulations and a thank-you, for getting the job nobody thought he'd get and giving her palpitating heart a rest for five earthly minutes. It was the tie he knotted himself into with shaking hands, only a few short weeks after he'd worn his last tie, his school tie, around his head, and then burned it with a lighter as a symbolic fuck-you to all those years of enforceable tie-wearing.

It was navy blue. Polyester. He didn't know another kind.

It was the tie he'd bought despite nobody telling him he needed to wear a tie, and although everyone else in the office wore their shirts open-necked and tucked into jeans, or else a slim-fit sweatshirt and no collar at all. Even the boss. It was the tie he continued to wear for six weeks straight, with his old school trousers and his cousin's hand-me-down blazer, until his new colleagues started to call him "Alan Partridge" behind his back. Then to his face.

It was the tie he continued to wear when he left the house, then stuffed into a pocket as he rounded the corner of the estate, away from his mum's beaming face at the window, and the tie he put on again as he retraced the same steps back each evening to be greeted by a torrent of questions and a warm fug of cooking smells, of spice and sugar and salt and fat.

It was the tie she continued ironing, lovingly, each morning. She could never understand how it got so crumpled.

# 8

"Excuse me! This doesn't have a cable."

A wiry middle-aged man placed something large, ornate and made from brass on the counter. A smirk played about his lips, as though he were about to make her look very foolish indeed.

"Ah," said Gwen, pretending to look.

"See, here." He pointed out the hole in the back where a cable should be, and where a cable wasn't.

"I see. I'm sorry."

"Well?" he demanded. "Do you have the cable?"

"I'm afraid not," she told him. "Sorry about that."

"But it's useless without the cable!" he spluttered.

"Mm. I suppose we're selling it more as a decorative item," ventured Gwen. She still wasn't sure what "it" was. "Or it could be a restoration project for someone?"

"I'd have to contact a specialist electrician!"

"I'm sorry," she tried again. "Thing is, we can only sell things in the state they're donated to us . . ."

"It could cost more than the lamp!"

". . . that's why the sticker says 'Sold as seen.'"

"They might not even make that style of cable anymore!"

"Right. Well, nobody's forcing you to buy it."

They had arrived at a stalemate and stood for a second, staring at the lamp, both of them with their arms folded across their chests as if waiting for a tardy genie to arrive.

"If you don't want it, then I'll—"

She made to pick up the lamp and carry it back to the bric-a-brac section, but the man was now pulling out his wallet and producing a ten-pound note.

"I suppose I'll take it," he muttered, as if doing her a great favor.

"Lovely," said Gwen.

This wasn't an unusual exchange, she was learning. Not everyone grasped the concept of a charity shop, and those who did often acted as though each item had been placed there specifically for their disappointment. Or as if Gwen had. Customers often spoke to her as though she were stupid, or as though her life must have hit the skids in dramatic fashion to have ended up here, working for free on a weekday afternoon. Which she supposed wasn't untrue.

But the more shifts she volunteered and the more her stage fright wore off, the more she was beginning to find the customers disappointed her too. On the whole there was less respect for the systems and routines that governed traditional retail—things like queuing, and putting clothes back on hangers, and deciding which items you wanted to buy *before* you got to the counter rather than holding up five people behind you while you deliberated at leisure. Maybe some people behaved that way in every shop; she didn't know. She did know that it was futile to ask them not to leave their rejected clothes on top of the pile at the end of the counter, explaining that this was in fact the *tagging* pile and not the *changing* pile, as though the subtle machinations of charity shop life meant anything to them. To them, it was all just piles.

Sometimes they were on the phone when they came to the counter and kept up the conversation throughout the whole transaction, not looking at her, not even looking at the total as it came up on the card reader. It was rude, but on balance probably no ruder than St. Michael serving customers with one hand while he did the crossword, or Brenda holding up ugly donations and shrieking with horror before the donor had even left the shop. In many ways it was worse when people wanted to engage. Like the man who spent ten minutes explaining, quite aggressively, why Gwen should keep a dream journal. Or when they asked her to help them choose between two items, and invariably bought the one she hadn't chosen.

The man with the lamp huffed his way out of the shop, and all was quiet again. Gwen eased her phone from her pocket.

As always, guilt throbbed at her from behind the glass. The guilt of unanswered messages, unread subscriptions, unsigned petitions, photos of missing children she hadn't shared and misunderstood memes she vowed to look up later and never did. She toyed with replying to Suze's message—three days and counting—but couldn't face the tyranny of the blank window. She checked her email. Ten percent off on algae supplements. She checked the weather. Sixteen degrees Celsius, cloud.

Gwen had left Instagram now, more or less. It hadn't been good for her but that wasn't the reason; she left because she wasn't good *at it*. She would agonize for hours over captions, rewriting each one until it felt overwrought and unfunny, like a modest bungalow crushed by a series of clumsy extensions. After a while she'd stopped posting anything at all, lurking and liking only, strumming at her screen like a miserable adult fidget spinner. Then one day she deleted the app to free up more storage, and had never reinstalled it, thus severing one of her last connections to all the friends she rarely saw in real life. Apparently this was healthier.

But Twitter still held some fascination. It felt like eavesdropping on strangers, which she loved to do in real life too. Sometimes she'd switch benches in the park to sit closer to a couple having an argument. Not for the schadenfreude, or not exactly. Just to know.

As she scrolled, a stranger's retweet caught her eye. "Devastated to announce that my darling wife, my best friend, died yesterday. She was thirty-seven. Life will never be the same without you, Rachel."

"What from though?" Gwen muttered. It was the question she couldn't ask and always wanted to, whenever she rubbernecked on a stranger's premature death. How did they die? *Why* did they die? And what was the precise percentage likelihood of it happening to her? She would fall into holes for hours, picking her way back through the digital footpaths of the deceased, looking for clues. Anything that might suggest they lived a thrill-seeking lifestyle, foraged ambiguous mushrooms or raised wolverines in badly constructed cages. That they smoked forty a day and ate bacon grease with a spoon. That their parents were first cousins, and also nephew and aunt. Anything that allowed her to gratefully exhale, set aside her selfish panic and get on with the business of feeling compassionate, like a good person, from a distance.

"Penny for them?" asked Brenda, appearing over her shoulder with an armful of men's shirts.

Gwen shoved her phone back into her pocket and recomposed her features. "Only death!" she replied. "Do these need tagging?" She took the shirts gratefully into her arms and hugged them to her chest for a second.

"Speaking of death," began Brenda, but was promptly cut off by a customer buying a cardigan.

This happened a lot with Brenda. Actually it happened to all of them, though Brenda—a retired flight attendant who seemed to have served vodka and peanuts to half the Forbes rich list—had the best stories to interrupt. She'd launch into what promised to be a long, juicy anecdote while they idled behind the counter, only to break off mid-sentence on an agonizing cliffhanger when someone came to the till. *So there we were, naked as a jaybird with this ferret on a lead, when WHO SHOULD— Oh hello there, the red jacket on the mannequin was it? Hold on, I'll fetch the stool . . .*

While St. Michael tended to rule over the shop in draconian fashion, telling them off for minor infringements like slouching over the counter or using "French sevens" on price tags, it was generally accepted that the volunteers were there to socialize as much as philanthropize.

"The chat is my wages," Brenda had told her last week, with the authority of a union president. "Nice to do our bit for the loonies, I know, but if I couldn't have a natter I wouldn't come."

"I'm only here because I have no life," she had told Brenda in reply. "It was this or the dentist."

Brenda had nodded, unquestioning. Gwen decided to let "loonies" lie.

Every volunteer seemed to move in their own orbit, crossing paths at random, some pledging regular days every week while others popped in on a whim every couple of months. The schedule that hung in the back room was a tangled net of scribbles, crossed-out names and weaving arrows to keep track of who was meant to be there and when, and the managers seemed genuinely surprised every time she arrived for her shift. It felt nice to be in a workplace where nobody was competing for promotion or jostling to be the crown prince of a pitch meeting. Here, people were grateful for the very fact of her turning up.

Was this the secret of volunteering, she wondered. Giving your free time in exchange for the guarantee that someone, at least, will look pleased to see you? Wasn't that the same reason people got dogs? Or escorts? Gwen had once accompanied an earnest former housemate to a sparsely attended talk on Why Altruism Doesn't Exist. For two hours, in a lecture theater that smelled of boiled potatoes, she had listened to a man with a soul patch explaining that every good deed was deeply selfish and that charity was a capitalist con. It had enraged her at the time, not least because the earnest housemate had fallen asleep and snored, but now she almost wished she'd paid more attention to the tip-off. Perhaps helping others was a canny life hack she had waited too long to try.

As well as Brenda and Lise, she had now worked alongside

Harvey, the waifish teen who never talked, and Gloria, a beautiful Trinidadian pharmacist who did nothing but talk. Gwen left their first shift together hoarse and slightly dazed, clutching a recommendation for the best off-brand multivitamins and a recipe for vegetable moussaka.

There was also Jeremy, a retired banker from Highgate with a Nigel Havers-ish air, who was volunteering to ease his overdue crisis of conscience and hide from his second wife. There was Yasmeen, a "dance-positive content creator," who, Gwen later learned, was famous to everyone under the age of twenty-five but to absolutely nobody over it. Finn, a doe-eyed barista-slash-something with an ironic curtained haircut. Brian, a former prison officer with a broom of a mustache, who liked to stake out the valuables cabinet as though starring in an Andy McNab novel. And a willowy blonde in harem pants who Gwen could only address as "Hello, you!" because when they had first been introduced she thought Michael had said "Harp"—and nobody, surely, could be called Harp.

But her favorite person so far was Asha, a lawyer in her late twenties with a disarming conversational style that involved pelting a person with questions both superficial ("How do you feel about Marmite hummus?") and deeply personal ("Do you believe in an afterlife?"). All answers were treated with equal reverence; with an unblinking gaze and a torrent of follow-up questions. Why did she come to that conclusion? How did it affect the way she lived her life? Did a breakfast spread have any right to infiltrate the picnic dip market, and would this set a dangerous precedent?

Something about the blend of low stakes and busy hands lent itself to lowered inhibitions, and Gwen found herself opening up to Asha with a candor she hadn't allowed herself in a long time. Not since all her friends stopped staying out past 9 p.m., and she started to feel like an adult chaperone among her colleagues. Chatting at length about herself felt stiff but satisfying, like stretching a long-dormant muscle. It felt, she noted with a guilty pang, like the exact opposite of talking to her mother.

*

It took several shifts to realize that while Asha now knew almost everything about Gwen, from her GCSE results to her preferred menstrual hygiene method, Gwen knew hardly anything about Asha. So one day, when the shop was almost empty and smelled of damp raincoats, she attempted to switch the direction of the current.

"Sooooo. What led you here?" she asked, cocking her head to one side in a way she hoped might welcome disclosure.

"The one-four-one," Asha replied without looking up. "Stunk of piss."

Asha was attempting to untangle a huge pile of necklaces. This was the Rubik's cube of charity shop work. Nobody ever expected to complete the task, but it was a relaxing way to keep your hands occupied.

Gwen laughed. She tried again.

"I meant, ah, why did you start volunteering?"

"Oh." Asha tensed slightly around the shoulders. "I . . . ha. I went briefly batshit and got sent home from work for a while. Signed off. So excessive!" She rolled her eyes. "I mean, they're fine when you're in the office until three a.m. chaining CBD gummies, but one tiny little sobbing meltdown in front of the clients and suddenly it's all 'concern' this and 'take some time to recalibrate' that. Anyway, after I'd rewatched the whole of *Gilmore Girls*, I needed to get out of the house. So."

She gestured to the shop, as though it was the obvious answer. Gwen nodded in recognition.

"That's tough. I'm sorry."

"Whatever. It's fine. Paid holiday! I'd rather be here than trying to convince my mum for the thousandth time that stress leave is a real thing, not code for 'sacked for mouthing off too much.' She's more concerned about what to tell the aunties at Christmas than she is about my fragile mental state."

"Can't she just tell them the truth?"

Asha grinned at Gwen. "You joking? More believable to tell them I've been visited by three ghosts and half the cast of the *Muppets*." She adopted a Ghanaian accent. "What have you to be sad about? Ashanti, there's nothing wrong with your brain that prayer and cleaning the bathroom cannot solve."

"Ah." She didn't know what else to say.

"Yeah." Asha shrugged. "Is what it is."

Gwen watched as she tugged firmly at a necklace and it came free, quite suddenly, from the knotted mass of chains. "GET INNNN," cheered Asha, holding it up to examine it in the light. It was a tarnished silver owl pendant; a relic from that time in the near-past when every second object had an owl on it.

"There," she said, fanning herself. "Can't say I'm not hitting my targets."

# Souvenir

Was it supposed to be ironic? She couldn't remember.

Was it ironic now? She wasn't sure.

Was it likely, that after the hours and hours and thousands of pounds of fees paid to smooth-voiced, slick-palmed lawyers to carve up their mutual assets like a pound of rump steak, to caw over the charred remains of their relationship like the vultures from *The Jungle Book* with less attractive haircuts, that he would fight her for custody of a fridge magnet shaped like a paella pan with *¡Te amo!* painted below it in red, black, and yellow?

Did she want it? No. She didn't want to see it there every time she opened a certain cupboard, to studiously overlook it every time she needed a serving dish, and even in the act of ignoring it to be caught off guard, winded, snagged by the sharp corner of a passing memory, of his skin on hers, the taste of sea and salt and blood and fire.

Did she want him to have it? Also no.

Now it sits on the shelf in the charity shop, next to a pair of wooden egg cups, a Denby sugar pot, and a metal wall plaque that reads YOU HAD ME AT PROSECCO. Where it will be bought, ten days later, by a man from Tottenham for his Valencian girlfriend, whose homesickness has been severe of late, causing her to cry silently on the sofa and him to lie wide awake at night panicking that she might be gone in the morning. She will stare at it blankly, brow furrowed. He will tell her it's supposed to be ironic.

## 9

She had been volunteering at the shop for three weeks when Asha asked her to the pub.

"You're coming to the pub yeah, Gwen?" she called across the shop floor at closing time. When Gwen opened her mouth to say she didn't know anything about the pub, Asha pressed her lips together and made her eyes very wide in a gesture of silent pleading.

"I . . . um, yes! Pub! 'Course I am," she played along. While Asha mimicked prayer hands, a tall man emerged from the back room, chanting "Pub! Pub! Pub!" as though the word might be short for public school initiation rite.

She'd guess he was twenty-seven, twenty-eight at most. He had sandy hair full of product, and the smooth, ruddy cheeks of a painted cherub. He was wearing turned-up chinos with bare ankles and a shirt striped like Aquafresh.

"Gwen, have you met Nicholas? He's just back from holiday."

She hadn't met him, on purpose. He'd been in and out of the back room all afternoon, cracking too-loud jokes and making small, self-conscious shows of buffoonery—trying on a feathered fascinator, reading out book titles to nobody in particular, playing air guitar on a mop. It had felt easier to busy herself with something each time and refuse to catch his eye than to do the whole painful hi-hi-how-are-you-don't-think-we've-met dance.

Volunteer turnover was high, and she'd begun to understand

that shift patterns changed so frequently that it might be weeks or even months before she saw someone again. Besides, this looked like the kind of man who would go in for a handshake. Or worse, a cheek kiss.

"Hello! *Gwen* was it? Nice to meet you, *Gwen*." He said her name as though it were the punch line to a joke he didn't understand. Then his own, in case she'd missed it. "Nicholas."

Gwen had never trusted people with obvious nicknames who chose to use their full name instead. Toms who preferred to be Thomases. Kims who insisted on Kimberley at all times. It seemed arrogant to her, to force everyone to say three whole syllables every time when one would do. This was probably the side effect of having an outlandish name herself: a silly, frou-frou, knitted loo-roll cover of a name, which she only ever used in full when bidden by law.

Then, there it was—Nicholas's hand, proffered with the air of a special invited guest at a prize evening. It was warm and childishly soft. She braced herself for the kiss-swoop, but he just pumped it up and down a few times and released her. "Puuuuub," he boomed, swiveling and leading them out of the door with a golf umbrella in an outstretched arm.

"Sorry," muttered Asha as the women followed in his wake. "It was a medical emergency."

Ten minutes later, the three of them were in a booth at the Coach & Horses, Gwen and Asha watching over their wine as Nicholas lovingly buffed a picture frame with a soft cloth and a tin of silver polish.

"It's what I do," he was explaining to Gwen. "Or rather, what my *company* does. We're an interiors consultancy, specializing in sourcing authentic bygone paraphernalia for the urban hospitality industry."

"He sells retro tat to gastropubs," translated Asha. She reached for a fistful of crisps from the split-open packet in the middle of the table. "Oil paintings, old clocks, tea cozies. Any time you've ordered a drink with a stuffed otter looming down at you, he put it there."

Nicholas flushed, then produced a business card from his wallet and handed it to Gwen, leaving oily marks on the matte charcoal finish from where his fingers had been in the Tyrrells.

"Restaurants, cafés, boutique hotels, bars, co-working spaces—they know the vibe they want, but they don't have the time to trawl charity shops and antiques markets, eBay, etc., looking for the perfect artifacts to complete their vintage aesthetic?"

"So you do the trawling for them?" asked Gwen.

"Yes! I mean, no. I have an intern," replied Nicholas. He said this with a little snort-laugh, as though the intern was a given. "But we provide them with a completely bespoke edit of items to fit their unique brand profile? Whether that's, y'know, Post-War Suburban Kitsch or Mid-Century Domestic . . . ah . . . Kitsch."

"Aren't they the same thing?" asked Asha, spraying crumbs.

"No," said Nicholas, incredulous. "Post-War Suburban has doilies."

Gwen had been looking for jobs. Ish. Every evening after she'd washed up her saucepan, she would take a deep breath, open her laptop on the sofa and trawl a merry-go-round of recruitment sites, hoping that new adverts would have appeared on the first site by the time she'd finished rejecting everything on the last.

Occasionally something would strike her—Project Strategist at an app for dogs, Systems Wizard at a start-up called Upstart, Chief Zesting Zsar at a company that made bespoke bottled juices based on your DNA—but she would usually lose enthusiasm before she was halfway through the covering letter.

Gwen had always argued—to herself, mostly—that the reason she never got her act together to finally leave Invigorate was that looking for a job *was* a full-time job, and she was too tired in the evenings after long days of supervising "ideation sessions" full of boisterous twenty-four-year-olds like a childminder at a shopping center daycare. But now that she didn't have a job, now that her week was a baggy, unwieldy thing held together only by four-hour stints in a charity shop, walks round the block and *Homes Under the Hammer*, it turned out that time hadn't been the problem after all.

The problem was that she didn't *want* to do anything.

She didn't want to *do* anything.

She didn't want to do *anything*.

She hadn't felt a calling toward a certain career when she was young. But plenty of people left university without a clue, and fell into the first job that would have them. But she hadn't had a calling during the next wave either, the mid-to-late-twenties reckoning, when all around her people had been making exhilarating leaps to new ladders and scrambling up a few rungs to safety. She'd missed the third boat too, the early thirties exodus when people who had earned too much in the City or not enough in Bloomsbury, jacked it in to retrain as primary school teachers or open a boutique selling hand-poured soy candles. She had waited for her passion to find her, and it hadn't, and now she was forced to confront the sad fact that her passion might not exist.

"What made you want to be a lawyer?" she asked Asha the next morning, as they dressed the window display "for Eurovision" (gold lamé leggings, a faux-fur *Doctor Zhivago* hat, and a bustier with a Union Jack across the boobs).

"I always loved paperwork," Asha replied. "Obsessed with forms. When the other children were out playing in the street, I'd be in my bedroom, drawing up imaginary contracts."

"Really?"

"No, you twat. *Ally McBeal*."

# Slippers

Why does anyone take hotel slippers?

Either you're a slipper person, which means you own slippers, probably better ones, already—or you are not a slipper person, which means the very idea of shuffling about your own home like an escapee from Champneys probably makes you gag a little. Either way, you're not going to wear those slippers.

You know you're not. You would be embarrassed if anyone came to the front door while you had them on. It would be like wearing a sign that said: "I stayed in a hotel once!!! Did I mention?"

And yet, you take them home. Of course you do, because there they are—all fresh and virginal, two fat white slices of pseudo-luxury in crinkly cellophane wrapping. Just trying to do their job, which is to make you feel special and also help justify the room charge. You take them home for the same reason you take the fleecy blanket from the airplane and the calendar from the Chinese takeaway and the tiny pen, once upon a time, from Argos. Because it's not often this world gives you anything for free, so when it does you might as well take it.

Only, the slippers transubstantiate in your suitcase, and by the time you're taking them out at the other end they're no longer pseudo-luxurious but actively annoying. Just another thing, another bundle of atoms and space dust to find room for in an over-stuffed cupboard.

"Why did I take these slippers?" you ask yourself, chuckling fondly at the you of several hours ago. But even as you toss them into a drawer or put them in the bag for the charity shop (at least you resealed the cellophane, you reason, they're more resaleable now), you know you'll take the next pair, and the next. If you're lucky enough to have a next.

Because who are *you*, to turn down free slippers? What if life never gets better than free slippers? Free slippers! Imagine.

## 10

It was funny, the way viewing the donations out of context sometimes made them uglier—stretched-out bodycon, green-tinged jewelery, empty notebooks, and whimsical placards from Generic Gifts R Us—but sometimes it gave them an opportunistic sort of beauty, like the kind of crush that develops across an airport lounge during a three-hour delay.

This afternoon, Gwen was dusting the bric-a-brac section and admiring the contours of a chipped enamel saucepan. She appraised its robust bottom, lifted and replaced the neat little lid. Did she need a chipped enamel saucepan? Did it need her?

Currently Gwen only used one saucepan. She had others, of course—a whole Tefal set, slightly dented, pilfered at Great Aunt Dor's wake while everybody else was tussling over Lladro figurines—but there seemed little point putting them all into circulation. Instead, she washed out the same small pan three times a day. Porridge, soup, pasta; repeat; so that it lived permanently on the draining rack and never saw the inside of a cupboard.

Thinking about this one day as she soaped and rinsed the pan, scraping off the burnt remnants of oats and/or onions, Gwen was reminded of the twenty-four-hour Betterbuy on Kentish Town Road. She and Suze had been obsessed with it for a time, when they were twenty-two and newly installed in the city.

"But it has a shutter," Suze had said once, voice fuzzed with gin, as they sat at the bus stop after one of their nights bothering the basement bars of N1.

She'd pointed, Gwen had looked. It had a shutter. "So?"

"So, the shop never closes! The shutter never comes down," Suze had replied. "*Never. Comes. Down,*" she added, as if it were the payoff in a campfire ghost story.

They had sat and pondered this for several minutes. It hurt their heads a little to think about it, although maybe that was the London Dry. Eventually the bus arrived and they had sat on the back row, quiet for a while longer, chip boxes warm and sweating in their laps.

Finally Gwen had said, "Maybe it comes down at Christmas."

Yes, Suze had conceded. Maybe at Christmas.

Susannah. Susie. Suze. Suzy Q. SuBo, for a short while after Susan Boyle's *Britain's Got Talent* performance had moved her to heaving sobs in the corner of a house party. Suze was her savior. She'd never asked to be, but had cast herself unwittingly in the role by saving Gwen a seat on a year nine field trip to Bignor Roman Villa, at precisely the point where thirteen-year-old Gwen's chronic friendlessness at their all-girls comprehensive was in danger of tipping her from "melancholy child" to "clinically depressed adolescent."

It had been a worry. There had been hushed conversations in the kitchen after bedtime, followed by meetings with teachers and kind-faced doctors in cardigans. Gwen hadn't resisted so much as let their concern wash over her, the way she let her classmates' noise and activity wash over her most of the time. Wondering how a person was supposed to become a vessel and catch a little of that life and vigor, contain it and hold it for herself.

It wasn't like she'd never made friends. She had, in her time; had joined in the shared classroom mythologies and whispered playground secrets, secured permission to sit on the fringes of a birthday sleepover, making sure she laughed when everyone else did. It was *retaining* friends she struggled with. They slipped through her fingers like water.

But then here was Susannah—clever, confident Susannah, with her Goal Defense stature and her impressive collection of gift shop snap bracelets, Susannah who disarmed teachers with her questions and charmed the canteen staff with her metallic smile—holding her own hands out to catch Gwen.

Or was she? Gwen remembered every beat of that first inter-action. Shuffling down the aisle of the coach, hearing her name called, expecting to see a sympathetic teacher, guilted out of their brief solitude to look after the misery kid—and instead seeing her there, braces glinting in the light, gesturing to the empty seat beside her. Gwen doing a cartoon double take, entirely serious, looking behind her to see who the real beneficiary was. Suze laughing at this as though it was intentional slapstick, pulling her into the seat by the cuff of her blazer, then producing a copy of J17 and opening a packet of Revels like it was the most natural thing in the world.

She remembered the warmth Suze had given off, a kind of force field, as though her body had too much kinetic potential for one lanky teenager and needed to transmit some to its surroundings. Gwen had basked in that heat, like a stray cat on a sunlit pavement. She remembered giggling together over the magazine, making a bitchy comment about Whigfield that Suze seemed to approve of. She remembered desperately not wanting to get off the couch and break the spell, then the rush of pure relief when Suze had grabbed her as a partner for some activity involving tracing the ruins of an underfloor heating system. She remembered the floating ease with which they had found each other in the form room the next day and filled it with chatter and laughter too, and the next day, and the next.

She had felt as though all the thoughts and observations that had been sitting stagnant within her for years could finally come spilling out, tumbling forth like a burst pipe or a torrent of tiny polystyrene balls from a split beanbag (it was, after all, the nineties). Starting with the cleanest and most innocuous, the least likely to drive Suze away—*How funny is it that the name is Manic Street Preachers, as in people who preach manically in the street, and yet we pronounce it Manic Street Preachers, as though they are in fact preachers who live on Manic Street?*—then drilling down, down, down into the well of herself until there was nothing left to share but her deepest and weirdest thoughts, the ones that had mutated in the darkness and were never supposed to see the light of day. *Do you ever worry you might accidentally pick your nose in public? Do you ever think about how if you got pregnant from a toilet seat, it would be your dad's baby?* Suze could handle even those. She'd laughed at them, agreed with them, offered up her own titbits of interior pond life as consolation. Gwen remembered it all.

Suze, it later turned out, after perhaps the fifteenth retelling of their origin story, didn't remember the seat-saving at all. "I dunno, I thought we just kind of . . . became friends," she'd said, shrugging. "Did I really save you a seat? How adorable was I!"

As though it was that easy. Suze made life easy.

She'd made it easy to follow her to university, begging Gwen to take up her place at the same northern redbrick "so we can keep each other sane and stop each other going to toga parties." True to one part of the vow at least, within a fortnight Suze was pulling the covers off Gwen's head at midnight and dragging her out of bed to attend whatever horrible kitchen rave thumped through her bones from the other end of the building. "It's okay I hate it too!" she would trill, dragging Gwen by the hand into the smoky throng and introducing her to a parade of Stus and Steves and Darrens and Nickis and Nadias and people called "Wazzo" who Suze had already swapped life stories with in the laundry room queue. Suze was eternally three paces ahead of Gwen. But it was okay, as long as she remembered to look back.

For a while, it had felt as though Gwen was catching up. Toward the end of uni, when fate would have it that she just started to feel comfortable and confident as things wound down for good. And when they joined the mass migration south toward the capital and went about squeezing themselves into any crevice of London that would have them. Finally, Gwen felt as though she walked in step alongside her friend instead of trotting on an eager half-beat behind.

For those joyful years she felt easy and confident in the friendship, able to phone Suze up whenever, summon her for emergency drinks and rest her head on her shoulder, plait that silky raven hair as though it were her own. Reassure her during the mornings when Suze would cringe "I was too *much*" into the kitchen table, while Gwen worried that she hadn't been enough.

When she started dating Ryan, six months before Suze met Paul, they would joke about them as the two little dickie birds from the nursery rhyme, being dumped one day in tandem. *Fly away Ryan! Fly away Paul!* Part of Gwen, though she would only admit this privately to herself, had assumed Suze actually would break up with Paul as soon as she broke up with Ryan. That they would laugh about their uniquely terrible taste in men, toast their bravery, and cheerfully start over again. Together.

But of course, Paul never did fly away. And Ryan never did come back. He had wasted no time finding and subsequently impregnating a crop-haired jewelry designer called Clea Frears, whose unpronounceable name was the only thing that stopped Gwen doing herself an injury when the news surfaced. Meanwhile, two years after washing Gwen's snotty tears off her sofa cushions and calling her brave, brilliant, a fearless woman of steel, Suze was walking down the aisle to a string quartet and honeymooning on Santorini. Gradually, what had felt like three paces widened to five, then ten, then a yawning distance that left her combing Suze's social-media tags for clues as to how she filled in the gaps.

When they saw each other now it was still warm, still familiar. Still fun, or whatever Pinot-steeped approximation passed for "fun" in their late thirties. But where Suze had once held out her hands to catch Gwen, it now felt as though she'd placed her fondly at the back of a cupboard, to be returned to less and less frequently; dusted off more out of nostalgia and novelty—guilt, perhaps—than genuine need. She was leftover junk from the past, just waiting to be a source of joy again.

By the time she finally replied to Suze's text, these thoughts had festered in the back of her mind for a week and mutated into a kind of defiance.

Sure, sounds lovely! I'll bring someone x.

She watched herself write it, and blithely hit "send."

# T-Shirt

Lindsay said she would buy the T-shirts herself.

They hadn't been going to have T-shirts, because Megan had said she didn't want them. "No T-shirts, no sashes, no penis straws," had been the party line for months of planning; it was the tuning fork they had orchestrated the whole weekend around.

Then, only two weeks before, she'd made an offhand comment—"Can't wait to see the whole squad in your matching tees!"—which had prompted panic and a flurry of messages in the adjoining group chat, followed by the careful extraction of the truth (Lindsay was always voted chief truth-extractor). Megan *did* want T-shirts, it turned out. Couldn't remember ever saying she didn't. And anyway if she *had* said it she'd assumed they'd ignore her, because that was the way these things went. Everyone knew that.

So: T-shirts. An extortionate fee was paid for a rush job, Lindsay holding her breath as she tapped her card details into a site from the third page of Google, on sixteen fuchsia tees with MEGZ'S MEGA HEN on the front and "Make ours an amaretto!!" on the back. This was a weak reference to a night involving a bottle of Disaronno six years earlier, and one they only prayed Megan remembered enough of to understand the joke. The wording had been settled on in some haste, after one of the previously silent cousins had piped up in the group chat requesting MEGA SLAGS for the back and had to be gently talked down on the basis that Megan probably didn't want to brand her future mother-in-law a Mega Slag, or really any size of slag, but at this point who even knew? Perhaps she did.

Lindsay had asked for a second opinion on apostrophe placement—did the Mega Hen *belong* to Megz, or was it Meg's Mega Hen and therefore Meg'z Mega Hen?—but none had been forth-coming.

The style of T-shirt had prompted some back-and-forth. Half the group favored the stretch fitted option ("more flattering") at £3 extra per unit, while the other half wanted traditional baggy tees, ostensibly to save money but really so that they could wear them tucked, knotted, slashed into crops or any other way that made them look gamine and pixielike. Lindsay, whose self-esteem had recently taken a bruising at a bridesmaid fitting, ponied up the extra for fitted tees herself.

Two of Megan's workmates, Carlotta and Neve, sent barbed comments about the T-shirts. Were they really necessary? Couldn't they compromise with Mega Slag tote bags instead? Wasn't there a risk that the matching T-shirts might get them turned away from venues for being The Wrong Sort of Hen? Though Lindsay privately agreed, the audacity from these interlopers only made the rest of the group dig their heels in more. Neve was already on rocky ground for suggesting they stay in yurts. The T-shirts were happening.

When the T-shirts still hadn't arrived by the preceding Thursday, she had called in sick in order to stay home, stuff pick-and-mix into floral gift bags and wait for the postman. By Friday morning she was frantic, looking up fabric pens on Amazon and wondering if she could turn the whole thing into a craft activity, shoehorned in between the cheese appreciation and aerial yoga. But the goddesses were smiling upon them and the Yodel courier rounded the corner with the parcel under his arm, a scant ten minutes before she needed to leave the house. All the way from Taiwan, smelling of sawdust and melted plastic, sixteen stretch-fit fuchsia T-shirts with "Meg'zs Megahen" printed across the chest.

In the end, it had rained so hard all weekend that the T-shirts remained mostly covered beneath coats and jumpers. This was probably just as well, because Megan had looked at them as they lined up, shivering, for the obligatory photo outside the archery and mixology workshop, and said with a wrinkled nose, "I didn't think you'd get that sort of T-shirt."

It was a comment that continued to torture Lindsay, until long after Megan's divorce had been finalized.

# 11

The next time Gwen encountered Nicholas, he was pricing vinyl in the back room while she tagged a heap of jackets. He whistled as he worked, pausing at every second or third album to read the tracklist on the back, nod approvingly, maybe slip the record out of the sleeve and peer at its surface, holding it carefully between two fingertips. A couple of times she heard him mutter, not quite under his breath, "Tuuuuuune."

Was this for her benefit? It didn't seem to be for Lise, who was eating microwaved pad thai and watching videos on her phone. While Gwen pondered the performance, Nicholas looked up and she accidentally caught his eye. *Shit.* He beamed at her.

"Some quality gems in today!"

"Oh yeah?" Gwen felt obliged to engage, so she leaned over to see what he was holding. It was *Making Waves* by The Nolans. "Are you . . . a fan?"

To his credit, Nicholas laughed. Gwen laughed too. Nicholas continued laughing, louder. Gwen stopped laughing. Nicholas slapped his thigh, wiped his eyes and wagged a knowing finger at her, as if to say "Foiled me this time, you minx!"

Gwen returned to the coats.

The next time that Gwen encountered Nicholas, he was wrapping a teapot in old copies of the *Metro*, and chuckling to himself. She didn't ask what about, though it was clear he wanted to tell her.

The next time that Gwen encountered Nicholas, he was wearing a felt fedora and offering her a doughnut from a paper bag marked 30p REDUCED TO CLEAR. The thing was, she really did want a doughnut.

The next time that Gwen encountered Nicholas, he loomed up behind her shoulder as she was flipping through a box of art postcards: the kind from gallery gift shops that she had hoarded when she was younger, and Blu Tacked across numerous rented bedrooms.

"Do you like art, Gwen?" he asked, and Gwen couldn't think of anything to say that didn't make her sound petulant or stupid. Except: "Yes."

"Where do you go to see art?" he asked, hoisting himself up to sit on the counter, legs swinging in what she imagined he thought was an impish way. There was an audible *clunk* as he swung his foot back too far and kicked the bin.

Gwen stalled, her brain replaying scenes from the film *Mona Lisa Smile*. "Galleries, mainly."

He laughed again at this, too hard and too loud. She didn't entirely hate it.

"Come on, *Gwen*,"—again, her name, as though it were ironic—"tell me your secrets."

She could feel a blotchy fluster begin to creep from her chest toward her neck.

"Oh, you know . . . the usuals." She momentarily weighed up the benefits of saying something niche and impressive—*the White Cube? An underground space beneath a Soho car park? The "exhibition opening party" Suze had once taken her to that turned out to be twelve people queuing up to look at a butt plug in a glass box?*—but in the end she decided honesty felt less like pandering to him.

"Oh god, I'm very basic. I like, er, The Tate? Ss. Both Tates! Except Modern always makes me need the loo. And Britain is . . . well, you know. In Pimlico."

He nodded solemnly. Apparently she was expected to go on.

"Dulwich Picture Gallery is good, by which I mean the cheese scones in the café are good. The Whitechapel Gallery has some . . . interesting ideas. I hear. And, um, the National Gallery. Obviously." Was this tragic? She tried to pull it back with a joke. "Every backpack-laden tourist's favorite time-kill."

"I've never been!" Nicholas suddenly sprang to life. "I know! MAD, isn't it? Born and raised in Fulham and yet somehow never stepped inside its hallowed doors."

Gwen agreed that it was, indeed, mad.

The next time that Gwen encountered Nicholas, he asked her on a date to the National Gallery. She said yes, which seemed madder.

# Travel Guides

Doug had been collecting travel guides for twenty-two years. He was proud of his collection—ordered by continent and then alphabetized, they took up four whole shelves on the wall of his living room. Lonely Planets were his favorite; he liked the way they didn't patronize the reader, and enjoyed the accessible depth in which they covered the political and social history of a place as well as the top-line tourist stuff. But he bought others too, the whistlestop "Top 10 Things to See in Turkmenistan"–style books, even flimsy pamphlets and battered old guides to countries that had long since been reshaped and renamed. *Roads Around Rhodesia. You Go! Yugoslavia.* Often those were the most interesting.

From his guides, Doug had learned everything. He knew the tipping etiquette in Tibet. He knew where best to catch a tuk-tuk at Angkor Wat, and precisely when to be naked in an Egyptian bathhouse. He craved Venezuelan corn cakes and Norwegian salted liquorice and a very specific type of Lithuanian potato dumpling; could imagine the way the starchy dough would yield in his mouth and the spiced filling would burst forth on his tongue.

Doug had an encyclopedic memory for details and rarely forgot anything he had read, though he would cross-reference between guides on any similarities or points of difference he found interesting. For example, did you know that there are only two escalators in the entire state of Wyoming? Doug hadn't. But now he did.

These details sometimes came in handy when he spoke to the women on his chat sites. Though he knew there was no obligation to impress them—indeed, he was paying to be blissfully free of that burden—it still felt good to drop in a comment that showed a little cultural awareness and worldly sensibility, before things progressed to a more universal form of communication. He felt they appreciated it.

From time to time Doug would pick up a guide to London. He read these as devotedly as the other books, marveling at the way the city changed from year to year, its edges creeping further out, its epicenters of cool shifting subtly from west to east, north to south and back again. Neighborhoods that never warranted mention a decade earlier suddenly had whole sections devoted to them, as though they'd wiggled their way through the cracks and sprung up into flowers overnight. At the same time, the cultural commentary was often so laughably inaccurate that it made him sad to wonder how many idiotic tips he was picking up from the other books without knowing. Doug made notes in the margins, either correcting outright errors (why did so many publishers think running the books past a real-life British citizen a needless luxury?) or reminding himself to engage in further research. *Is "adult ball pit" code for something? Find out what cruffin is. Deptford?*

Doug bought his guides at the charity shop around the corner, and he preferred it this way—he liked the surprise element, not knowing what he would find on each visit and whether there would be any duplicates. As a child in the seventies he'd collected football stickers and enjoyed a similar thrill each time he tore open a fresh packet. Doug liked having the choice made for him. The idea of walking into a high street bookshop and choosing from shelves and shelves of brand-new books seemed absurd, for a number of reasons.

The staff at the shop didn't greet him in familiar tones the way they did with other customers—he didn't visit often enough for that, and the volunteers seemed to change as regularly as the window display—but they would sometimes comment on the books he was buying. People can't resist telling you when they've been somewhere, Doug had noticed.

"Such great food!" they would say, or "You MUST do the bus trip out to the ruins, they're worth it," or "Whatever you do, watch your wallet on the piazza." And Doug would smile and thank them for the insightful tips, and agree that yes, he was very lucky, it would be so nice to escape all this rain, and he'd be sure to remember them to Tony in the kiosk by the old monastery.

He never would, of course, but then he made it to the shop infrequently enough that it wasn't likely they'd ever remember to check. Sometimes weeks would pass without him getting further than the end of the path. Each time he did was a personal victory, and each book a small trophy for his efforts. Back home, he would lock the door and make a tea and sit down to read for several hours which sometimes stretched into days, telling himself as he did so that he *was* very lucky. It was so nice to escape all this rain.

# 12

Ahead of her at Leicester Square, an American man was Face-Timing someone from the Tube escalator.

"Oh, you would hate this!" he cried, gleefully, at the pixelated shape on the screen. "You would just HATE it!"

What the recipient would hate was unclear: the escalator, the London Underground, or the city itself? Gwen wondered why everyone else always seemed to be able to get Wi-Fi on the Tube except her.

Nicholas met her under the Hippodrome awning, which contrived—along with the Saturday crowds and his baby-smooth jawline being bumped against hers with a narrative "mwah"—to make her feel about fourteen, as though he might be about to buy her a McFlurry and feel her up on the bumper cars. This was counteracted starkly by the fact he was wearing a white shirt and rolled-up chinos with brown loafers (what else had she expected?) and carrying a battered leather satchel, to remind the world that even in a freak spring heat wave, he was still a man of discernment.

In the gallery, Nicholas's hand made friends with the small of her back and it was soon clear the pair were inseparable. He touched it to tell her something. He touched it to acknowledge her reply. He touched it to steer her this way and that through the crowded building, as though demonstrating expert command of a golf buggy. It might have been a smoother move if Gwen had been wearing, say, a clinging silk slip and not a baggy linen smock dress, but she almost admired his dedication to the cause.

Nicholas had his gallery patter down to a fine art. Confident, considered, with smatterings of showy knowledge ("Of course, the Spanish Armada was only the previous year . . ."; "It's actually a type of Japanese citrus . . .") tempered by careful dollops of what she supposed he thought was self-deprecation ("I can never remember the difference between the Huguenots and the Argonauts!"). He studied some paintings for longer than really seemed necessary—arms folded, head at an angle—until she worried he might be having some kind of emotional response.

And while he appraised the works, Gwen appraised him. She tried to find things to be attracted to, coaxing herself the way one would a child to eat vegetables. She tried to focus on his nice forearms, or his extensive knowledge of the use of the camera obscura in seventeenth-century Dutch Baroque, and not the way he said "obviously" three times per sentence or blew his nose on a wad of Pret napkins instead of a tissue. When he paused in one of the long halls to read the benefactor's double-barreled name embossed in gold above the archway, she was relieved to hear him say, "Lol, imagine being called *that*," rather than "Oh look, Uncle Topsy!" Gwen knew she was grasping.

Going out with (allowing herself to be courted by?) Nicholas felt so improbable she could barely admit to herself it was happening—it was easier to believe her legs had simply brought her here of their own accord, as some kind of prank. Maybe the sheer novelty of someone so young, and so posh, and so overtly, unashamedly interested in her was enough to sub in for genuine feelings. Or maybe she was just that bored.

Still, he laughed hard at all of her jokes and that wasn't *not* nice. He smelled spicy and heady, of something undoubtedly more expensive than Lynx Africa, but which nonetheless activated the same long-buried part of her that used to believe she could smell testosterone from the end of a school corridor. He made her feel queasy and intrigued in equal parts, and she was curious to see which would win out.

After an hour and forty-five minutes of doing that special, slow meandering-around-a-gallery walk, Gwen's lower back was aching and all the touching it wasn't helping. Her face ached too, from holding it in her "wryly thoughtful" expression. Her contact lenses itched. As they emerged from one of the endless rooms into a familiar stairwell, she took the opportunity to stretch out her neck (it crunched, which she hoped he didn't hear) and issue a demonstrative "soooooo."

"Are you hungry?" he asked.

She forgot to lie. "Yes."

"Do you like ramen?"

Gwen did like ramen. Instant noodles were one of her most dependable dinners. If you bought them from the Asian supermarket and added a soft-boiled egg, you could kid yourself it was a nutritious, restorative meal. And if they went for ramen, she reasoned, then he couldn't take her to Simpson's, or Rules, or any other faintly terrifying place with a £30 fish pie and a disgraced Tory peer in the corner. Ramen also meant no dessert, so she could buy a box of Billionaire Magnums on the way home.

"Love ramen!" she replied.

But as soon as they stepped from the marbled cool of the gallery into the thick, blanketing heat of the afternoon, she realized her mistake.

Gwen continued realizing her mistake as he led her through the steaming hordes outside M&M's World, past the happy thrum of Chinatown and onto the heaving, gilt-edged expanse of Haymarket. Her thighs began to chafe as they walked. She wondered if he could tell.

Finally they stopped in front of a noodle bar and Gwen prayed for aircon as Nicholas made a strenuous show of holding the door open for her while simultaneously trying to lead her through it. There was no aircon. Or maybe there was, but its effects were negated by the great clouds of steam billowing from everyone's bowls. Either way, she was sweating by the time they sat down. Her mistake ran in rivulets from her hairline.

One good thing about Nicholas was that he was well-bred enough to pretend he hadn't noticed. Like the queen drinking her own finger bowl, thought Gwen. As he talked about his business and his friends and his love of *The Sopranos* and his hatred of his Australian flatmate and his opinions on various Alpine ski resorts and recounted several choice stories about the family Dobermans, Jeeves and Wooster, Gwen could only focus on the sweat. It was streaming, now—not from her armpits, which would at least be the conventional place, but from quirky locales such as her neck, her elbow creases, and the backs of her knees. The curly baby hairs at her temples would be plastered to her face now, she knew without reaching a hand up to check. Her underboob had become a garden water feature, which felt like a cruel irony, considering she and Suze had used to refer to going braless as "the full Dimmock."

As he spoke, she nodded her head the minimum amount she thought she could get away with. Moving as little as humanly possible was surely the best tactic, aiding the evaporation process without triggering any new secretions. Maybe he would find it mysterious and coquettish? Did straight men secretly love a really, really still woman? Her mind strayed to the checklist she had to complete every time she went back to the doctor for a repeat prescription of Citalopram. "Moving or speaking so slowly that other people could have noticed." How slow was noticeably slow, she'd always wondered? Was it possible people were being misdiagnosed with depression when they were simply trying to will their own glands closed?

"You're a *really* good listener," he said. "Shall we order?"

If Nicholas's satchel was chosen to recall a bygone era, then his cultural awareness gave the illusion of a man frozen in the nearish past. He said "doggo." He talked about loving Woody Allen without grimace or caveat. He'd never been on TikTok.

He swore a lot, and disproportionately, and too loudly, with the self-conscious swagger of a schoolboy who has only recently learned the words. The miso broth was "actually FUCKING tremendos." The man two tables over who had his phone on loud was "a grade-A CUNT." He hesitated for a millisecond before each expletive in a way that Gwen found deeply unsexy. At one low point he responded to her suggestion they share an order of gyoza with an unconvincing "SHIT yes."

Yet there was something—something in his sincerity and boundless enthusiasm, which she found appealing in spite of herself. He was incredibly polite to the waitress, without any hint of sleaze. And he wanted to know about Gwen; really, genuinely seemed to want to know things about her. Any bone she cared to throw—her career, her favorite crisps, her parents, her imaginary childhood friend—he caught gratefully and held aloft, repeating words back to her to make clear he was paying attention.

"Dorking," he rolled the word around his mouth as though it were a fine Merlot. "Doooorkkkkinnng." "Scaaampi Friiies." "Strategic creative content solutionssss."

Perhaps it was their age gap, or the fact he thought selling chintz lampshades with a 500 percent markup could be passed off as dazzling entrepreneurship, but there was something about Nicholas that gave the truth a rosy spin. When she told him that she'd recently been made redundant and was "taking a short career break" while she figured things out, it didn't sound like a tragic bluff. It sounded self-assured. He asked if she'd considered starting her own consultancy. "Perhaps," she replied, and briefly believed it.

Any respite from the sweating ended as soon as their food arrived. Despite the nice, cool, dull salads calling to her from the opposite side of the menu, Gwen had felt obliged to order ramen to save face—which was ironic seeing as hers was now sliding rapidly down her cheeks and into her soup. She shifted in her seat, wondering if she would leave a strip of visible condensation on the plastic when she got up to go to the toilet. She decided to risk it, shuffling her bottom around to wipe away the evidence before she stood up.

In the bathroom, she held damp paper towels to the back of her neck and repaired what she could of her makeup in the dimly lit nightclub mirror. It was pathetic, she thought, that she could be repelled by a person on nearly every level, yet still worry that a rogue glob of mascara might turn him off forever.

When they left the restaurant, hazy daylight still streaked the horizon but the air was mercifully cooler. They walked for a few paces in no particular direction, trying not to get tangled in the crowds racing for the *Jersey Boys* stage door.

"There's a cool little place I know near here, we could . . . ah, get a nightcap?" he suggested, and in his voice for the first time was a discernible twang of nerves. For a moment she considered it. She was almost curious to find out what would happen, or at least to find out whether Nicholas's definition of "a cool little place" was the Garrick Club or the Rainforest Café. But then, just as he leaned in to reunite his hand with her lower back, Gwen felt a fat, solitary drop of sweat leave the crease below her right buttock and begin a leisurely journey down the back of her thigh. A vision of her own shower flashed before her eyes. Taking her clothes off and sitting on the bathroom tiles. The cool crack and slurp of a Magnum.

"Not tonight . . . tired . . . hot . . sorry . . . lovely, um, time!" she replied, barely bothering to form the whole sentence. She clasped his hand in both of hers and waggled it like a fond aunt. "Bye, Nick."

Gwen turned and made a bid for freedom. In her peripheral vision, she saw Nicholas take a wad of napkins from his pocket and dab his own forehead.

# Paperback

In the same way a farmer can't get too attached to their lambs, Michael was rarely sentimental about stock the way the volunteers were. But there was something about book inscriptions that got him every time.

The older ones were the most romantic, with their curlicued handwriting and quaint formality—*With fondest regards on this most auspicious occasion, Pater*, etc.—but the newest were the most tragic, being as those books had been kept and loved for the shortest time. His heart broke imagining the confidence with which the inscription had been written, the pride with which the book had been handed over and then the cold detachment with which it had been given away, only a year or two later, maybe unread.

He understood it, of course, the giving away. People's houses were overflowing with crap, and they probably weren't going to look at *The Little Book of Historical Biscuits* again beyond Boxing Day. Sure. But the inscriptions still choked him every time. He absorbed that micro-dose of rejection on behalf of all the gifters who would never know. Who might be out there browsing *The Big Book of Cactus Facts* for your next birthday as we speak. He took it for the team, swallowed it down, and held that bitterness in his gut. As a favor.

His gut had long been bitter, anyhow. Much as he'd tried to dilute it with cold white wine and effervescent vitamins, with candy-sweet pop culture and buttery-rich arts. For all he'd nourished himself better with wholesome acts for the outside world, by sacrificing the lucrative career for the charitable one, the comfortable life for the one that was always slightly too tight in the crotch. He kept to a rigid schedule of self-flagellation in the way his friends did Pilates and spinning. St. Michael the martyr. Still bitter.

It had started with a book.

*Brideshead Revisited*, which was such a cliché. He wished it were *The Line of Beauty*, *Giovanni's Room*, something sexy with more confidence and less Catholicism, but there you are. First he'd been drawn to the cover in the school library—the soft Penguin Classic with its elegant art deco illustration. Then he'd been drawn to its world; the velvet-cushioned luxury of a life with room for eccentricities and teddy bears' picnics and spiritual crises, without the immediate threat of having one's face bashed in behind the Erdington Costcutter. There was nothing explicit in it, but that was good because back then, explicit still scared him. He craved the delicious ambiguity, cosseted himself quite happily in the gray area where nothing was confirmed but everything was implied.

Reading about Sebastian through the lens of Charles's infatuation had felt so familiar to him that it almost felt like nothing at all. Like sinking into a perfectly warm bath, released for a few blessed minutes from the gravel and friction of almost everything else in his life. He read, and reread, and it was enough, and then it wasn't. After a while, the pages were dog-eared and the spine was peeling and the warm bath was rapidly cooling around him, leaving Michael goosefleshed and vulnerable once more. He needed to share it. He needed someone else to feel the same way.

So he went to the bookshop in town one day after school and bought a fresh copy, small enough to shove into the inside pocket of his blazer. It didn't look small when he slid it across the Formica table of the all-night builders' café they always went to on Fridays, circumnavigating coffee splashes and the dark, sticky remains of historical ketchup spillage. The book looked huge, sitting there, between them. It threatened to grow as big as the room and smother them all. For a second he wanted to snatch it back and run away, but something made him believe he'd buckle under its weight.

Greg picked it up. "Thanks, man."

"Just thought you'd like it. I dunno. I like it."

"Cool. Sure I will."

"Happy birthday."

He'd spotted the paperback again some years later while helping with the admin effort needed to get Greg out of his ill-advised first marriage and, shortly after, into his second. It was in a box marked BOOKS—GET RID, nestled between *The Microwave Gourmet* and *Infinite Jest*.

When he picked it out, he was comforted, at least, to see the spine was cracked and the pages were creased at the corners. But on the yellowed flyleaf, the inscription stung like Friday night's salt and vinegar splashed into an open wound.

*To Greg,*
*Always yours,*
*Michael*

# 13

The steamer was on in the back room and Gwen was working her way through a rail of men's sweaters.

She methodically blasted each one, relishing the noise of the machine and watching as the hot droplets evaporated in a cloud that smelled slightly different each time. Sometimes sweet or tangy with perfume. Sometimes the musty warmth of dark wood, like playing hide and seek in the back of a grandparent's wardrobe. Sometimes wafts of unfamiliar fabric conditioner, which reminded her of going round for tea at schoolmates' houses; the crippling anxiety over how one's own home might smell to other people and whether or not it was possible to know.

Sometimes the steamer released a gust of BO that was so curiously close to a cooking smell—maybe falafel?—that it made her hungry, which then made her nauseous. It was at one of these moments, holding her breath as she doused a Good Charlotte tour sweatshirt from 2002, that Nicholas walked in.

Gwen had been avoiding him all morning. Just as she'd avoided opening his follow-up text ("Hey pal," it had started, which was somehow worse than the "m'lady" she had braced herself for) on Sunday. But now here he was, and all she could think about was her shiny pink face and the way the steam had made her fringe stick to her forehead in clammy strands. Why could she never encounter this man in situations with less than 70 percent humidity?

"Gwen! Hello!" He affected a little backward stagger, as though her presence was a delightful shock.

"Hey, hi." She flapped a hand at him from behind the rail, grateful for the row of invisible ghost men providing a buffer.

"How are you today?"

Nicholas didn't have the good grace to busy himself with something, the way a normal person would. Instead he stood completely still and stared at her, waiting for an answer.

"Steaming!" she replied, which wasn't an answer but seemed close enough.

"You never texted me back."

Was this—Hang on, did people just . . . say these things, now? What happened to letting the awkward facts hang between you, unspoken? Was the contemporary dating scene full of people baldly airing the truth alongside their dick pics?

"I, ah—No? No. Sorry. Busy week!" She fluffed a pullover, as if to illustrate her point.

Nicholas was still smiling, which unnerved her. "It's fine. Absolutely cool. I totally get it."

What did he get, though? And could he please explain it to her?

Gwen smiled back in what she hoped was a firm, conciliatory manner. But Nicholas had cocked an eyebrow—of course he was an eyebrow-cocker—and was still looking at her, quizzically, in a way that made her neck prickle. Just as she cleared her throat to speak, with no idea what she was about to say, the steamer ran dry and began to rasp loudly for attention.

"I should . . ." She reached for the plastic jug they used for refills. Nicholas nodded, as though this was the answer he'd been anticipating all along, turned on his heel and left the room again.

On the way home, she took a deep breath and opened his text.

Hi pal, it read. Yesterday was fun. Got home and read entire Wikipedia on the Huguenots, wild fucking times! Anyway just wondered what you're doing Friday? Nx

Actually, I'm going to a thing, she watched herself reply.

This was odd.

Want to come? x

# Ring

Like most long-term relationships, the later years of Gwen and Ryan's had been soundtracked by comfortable silence and superfluous commentary. *"Are you not eating those crusts?"* *"Oh, you've got that shirt on."* *"It's raining."* They would narrate the world to each other as they saw it, and enjoy the sound of their own voices bouncing back.

In front of other people they had their setlist of stories, polished and refined through rounds and rounds of retelling. Together they maintained mutually agreed fallacies—such as that he was tight with money, which was only occasionally true, or that she was terrible with directions, which she definitely wasn't. They would trot out the same stories, personal news headlines, and two-person comedy bits from an ever-rotating selection, adding new ones as they occurred and retiring older ones once they'd been heard by everyone they saw socially. The time Ryan lost his wallet on a canal boat. The time Gwen fell down the gap on the Tube. The film they'd seen last week, the holiday they took last year. She assumed every other couple did the same.

They had achieved true physical intimacy around the two-year mark, and that was nice. They nuzzled and nestled into each other at night like newborn puppies. They peed freely with the bathroom door open, and she no longer cared if he saw her scratch herself or pluck the long, wiry hair that grew like the pantomime beanstalk, seemingly overnight, from her chin.

But emotional intimacy was the problem. Even three, four years down the line, Gwen was still anxiously sucking in her full personality. She still edited sentences in her head before she said them out loud to him, still dithered over whether or not to bore him with some minor episode from her day. Instead of all her thoughts pouring out, half-formed, as she thought them, she would do her best to ration them out, releasing one only when he seemed in the best mood and most likely to humor her. It wasn't the way she imagined love should be.

Sometimes he would answer the phone to her by saying "Hello?" with a rising inflection. Question mark implied, the way a person answered the phone to an unknown number. Sometimes he said "Hi, Gwen," which was almost worse. Because nobody calls a person they love by their name when they answer the phone. They call them *sweetie*, *babe*, *honey*, *fuckface*. They sing "Hiyaaaa," or they skip the greeting altogether and simply launch into the conversation at the place they left off. She had tried to explain this to him once, but she sounded insane.

"You want me to call you fuckface?" he'd said, earnestly. Trying to understand his latest misstep into an invisible relationship pothole.

"No. No! I just think it's weird when you use my actual name, don't you? It's very formal."

"Should I use a pseudonym?"

"I think other couples call them pet names."

"But we don't have pet names. Do you want pet names?"

She'd released a long, uneven exhale.

"No."

The trouble was, she had no point of comparison. Nobody talked about this. Her friends and colleagues complained about their partners staying out too late or failing to buy decent birthday presents, and later on, about their inability to load the dishwasher correctly or pick up a recipe book, choose a recipe, and make it for dinner. They complained about the weight of emotional labor and carrying the mental load, at first not in those exact words—and, later, once they'd all read the articles, in those exact words. But it was always recreational complaining, complaining as sport, complaining as bonding rite. Those complaints were never presented as deal-breakers because the deals had apparently been struck and signed in blood, long before anyone put a ring on it.

It was generally assumed that anyone you went out with for longer than two years in your early twenties, one year in your late twenties or six months in your thirties, was The One until proven otherwise. You could often sense the relief when a formerly single person started dating someone; the palpable fast-tracking of their relationship in everyone else's minds. It would be a matter of weeks before joint invites started arriving, along with eager comments about future plans, group holidays, game nights, sporting activities, professional advice, loans of DIY equipment, and all the other ways in which the new person would take their place in the social tableau. Nobody ever said "If you're still together by then . . . ," because of course they didn't. It would be rude.

From time to time, someone—usually some peripheral friend of a friend—would go through a catastrophic breakup, and Gwen would get crumbs of third-hand gossip about rumored infidelities and custody battles over cockapoos and custom-made sofas. *Then*, people would talk. Then, they would refill their tumblers of wine and smirk through feigned concern and barely bother to mask their real thoughts, which were: thank god it's not us.

But nobody ever talked about doubting that their partner was The One, or even A One. Gwen would search in vain for the gap in conversation into which a person might slide the question, but it never appeared. It became harder as they got older and social occasions became shorter, more civilized and, crucially, more coupled. You might be able to loll drunkenly on someone's shoulder on a night bus and whisper "I don't know if I love him enough," but you couldn't announce it over the dips at a birthday barbecue.

Nobody wanted to talk about it, she suspected, in case the doubt was infectious. Because if you presented your casefile of evidence, if you set out your meager tray of insecurities and reservations and it turned out they were no worse than the things *they* felt and thought about *their* own relationships, then what? Chaos? Everyone would have to break up and start all over again? They couldn't risk it.

Cheating, lying, emotional or physical abuse, screaming matches in supermarkets: they were reasons to break up a long-term relationship. Flimsy, half-formed worries were not. A vague itch of dissatisfaction was not. The way they answered your phone calls definitely wasn't. Until it was.

She had broken up with Ryan almost by accident, during a conversation that wasn't a fight or even a particularly serious discussion. Until it was.

It was so far from a fight or a serious discussion that they still had the TV on, and so she ended up breaking off their engagement and ending their seven-year relationship while an episode of *Grand Designs* played out in the background.

He had lost something: a pair of goalkeeper gloves that Gwen had never seen in her life. Ryan insisted she knew the ones (she didn't), that she must have moved them from the spot in the bottom of the wardrobe where they were always (never) kept. He wasn't particularly angry, just utterly sure.

"It's not a big deal, but you definitely *have* moved them," he kept saying. "There's no other explanation."

Then, poking a finger into her cheek, trying to be cute: "It's fine, future wife. You have our whole lives together to admit it."

Reflected in his rock-solid conviction, Gwen suddenly saw her own uncertainty. She saw their whole lives together, decade after decade of him being utterly sure and her wavering, crumbling like limestone under granite, only a small band of metal to hold her in place. And so instead of telling him, once more, that she hadn't moved the goalkeeper gloves, had never *seen* the sodding goalkeeper gloves and since when did he play football anyway, she told him it was over.

While she cried, her reasons falling out in snotty, half-formed sentences, Kevin McCloud interviewed a beaming couple in hi-vis jackets beneath a tarpaulin in the rain. She tried her best to narrate the world to him as she saw it, and Ryan tried his best to pick up his cues in this conversation that was nowhere in their shared repertoire, nowhere at all.

By the time she'd convinced him that it wasn't an exasperated tantrum, that she was serious, that she couldn't marry him, that he had done nothing wrong but somehow still nothing was right, Kevin and the couple were touring a glass-walled palace against a backdrop of blue sky with a sleeping baby in their arms.

By the time she'd convinced *herself* that she was serious, Ryan had left for his parents' house, and succumbing to silence felt more terrifying than anything else she had done. Gwen had taken the ring off immediately. But she left the TV on for several days.

# 14

It was on the day of Suze's thing, just as she was working out the most convincing but least infuriating time to send a cancellation text, that Gwen met Connie.

The shop was busy, seemingly for no reason. These flurries would happen on an otherwise dead day—a clump of customers suddenly drawn toward the counter all at once, like iron filings to a magnet. Gwen was having a panic attack, also seemingly for no reason. A lump bobbed in her throat, resistant against even the biggest gulps of water. Her chest was tight, her breathing ragged with the conscious effort of filling her lungs up again, and again, and yet again. Breathing was relentless, when you thought about it.

A woman held up a sweatshirt halfway across the shop and called over to ask if it came in any other colors. A man slapped a paperback down on the counter with an impatient "Only this!," as though the insignificance of a £1 purchase meant he should be allowed to jump the queue.

The line had reached four deep now, and she dug her nails into the flesh of her palm while the customer at the front of it dithered over their selection—a denim jacket, a porcelain shepherdess, and a toaster that printed each slice with a heart-eye emoji. *Did the toaster work?* It had been safety tested, but not on bread. *Was the shepherdess a collector's item?* Hard to say. *Would my niece like the denim jacket?* Well—Gwen's jaw was growing tight now, pins and needles spreading in her cheeks as yet more customers joined the queue—who doesn't love acid-wash?

Then, just as the room went swimmy and she began to conclude that she was, in fact, drowning on dry land beneath a strip light while "Wichita Lineman" played on the radio, there was suddenly a woman by her side, wrapping the shepherdess in newspaper and bundling everything matter-of-factly into a paper bag.

"Lovely choices! What excellent taste! Sixteen pounds fifty please thankyooooou there you go, next!"

Gwen meekly stepped aside and began straightening the spare hangers while the woman whisked her way through the rest of the queue, maintaining a steady stream of patter and benign pleasantries without pausing long enough for anyone to interrupt her flow. "A classic belt! Brown goes with everything doesn't it? Well, best of luck with the funeral *and* the interview. Hello, what a charming anorak!"

Eventually they reached a lull, and the woman flopped dramatically onto the counter in feigned exhaustion. Her thick, salt-and-pepper hair was wound into a loose topknot, which bobbed forward a fraction of a second later than her head did. Probably in her early sixties, she was wearing cropped palazzo trousers and a linen shirt, which was half untucked in the elegant way that Gwen had never been able to master. Her wrists clanked with silver bangles and she smelled like tobacco—fragrance, not fags. Or maybe both. The woman hauled herself back up and turned to Gwen.

"Hi! Hello. Connie. Who are you?"

Gwen told her.

"Nice to meet you, Gwen! You look half-dead, are you having some sort of episode?"

Gwen would discover this to be textbook Connie. She took pride in the kind of deadpan bluntness that might seem rude in someone younger, or poorer, but which her brisk, Radio 4 voice and statement earrings managed to put across as fresh and charismatic. The sort of person you expected to find disarming the author at a literary Q&A, or charming her way to a refund in Marks & Spencer. Behind hip, thick-rimmed glasses her eyes were crinkled in shrewd observation. Yes, Gwen confirmed. She was having some sort of episode.

Within an hour, Connie had not so much calmed her down as chivvied her back to health. Coffee was made ("Decaf for you, I think"), biscuits deployed, and potted biographies exchanged. Connie was newly retired and furious about it, and newly divorced and delighted about it. She had lived in Tufnell Park for thirty years, in a house she had bought for "about two pounds fifty, I'm sorry to say, but we did used to find syringes in the rhododendrons." It was only her second shift at the shop, and Gwen marveled at her rookie competence.

Connie had started volunteering out of boredom, and to give her an excuse when friends tried to get her to join their community choirs or urban hiking groups.

"Honestly I can't go for a *mammogram* these days without one of them leaping out from behind a screen with some purple-nosed prick called Nigel who wants a new wife to stoke the dying embers of his ego," she sighed. "I keep telling them, I like being alone! Being alone is bliss! I belch like a trucker and sleep like a queen."

Gwen, meanwhile, was newly redundant and ambivalent about it, single and resigned to it, and having a panic attack because tonight she had to go to a thing at her best friend's house with a man-boy who made her feel . . . confused. She wasn't sure whether Connie had encountered Nicholas yet, so she kept the details vague.

"I just . . . why am I forcing myself to go?" she laughed weakly. "What's the point?"

Connie paused, seriously considering what the point might be.

"You want me to tell you not to go," she surmised, as Gwen stabbed at a pair of men's shorts with a pricing gun. "You want me to say: 'Just cry off! Stay home, get a pizza, have a bath, be kind to yourself.'"

"I don't," Gwen protested. She did.

"Well, I'm not going to," Connie continued. "You should go. You never regret going out, not really. Either it's better than you're expecting and you're glad you went, or it's a nightmare and you get a good story out of it to tell at the next thing. But usually the former, I find. Always better to do something than nothing."

Gwen considered this. There was a time she might have turned up on Suze's doorstep in a worse state—or rather, crawled across the landing to her bedroom and whimpered, stretched across her rug amid the discarded pants, demanded tea and sympathy and someone to put her leaden legs across while they watched *Come Dine with Me*. But now, the idea of presenting as anything less than the lightest, sparkliest, lowest-maintenance version of herself felt like bad etiquette.

"What if . . . what if I'm terrible company though? Like this, I mean?"

"Well, so what if you are?" Connie was replying in between serving customers, while Gwen sorted through a pile of new donations. Just as it had with Brenda, Asha, and the others, something about their side-by-side positioning at the counter made it feel less strange to be airing her insecurities so openly to a woman she had only just met. That, plus the fact Connie had the vibe—it suddenly dawned on her—of the kind of non-NHS therapist that Gwen couldn't afford.

"Nobody will notice. Everyone is far too self-absorbed, in my experience," added Connie, in a way that suggested Gwen wasn't necessarily excluded from the statement. "And hey, if it comes to it, people like to see other people having a tough time. It makes them feel better about themselves. The worst kind of company is the company that doesn't turn up at all."

Gwen wasn't sure she agreed, but the pep talk was invigorating in its harshness. Connie went on.

"What is that thing my niece has written on a hideous cushion? *It's okay not to be okay.*"

Gwen secretly hated this adage, which had swelled up in the past few years through online thinkpieces and pop lyrics and entire Disney Pixar movies, until it often felt to her that a whole generation was more concerned with reassuring each other it was fine to stay in their mutual pits of gloom than with helping each other climb out of them.

She understood what it meant, technically—the need to destigmatize the struggle, the need to accept that sadness and insecurity and anxiety and indigestion were all part of humanity's rich emotional tapestry and shouldn't be choked down or bottled up in case they fermented inside you and burst out one day in a torrent like overripe kombucha. She got it. And yet, every time she read or heard that phrase, she wanted to scream. It *wasn't* okay to not be okay, that was the very definition of not-okayness. Please, a smaller voice deeper within her would whisper in the scream's wake. Don't tell me this is normal. Don't leave me here.

Gwen swallowed, felt the lump bob back up again. A lifebuoy adrift in the ocean. But her face had stopped tingling, and she hadn't counted her breaths for the past few minutes. Instead she felt the reassuring heaviness of her limbs, the bone-tired ache that usually descended on her once she was Over the Worst of It.

"All right! You're right. I'll go." Fifteen minutes to closing time, which meant she had forty-five to pull herself together, put on a nicer top in the loos, dab tester perfume over the musky hum of panic that lingered around her body, and wolf a baguette on the tube in case Suze's latest interpretation of "a thing" was martinis 'n' sashimi. "But I will be holding you personally responsible if it's a disaster."

Connie gave her a sporting clap on the shoulder. "If it's a disaster, I will cook you dinner myself."

Gwen actually believed she might.

# Brooch

Shaped like a small silver ship, glinting with marcasite, it has ridden the waves of fashion for near seven decades, sinking to unfashionable depths and then being dredged up again—for irony, for novelty, for fancy dress, for a new decree in *Vogue* that says brooches are back again. Hadn't you heard?

It first belongs to Dorothy, who buys it from a small gift shop on her honeymoon in Suffolk in 1952. Then to her daughter, Barbara, who passes it onto her sister, Judith, who hates it and gives it to the church jumble sale, where it is bought by the butcher's wife, who likes to pin it to her white coat before she notices that remnants of giblet have attached themselves to its mast like a gruesome mermaid.

Next it is wiped down, wrapped up and gifted to her sister-in-law Esther at Christmas, who would have preferred a bottle of Cinzano. The brooch is submerged in her jewelry box for several years, until her New Romantic son extracts it from the tangle and pins it to his frilliest shirt. From which it promptly falls, thanks to a weak clasp or vigorous dancing, in the corner of a basement club, to be fished out of the lost property box by a bouncer, who gives it to his girlfriend, who later leaves it behind in an abandoned houseshare, where it is subsequently discovered in the bottom of an old chest of drawers by a seven-year-old girl, and added to her collection of various treasures: a lip balm, a mood ring, and a turtle in a bow tie from a Kinder Surprise egg.

When she moves on to other prizes, the brooch washes up in a charity shop—where it is bought by Bola, who loves brooches, who wears it pinned to her best coat for several years, until arthritic fingers force her to move from buttons to more practical zip-and-velcro. The brooch flounders in another jewelry box for several years longer, before being passed to Bola's granddaughter, Maya, who would never be seen dead in a brooch.

Then onward to a car boot sale, where it is bought by Ahmet, who sells job lots of old jewelry on a newfangled website called eBay—to people like Pauline, who has a stall on the Portobello Road, selling vintage trinkets to tourists while they juggle camera phones and extravagantly frosted cupcakes in their eager hands.

To tourists like Emily, down from Northamptonshire for the day, who pins the ship to her velvet blazer alongside badges and buttons and a patch that reads "Normal people scare me." The brooch stows away with her as she moves her earthly possessions to London and becomes, in time, disappointingly, normal.

Over the course of a decade it surfaces for precisely two Halloweens and one funeral. Eventually the small silver ship ends up the victim of a "mindful spring clean," thanked for its service and launched back into the choppy waters of charity retail, to be exhumed by Gloria on a quiet Wednesday morning, wiped down, labeled, and placed in a black velvet tray on the counter next to a swirled plastic bubble ring and a bracelet made out of a fork.

St. Michael later takes a Sharpie and ups the price by £3, because *Vogue* says brooches are back again. Spread the word.

# 15

The Tube smelled of wet dog. Rain rose gently off damp denim and umbrellas in the heat of the carriage, and Gwen breathed through her mouth as she balanced in the aisle, her feet wedged between a tourist rucksack and a heap of sodden, partially decomposed Primark carrier bags. Three seats away, a man was looking at her. Not furtively, or aggressively, or even what could be called appreciatively—just a leisurely appraisal, taking in her legs, her chest, her face, before his eyes slid calmly to the advert for fiber optic broadband above her head. She swapped hands on the pole and turned to face the other way.

The panic had abated, for now, or perhaps she'd smothered it with *jambon-beurre*. But in its place was that queasy curiosity again. The Nicholas effect. She felt somehow both detached and invested in the whole thing, as though watching it play out at a safe distance with a bucket of popcorn. She was curious enough to leave him in the middle of Suze and Paul's immaculate kitchen extension, ignite him like a firework, and step back to see what happened.

Maybe he would distract everyone from her joblessness, her aimlessness, the unfashionable wine she was about to buy from the corner shop. "Don't look at me! Look over here, at this twat!" Or maybe—a comforting thought—he wouldn't turn up.

*

Gwen hadn't known how to tell Suze about her job. All it would have taken was a "how are you?" text, but none had arrived because Suze wasn't a mind reader and this had never been their style. To spill her guts unbidden felt intrusive, somehow. Rude.

In the end she had tagged it on to her RSVP, hoping it worked as a kind of excuse for her late correspondence.

> Great! So glad you're coming! Suze had said.

> Me too, looking forward to it! Gwen had messaged back. Funny story: I've been fired x

> Whaaaaaaat. Fired?? You?! came the reply, which wasn't the concerned phone call she might have liked, but was at least engaged. More typing, then:

> Dipping a hand in the Coutts account was it?

Gwen had dithered, then replied.

> Yeah, went crazy with the company card in Whole Foods. Bought one of those buckets of almond butter

> You grifter!

A pause. Suze was typing . . . then she wasn't. Gwen had messaged again.

Technically, made redundant. Less sexy than fired. But I think it's because I told a client we were secretly overcharging them . . .

Ah.

. . . in front of my boss.

Yeah, that'd do it. Bastards.

Bastards.

A pause. Then:

Shit though! Love! Are you ok? You'll be fine right?

I'm ok! I'll be fine. Got enough redundancy money to last a few months. Maybe four if I cancel that gym I haven't been to since 2016.

Good! You'll be fiiiiine. Four months on pay is basically gardening leave. Tell people that.

Gardening leave! The dream!

THE DREAM.

No more typing. Gwen had put her phone away and stared out of the window at the gray sludge of sky sweeping by. Then she'd taken it back out again, and added:

I've started volunteering in a charity shop.

Three minutes had passed.

> Amazing!! Look at you, Mother Teresa.

> Actually Mother Teresa was a cult leader.

> I'm sorry, what?

> I read a thing.

Then, as Gwen was typing further explanation:

> Will you save me the good swag? Paul's sister
> found a Chloe Paddington in Cancer Research and
> never fucking shuts up about it.

> Of course, of course. The plan is to pull a priceless
> antique out of a rag bag and never have to
> work again.

> That's the spirit!

More typing. A pause. Then, nothing.

Suze must have told other people, because in the days that followed, a dribble of messages had arrived from mutual friends. One old housemate, a uni friend, even one of the school people who existed to her now only as Facebook birthday well-wishers but with whom Suze seemed to maintain an easy dialogue. But since none of them had ever really known what her job was to begin with, the commiserations felt hollow. Hope you're ok! looked more like an order than a question. So she kept up her end of the deal, and reassured them she was. It may be okay not to be okay, but it was easier to pretend to be it.

Gwen turned the corner onto Suze's street. She was relieved to see no sign of Nicholas, having half-expected him to be standing outside the house in a top hat. She hastily chewed a couple of Gaviscon, digging the chalky globs from her back molars with her tongue as she shook out her umbrella and approached Suze and Paul's redbrick Walthamstow terrace ("How?!" "He had an old dead aunt." "Ah, the best kind.").

She took a deep breath—*a good decision, a good decision*—and rang the doorbell.

# Watch

---

For seven years, she had kept the room exactly as he'd left it. Which meant disgusting.

This went against all of her natural inclinations for cleanliness and order, and as such she considered it a point of personal pride. A sacrifice to his memory. Her boy was commemorated as he had lived: in chaos, color, and squalor.

Sometimes, on the lowest days, she would climb into his bed and bury her face in his pillow. The scent of him was all but imaginary now, and yet she could still conjure it if she tried hard enough. The faint tang of body spray and the spicy hum of ripe testosterone. The cloying top note of marijuana that she'd hated then, but inhaled now with fond indulgence. The smell of the neck she had used to kiss, pulling him into a headlock and landing somewhere south of his earlobe, because he was too tall, her beanstalk of a boy, to reach his face. Unless it was her birthday or Mother's Day, when he deigned to stoop.

Maybe she'd have tackled the room sooner if any of his possessions had been worth passing on, handing out to family members as heirlooms—but what ordinary nineteen-year-old boy has things that anyone else in their right mind would want? Festering sports kit and battered A level paperbacks. The CDs and DVDs that had made such useful Christmas and birthday presents in the days before streaming services. A games console that had been on the verge of obsolescence then, let alone now.

Old sticker albums from childhood, the dusty vestiges of multiple magazine partworks—*Build a dinosaur! First issue only 99p, all subsequent issues £8.99*—begun and never completed. Jumpers with purposeful rips in the cuffs, faded jeans with fraying hems. A pair of trainers with a hole where a toe poked out, and which she had begged to be allowed to replace for him. Hidden them once, even, waving £30 cash at him before giving up the fight in embarrassment once he explained how much trainers cost these days. Who would want any of it?

This left them in a kind of limbo. She couldn't bear to dismantle his room, the swampy shrine, because she couldn't bear to have it confirmed that each piece was worth so much less than the sum of its parts. How could they parcel up each lousy piece of detritus and scrub him away?

Yet with each passing year the need became greater, and the task became more impossible. They'd left it too late. They should have been organized, acted quickly—started passing things out at the wake, or soon afterward. They could have made a day of it; invited all his friends round to choose mementos, then taken them out for beers and milked them for stories and secrets. Gathered all the tiny parts of him together in their arms and held them close, before they drifted off into the ether. "A celebration of life." But nobody had told them to do this at the time.

At the time, they'd been too wrecked by grief. Too hollow; sleepwalking through the admin of it all, barely mustering the energy for what had to be done. Willing each day over as soon as it had begun, and the next, and the next, doggedly putting one foot in front of the other, scared to snatch a glance at the horizon. Praying desperately for the moment that the anesthetic cocktail of time and distance would finally kick in.

And now so much time had passed that it would feel silly to start dredging it all up. His friends were grown men now, with jobs—families even, one or two of them, who she saw from time to time in the precinct, wearing babies in slings like chubby medals around their necks, and she had to step hurriedly away, blinking hard. It would be silly to think they'd want to come round now and claim a piece of the adolescent friend they might barely remember. Or unfair, perhaps, to stir up the pain again if they did.

These were the things she told herself, as she wrapped herself in his duvet—fresh from the wash only a couple of days before it happened, thank god—and stared at the ceiling. The one place where all was calm and clear and clean.

His sister had offered to help, of course. Many times, in the early days. But she'd stopped after a while, perhaps not wanting her parents to think she was being callous. Perhaps not wanting to do it at all. Perhaps even assuming they'd done it without her by now, which would be a fair assumption, because it had been seven years and her mother was usually notorious as the kind of person who cleaned the table down with a wet wipe while you were still chewing your last bite of dinner. But to do it without her would be unthinkable, just as doing it with her was unthinkable.

"No," she'd told her daughter, tight-lipped, before moving swiftly on to some other topic. "No, I don't think so. Thank you. Not yet."

It had been easier to bristle and feign offense than it had been to admit the truth—that his room had slipped into some unreachable, iron-clad part of her mind that she, a weak human, could not access. Even as she lay here in it, watching the swirling dust motes catching the late afternoon light that streamed through a crack in the curtains, the room felt unworldly. She was through the looking glass, down the rabbit hole, in the magical world at the back of the wardrobe where time stood still.

Experimentally, she reached for the nearest object on his scrappy plywood bedside table—a watch, Casio, with a steel chainlink strap. She didn't remember him wearing it. Or perhaps the memory had been surpassed by the image of it lying here, a historical artifact.

She blew the dust off its retro digital face and passed it slowly from one hand to the other, feeling its weight, half-expecting tears to come. But they didn't. So after a while she slipped the watch into her pocket, heaved herself slowly off the bed, and left the room.

Downstairs, where Derek was busy in the kitchen adding too much red wine to his Saturday bolognese, she slipped it into the fold-up shopping bag that hung in the porch. She added a few unwanted paperbacks for good measure, and quietly congratulated herself on this effort. Progress.

**16**

Somewhere from the left of her head came the reassuring *plink-fizz* of a Berocca being dropped into a glass of water. Gwen's mouth twitched. Someone appeared to have snuck in in the night and carpeted her tongue.

She reached up a tentative hand, eyes still closed, but Suze's voice came back curt and schoolmarmish. "Not unless you sit up, this bedding is White Company."

Gwen grimaced into the pillow, and inhaled the telltale scent of pomegranate and fig ironing water. "Why am I in your bed?"

"You were hiding."

"Hiding?" She winched herself off Suze's crisp cotton and took the glass.

"From the young David Dickinson."

The night before lurched into focus, like a pixelated image on a TV gameshow. She remembered. She groaned. "*Nicholas* came."

"Not just Nicholas, from the sounds of things."

Gwen choked, and sprayed a fluorescent mouthful across the bed.

"What? In *here*?" They couldn't have. Not in the pristine honeymoon suite. It would be a sullying worse than the yellow stain now seeping 700 percent of her vitamin C RDA into the duvet cover.

"No no, no. In the garden, if you please! A lovely treat for the neighbors. It'll be all over the Facebook page."

Suze was trying to sound scathing, trying to set her face into a scowl of disapproval, but there was too much of the old gossip-hound escaping through. She had always loved living vicariously through other people's mistakes. Connie had been spot on in that regard, at least.

"Then you disappeared up here and didn't come down again," Suze went on. "We had to listen to him talk about business coaching seminars for forty-five minutes until he finally left."

"Oh god, I'm sorry."

"He tried to sell us a stuffed weasel wearing boxing gloves."

"I'm so sorry."

"Then I came up here and found you curled up in a ball in our bed with no jeans on. Quite like a little weasel yourself, actually. Maybe a stoat. I had to send Paul to sleep on the futon."

"I'm so, *so* sorry."

"Ach, it's fine." Suze was grinning now. "Unlike Paul, you're happy to be the big spoon."

"She is risen indeed! Alleluia!" bellowed Paul as Gwen emerged at the bottom of the stairs some time later. He was in the kitchen, spreading marmalade thickly on a hot cross bun. Weekend papers on the table, radio burbling in the background. A domestic diorama. An artist's impression of a grown-up.

"So. Gwen." He paused, took a languorous bite, wiped the crumbs from his chin, surveyed her through the round wire frames that she had always privately suspected had no prescription in them, and asked: "Is it love?"

Suze hooted from somewhere behind her, pushed her roughly into a kitchen chair and began pouring coffee into a matte charcoal cup. Everything Suze owned was matte charcoal now. And to think, not so long ago they had both agreed that the most personally relatable thing in the whole of *Sex and the City* was Miranda telling Steve that her sponges smelled.

"Come on, we're in suspense!" he went on. "Is he . . . *the one*?

Will he be making you *Mrs*. Stuffed Weasel? Have you taken him home to meet the parents yet, or"—he'd thought this up in advance, she could tell—"will the only *Dorking* be happening in our shrubbery?"

Gwen belched softly and apologized.

Paul was, as a mutual friend had once put it, the kind of man who might sing Gilbert and Sullivan at any moment for no reason at all. "I am the very model of the modern major prick," the friend had muttered, every time Paul launched into one of his Open University–style lectures on which planets were planets and which were just gaseous orbs.

"*You're a gaseous orb*." The same friend had slept with Suze once, and very much hoped to again some day.

In truth Paul wasn't a major prick, or really one at all. But it was easier to call him a prick and believe it than it was to get one's head around Suze genuinely loving him. It made no sense.

Paul had little to endear him as a friend, but even less to recommend him as a partner. If he'd been a loose acquaintance, he might have been the kind of person they'd have enjoyed having around purely to bitch about in taxis home. But as it was, as Suze's eternal plus one, his lack of charm was confounding; it felt like an administrative error. As though at any moment a different man, one who didn't go to Cheltenham Races every year "for the networking," might rush in and apologize for the mix-up.

For the first few months that they were going out, Gwen had to fight the urge to bat Paul's arm away every time he snaked it publicly around her friend's waist. She kept waiting for Suze to recoil at his touch, but Suze never did. So Gwen recoiled for her. Eventually she recoiled halfway across London.

She'd married him, of course, eventually, in a National Trust place near Chalfont St. Giles. Suze had two sisters and Paul had a legion of Shirley Temple–esque nieces, and Gwen had been relieved about that. It meant that she wasn't asked to be a bridesmaid, but that technically she wasn't *not* asked to be one either.

As it was, she'd spent the day hovering on the fringes of a discordant crowd, made up of people who once upon a time had things like "Halls" or "SickInBush" listed as their last names on her phone, but who now limited their contact to housewarming invites and reciprocal endorsements on LinkedIn. She had asked all the polite questions about recent holidays and home renovations, remembered the names of their various offspring, hugged the weepy ones in the loos and fetched the pregnant ones ginger ales from the bar. She'd felt the old friendships warm up as the night went on, brittle connections growing softer and more malleable in the heat of the occasion. She murmured affectionate old nicknames into their hair, and they told the skin just left of her ear that she really must come round for dinner soon.

By 9 p.m. they were bellowing lyrics at each other across the dance floor—songs from way back, absorbed through repeated exposure until each beat from *Now That's What I Call Music 49* was stored as vital data in their cells. Sonique. Basement Jaxx. Groovejet ft. Sophie Ellis Bextor. Paul's preapproved list of big band swing tunes was swiftly abandoned once the DJ saw the response he could get from "Let Me Blow Ya Mind" by Eve and Gwen Stefani.

Then, during the brief scuffle around a false labor scare that turned out to be the elastic giving out in a pair of pregnancy Spanx, Gwen had looked up and seen Suze walking toward her. Flower crown askew, barefoot, with a fistful of cheese. Grinning.

Gwen never knew what to say to people on their wedding day. The whole thing was too stressful. After the obvious scripted pleasantries—congraaaaats, you look amazing, such a gorgeous ceremony, let's see the ring, what a speech, aren't we lucky with the weather, how does it feel, are you floating on a cloud of celestial happiness, etc., etc.—no conversation ever felt special enough. You couldn't start talking about work, TV, or your ongoing hunt for the perfect bath mat on what was supposed to be the most magical day of someone's life. You couldn't hog the blessed couple with your lackluster, workaday chat. She tended to clam up and move on quickly to let other guests have their piece of the bridal pie, then feel sad about it in the taxi home. Sad that she hadn't delivered some sparkling nugget of wisdom for them to cherish for years to come. A real friend would manage to think of something better than congratsyoulookamazingluckyweatherhowdoesitfeel.

"I fucking hate it, nobody's talking to me," Suze had announced before Gwen had a chance to say anything, picking a nugget of Stilton out of her lacy cleavage. "They just take photos of me and coo. I feel like one of those sodding meet-and-greets in Vegas where you pay a grand to get a selfie with Britney."

At this, Gwen had taken Suze's beautiful bridal face in her hands, and stared deep into her beautiful bridal eyes. The two had swayed slightly, while Train's "Drops of Jupiter" reached its crescendo. She had hiccupped, and watched a single bead of sweat roll down the beautiful bridal forehead.

"Wanna hear about my new bath mat?"

"Please," Suze had replied.

And now here she was in the immaculate bridal kitchen, being tentatively offered marmalade. *Please look after this woman.* Gwen declined the marmalade, because her mouth already tasted of bile.

"I'm sorry about Nicholas," she said lamely, again. She felt mildly hysterical. "He's—Oh *god*, I can't even—I don't know what—"

Except she did know what. It was replaying in her head now, images juddering round at triple speed like one of those Victorian story carousels. The other couples—no, not "other,"—the *couples*, only three of them, more a thing than A Thing after all, laughing around a Lebanese sharing platter, pure Sunday supplement magazine. Complimenting the fattoush, asking about the table runner. Asking Gwen what she did. What *did* she do? What does the fact we use that word as shorthand for "work" say about the national psyche? Her answer, self-mocking. Her mouth, dry. Her fringe, feathery and chaotic from the rain. Nicholas, arriving late, beaming and swearing, brandishing a bottle of something expensive but embarrassing, like cognac or, god forbid, Goldschläger. Gamely chipping into every conversation with a story that was too long, or too loud, or ended with someone crashing through a stained-glass window in a dinner jacket. Paul, topping up her wine with an air of largesse. Suze, topping up her wine with glee. Nicholas, topping up her wine while his free hand stroked her thigh, first timidly, then idly, then purposefully, under the table. Hearing his remarks come crashing down like distant waves. Topping up her own wine this time. Letting it all wash over her. Moving to the lounge for dessert, something gooey and impressive that curdled on impact with her stomach. Music. Vinyl, naturally. Not The Nolans. Escaping to the loo, sitting there and staring at the towel ladder, letting her eyes slip out of focus for a few minutes, as a treat. Leaving the bathroom to find Nicholas waiting for her outside, a move that would have seemed almost smooth, were it not happening to her. With him. Paul's framed *New Yorker* covers bearing down on them in the hallway: too many pairs of illustrated eyes for her liking. Him steering her into the garden for a smoke—no, hang on, a vape, of course a vape—and the muffled squawk of Cards Against Humanity unfolding from the other side of the wall as she willingly pressed her back into the ivy trellis, feeling its dampness begin to seep through her top, wondering at what point she might put a stop to things. The eager hand beneath her skirt. The cloud of sweet condensation on her neck, and then the taste—it still lingered faintly in her mouth, she noticed, beneath the acrid tang—of synthetic lemon meringue.

"Leave her alone, you dick," ordered Suze, swatting at her husband with the Culture section. "If she's going to start messing around with boys, I'd rather she did it under our roof. Or, you know, our porch light."

They were both enjoying this a lot, smirking into their coffee cups like scandalized Regency mamas. A little taste of youthful indiscretion to cut through the creamy richness of their weekend. Gwen forced a self-deprecating laugh. Her mouth felt tingly and swollen.

"Honestly though, Gee," Suze said, turning solemn; Gwen sensed a polite back-pedal in motion. "He seems really . . . ah, sweet."

"Agghh, don't," Gwen protested. "Please do not."

"No but seriously! We're happy for you. It's great that you're . . . you know. Dating?" Her voice rose at the end, seeking confirmation.

Gwen bristled at this, although bristling hurt her head. "I mean, I've *been* dating . . . for years, I've been—"

"Sure! Sure. But we've never got to meet any of them." She said this as though perhaps the men up till now had been imaginary. "And after everything with Ryan . . ." Suze hesitated, took a breath. "And . . . your family."

Gwen's gut lurched perilously at this. She had the sensation of water rushing into her ears, a tipping of everything off-kilter. Suze continued.

"It's been so long and it just felt . . . I dunno. I worried you were . . . punishing yourself. Like you'd put your whole life on pause."

Paul stayed silent behind his newspaper, raised unnaturally high. Not because he felt awkward, she suspected—Paul never felt awkward—but because he didn't want to taunt her with his presence at this delicate moment. The dutiful husband. The trophy spouse. *Here's what you could have won.*

Acquiescence seemed easier, both on Suze and her stomach. "You're right," Gwen sighed, and nodded. "Maybe I was punishing myself. Hell, you met Nicholas—maybe I still am."

It was supposed to be funny, but it came out sounding tragic. Besides, it wasn't even true. That realization dropped into her head a mere beat before—ba-dum—the realization that she was probably, definitely, about to throw up. She didn't regret it.

# Huge Hits '97

On slow days, Finn passed the time by developing crushes on the customers.

He often tried flirting with the customers too, though they weren't always receptive. A particular low point had been the time he'd smiled at a woman with a winsome, faraway look in her eye and asked, "What's on your mind?" and she'd replied, "My father-in-law's bowel cancer."

Still, it felt exciting to have this outlet that nobody else he knew had. Beyond the usual trifecta of work, friends, and apps, the shop was a secret, bonus reserve of possible . . . what? Romance. Excitement. Sex. Love. Distraction. Having no particular preference on gender or age gave Finn good odds to begin with ("Like those meat-eaters who take all the Quorn sausages," his friend Li had once grumbled the morning after an especially libidinous house party, prompting an argument about why the "pansexuality as greediness" trope was problematic that neither of them really had the energy to get into) and he got a kick out of the idea of a charity shop meet-cute: his eyes locking with theirs over a rack of polyester blouses or a basket of cracked CDs.

Finn was twenty-two and found CDs and cassette tapes alluring in the same way people two decades older fetishized vinyl and rotary dial telephones. Today he was wiping the sticky residue of an ancient price label off a copy of *Huge Hits '97* and gazing fondly at a man—tall, tubby, handsome, graying at the temples—who was rifling through the shirts with a profound sense of urgency. This was common in the shop. For every person who saw charity shops as a place to idle away time, there was always someone else on a deadline. A fancy-dress party, a funeral, an impending job interview with a large slop of pizza sauce down their front.

"Do you need any help there?" called Finn. The man turned around looking grateful, which was rare. Most people, when asked if they needed help, did the normal thing and left the shop.

"Which one?" the man asked, holding up two near-identical checked shirts. Finn knew without seeing the labels that both were from Uniqlo.

He pretended to consider them carefully. "The green one. It will make your eyes pop."

"Is that . . . good?" asked the man, his eyes bugging involuntarily behind his tortoiseshell-rimmed glasses.

"Very good," Finn assured him. He enjoyed dispensing advice to the needy. Last week Jeremy had brought in a stack of Pringle golf sweaters, and was forced to admit that his new wife was in the process of rebranding him.

"You can dress a horse in Arket but you cannot make it drink," Finn had told him sagely. "Drink what?" Jeremy asked.

"Orange wine," Finn had replied.

"It's a d-date," this man admitted now, tripping slightly over the word. He tugged at his sweatshirt. "I was wearing this—I mean, *am* wearing this—but you know . . . you know when you leave the house and you see your reflection in a shop window and you think 'god, what a total shitshow'?"

Finn had never experienced this. "All the time!" he said.

The man continued. "So I thought maybe I'd do a quick change. Superman-style."

"Pants over your trousers?"

He chuckled nervously. "If you think they'd make my eyes pop."

Having settled on the green shirt and been talked into a belt too, the man executed his self-conscious quick change in front of the mirror. Finn advised him to leave the shirt undone over his T-shirt, not buttoned up, which he did. The result was distinctly more Clark Kent than Superman, but that was no bad thing. He looked himself up and down; gave his reflection a coy nod of approval.

"And hey, if the date doesn't work out . . ." called Finn, breezy, from behind the counter. The words hung in the air between them for a delicious moment before he added, ". . . keep the tag on, we have a thirty-day returns policy."

The man looked briefly alarmed. Then he smiled, deposited his reject sweatshirt on the counter—still warm—and left the shop.

## 17

Other people griped about Sunday evenings. The looming black cloud of bath time and unfinished homework that never quite dissipated, no matter how many years had passed since your last exam, no matter how much you bloody loved baths now.

But for Gwen, it was Saturday afternoons. To her mildly synesthetic mind, Saturday afternoons were always gray scale. They were black-and-white films on TV and the soporific drone of the football scores. Rain lashing against a coat hood on the walk home from town. Saturday mornings were blank white pages of possibility, and Saturday nights were razzle-dazzle, the gaudy cruise ship of light entertainment that would carry you through to bedtime. But first you had to endure approximately thirty-five hours of nothing. Even during the most fun-packed Saturdays of her adult life, she'd swear she could still hear it, on some distant plane, the heart beneath the floorboards. *Peterborough United, one. Accrington Stanley, nil.*

Even sunny Saturday afternoons like this one were a false friend, too full of pressure to be *out and about*. Not, as Gwen thought to herself, crawling into bed with her coat still on, *in and a . . . bin.*

"Look after yourself" was the last thing Suze had said when she closed the door, and it had replayed on a loop in Gwen's head as she stumbled home, wine sweat seeping from her pores, tote bag of leftover mezze bashing against her calf. It was cheerful and innocuous enough, especially from the woman who'd just spent twenty minutes making sympathetic noises at her through the door of her own downstairs toilet—but she couldn't help scanning the intonation for any undercurrent of threat. Or plea? *Look after yourself . . . because you're valuable. Look after yourself . . . because I don't care enough to do it for you. Look after yourself . . . because if you can't, how in the hell are you going to love somebody else?* No, that was RuPaul.

Gwen belched, and felt slightly better.

It had been so long since her last real hangover that she'd started to miss them, almost, in a nostalgic way—the free-pass, snow day-ish feeling of a seriously bad weekend hangover, when there's nothing to be done but sack everything off and wallow in it. The days when she could use carbohydrates as a form of fire blanket, quelling the stormy seas effectively enough to get back on the horse by lunchtime. Before her insides staged their early thirties revolt. After that, as little as two glasses of corner shop Sauvignon was enough to require a multi-stage management plan involving Gaviscon, Lucozade, and strategic deployment of Nairn's ginger oat biscuits.

"Your hangovers are like early-stage pregnancy," Suze had said once, after Gwen had dragged them both off a bus so that she could stand queasily with her face against a cool, tiled surface. "Also late-stage pregnancy," she'd added, as Gwen started breathing heavily, eyes closed, her nails digging into Suze's forearm.

They'd joked a lot about pregnancy back then, with the easy arrogance of those who haven't attempted it yet. They tossed it back and forth between them like a playground game. "You have a baby!" "No, YOU have a baby!" Before the very word became something hot and combustible, to be handled with care. Drop it in the wrong conversation and you never knew who might get hurt.

Gwen had watched for a decade now, as friends and colleagues parted around her into two distinct camps: the haves and the have-nots. She had learned to recognize the black-and-white whorl of a sonogram photo before it even downloaded. Learned to detect the cadence of a voice that came bearing "some news!" and cushion herself, mentally, against the blow. There were smaller factions within the have-nots, of course—the don't-wants, the do-wants, the tryings, the grievings, the quietly undecideds—but none of them seemed to have room for her, the person who had wilfully blown her chances. Given up her happily-ever-after. And for what?

These days the haves tended to treat her delicately and warily, dragging their sticky-fingered progeny off her skirt every two minutes and apologizing in frantic tones. *"Leave Auntie Gwen alone!"* She was never sure if this was because they assumed she hated children, or because they assumed she might try to tuck one into her handbag at the first opportunity.

"Auntie Gwen is generally covered in melted chocolate, it's fine!" she'd quipped the last time it had happened, at a colleague's baby shower. The parent had wrinkled their nose and said nothing.

People sometimes lost their sense of humor for a year or two after having a baby, she'd noticed. It was probably just sleep deprivation, though Gwen sometimes wondered if it were something deeper too. Maybe their world had become more earnest, more sincere? Maybe it was harder to be flippant about things now that their feelings were made flesh and moving around in it, vulnerable and exposed. Or maybe they had mum jokes now, brilliant quips about pumping and teething and perineum stitches that they saved for people who would better understand? Hard to know.

Now, Suze was another great unknown. Or she was to Gwen. Perhaps there were other friends, legions of supportive WhatsAppers, who knew exactly what the deal was with Suze's reproductive plans or lack thereof. It hurt a little to think about that. But as the years had passed and they'd grown incrementally more distant, more formal with each other, as their contact was relegated to proper calendar occasions—birthdays, housewarm-ings, New Year's Eve, Eurovision—and Paul's presence became a given, an implied plus one on every invite, Gwen was never alone with her for long enough to ask.

Would she have asked, if she'd had the chance? Was that even allowed? It was a question feminist principles forbade, and social awkwardness even more so. Women's bodies were not up for public discussion. Their wombs were not Big Yellow Storage units. Each time someone asked that question it felt like an un-solicited prod, the sharp finger of societal expectation needling into their choices.

Gwen knew from personal experience that the hardest thing about being asked, relentlessly, when you would have children, if you wanted children, whether you wanted to get married too and if so in which order, wasn't always the exposure of your private feelings, so much as being forced to identify those feelings at all. When much of the time the honest answer is: "I don't know, and please don't make me think about it." Don't make me think about it now, here, in this bar, at this picnic, on this hard plastic chair in this doctor's surgery. Don't throw a live grenade at me in the office kitchen. Don't expect me to pack up the shifting sands of my hopes, dreams, maternal instinct, and biological clock into a neat parcel that can be unwrapped in the gap between starters and mains.

And yet, there was still the part of her that wanted to ask. Hon-esty was intimacy, wasn't it? Knowing the grisly truth was what really tethered you to a person, and not only in crime novels. It was hard to trace the point in their friendship at which Gwen had gone from knowing her best friend's pin number and IBS triggers to not knowing whether or not she wanted children, and it was even harder to know how to go back again, if she could at all.

But she was fairly sure getting fingered on Suze's decking wasn't the answer.

*

The weekend passed in uneven lumps. No communication from Nicholas arrived, which should have been a relief but actually felt worse, like needing to vomit again but not being able to. Even by Sunday morning, once her hangover had subsided to a dull throb, the bilious gnawing in the pit of her stomach remained. It remained even after she'd doused it in Purdey's from the corner shop and submerged it under a blanket of Deliverooed katsu curry. It was, she realized with some annoyance, shame.

Not shame from what she'd done *with* Nicholas, rather what she'd done *to* him. And how dare he, frankly, for that. He'd put her in a position where she was forced to reject him, and now *she* had to feel bad about that. Hadn't he? Didn't she?

She stewed on this for a while, wiping a smear of luminous curry sauce off the kitchen counter with her hand. She was forced to admit that no, he hadn't.

Though the idea of her purposely leading anyone on (oh god, was she a fuckboy now?) seemed hilarious, there was a pang of . . . not quite regret—was it almost . . . *maternal* concern? Images loomed like a gruesome pop-up book. Nicholas as little orphan Oliver, chased out of the workhouse for asking for more. Nicholas as Roger the spurned neighbor in *Sister, Sister.* Nicholas cry-wanking bitterly in a storage unit full of stag's heads and Hornsea teapots.

As punishment, Gwen hung her washing out in silence instead of turning on one of the podcasts that usually soundtracked her waking hours. She forced herself to empty the food waste bin that had a snowy white layer of mold across the top. She pushed herself through a series of boring domestic tasks and grudgingly past each of the hourly milestones that made up another empty weekend, until finally she arrived at her greatest act of penance.

"Hello?"

"Hi, Mum, it's me."

"Oh! Hello." Then, alarmed, "Is everything okay?"

"Fine! Fine. Are you okay?"

"Oh yes," said Marjorie, as though the question was mildly insulting. "Fine! Fine."

A brief pause, then she was off. "We've had the plumber here this week, it's been a complete nightmare. Refused to take his boots off, trod mud up the stairs, then did himself an injury with a pipe cutter, went off to find a bandage and didn't come back for three days."

"What for?"

"Well it was an accident, or at least I assume so. He was cutting a piece of pipe."

"No, I mean what did you call the plumber for?"

"Oh. Dad thought there was a leak in the airing cupboard."

"Oh." Gwen couldn't think of anything to say to this. "Oh dear."

"Yes, well. Anyway, he was somebody Teresa Hibbert recommended but we shan't be using him again. Between you and me I half-wonder if he's some relation she's trying to foist on people, like the time she let her goddaughter give me those highlights."

"Mm." An old image of Marjorie with copper-hued tiger stripes loomed into view. Gwen's head throbbed and she winced, audibly.

"What's wrong?" demanded her mother. "You sound like you're in pain. Are you in pain?"

"Toothache," Gwen told her. "I need to go to the denti—"

"Well, make sure you go to the dentist!" Marjorie cut across her.

"I just said, I'm going to."

"Make sure you do!"

A pause.

"Any word on the promotion?"

"Not yet. There's some kind of holdup, I think. An HR freeze. Actually, Mum, I—"

Marjorie interrupted again. "I thought maybe that's why you were phoning. To tell us the news."

"No, I was just . . . phoning."

"So no news?"

"No news."

"Oh. Right you are then. Well, I'll let you go."

# Coat

It was a quilted anorak, but not the trendy kind. It had a drawstring waist with plastic toggles, and a hood lined in ratty fake fur. There were white and yellow flowers embroidered on the pockets, and when Lise put her hands in them she found a couple of train tickets dated 2011 for journeys to Godalming and Box Hill & Westhumble. Places that sounded almost satirical in their flavorless English way.

The coat was a purplish color that could not be called lilac or lavender or violet or anything else floral; it was more anatomical. Bruise. It was a bruise-colored coat. It looked like the old blood that pooled beneath her tracing-paper skin. It wasn't her style, and this bothered her, and it bothered her that she wasn't supposed to be bothered. She was supposed to be so glad of any crumb of comfort she was thrown that she could override personal taste and rejoice in a coat that looked like something her mother would walk the dogs in. As though gratitude should be her personal style now. *Here we have Lise, in this season's latest shade of pity. Note the virtue signaling around the hem.*

But no. Lise was still Lise was still Lise, and now she had to be Lise in a coat she hated.

It was hard to shake the idea of the coat smothering her, concealing her real identity even as it was warming her bones. She worried that if Jakob ever came back to find her, he wouldn't recognize her in this ugly-ass coat. That he, like everyone else, would walk straight past.

That morning a man had given her a tenner and explained he had "nothing against the Poles, they work hard when they're not drinking hard." When she had corrected him—she was Norwegian, a nationality that didn't appear to have a place on the snakes and ladders board of prejudice and sympathy—he had looked for a moment as though he might take the money back.

She'd seen people get abusive, plenty of times, when a homeless person declined their charity. Usually a cold box of chips, or something unholy like a tuna melt or an egg sandwich. She'd seen the spark of victory in their eyes, watched it burn up their momentary embarrassment. In only a few seconds, the smart of that rejection would become something else: contempt. Even the ones who didn't spit or yell would use it, she imagined, as evidence against you. A little strike in the mental column headed "reasons to keep on walking." *Nothing worse than an ungrateful beggar.*

Lise had pretended to be grateful for the coat for several minutes at least, long enough to give the volunteer her warm fuzzies: the mental photo opp that comprised Lise's part of the bargain. Not a real photo opp, thank god, although that had happened too.

"D'you mind if I . . . ?" one guy had asked after he chucked a fiver into her cup, brandishing his iPhone at arm's length in the universal sign for selfie. *If you're too embarrassed to finish the sentence then that's your answer, buddy*, she had thought. But she hadn't had time to say it before he'd lurched toward her—his head not touching hers, but close enough that she could smell his coffee breath—and snapped the photo.

"Thanks," he'd said as he pocketed the phone quickly without showing her the results. "It's for this, like, thing I'm working on?"

Lise had thought about the photo for a long time after that. She thought about it as she closed her eyes to sleep, swaddled in the coat, with her face turned toward the slimy brick of the underpass and the rattle of the 1 a.m. freight train passing overhead. Wondering how her hair had looked, and hoping the guy had died.

## 18

The heat wave had abated now, and outside the world was divided into two camps: the underdressed and the overdressed. Both groups were brazening it out, in duvet coats and micro-shorts, refusing to cave. Fallen camellias like fat pink shower puffs littered the pavement and walking through this part of town felt, to Gwen, despite being barely twenty minutes away from home, like a holiday.

She had often walked through these roads during the first winter after she moved to London. Back then she had loved peering into brightly lit windows in the dark, the glimpses of high ceilings and white walls and cool, spartan luxury making her shiver in a way she couldn't quite explain. "Imagine being this rich!" Suze used to say, a little too loudly, as though hoping the owner would hear them from behind a hedge and . . . what? Feel a pang of bourgeois guilt, presumably. Or leave them the house in a will.

These days Gwen preferred looking down into the basement flats that were tucked below street level, enjoying the curious intimacy of seeing straight into a stranger's washing-up bowl.

Connie's house was a whole house on a street full of houses converted into flats, which gave it instant gravitas. It was tall, Victorian, in biscuit-colored brick with an original tiled path—cracked and chipped in places, not the gleaming new restorations of some of her neighbors. It had a front garden full of hydrangeas and climbers in glazed blue pots and terracotta urns, plus an attractively rusted iron bench. The door had panes of mismatched stained glass and Gwen found herself holding her breath automatically as she tapped at the knocker (were doorbells gauche now?) and waited for Connie's form to appear from the end of the long hallway, distorted into a Picasso by the jewel-colored swirls.

"Hello! There you are! Come in then, come in." Gwen had timed herself to the minute but Connie somehow made her feel both late and embarrassingly early. She was wearing a long wrap-around skirt with a linen shirt, a hefty amber necklace, and an apron in faded Liberty print that looked like a deliberate part of the outfit. A tortoiseshell cat appeared, weaving prettily around her ankles. "Bugger off, you mangy mog," she told it and swept Gwen inside.

A vast hallway stretched before them, bathed in early evening light. On the floor, a series of long rugs lead the way to a sunken kitchen beyond, full of terra-cotta tiles and honey-colored wood, from which music and complex smells were drifting. The walls were covered in art, photography, sketches, framed posters: clustered in a way that gave the impression of decades of leisurely evolution. Nothing so strategic as a "gallery wall." Nothing so crass as "decorating." In fact the whole house gave the impression of not so much having been built and designed as birthed, and cultivated. It only bore evidence of the very best, most tasteful parts of each decade: no rogue floral borders or *Changing Rooms* hangovers. The years had settled on it gently, like dust.

There was actual dust too, a light coating on a nearby vase and a few elegant, looping cobwebs that somehow only served to emphasize how high the ceilings were. Through the open door to the living room, Gwen could see more faded Persian rugs, a vast green-tiled fireplace and a battered old Chesterfield covered in blankets and embellished cushions of the kind her mother would call "ethnic." Piles of books, magazines, and newspapers on rickety side tables stopped safely short of looking hoarderish. They looked as though they might even get read.

Not even Connie's downstairs loo, where Gwen ended up almost immediately since it was her bladder's habit to grant her the length of precisely one Tube journey and not a second more, showed any sign of squarely prim functionality. Its walls were covered in framed newspaper clippings, political cartoons and private jokes—a caricature of Connie dressed as Blonde Ambition–era Madonna; a handwritten limerick on a scrap of brown paper bag. There was Molton Brown hand cream perched on the side of the sink, but the soap was a bar of Imperial Leather, slightly ridged, in an olive green dish that brought to mind church hall crockery. The tap was lightly crusted with limescale in a way Marjorie would never have permitted.

Gwen's parents lived in a small, spotless 1950s semi-detached, which they had spent the past four decades carefully and methodically stripping of anything that could be classed as character. The house she remembered as once being warmly cluttered with the debris of family life, with various loud floral sofas, shoes strewn in the tiny hallway and peeling stencils on the dated kitchen tiles, had been steadfastly cleared out and cleaned up and lacquered over, bit by bit, with thick carpets and laminate flooring and so many coats of white gloss paint that it felt incrementally smaller and more claustrophobic every time she went home.

On her most recent visit, which wasn't very recent at all, two large, perfectly spherical balls of fake plastic foliage had appeared either side of the front door. Gwen had always wondered who bought those, and why.

"But you *garden*. You grow *real* plants," she had said, and her mother had looked at the balls in confusion, as though perhaps a stranger might have crept up and hung them there in the night.

"Yvonne has them too," she'd said eventually. Defensive. "I thought they looked nice."

Now, Gwen suddenly burned with embarrassment at the image

of Connie eyeing the balls. Or her parents' beanbag lap trays, or the *no junk mail please* sticker on the letterbox that they carefully replaced every couple of years. Or knowing that her mother kept every little pre-wrapped biscuit she was ever served with coffee, "to give to guests." They never had guests.

She had assumed reading while cooking was something people only did in books. But when she returned to the kitchen there was Connie, barefoot and swaying, with a paperback in one hand, a wooden spoon in the other and a sputtering pot before her, every inch the manic boomer dream girl. Titania by way of the Toast catalog. The effect was slightly reduced when she noticed the book was a Lee Child and not a battered paperback of *Madame Bovary*, but only slightly.

Connie was cooking something intensely spiced, involving one big, bubbling Le Creuset and several other pans of mysterious additions. Crisping onions, toasted nuts. Several small heaps of chopped herbs sat on the counter like summer grass cuttings, and Gwen felt another pang of shame thinking about the dusty jar of all-purpose "mixed herbs" she sprinkled into everything these days, half-enjoying the way it made all her meals taste like a Pizza Hut buffet.

"Sit! Sit!" Connie ordered. So she perched on a stool at the breakfast bar, and waited in silence as her hostess held up a stern finger, finished her chapter and then closed the book with a flourish.

Connie slid a large glass of red wine along the counter toward her, still stirring with her other hand, and then produced a bowl of fat olives with a little dish for stones.

"I hope you like lamb," said Connie, though it was a statement rather than a question. "I never even asked if you were vegetarian! You don't look vegetarian." She turned to appraise Gwen over her glasses, which had slipped halfway down her nose in the steam. "Or not vegan, anyway."

Gwen was flexitarian, in that she was vegetarian when dining with people who might judge her, and not when she wasn't. She felt like this about most hot issues of the day, and sometimes worried that if she lived in a vacuum without access to anybody else's opinions, she wouldn't have principles at all.

But she didn't tell Connie this. She only agreed that she didn't, and she wasn't, and yes, she did like lamb.

"Good!" Connie seemed appeased rather than relieved. "Our sacrificial lamb."

During the meal they talked shop. Connie was full of theories and observations and gossip—things that Gwen, who had three more weeks of volunteering under her belt than Connie did, hadn't noticed, or felt stupid for not knowing. Things like, did St. Michael get fillers or was it just his personality? Why did Brian always say yes to a cup of tea but never, ever drink it?

Connie told her that Silent Harvey was helplessly in love with Yasmeen, which Yasmeen encouraged by occasionally giving him her used eyelash extensions ("It's fine, they're a tax write-off," she'd told Connie). That Gloria had apprehended a shoplifter single-handed last Tuesday, and talked to him at such length that he'd ended up apologizing and donating his own belt to the shop. That several celebrities who lived locally had been known to drop off bags of clothes, but the spoils vanished so quickly that there was speculation Head Office might be running an Only Fans account.

At this point, when they were both two glasses of not-orange down and had chewed the meat off their lamb bones with carnal relish, Connie sat back in her chair and said, "Right. Now tell me why you're here."

Gwen panicked for a second. Had she hallucinated the invitation? Got the wrong end of the stick? Had she wandered in like a drooling sleepwalker and Connie was simply too polite to turn her away?

"The disastrous dinner party!" said Connie. "Come on, you've left me hanging long enough. I want all the sordid details. You must sing for your supper."

"Oh god." Gwen winced at the memory of the evening as it bobbed back up, fully formed, yet another unflushable taken up residence in her mental U-bend.

"It was brutal. I mean, it left *me* hanging for long enough . . ."

Connie didn't dignify this weak joke with a smile. She wanted the juice. On their last shift together she had been brisk and businesslike about this consolation dinner, as though her jokey promise had been a binding contract. She had taken out her diary—a Moleskine, not a phone calendar—to suggest dates practically before the words "It was . . . *not good*" had left Gwen's mouth. Connie seemed to think it the most normal thing in the world, to make a social commitment and actually see it through.

"Your friend, the one with the awful husband. Is it her fault? Did she try to set you up with somebody odious? Car keys in a bowl? Oh god, she didn't ask you to waitress . . . ?"

"Ha! No. None of it was her fault. Except hosting the thing in the first place, I suppose. And telling me to bring someone."

Connie nodded, encouragingly. Gwen went on.

"So anyway, I took . . . ahem, Nicholas. Have you met Nicholas, from the shop?"

Connie frowned. "The loud boy with the briefcase? Pink face? Pockets full of antimacassars?"

"That's him."

"Oh, Gwen."

"I know. I don't know why the hell I asked him. Except I couldn't face another evening sat at the end of the table—or worse, right in the center, like the exotic filling in the middle of a couple sandwich—just . . . just answering all the polite questions and making sympathetic noises about childcare costs and waiting for the inevitable point in the night where they all ask to have a go on my Tinder."

"Ugh," Connie barked with sympathy, though Gwen suspected this wasn't how her own dinner parties went.

"I'm not even on Tinder," she added.

"Of course you're not," said Connie. "Anyway, go on."

As well as a therapist, Connie also had the energy of a friend's liberal mother who you would go to with your first UTI. The sheer adolescence of the story felt fitting, and so Gwen sunk into it, recounting each part with groans and squeals of mortification. When they reached the garden part, Connie rewarded her with a cartoonish spit take, spraying Cabernet Sauvignon across the dinner table but somehow missing her own white blouse.

"You *hussy*!" she screeched in mock-horror. "Lucky Nicholas! Poor Nicholas! Poor you. I was right though, wasn't I?" Connie added. "You always get a good story out of it."

"Nobody is *ever* hearing this story," said Gwen, her own laughter turning to spluttering panic as she pictured Brenda, Brian, and Harp all tutting over it in the back room of the shop. An unlikely image, but not an impossible one.

"You have to promise me you won't tell anyone. *Promise me*."

"Oh you're fine, I won't. I promise. I'm a very good secret-keeper," said Connie. "Never told anybody about my husband's tax evasion in thirty-two years of marriage. Although now I can't seem to stop telling people. Anyway, then what?"

"Then I woke up the next day in my friend's bed. Apparently I'd hidden there until he left, and fell asleep."

"That's it?"

"Isn't that enough?"

Connie had a way of switching suddenly from speaking to her like a trusted confidante, to speaking to her as though she were an exasperating child.

"*That's* the great source of existential anguish, you humped him in the garden and passed out?" She stopped just short of adding "in my day it wasn't a *party* unless . . ." but Gwen sensed it anyway.

Perhaps she was supposed to feel stupid, but for the first time in days, she felt better. She took a jubilant swig of wine.

Then Connie asked: "What about love?"

Gwen swallowed. "I barely even like him!"

"Not Nicholas, I mean in general. Are you in it? Ever been in it?"

"No," she said, after a pause. "And yes. Or . . . well, ish. I thought I was. Whatever love means."

"If you're quoting Prince Charles then it can't have been good," said Connie.

"No, it was—for a while," she replied, honestly. "Just not quite good enough. Not in the end."

After dinner was finished, Gwen was thrilled when Connie went to the fridge and produced a huge tiramisu. She'd assumed Connie to be the kind of person who thought cheese was a legitimate dessert, who looked scandalized if you asked for sugar in your tea, and dug a crusted old tin of golden syrup out of the back of a cupboard. Whereas Gwen secretly and childishly still saw all meals as the tithe one must pay to get to pudding.

It was good tiramisu. The sloppy kind, not the kind like damp cake. They ate quickly and messily with big spoons, shoveling it in first from a pair of speckled earthenware bowls and then, for second helpings, straight from the dish. Afterward Connie made coffee and served it in small glazed cups, the kind bigger than an espresso cup but smaller than a plebeian mug. She refused to let Gwen wash up, or help stack the dishwasher, and made no move to do either herself. Instead she opened the large French windows at the end of the kitchen and lit a cigarette, using an empty olive tin as an ashtray.

"Terrible," she muttered after every drag, looking delighted.

At 11 p.m., Connie suddenly announced: "Right, it's past my bedtime! Let's get you a taxi."

This was the smoothest, most assertive getting-rid-of-a-guest

Gwen had ever witnessed. For a moment she just sat, gazing at her in admiration, before remembering she was the one being got rid of.

"Safe home!" called Connie from the doorway as the Uber pulled away. Gwen nodded off on the drive, and woke up as the car stopped outside her flat.

When she got upstairs, there was a dead mouse in the trap next to the kitchen door. Its eyes were open, glassy and accusing. She shut the kitchen door and went to bed, resolving to deal with it in the morning.

Gwen turned the light off in her bedroom and shuffled carefully back to her bed in the dark. She did this every night. Probably about once every ten times, she would stub her toe on the way. She knew she should buy a bedside lamp, but one stub in every ten shuffles wasn't quite enough to force her to actually do it.

Just as she was dozing off, her phone lit up. It was Nicholas.

> I've played it cool for long enough, he wrote.
> Gwen, let me buy you a martini.

She groaned aloud, to nobody. For a long while she lay in the dark, pressing her knuckles into her eyes until brown geometric shapes began to appear like retro wallpaper. Then she turned her phone over, got out of bed again, and went to dispose of the mouse.

# Hoodie

Alicia loved watching them grow up. Each newly learned word and personality quirk a notch on their beautiful, evolving identities. That's what you were supposed to say, wasn't it? It was the parental party line.

But the truth was she also hated watching them grow up. Each newly learned word and personality quirk putting more distance between them and her, the petals of a blooming rosebud curling ever further away from the core. Sometimes in her less rational moments she wanted to grab them and smoosh them both to her stomach, hard, so they could all become one again. Like wet clay, smoothed back into a ball.

Whenever Alicia found herself having that thought, she took a Valium and sent a bag of things to the charity shop. Before she found herself becoming the kind of mother who sobbed over milk teeth and old bits of hair, kept their bedrooms as shrines. She would whirl around the house with a blue Ikea bag in hand, picking up any abandoned item, anything on the floor or under a bed or covered in a light layer of dust, and demanding the owner plead its case.

"I've never seen you wear this!"

"You begged for this for Christmas and barely looked twice at it!"

"There are poor children in the world who would be *delighted* with all your crap."

And if the owner didn't happen to be in the vicinity, well then that was just too bad. Her children had become used to finding their possessions disappeared overnight, to the extent that they hardly bothered to put up a fight anymore. The screams and door slams only lasted a few minutes. She feared that overall the practice was making them value their things less, not more.

Alicia often heard her own mother's voice in her head as she did it, felt her on her shoulder, breathing hot scorn into her ear. But she couldn't stop herself. A dog-eared paperback. A plasticky party game. A gray hoodie with a motif on it, of a dirt-track race or a beach shack or a cattle ranch or some other bullshit piece of made-up Americana via the Great British high street. She would shovel them into the bag and keep going until it was full. Then she would march out of the house, letting the whines of protest—all those newly learned words, so coarse these days—dissolve behind her.

She would march along the road and round the corner and up the high street, sidestepping the fried chicken boxes and swerving around pedestrians until she reached the shop, where often she wouldn't even bother to walk all the way up to the counter and wait her turn; she would merely shout "Donations!" in a singsong voice and plonk the bag down inside the door. The quicker the better. She never stopped to browse.

Back home, now that the bedroom floors were clear and the children were sulking and the pill was wearing off but the residual glow of philanthropy still enveloped her, she always felt better. She would hug them and laugh at their sad, spoiled faces and order their favorite dinner by way of apology. She would beg them to stay in tonight, put their devices down, watch a film with her on the sofa, scooping them into the crook of her body and laughing, laughing, laughing as they struggled to be free.

"Just you and me, kiddos," she would say to them, the way she had for years. "That's all we need."

## 19

"I've made a friend," she told her mother on the phone, and immediately regretted it.

"Who?" asked Marjorie, instantly suspicious. "They're not trying to sell you anything are they?"

"No! She's . . . a person. She's nice. She's about your age, actually."

"*My* age? Why on earth would you want a friend my age? You'll never hear the end of the menopause." Marjorie prided herself on having weathered seven years of debilitating hot flushes, night sweats, and mood swings without ever having mentioned it once.

"I think she's, um, completed it," Gwen replied, as if the menopause were a platform game.

"Well." A pause. "Good for her."

Then: "Have you seen Susannah recently?"

She had not. Their follow-up after the dinner party had been funny and affectionate—one more flurry of apologies from Gwen for good measure, one more reassurance from Suze that if anything she was grateful, it had livened up proceedings—but the messages had run dry after a few rounds. Now, nothing. Gwen was back at the point she had been before, of looking around her life with a forensic eye in case anything was funny or interesting enough to bother her best friend with. She felt like a cat, hunting for a dead bird to drop on the doormat.

"Everyone secretly worries all their friends hate them," Connie shrugged when she vocalized this fear. "That's normal. And the ones you're *not* worried about are almost certainly worrying that you hate them instead."

It had sounded so blissfully simple, the way she'd said it in that moment, her head bowed over a pair of jeans and a pot of Vanish Oxi Action. But as soon as Gwen was alone again, she'd begun worrying that Connie hated her too.

"Suze? Yes, I was round there for dinner the other weekend," she told her mother. "She's well! Paul did something complicated with an aubergine. They have a new bio-ethanol fireplace."

Her mother asked what a bio-ethanol fireplace was. Gwen was forced to admit she didn't know.

The next time Gwen encountered Connie they were both working the Friday afternoon shift, which tended to have a bacchanalian air. Brian had brought in a bucket of chocolate mini rolls. They sang along tunelessly to Heart FM, and had a long discussion about the various flaws and plot holes in the film *My Best Friend's Wedding*, which Connie had recently watched for the first time and was clearly still processing.

"She's supposed to be twenty bloody seven!" Connie had raged, brandishing a pricing gun. "Twenty-seven!"

And "The main chap has all the charisma of a breeze block!"—yelled from up a stepladder.

And "And we're supposed to believe Carmen Whatsit, Diaz, is going to drop out of college to open his beers?"—while helping a customer wrestle a pair of cargo pants off an armless mannequin.

"I know," Gwen said each time, in a soothing tone. "You're very right." Although they both agreed the musical lunch scene was perfect.

A little later, Connie talked Gwen into buying a pair of shoes. They were white with vertiginous stiletto heels, pointed toes and slim, buckled straps that crisscrossed over her arches. Shoes of a kind Gwen had never worn, not even at Peak Clubbing or, a decade later, Peak Wedding. She was stroking them absentmindedly, more as a piece of art than a wearable prospect, when Connie pounced and forced her to try them on.

"They're ridiculous," she told Connie, as they both looked at her reflection, one hip jutting out in a parody of music video sex appeal.

"They're fabulous," Connie insisted, although Connie wasn't the kind of person who said "fabulous." "Not my taste of course, but *you* look tremendous in them. And look! Look at your face, you clearly love them."

Did she? She really didn't think she did.

"Honestly, Gwen," Connie went on, "buy all the heels! Wear all the heels. Fuck your feet up until they are gnarled little trotters, life is short." She said this with the breezy conviction of a woman in £300 loafers. Connie would never wear shoes like this, Gwen was sure.

"Really, Connie, I do not lead a killer heels life. I barely lead a clogs life."

"Well that's because you don't have the shoes." She was grabbing skirts and dresses from the rails now, holding them up in front of Gwen for consideration. Cheryl Lynn's "Got to Be Real" was playing over the shop speakers and suddenly the effect was so acutely that of a rom-com makeover montage that it felt rude to ruin the moment.

"They're not *me*," she tried again.

"Then don't *be* you! Be someone else for a night. Run riot."

"I can barely hobble riot."

Connie laughed her signature laugh, which was a loud, monosyllabic bark. But she was in full flow now, boxing the shoes up, ringing them through the till and writing them down for her in the volunteers' purchase log.

"You want them, I can see it in your eyes. Now drop the sexless self-denial bit and give yourself permission." It seemed easier to give in before Connie tried to make her recite any affirmations. Obediently, Gwen tapped her card.

The jury was out on the sexless self-denial bit, because she had agreed to see Nicholas tomorrow night. Somehow, after the ick factor of the dinner party had faded, the morbid curiosity remained. "Okay," she'd said quietly, walking up behind him as he shook warm rain from his trench coat at the start of their Tuesday shift. "One drink. But please know if there is a single Ian Fleming reference, I will leave."

Nicholas had laughed, and promised, and spent the rest of the afternoon whistling "Nobody Does It Better" while he baby-wiped a pile of Mills & Boon romances. Gwen had spent the rest of the afternoon pretending he wasn't there.

Only when he'd said "See you Saturday, Gwen," in front of Lise at the end of the day, and Lise had dropped her usual cool demeanor to yelp "I am sorry, *what*?," and Gwen had stammered something unconvincing about him sounding her out for work consultation on his retro-tat business, and Lise had told Brian, who had told Brenda, who had told Connie, who had greeted her arrival for the Wednesday afternoon shift with a cheerful "Here she is, Mrs. Robinson!," had she admitted that the drink was a thing that was happening. She admitted it more fully the next evening as she gave herself an at-home bikini wax.

It itched, now, the whole region did, and she performed a series of discreet lunges behind the counter to try to deal with the problem. It didn't work. By closing time she felt like one giant, walking crotch.

"Go, have fun! Make his year! Tell me all the sordid details please," Connie said, winking, giving her a little push out of the door. "Wear the shoes."

# Handbag

---

It was the first thing Asha bought when her first month's salary came through. Before lunch, even, or a new pair of tights to replace the ones that had laddered halfway up her thigh on the escalator at Turnpike Lane that morning. A bag. The right kind of bag.

She didn't love it, but that didn't seem relevant. Asha wasn't sure what it meant to love a bag, or how she would know if it happened to her. She loved people, music, intense conversations, and mediocre Thai food. Loved finding the perfect question to pry a case, or a person, wide open. The other junior associates knew how to love bags. They knew how to identify each model (make? Flavor?) by its proper name or number, and appreciate the tiny design evolutions that could add three hundred pounds to a price tag. They knew how to talk about gold "hardware" and pocket capacity and exclusivity—mainly the last thing—while stroking each other's buttery-soft full-grain leather, cooing over new acquisitions as though they were lapdogs with straps.

Some of them had been toting expensive bags since they were undergrads, or school kids. She could tell. It came easily to them. They carried them casually, tossing them onto sticky pub floors and swinging them from the crooks of their elbows as though they weighed nothing at all.

Some hadn't, and she could tell that too. They carried theirs a little too carefully, held them a little too tightly in the Itsu queue. She could see the glimmer of awe and defiance in their eyes, reflecting the gold embossed label that proved it definitely wasn't a knockoff from the market. Asha held her bag like it was someone else's newborn baby, or a bomb that could go off at any second (though honestly, weren't they the same thing?). She couldn't not hear her mother's voice, squawking that there were thieves everywhere, that pride was sinful, and the world was queueing up to knock her off her perch.

Truth was, she barely even liked the bag she chose. But that seemed the best strategy—playing against all her natural inclinations, going too far the other way. She hoped she could use the bag as a corrective device, against which she would grow in the right direction. It might help counteract her accent, her shoes, the nails that clicked against her keyboard as she typed and which somehow sounded different in their timbre and pitch to everyone else's nails clicking against *their* keyboards as *they* typed.

She had swelled with pride as she left the shop with her bag (inside another bag, inside a box, inside yet another bag because that was how this lunacy worked). Pride, not so much for having earned it herself, but more for having successfully overridden her own instincts. And while buying an overpriced bag she barely liked might be small fry compared to the other modifications on her Be Less Asha checklist—talk less, talk more quietly, ask fewer questions, learn to ski—it felt like as good a place as any to start.

Within a couple of weeks she had filled the bag as she had filled every bag before it: with tissues; lip gloss and loose, fuzzy lozenges; wadded-up receipts with gum spat into them; wrapperless tampons roaming free like escaped mice; and a quantity of that mysterious gritty sand that will line every handbag until the end of time. Her plastic lunch box had leaked oil into one corner of the monogrammed lining. She would scrub furiously at this stain several years later, knowing it meant that there was no point trying a fancy resale site, that it was consigned to the charity bin liner instead. She would see the handbag as a symbol of everything she'd tried so hard to carry, and everything she'd let fall. For now, she shrugged.

The bag was soon scuffed around its edges in a way that she'd hoped, as she hurled it cheerfully into the backs of taxis and onto the toilet floor when she had her customary 4 p.m. cry, might give her a little of the same easy nonchalance as the others.

But it didn't. And it wouldn't. It wasn't the right kind of scuffed, somehow.

Maybe it wasn't the right kind of bag.

## 20

Gwen wore the shoes.

She felt absurd, teetering on their spikes along Seven Sisters Road, feeling every bump and swell in the pavement through the tender balls of her feet. It had been a while. She'd almost forgotten about heels. Forgotten the way they made you feel fragile, but somehow brave in your fragility. The same way red lipstick made you self-conscious about your mouth, and that was supposedly its power.

She'd forgotten the way each street and staircase you click-clacked down without falling over felt like a victory, and so maybe that was the secret: to spend a day in heels was to cheat death over and over again. Who wouldn't feel strong after that?

In the Tube station, a busker was playing a maudlin acoustic version of "Clint Eastwood" by Gorillaz and Gwen pictured herself falling down the Tube escalator. She did this a lot, even when she was wearing trainers. She pictured the way she would fall, imagining each thud and crunch as her limbs hit the stairs. The way her body would fold and flail like a defective Slinky. She would replay it over and over in her mind, zooming in on different details—the wobbly ankle that started it, the faces of people around her changing in slow motion as she made her descent—and imagining all the variables of pain and injury, from small grazes and bruises to instant death. The more she imagined it, somehow, the safer she felt.

This wasn't the same as imagining leaping in front of a train as it pulled into the platform, or hurling somebody else's baby across the room like a rugby ball, or the urge to kiss the back of a stranger's neck, tenderly, while she stood behind them on the Tube. The more she thought about those things, the more she worried she *would* do them. But because the falling would be involuntary, the act of a sadistic god, it felt like the best way to protect herself against it happening was to mentally practice, again and again, until she almost started to wish it would happen, just to get it over with. And then it wouldn't. This all made sense in her head.

The bar turned out to be one of Nicholas's clients, which meant she had to endure the painful ordeal of watching him greet the barman like an old friend, then asking after "Tom" once it was clear the barman didn't remember him, then discovering the barman *was* Tom, then carefully explaining who he was by saying "I sourced your musket" several times.

"The muscat?" asked Tom, helpfully.

No, insisted Nicholas, and pointed to the wall above the pool table, where a long replica gun was mounted alongside framed sepia photos of Wild West pioneers. "The musket."

Once that was settled, he steered her toward a cozy corner booth—the hand on her lower back was welcome for once, as ballast—and the two of them sat in silence for a moment, sipping their martinis and making "ah" noises. She was determined not to crack first.

"So Gwen, how's the career break going?" he asked, finally.

"Still broken!" she joked.

"But are you feeling, like, creatively refueled?"

She studied his face for signs that he was joking, and found none.

"Not entirely, ah, *refueled* yet, no . . . but certainly in the process of . . . um . . ." She stalled. "It's nice to have more, y'know, headspace? I've got a much better idea of what I don't want to do, at least."

"Which is?" Nicholas asked.

"So far, everything."

He shook his head and wagged his finger. "That's a defeatist attitude, Gwen. I thought you were more driven than that."

"Nope, sorry. Really not."

"Your friend Susan said that at school you were voted Girl Most Likely to Be Prime Minister."

"That's because I used to take a newspaper with me to house parties."

Nicholas didn't seem to know what to say to this, so he launched into a long story about a debate tournament in which he'd once beaten Richard Branson's nephew. Gwen fished the olives out of her drink and ate them, suddenly starving. She willed the numbing warmth of the vodka down toward her throbbing toes.

She was almost glad he'd used the martini gimmick, because it made the whole thing feel more like elaborate roleplay than actual dating. So long as he kept up his schtick with the galleries and cocktails and trench coats and antique armory, Gwen could pretend she wasn't going out with him so much as taking part in a murder mystery weekend, or an amateur dramatic Noël Coward. And for as long as she was unemployed, this odd diversion seemed to fit the bill.

For as long as she was fraternizing with Nicholas and failing to get herself hired as Special Client Envoy for a dynamic design agency who did the blackboards outside coffee shops ("curbside straight-to-consumer marketing, must have GSOH and proven chalk skills"), she could write this whole time off as an aberration. Post-redundancy decision-making disorder. It could also explain why she'd started watching old reruns of *Watercolour Challenge* on YouTube at 3 a.m. And when she had mortifying sex with him later, which she was already fairly sure she was going to do, it would explain that too.

Nicholas finished his story. But just as he shuffled closer to her on the banquette in what had all the overtures of A Move, a voice cut through the buzz.

"Oh hey! Gwen!"

It was one of the Gemmas from her office. A lesser-known Gemma—possibly a Jemma, or even a Jenna?—dangling off the arm of a man who was wearing two shirts, one on top of the other.

"Hi! Hey! How are you?" Gwen attempted to match her enthusiasm without necessitating introductions.

"How are *you*? Funny, I was saying to Claire H. the other day, we needed to catch up with you and find out how things were going." G/Jemma tilted her head sympathetically to one side. "Honestly it was so unfair what happened to you, we were all *fuming* after you left. After all those years you'd been there and everything. A few people even thought about seriously kicking off to the directors."

"Did they?" Gwen replied. "That's . . . sweet."

J/Gemma nodded emphatically. "They really did."

"I'm fine though, honestly!" Gwen hurried on, lifting her martini in a Gatsbyish pose while praying Nicholas would keep quiet. "I'm actually doing a bit of, ah, volunteering. Taking some time off while I figure out what I want to do next."

Somehow it sounded less convincing than when she'd said it to Nicholas. It sounded like a disgraced politician doing photo ops at a soup kitchen.

"Wow, good for you!" replied Jemma, because that's what people have to say. "So selfless! Is it, like, a mentoring thing?"

"No, it's . . . it's a cha—" Her lips were forming the word when Nicholas jumped in.

"It's more a kind of retail consultancy, isn't it. Gwen?" he said. "Social enterprise combined with strategic post-consumer waste management solutions. Fuelling the circular economy while parlaying the profits into a range of vital community causes. As a small business owner myself I've really found her support invaluable."

Jenna blinked. "Amazing! Wow. So cool. I really must give

something back, I'm always saying that, aren't I, Felix?" Felix dutifully nodded. "I love the sound of the one where you take old people out to tea."

She turned back to Gwen. "Really glad you're okay though, Gwen. Honestly it's their loss. And you didn't hear this from me, but . . ." She leaned in, after casting a quick glance over each shoulder. "We lost the New Roots account after you let slip about the rates. They went to find an agency that wasn't stiffing them. Chris was raging. It was fucking brilliant. So there's another legacy for you."

Then after the requisite chorus of *byebyebyeeee*s and hollow pledges to go for coffee soon, Maybe-Gemma turned and weaved her way out through the crowd with Felix Two-Shirts in tow. Gwen slowly drained the rest of her drink, watching them through the glass. When she finished, she put it down and found Nicholas staring at her.

"So what—" he began.

"Can we not talk about it, please?"

"Obviously, yeah, of course," he replied, then proceeded to talk about it. "But did y—"

"Really, I'd rather not."

"But I just w—"

"*Seriously.*"

"Okay, fine, whatever," he said, affecting a sulky pout. "But you're going to have to suggest something else for us to do instead, Gwen. I think you owe me for that lie, which was pretty fucking good, if I do say so myself. Did I tell you I used to do improv?"

Gwen looked at him. His hair was rumpled, his cheeks flushed. He was smirking at her teasingly, but also hopefully, and she had the sensation of being an old cad come to corrupt the petal-lipped ingénue. She couldn't bring herself to deliver the obvious dialogue—"I have a few ideas . . ." or something to that effect—but she leaned in and kissed him anyway, cutting him off right in the middle of a sentence about the St. Andrews university sketch group.

There was an inevitability to the situation that was oddly comforting. Because she'd tortured herself by imagining how it might happen, so many times now that she'd almost started to wish that it would.

# Dress

The dress was too tight across her chest. Not so tight that she couldn't get the zip done up, just tight enough that Bronagh was compelled to take her bra off and manipulate her breasts into place, one then the other. Were they better in the middle, nipples tweaked to point purposefully forward rather than down? Or—she inched a hand beneath the neckline, rummaged around again—tucked away to the sides so they sat almost beneath her armpits? Mix and match? No.

She took a deep, experimental breath, felt the stitches tauten and dig into her flesh as her ribs expanded against their fabric casing. Was she light-headed, or was that psychosomatic? Would she be forced to escape to the toilet every thirty minutes, to sit and unzip and inhale?

Not for the first time, Bronagh entertained a fantasy about cutting into her skin and scooping out a few extraneous fat cells. Not as an act of self-loathing, because she loved her breasts perfectly well most of the time; loved to see them bouncing and assertive in a bikini top or emerging from the bathwater in glossy white mounds like two triumphant, family-sized panna cotte. She'd come a long way since her teens, when she would fill the great, hungry chasms of her waking hours googling "are there calories in phlegm" and wondering which food group silica gel fell into.

No, she'd like to cut it out as a mere practicality. A simple workaround. Not many things left in the world could make her hate her body, but clothes were one of them.

She had bought the dress in a panic, which was how she bought most of her clothes. Notions of shopping as "retail therapy" had always baffled her, because to Bronagh it felt more like administering an emergency drug.

She shopped on her lunch hour, when whatever she'd left the house wearing that morning felt wrong—socially wrong, aesthetically wrong, morally wrong, but also physically wrong, digging and slipping and riding up as though the clothes were trying to crawl off her body and escape. She shopped after work too, grabbing things she was too exhausted to try on and knew she'd be too lazy to return. She shopped at night, bathed in the blue light of her phone screen as her boyfriend slept beside her. She shopped alone, always, and couldn't remember the last time it had been fun.

This dress was a midi in a vivid floral print that had looked playful and stylish on the mannequin but somehow both clownish and dowdy on her, like a toddler dressed as a pensioner for a play. She'd bought it anyway. It had joined the legion of dresses in her wardrobe that were worn resentfully, and which only looked good in the mornings.

This morning, "good" was too high a bar but she was willing to settle for fine. "You look fine" was how her sister answered the phone when Bronagh called to say she wasn't going to the party. Actually she said, "You look fiiiiiiiiiiiinnne," stretching the vowel out until the word collapsed into an exasperated grunt. Not "fine" as in beautiful. Fine as in adequate. Fine as in, nobody is looking at you anyway.

"I can't fully breathe," she had said.

"How fully is not fully?" Siobhan had replied.

"Maybe fifty percent lung capacity?"

"Any pain under your ribs?"

"Not yet."

"Good girl. Pop a Brufen."

Bronagh clenched a fistful of fabric. "Shiv, I'm not coming."

"You are though."

"I'm not."

"Except you are."

"Nobody will care."

"I care. You're coming for me."

"Do it for me" was the sibling trump card they agreed could be played once a year each, no more. In their teens Siobhan had even kept a tally in the back of an exercise book to ensure neither exceeded their quota.

Back then, their duties mostly involved lying for each other to their parents, accompanying each other on trips to R-rated films and taking it in turns to stand guard as they got off with the same boy round the back of the big Safeway. Being so close in age meant the sisters tended to swap and share everything indiscriminately—clothes, razors, lovers—until either felt the slightest tug of competition from the other, at which point they'd mark out their territory with sudden ferocity and snarls.

Two decades later, their obligations were more complicated. They had involved, over the years, lawyers, landlords, removal vans, hospital waiting rooms, the invention of fake email addresses and the destruction of incriminating property. Sometimes when her phone pinged and it was her sister, resurfacing after months of silence with the words "Do me a favor?," her palms would sweat and she would curse the day her parents came home with the new baby and condemned her to a life of familial servitude. Sometimes, though she'd never admit it, she was thrilled.

Today, Bronagh was defeated. "Fine" was all she said, and hung up the phone.

Then she unzipped the dress to her waist, inhaled greedily, and put an old cardigan on top. She turned back to the mirror. Fine. Fiiiine.

# 21

When it came to sex, Gwen usually struggled to focus on the job in hand.

This had been especially true with Ryan after years of the same set menu, but it had happened with her few casual flings in the years since, too. Her mind wandered. Pragmatically, through pieces of life admin—whether she'd hung that washing out, had she canceled the Sky Cinema trial—but also surreally, to snapshots of places long since forgotten during her upright hours. The kitchen of a childhood friend, the cool atrium of a ceramics shop she'd once visited in Mallorca, the thickly carpeted foyer of her local bank branch. Faces of former teachers and colleagues, long-dead relatives and daytime TV hosts would loom up out of nowhere. She would find herself running through lists of trivia or trying to retrace her footsteps around a local TK Maxx, only stopping when some shift would occur in proceedings that jolted her back into her body.

In this respect it wasn't that the sex she had was bad, only that it functioned less as sex and more as an exercise in meditation: allowing the weird flotsam and jetsam thoughts that were usually held back all day behind makeshift mental barriers to surge forward and flood her brain. She always slept soundly afterward.

But this time was different. For the first few minutes, her embarrassment acted like a shot of adrenaline. Every noise seemed amplified, every awkward maneuver and logistical shuffle and oop-my-hair-is-caught was magnified times ten. She felt electrified by the strangeness of the situation. Lit up by a thousand fluorescent bulbs, naked in the middle of a soundstage. Burning with the fear that after twenty-odd years, you might still be doing sex wrong.

Then she forced herself to look at Nicholas, who was pinker-cheeked than she had ever seen him, grinning like a kid at a funfair, and something brilliant happened.

Something awful happened first—his growling "You love that, don't you," while kneading at her tits like bread dough, which she absolutely didn't love—but suddenly, Gwen didn't care what he thought, and that was energizing in a different way altogether. She didn't care about inhaling as she arched her back to unclasp the bra he was struggling to remove; didn't care about the stretch marks that laced across the tops of her thighs, or the minimal depilatory efforts that drew a firm landing strip, as far as she'd heard, between her generation and his. With a confidence Gwen had never had in bed before—not with Ryan, who tended to take sexual stage directions as a personal insult—she told him what she wanted, and what she didn't, and where and when and how and nope, not that, stop it, stay still, yes, no, yes, yes yes. For once she made no effort to rush things along; didn't feel obliged to start the encouraging fanfare too early, to make things sound more imminent than they really were. The coital equivalent of texting "there in five!" when you're still upside down with a hairdryer. No. Let him wait.

Nicholas didn't seem to have a problem with this. In fact, he seemed to prefer it.

Afterward, Gwen sat on the toilet, praying he would leave of his own accord. Her mouth felt swollen again, and alien. She pulled at her lower lip, maneuvering it until it covered her top lip completely, enjoying the warm, wet flump of it against her skin. Gwen often did things like this in private. It was a kind of sensuality that didn't exist in porn or perfume adverts.

She sat for another minute, or maybe three, not caring if her absence started to look suspect. Two short, dark hairs lay on the side of the bath, she noticed, curled one within the other like quotation marks. She left them there. In the mirror, she wiped away the mascara gunk that had collected under her eyes. Then she took out her lenses, pulled her hair into a topknot and proceeded to remove what was left of her makeup, slowly and methodically, until all she could see in the mirror was a round, pink balloon with ears.

Eventually, Nicholas's voice punctured the silence. Not from the next room but from right up against the other side of the bathroom door. It felt presumptuously intimate, in spite of everything they'd just done.

"Uh, hi, Gwen? I was thinking, I'm going to order a pizza," it said. Then, "What would you like on yours?"

# Clock

By the time Janet was eight years old, she was well known to the counter staff at the pawnshop.

Her father was in the habit of taking the smallest and most adorable of his six children along with him on each visit, as a kind of insurance. Cross words might still be spoken, veiled threats might still be exchanged, but while Janet stood there in her gymslip and best school socks, smiling her gap-toothed smile like her sister Linda before her, and her brother Ralph before her, and Rita and Bernie and Phyllis before him, he knew that no punches would be thrown and the curses would be kept to a minimum. Reggie preferred it that way because he was, as he was fond of telling everyone at the dog track as yet another prayer was lost in the dust, a deeply pious man.

Besides, Reggie McAffery was good for business and it didn't do to let them forget that. Grimes & Son, meanwhile, made money off the downturn of other people's fortunes. Underneath all the niceties and yessirs and shiny cufflinks and biscuits at Christmas they were nothing but a pair of jackals feasting on other people's bad luck, and if Reggie shook their hands and took the biscuits, well that was only because it paid to keep them on side. Also, he loved the pink wafers.

"It's never really their money," he would tell Janet, or Ellen or Bernie, with emphasis. "But it's never really ours, neither."

And so the family lived in a state of eternal seesaw, like so many on their street, using the life raft of their possessions to keep their heads above water on a weekly or monthly basis. During the leanest months, Reggie would pawn his best Sunday suit on a Monday before buying it back with his Saturday pay packet. On the few occasions the money wouldn't stretch to get it back in time, he would wear his overalls and boots to the churchyard and sing along from the end of the path, his gruff, tuneless baritone still managing to drown out most of the indoor congregation.

But the clock was the real barometer for the family's fortunes. Janet had still been a baby when Reggie had been given it as part payment for a plastering job at the smarter end of the Roman Road, where a young French couple had vacated the property in a hurry and the landlord didn't want to cough up the full amount for their extensive—and somewhat mysterious—damage. It was a hulking great thing in gilded wood; a brass-ringed face buried in an ornate sunburst design, layers of rays in deep relief, intricately carved to look like so many golden feathers. The back was stamped with the name: *Japy Frères*. Improbably, given the scene of wanton destruction around it, the clock kept perfect time.

"I took a shine to it," he'd told his wife when he brought it home that night. "Jappy Freers knows his stuff." She'd wrinkled her nose at its gaudiness and old-fashioned heft, at a time when everyone wanted Bakelite. And when Reg's cousin, who sold antiques on Camden Passage, had told him it dated back to the late Belle Époque and might be worth a serious bob or two, she had tried to insist he sell it outright. But Reggie dug his heels in. He was an aesthete when he could afford to be, and he wanted the sunburst on his wall where all the neighbors could see it glinting through the net curtains. He was, as he was fond of telling the curate when he called with his cautionary pamphlets, a deeply modern man.

"It'll brighten our gray days, Vi," he'd said, whistling a few bars of "You Are My Sunshine" and dancing her around the kitchen. She called him a big daft beggar, but she let the clock stay.

Of course, it ended up at Grimes & Son. In fact, the sunburst went in and out with such regularity over the years that it started to mimic the East End sky. "When times are good, the clock hangs on the wall," Reg liked to say. "When times are bad, we don't need a clock to tell us."

He was proud of this poetic bent. He fancied himself a latter-day Alfred P. Doolittle without the loose morals.

Then one day Reggie's wrist turned on a tricky ceiling job, and his little bit of luck went with it. Away went the sun for a longer stretch, and then a longer one still, and by the time Janet was eight and her eldest siblings were out at work themselves, money was so tight she could feel it—in the shoes that pinched, the skirt that cut into her waist, and the gristle that caught in her throat. It was the mid-sixties and elsewhere the city was starting to swing, but within their four walls life had almost ground to a halt.

Until she found the cash. A slim bundle of notes tied up with a piece of butcher's string, hidden inside an old Huntley & Palmer's tin right at the back of the wardrobe. Janet liked to climb in there periodically, to escape her siblings, crunch cola cubes and contemplate life. Her friend Nancy sometimes lent her a *Bunty* comic when she was finished with it. Last week, one of the stories had featured a gang of gung-ho schoolgirls coming across a hidden stash of money in a smuggler's cave during a pony trek (or was it in a circus wagon during a thunderstorm?), so when she opened the tin and saw it there, she simply thought: *treasure, of course.*

Wary of getting herself caught up in criminal activity that might not end as well for Janet as it did for the girls in straw boaters, she had felt it sensible to dispense of the loot quickly and in the most noble way she could think of. So she'd taken the money in secret, gone along to the pawnshop, flashed that gummy grin and asked very nicely if she could buy the clock back, please. It was her dad's favorite and it would make him so happy to have it on the wall for his birthday.

To his credit, Reggie only screamed and raged and kicked the bins along the alleyway later, after Janet had gone to bed. In front of his youngest daughter he simply clasped his hands together and said, "Well now. How about that. What a lovely thing you've done, old girl."

The clock never left the wall again after that. He was, as he was fond of telling them down the Dover Castle at chucking out time, a deeply sentimental man.

## 22

Nicholas was staring into her fridge, of all places.

"Why do you have so many types of vinegar?"

Gwen often stared into her fridge herself, imagining how it would look were she to be interviewed for a tabloid newspaper's "What's in your fridge?" feature.

What would a celebrity nutritionist make of the two whole shelves of pickles and gherkins and Christmas present jams and chutneys and chili oils and continental mustards with precisely one spoonful missing from each? The old yogurt pot suspended in ice like a dead explorer, or the clouded Tupperware of mystery leftovers so forbidding that she now thought of it only as "The Box"? What story could be gleaned from the graveyard of half-eaten apples, packets of parched coriander, stumps of carrot shriveled like witch's fingers, and fossilized quarters of lemon?

Optimism, she liked to think. Only an optimist buys a whole pot of buttermilk when the recipe calls for two tablespoons. An optimist believes they will genuinely use the rest.

Of course, the imaginary readers wouldn't know that the fridge also had an indeterminate smell, the source of which Gwen never managed to find. Every so often she'd turf out a mold-capped jar of pesto or a slimy spring onion and think she'd beheaded the beast, but the smell would return. They wouldn't know that when hungover or sad, she liked to crush up a family-sized bag of Doritos and eat them with a spoon, like cornflakes.

Every couple of months Gwen would take herself to the organic minimarket in the next postcode over and spend a pleasant hour breathing in the scent of burlap and botanical hand cream, squeezing bags of ancient grains, and looking at exotic fruits as though they were gallery installations. She never picked up a basket—a basket was too big a statement of intent—and so instead would gather a pile of things in her arms as she walked around, holding them in place with her chin.

At the counter, she would dump them all down and try to look like a person who knew *exactly* what she was going to do with a bag of blue maize flour, pickled plums, and a spirulina Bounce ball. While the cashier rang up her purchases she would do a frantic appraisal of the chocolate bars, the way she did in every shop, scanning the rows with urgency, as though it might be her last ever chance to buy chocolate. Occasionally she would grab one in the final seconds before the cashier announced the total, and then she would regret it when the chocolate cost £4.79 and tasted of soap. More often she wouldn't, and she'd regret that too.

Gwen would take her spoils home and line them up on the kitchen counter, hoping Nigel Slater might manifest and offer instructions in a soothing voice. She would nibble a cautious corner of something, open a packet of something else, dunk a Hobnob into a jar of apple butter and discover sadly that it wasn't butter at all, but a kind of sweet, viscous tar. Then she would bundle everything into the back of the cupboards and take the pasta saucepan out again.

All of which explained, but only just, how Nicholas came to be standing in her kitchen, asking why she had so many types of vinegar.

"Obviously don't get me wrong, love a bit of bal-sal," he was saying. "But *Gwen*, I didn't have you down as such a gourmand."

"I'm not," she told him. "I use it for . . . limescale."

They had finished their pizzas twenty minutes ago—eaten not in bed, but stood awkwardly at the kitchen counter like a pair of Italian businessmen—and though he was showing no sign of trying to settle in for a sleepover, he wasn't showing any sign of leaving either.

Having finally finished the fridge inspection, he was now walking around her flat, identifying items out loud to nobody in particular—"Curtains . . . nice . . . oh, a spider plant . . . HG Mould Remover Spray . . . cool . . ."—while Gwen yawned and tugged at the hem of her pajama shorts and agreed that yes, he was correct, that was a heated drying rack.

There should be music playing, she realized. It was strange, wasn't it, that neither of them had put music on? Didn't that say something, about something? She could put some music on now, but it was too late for that and might look like she was vying for an encore.

Then, just as he began a second lap of the room ("cushions"), she remembered Connie.

"Right, it's past my bedtime!" Gwen announced, slapping two assertive hands on her thighs. "Let's get you a taxi."

Mercifully, it worked.

The next day, Gwen re-donated the shoes.

She wiped them down carefully, checking the leather for nicks and marks—a sum total of two hours and one taxi had hardly been enough to trash them—then wrapped them back up in their dust bag and dropped them in the donation bin at the start of her shift.

Connie would be furious with her, but Connie wasn't there this afternoon. St. Michael was, however, and he raised an eyebrow at the shoes in recognition.

"You know, we're not a lending library," he called after her, in what sounded like genuine annoyance. "Does nobody *commit to anything anymore?*"

Gwen stammered an apology, while Finn helpfully pointed out that the shop would now profit from them twice. "Like, everyone rents clothes now? We should totally be cashing in on that market."

"Hmmph" was Michael's only reply. He marked up the price on the shoes by a fiver, and put them back out on display.

# Disposable Camera

"Thumb!" her family yelled at her, their faces frozen in a kind of happy claymation grimace.

"What?" Stephanie yelled back, over the din of Europop being pumped out of a nearby amusement arcade.

"Thumb!!!" they yelled again, and this time she understood. She had learned the hard way, the last time they had had photos developed. Twenty-eight shots of a blurry pink eclipse, two of the inside of Lee's mouth displaying a quantity of chewed digestive biscuit, and one of the car park at Happy Shopper, to use up the rest of the film.

Still, she was determined to be the documentarian on this holiday. Gatekeeper of memories. That would be her role, as she saw it, and the camera was integral. Each time Stephanie wound the film on, she felt a small rush of achievement. The little serrated wheel would hurt her thumb, but even that felt cool, like the way her music teacher had calluses on his thumbs from playing guitar.

Behind the camera, she was not only useful but protected. It didn't matter if the other kids at the holiday park didn't ask her to join in the games when they asked Lee and Kelly, didn't matter if her stepmother made comments when she reached for a second choc ice, or if she tried to get her to go for a "fun run along the beach, just you and me." It didn't matter if her dad disappeared for hours every evening and crept back into the chalet when he thought she was asleep, stumbling into the furniture as he tried to take his trainers off. It didn't matter because she wasn't an active participant, merely an impartial observer. She was wallpaper. Nobody could be angry at wallpaper.

And who cared if the rich kids at school were starting to acquire digital cameras, which let you see, actually *see* the photo on the back of the camera after you'd taken it? Stephanie liked the feverish wait for the slim paper envelope at the chemist. She loved the suspense and delight of it all, reliving the memories weeks later, usually in the rain. If her stepmother was in a good mood she might take her to Spud-u-Like afterward and pick at a portion of coleslaw while Stephanie talked her through each photo with detailed commentary. If she was in a bad mood there would be no potatoes and Celine Dion in the car the whole way home. But even then, it didn't matter because Stephanie had the photos.

In the past she had taken them into school with her, although generally nobody was interested if the photos didn't feature themselves, or the pouty senior school rugby captain they referred to as "Phil Lips." Perhaps this time they would care, though. Perhaps when she showed them the scene she had captured last night round the back of the Swim-o-dome, they would sit up and pay attention.

She remembered it with a shiver, the curious sicky-excited feeling in her stomach again, and wondered for the hundredth time how it would translate on gloss paper in the cold light of day. Where she'd hide it in her bedroom. How much she'd charge Lee and Kelly for a look.

Stephanie carefully removed her thumb from the lens, checked her viewfinder—their smiles were sagging fast now—and pressed the button. *Click*.

# 23

Up the road there was another charity shop. But you might not immediately know that, since it called itself a "Kindfulness Hub" and was styled after the sort of minimalist boutique Gwen was generally too afraid to go into in case she sneezed on something and had to buy it.

The floors were polished concrete, the walls daubed with work by a local community art collective, and they hung their stock from the ceiling on a complicated wire pulley system that meant the staff were forced to stage a kind of low-budget Cirque du Soleil performance every time someone wanted to try on a jumper.

St. Michael had been on a fishing mission ever since the other shop had opened, sending volunteers along to spy and report back. How many customers were browsing? How were they pricing their men's jeans? Was it true they were using part of the store to host a stick-and-poke tattoo pop-up? He discovered titbits of intelligence on the charity retail grapevine and would often arrive smirking, lips pursed around the gossip as though it were a delicious plum he was struggling to keep in his mouth.

"Bruce at Ethelred's Hospice says they only took £200 last Saturday, and half of that was for a sculpture someone knocked over with their tote bag."

"Christoph at Help Hamsters International saw an Atmosphere tea dress priced at £30 and labeled 'vintage.'"

"Melly from Pain UK heard that they're not allowed to call them receipts, they have to call them 'commitment slips.'"

These were the days Michael was in his best moods.

Volunteers were advised that if anybody suspiciously hip or assertive came into the shop, they should be watched closely for signs that they might be Kindfulness Hub staff, sent to buy all their best stock and hoist it up in the window to taunt them. What they were supposed to do about this if it happened, or why it was technically a problem so long as they paid for it, was unclear. But it gave them all a joint object of resentment. Nothing bonds people so swiftly or tenderly as finding something to hate.

Gwen was disappointed, after seven years of hating various rivals in the strategic content solutions sphere—agencies that always had names like a Leicester Square nightclub run by five-year-olds, names like "Strawberry Zoo" or "Rainbow Soup" or "Fun Fun Incorporated"—to find that the same dynamic existed here too, in the land of philanthropy and cardigans. Or at least, she had been at first. Then she got into it.

"Misplaced apostrophes in the Hub window today, Michael!" she called into the office as she arrived for the Monday afternoon shift, the way she had practiced it on her walk up the road. "Record's and book's. Laminated and everything."

"How mortifying for them," came his delighted reply. Gwen glowed a little.

But as she whipped out the photo she'd taken on her phone for his enjoyment, Asha appeared from the back room instead. She looked tired, her eyes bloodshot and missing their usual precision eyeliner, her hair shoved under a baseball cap. It had been nearly three weeks since Gwen had last seen her, she calculated now. She felt bad for not having noticed sooner.

"Been away?" Gwen asked.

"Ill," said Asha.

"Ah, shit," she replied. "What with?"

"Oh, you know. An attack of the vapors. My energies were

misaligned." Asha smiled wanly. "Nah, I just . . . couldn't get out of bed for a while, you know?"

Gwen did know.

"Well it's good to have you back! We've missed you." Was this too much? Possibly, but Asha seemed grateful to hear it.

"Oh, same," she replied. "Just thinking about changing that window display was all that kept me going, some days. I lay there in the dark, doing my four-square breathing and dreaming of color-coding the men's cargo shorts."

"Can't squander that gift," said Gwen. Asha grinned.

Still, she was subdued and distracted throughout the afternoon. When a customer called across the floor to ask what size a jacket was—they did this often, as though volunteers might have the ever-shifting inventory of the shop committed to memory—Asha looked almost tearful and apologized for not knowing, rather than her standard response: "Your guess is as good as mine, babe!" When St. Michael gave her a huge box of scarves to price, she spent an hour working her way through them all before realizing she'd written the wrong week number on every single label.

But instead of a caustic remark, Michael hummed a few bars of Cher's "If I Could Turn Back Time" and patted Asha gently on the arm.

"If we go back a week then it means I wouldn't have eaten that dubious prawn last Tuesday," he told her. "Good idea."

"Dubious Prawn sounds like something that would be on the Spotify at the Kindfulness Hub," Gwen ventured. No one said anything.

# Shirt

Deep down, Denise had been prepared for this. He was a charming guy, always had been—a ladies' man, her mother would have called him, although Denise never thought of his vast galaxy of female friends and associates as "ladies" but another, shorter, word. He was quick with a compliment, smooth as anything when it came to opening doors, pulling out chairs, remembering a favorite drink order, and recognizing a signature scent. Combined, all this overrode his average looks to make him an unlikely, but highly effective, player. She'd known that when she moved in with him.

So yes, she was prepared for the clichéd moment—the lipstick on the collar, the faint whiff of sweet, celeb-endorsed perfume, a receipt in a pocket for the same bistro she'd been hoping he'd book for her birthday.

What she hadn't expected, though, was to be betrayed by a shirt itself. A shirt she found stuffed beneath the bed, in a holdall she didn't recognize. This shirt was a curveball.

It was—well, how to describe it? Blousy. Blousy, but not *a blouse*. It had billowing sleeves and a leather thong tie that crisscrossed over a plunging V-neck. Medieval. Or was it Middle Ages? What was the difference? What did it bloody matter, when suddenly all those Thursday night "working dinners" and weekend "golfing trips" to Wiltshire were looming into view? All the clues she'd turned a blind eye to—the ponytail, the sudden taste for mead, the peculiar leather vest he'd said was for sciatica.

"So are you saying he's a cross-dresser?" asked her friend Mandie, who wasn't well versed in modern lexicon.

"God no, I *wish*. You know how much I love Grayson Perry." Denise steeled herself.

"Mand, I think he's . . . a cosplayer."

24

When she told Connie about Nicholas, Connie looked both appalled and delighted.

"I didn't think you'd actually go through with it, you maniac! Spare me the details, puhhlease."

Gwen promised no details were forthcoming, but Connie carried on shrieking.

"Oh Gwen, honestly." As though she were a puppy who'd soiled the doormat. "What are we going to do with you?"

It would be ridiculous to say she'd slept with Nicholas only because Connie had egged her on—was she not, after all, an autonomous adult woman?—and yet Gwen couldn't stop thinking about the time Eliza May Fletcher from the year above had dared her to suck on a scented gel pen cartridge during a Princess Diana memorial assembly. "Go on," she'd said, "it'd be really funny." Then, when Gwen had violent green ink coating her teeth and tongue and bubbling from the sides of her lips like a B-movie swamp creature, Eliza May Fletcher hadn't laughed, had instead looked at her with a mix of revulsion, pity, and something else—wonder. Wonder at her own power, and the tragic weakness of others.

"I can't believe you actually did it," she had said, while Gwen gagged on the chemical fetor of nearly-not-quite apple. "That's so gross."

Then she had added, almost kindly: "You know, you shouldn't do things just because other people tell you to."

"We need to do something about your self-worth," Connie was saying.

They were back in her kitchen again, a spontaneous late lunch after a dull Wednesday morning shift. ("I get too hungry for lunch at two," Gwen had protested on her third biscuit run. "That's why the lady is a tramp," Connie had replied).

It was hot out, which Connie—who never seemed to sweat— had exacerbated by putting the oven on for an hour and a half. Now her French windows were open onto a long, tastefully overgrown garden, a warm breeze licking Gwen's damp forehead as Jackson Browne played from a CD stereo. The remains of a harissa-coated chicken lay splayed between them like a patient on an operating table. Connie burped, softly, and went on.

"Where are all the friends your own age who should be telling you not to sleep with terrible men, and then telling you off when you do?" she asked. Gwen blushed, feeling exposed.

"They're . . . well, you know what it's like," she replied. "I definitely had some, once! Good ones. Or—fine ones. But some moved away for work and some moved away to have babies, and some stayed here and had babies . . . and what with all the work and the babies and the moving, over time I suppose we just . . . drifted."

What felt like a deeply personal issue, one that had brewed and festered for years, sounded like a stale cliché as soon as it hit the air. She felt like she was reading aloud from a magazine problem page.

"It's probably my fault," she added. "I let them drift."

"But you still have the friend who has the dinner parties, yes?" said Connie. "Or has she spawned and sold up in the past fortnight?"

Gwen sensed that Suze and Connie would adore each other. She could never let them meet.

"Suze. Yes. I have Suze. Geographically, if not always emotionally."

"So that's your problem then, geography?"

Gwen shrugged.

Her thoughts returned to Eliza May Fletcher (she had insisted on three names at all times, an affectation that had survived even after one of the other girls found out her middle name wasn't May at all, it was Margaret). She now lived in Ibiza and ran some sort of fitness empire that operated out of a nightclub. When she'd launched her company Facebook page, she had invited Gwen to like it. Gwen had accepted.

"Neighbors?" asked Connie, now in troubleshooting mode. "You said you've lived in your place for a few years, surely there are other people around you could be chums with?"

A small part of Gwen withered at "chums."

"Probably," she replied. "I have wondered about, well . . . looking into it at least. There must be a forum or something I could join. A few—I don't know—committees."

Connie hooted. "That's your plan, join a friendship committee? For god's sake, Gwen, you sound like *my* friends. Rotary clubs and parish councils and NIMBY Anonymous meetings for the over sixty and terminally constipated."

"Well, it's London," Gwen protested. "You can't just walk up to people at the bin shed and say, 'Be my friend?'"

"Why the hell not? It worked well enough for us in primary school, I've always thought it rather a shame that grown-ups get out of the habit. I used to tell my daughter—"

Gwen jolted at this. Connie had never mentioned a daughter. No story of the feckless ex-husband, and there were plenty of those, had ever featured children in the mix. Even her house bore no evidence, or not in the rooms Gwen had seen: no clumsy infant handicrafts, no Mother's Day cards or graduation photos. No family photos at all, she now realized—only a few glamorous snapshots of Connie in the seventies looking like a young Carrie

Fisher, standing on the beach in a high-legged swimsuit, smoking at a restaurant table, laughing astride a bike, the wind whipping her hair toward the camera.

"I didn't know you had a daughter," she said.

"Well, you didn't ask," said Connie. Then before Gwen could say anything else, she went on. "We're not close. She's"—Connie flapped a dismissive hand—"difficult. Anyway, when she was a child, I used to send her off to the park with a *himitsu-bako*"—she pronounced it with a generically "cultured" accent—"which is a Japanese puzzle box, and I would tell her to dare the other kids to try to solve it. Whoever figured it out would win the Malteser I'd hidden in the middle—and ta-da! Instant friend."

Gwen spared a thought for Connie's daughter, wherever she was.

"When she was older, I did the same thing with alcopops," Connie went on, airily. "Although she was such a little square that often she came back from parties with them still sloshing about in her backpack."

Gwen had so many questions, but found herself reluctant to ask them. Instead, she said: "I'm pretty sure if I approached my neighbors with a Japanese puzzle box, they'd double-lock the door and post their security footage on Facebook."

"It was only an example, Gwen! God! *My point is*, life is too short to wait for people to turn up on your doorstep. Sometimes you have to turn up on theirs. Speaking of which," Connie went on, "I need a walk after all that food, I can feel gout setting in. Why don't I walk you home? Wouldn't that be romantic of me!"

Gwen wanted to fight this. She wanted to go home via Superdrug and spend half an hour shuffling up and down the air-conditioned aisles, buying pointless serums in clean, bright bottles that might make her feel cleaner and brighter too. She wanted to sit quietly on a bench with her legs apart, airing the spot where her knicker elastic was turning her skin to steak tartare. On no account could she have Connie making an impromptu visit to her flat, certainly not *inside* the flat, where the bin was overflowing and the lamps were from Dunelm and her towels existed only in two states: crispy or damp.

But Connie was already fetching her handbag, and the trouble with confiding in someone about being friendless and aimless is that you can't suddenly pretend you have places to be and people to see. Gwen knew that if she told her the truth, she would end up with Connie in Superdrug, advising her on retinol, and Connie on the park bench, counseling her overheated crotch.

So, they walked.

# Clock

Janet hadn't meant to give it away. She hadn't meant to wrap it carefully in a cardigan and place it at the bottom of a sturdy shopping bag, then fill the rest of the bag with socks and undershirts and the soft old slacks that her soft old husband had left behind when he'd abandoned her for the great beyond. She hadn't meant to carry it around to the charity shop, leave it with the nice tattooed girl in the back room, assuring her it was mostly junk and probably not worth their time, and walk home again, stopping to buy mince and yogurt and bleach and tea bags and a lottery ticket on the way.

She hadn't meant to let a day and a half slip by before she looked up from the television and noticed the bright patch in the middle of the faded wallpaper; felt the bottom drop out of her stomach as she processed the violation. *Burgled! Stop, thieves!* If Henry had been here instead of selfishly dead, he might have . . . well, he'd have been useless. But he'd have screamed with her.

Janet had meant to run to the window to shout for help from the neighbors—not police, never the police—but then, as she fiddled with the knob on the sash window, something in her mind dislodged and half a memory emerged, glinting through a trickle of sand.

She could see it now, the clock, being wrapped up and stashed at the back of the old wardrobe so that the heavies at the door would never find it. Her mother bleating at her to be careful, it was valuable, but also to be quick, *quick quick quick*. Her mother would be furious that Janet had let them take it after all. But she hadn't meant to let them. Hadn't she done her best? Hadn't she wrapped it up so carefully, in her best cardigan?

When times were bad, she didn't need a clock to tell her. Soft old Janet.

## 25

Up ahead, a man was passed out on the pavement. His legs were splayed at improbable angles, his face red and waxen from the sun. There was a can of Black Ace next to him, standing perfectly upright like a prop in an advert.

As they approached, a woman appeared from the nearest shop and crouched over him for several seconds. "He's fine! He's breathing," she announced to the world at large, sounding almost disappointed. A few people in the vicinity nodded at her, as though to suggest they'd been on the brink of launching into CPR. Gwen and Connie walked on.

As they rounded the corner into Gwen's street, they saw the family from the ground floor assembled in their garden, a scrubby but neatly kept patch of lawn next to the bin shed. They were having a barbecue. A folding trestle table of food was set up against the wall of the building, next to a small inflatable paddling pool filled with ice and drinks. Toots and the Maytals played tinnily from a small Bluetooth speaker. It was the kind of scene Gwen had always romanticized, one of the things on her mental list of Reasons to Love London, along with coffee shops on canal boats and children's birthday parties held under trees. The list was, admittedly, becoming more academic and less applied with each passing year.

"A party, excellent! Who are they?" Connie asked, and for

a second Gwen wondered if Connie had somehow set this up herself.

"I'm not actually sure," admitted Gwen. She felt like a politician who doesn't know the price of milk. "I've never quite managed to get chatting. I mean, always wanted to! But you know . . . after the first year it started to seem awkward."

"Everybody needs good neighbors," Connie said. "I'm sure I've heard that somewhere." And before Gwen could stop her, she had walked over and started talking to them.

She was pointing at her now, and vigorously beckoning her over. "That's Gwen." By the time Gwen reached them, Connie was brandishing a chicken drumstick. "Gwen has lived in this building for five years!" It was almost four. "And she claims she doesn't know any of her neighbors, and I thought that was *ridiculous*. Don't you think that's ridiculous?"

The adults in the family smiled, albeit warily. The children—about eleven and nine, she'd guess—just stared.

"Hi," she said. "Sorry to interrupt! I'm Gwen, I live on the third floor." She did a little flourishy hand gesture to illustrate the concept of "upstairs." They nodded. "But you already know that," she added, lamely. They nodded again.

Then the man wiped his hand on his shorts and stuck it out in her direction. "Darrell," he said. "Nice to meet you properly, Gwen. This is Jackson, and Summer,"—the kids waved shyly—"and my wife Heather, and her sister Rochelle, and Rochelle's husband Nathan." He'd adopted the cadence of a team captain on *Family Fortunes*. Rochelle, who was reclining on a floral sun lounger, gave her a little salute with a gin tin.

"And I'm Connie," announced Connie. "I don't live here, I'm just a facilitator." The facilitator helped herself to coleslaw.

Darrell and Heather were gracious about having their barbecue gatecrashed, especially after Gwen declined to eat the last remaining burger. They chatted about how long they'd lived in the building, and in the area, and whether they'd tried the new pizza place up the road yet and how brazen the foxes were getting these days, and had they heard the guy who rode his motorbike around the block at 4 a.m. every Tuesday, and did she also think the ceiling fan showroom up the street was a front for a crack den? Benign, neighborly fare.

It might have been nicer were Connie not watching from behind her varifocals, nodding at Gwen like a pushy gymnastics coach and leaping in to make supportive comments. *"It's true!"* *"She does, you know."* When Darrell mentioned a community group chat and asked if Gwen would like to join (she wouldn't, but pretended she would), Connie looked as though she might cheer and applaud. She wondered if Darrell and Heather might think Connie was some kind of support worker. Perhaps it would be better if they did.

The whole endeavor was painful, and yet she couldn't say she wasn't grateful it had happened. As the sky cracked overhead and the first fat pellets of warm summer rain started to fall, Gwen found she was equal parts relieved and disappointed to say goodbye.

"I told you it was easy," said Connie, putting up her umbrella and slipping a wedge of Rochelle's coconut cake into her Longchamp tote. "All you have to do is ask."

Back inside, Gwen lay on the sofa and stared at the wall for a while. She was groggy from the daytime drinking and the social exertion; tired in the kind of way one only ever is after being out in warm weather, energy evaporating along with the sweat and a cool blanket of lethargy settling on her instead like fallen snow.

She knew she ought to use the evening to apply for jobs, and yet currently even taking off her left sandal felt beyond her. So she lay perfectly still, one arm draped across her forehead like a classical statue, breathing in the heady, mineral scent of wet tarmac, burnt charcoal, and stewed garbage that was drifting in through the open window. If she died right here, how long would it take for anyone to find her? Maybe it would be better to go outside and lie down in front of a shop.

When she finally reached for her phone a little while later, her heart leaped pathetically to see a LinkedIn notification. She opened it. Nicholas had endorsed her for "interpersonal skills."

# Jeans

---

They weren't really jeans. Jean-like, from a distance. Jean-adjacent, at a stretch. And stretch was the operative word, because what they lacked in authenticity and Bruce Springsteen associations, they made up for in Lycra. They sagged, apologetically, at the knees.

She had bought them online, or she assumed she must have done. Although when the deliveryman arrived, winking at her as he always did, as though he were a cheerful co-conspirator in her crime, she had only the faintest memory of hitting add-to-basket and wondered if she'd been shopping in her sleep again.

She had sat in the bath to shrink them perfectly to her body, the way her mum used to in the seventies. But indigo dye had leached out of the fabric and left a grubby tide mark around the enamel, and the jeans still sagged. Her mum never told her you weren't supposed to use bubble bath.

## 26

Gwen's days had begun to blur into one, in a way that was not unpleasant.

Volunteering at weekends meant that the conventional rhythm of her week had been upended, those once-echoing Saturday afternoons now carved up neatly between customers and tasks. A ten-minute tea break. A forty-minute conversation with Gloria about the best way to ball socks. An hour of steaming, an hour of tagging, an hour of sorting donations under Michael's critical eye. *Yes sir, yes sir, three bags full, sir.* Home again via Sainsbury's, eleven minutes for al dente pasta, and three, four, five episodes of something before bed.

But on the days she wasn't at the shop—and Head Office policy insisted there be some—time was mercurial. Whole afternoons could pass just trying to get her dodgy hip to click. Hours were shorter than minutes, and it was always too long until lunch.

She would force herself out for long walks like a convalescent, tramping the same familiar route around the same few streets, watching everyone else meeting friends for a dog walk like it was the easiest thing in the world. On those endless in-between days, Gwen worried she was losing the power of speech. She found it easier to swerve around someone on the pavement, stepping right out into the road, than to cough up the words: "excuse me."

When she wanted to feel productive and vital, she took her laptop to coffee shops, read essays on American news sites for as long as she could focus, and occasionally typed the word "jobs" into Google. Inevitably the coffee shops would be filled with parents and babies, great swarms of them multiplying across the morning, their steady stream of nonsense babble and nursery rhymes only serving, somehow, to make her own endeavors seem childish and ridiculous.

Twice now, Suze had messaged—Gwen's heart leaping at the sight of her name on the screen before plummeting again once she saw that it said: How's the job hunt going?x

These felt like emotional tick-boxes of texts. Suze doing her due diligence by checking the only quantifiable fact she could think of. Perhaps in another few years they'd log all vital statistics in a public database to save people the bother of asking. Engaged yet? Pregnant? New house? New job? Divorce? Cancer? Dead?

She had nothing to tell her. Besides a preliminary telephone interview for a role as Shoulder of Content Strategy at a comms consultancy ("We don't believe in heads of department, too hierarchical," the HR Sternum had explained), none of her efforts so far had been fruitful and so the efforts had ground to a halt. Several places had told her she was overqualified. Gwen tried to hold the word "overqualified" in her mind each time she made a mess of wrapping a teapot in newspaper, mangling the sellotape around her fingers while an unimpressed customer looked on.

It wouldn't quite be accurate to say that the shop had become her main source of excitement, given how much of her time there was spent rifling through a box of small plastic cubes marked *S*, *M*, *L*, and *XL*—but there were moments of levity and drama that sustained her for days. Shoplifters were surprisingly common, and although the crime itself often went unnoticed by the staff, it was usually accompanied by a good forty-five minutes of speculation and gossip. There were conspiracies and intrigue. Petty feuds and small-town politics.

Last week, Gwen had arrived for her shift to find treachery in the air. Treachery and a new vanilla reed diffuser, which was making the shop smell like a fudge pantry. Lise was holding a muttered conversation with St. Michael, who was pummeling a stress ball shaped like a Minion.

"What's going on?" she had asked Brian.

"Yasmeen's defected," Brian whispered. "Gone behind enemy lines."

"Not to . . . ?"

"The Niceness Hive, yes indeed."

"Kindfulness Hub," Asha corrected him, joining the huddle. "Said it aligned more with her personal value system."

"Yikes," said Gwen.

"So Michael blanked her in the corner shop."

"Wow. Shit."

"I know."

Two days later, a local Turkish restaurant had come by and donated their unsold mezze to the volunteers. "For all the good that you do!" the beaming teenage waiter had said, pushing a vat of taramasalata into Gwen's hands. "Eat, please, before midnight."

The Kindfulness Hub, Finn had heard via an unconfirmed source, received weekly deliveries of vegan pastries and cold brew from a benevolent sponsor. But as he, Gwen, Lise, and Jeremy sat on the brown carpet after closing time and toasted each other with fistfuls of stuffed vine leaves, all agreed that they could never go over to the dark side.

Then there were moments like today, when Gwen plunged her hand into an unassuming bag of T-shirts and pulled out, Excalibur-style, a huge purple dildo.

For a second she looked at it, wondering if it were perhaps a bike pump or a particularly sculptural pepper grinder. Then the truth dawned and she screamed and flung it across the back room, where it rolled gaily across the carpet and came to a halt next to the printer.

St. Michael stuck his head around the door and surveyed the scene. Gwen braced herself for a telling-off, but instead he looked from her to the dildo and back, then said, "Congratulations! Is it your first time?"

Before Gwen could reply, Lise had popped up behind him, followed by Brenda on tiptoes.

"Gwen found a golden ticket," Michael told them. Lise giggled and took her phone out to capture the moment.

"I'm sorry, a *what*?"

"It's a rite of passage," he crowed. Michael had never paid her this much attention before. For a worrying moment she thought he might hug her.

Brenda nodded solemnly in agreement. "You never forget your first dildo."

Gwen fashioned a protective hand mitt from a length of paper towel, and tried to sound stoical. "Well if this is as bad as it gets, then I'm glad I've passed the test."

"Oh bless your heart! This isn't as bad as it gets," said Brenda, cheerily. Then they all started chipping in with their most memorable donations, both intentional and accidental.

"Sets of dentures, lockets with human hair in them," began Michael.

"Used brushes for the toilet," said Lise, miming in horror. "Nipple rings."

"A mummified hamster," said Michael, "several inhalers, a rucksack containing a bag of dog poo—"

"Still warm," added Lise.

"A full set of adult lederhosen, a box of diabetic needles," continued Michael. "A VHS tape containing every Granada weather forecast from 1989 to 1993—"

"Someone's dead nan, in a jar," said Brenda.

"—multiple pregnancy tests in multiple handbag pockets—"

"We only realized because it said 'nan' on the side."

"—a copy of *50 Shades* with all the sex redacted in marker pen."

"—and a bag of broken biscuits," finished Brenda. "Three years past the sell-by."

"What do we *do* with them all?" asked Gwen.

"Well," Brenda paused, thinking for a moment. "The biscuits we ate."

# **Jumper**

Derek hadn't known what to do with the jumper.

He had grabbed it before he ran out of the house, because it was early evening and the weather had been unseasonably cold for late August, and there was nothing Derek hated more than being chilly. He had cursed the jumper ever since, for those lost seconds. Precious seconds he had wasted rifling through the hooks in the hallway (they needed to clear out those hooks, he'd been saying it for years), seconds which could instead have been spent cradling his son to his chest before the paramedics arrived. Before Derek was jostled out of the way and relegated to the role of "useless bystander, clutching jumper."

He could pretend that he'd grabbed it for his son, in a moment of foresight. To keep him warm as he lay there on the pavement, the chalky pallor of his skin already making him look like a crude imitation of a person. But that wasn't true. He had definitely grabbed it for himself. It tormented Derek to know that he was the kind of man who could hear the words "your son, he's collapsed, come quick" and think "better take layers."

He hadn't known what to do with it at the hospital either; had been ashamed to be holding it when his wife arrived, in case she noticed and knew immediately about those stupid, wasted seconds. His wife wouldn't have stopped to find a jumper. Or perhaps she would have?

In the end she hadn't noticed. She hadn't been able to see anything at all, it seemed, as she stumbled across the room toward him, arms outstretched as though groping through darkness. But he was aware of it as he held her, as they both shook with the sobs that seemed to come not from her but from elsewhere; from deep within the ground below them, as though their orange plastic chairs were sat atop a fault line. His arm had been at an awkward angle, he remembered, as he held her. It had gone completely dead but he had been too scared to move it. As though the tiniest shift would shatter everything anew.

When his daughter had arrived some time later, gasping for breath, with her boyfriend hovering mutely behind, she had looked down at his jumper in the empty chair and sat, confusedly, next to it. The gap it left in the family lineup felt at once both macabre and appropriate. *I'm sorry, that seat is saved.*

Later still, as he began shivering—it was cold, after all; in the hospital, Derek had been right—he didn't put the jumper on. Because what use was warmth to him now? But even as shock coursed like ice through his veins, he was turning to see if Luke was cold and if Luke wanted his jumper. Despite knowing that Luke would undoubtedly consider himself too cool to wear his dad's jumper. Despite also knowing, in the very same heartbeat, that Luke wasn't there.

Derek saw someone else in the hospital wearing flip-flops and another in pajama trousers and a tank top, and felt another rush of shame. What if he'd been in the shower when the doorbell rang? Would a good father have run outside in only a towel?

He must have brought the jumper home with them, though he didn't remember doing this. Must have folded it carefully and put it away in a drawer, which he didn't remember doing either. Derek had thrown away all the clothes he had been wearing that day, right down to his socks and underwear—had made a tight wad of them all and buried it deep in the outside wheelie bin. A move that his wife would have found sinfully wasteful, if she'd known. Or perhaps she wouldn't have.

But he hadn't thrown away the jumper, because he hadn't worn the jumper. It seemed nonsensical to get rid of it too. He didn't want to wear the jumper ever again, but keeping it felt like an act of small penance, a reminder every time he opened that drawer. A reminder of what? Derek wasn't sure, but it seemed important nonetheless.

It seemed important, like the hours he spent agonizing over the bottle of beer he took round to the neighbor that had called the ambulance. Important like claiming back the deposit on the room at the university that Luke wouldn't, after all, be attending. Important like the pinched nerve in his shoulder that bothered him for months, years even, after he had shouldered the coffin down the aisle at the funeral—something Derek hadn't wanted to do, desperately hadn't wanted to, but couldn't find the words to get himself out of. He never sought treatment for the shoulder, because it seemed important to live with the pain.

People like to say that you never know when it's the last time you will pick your child up and carry them. Sometimes they're wrong.

## 27

Their dinners had become weekly, and Gwen wasn't sure how.

There were lunches and coffees and drinks too, tacked onto their shifts at the shop. As with everything Connie did, from the way she ate a sandwich to the way she could take a scarf off in one clean, fluid motion or open a yogurt without it spurting into her face, there was a graceful ease to the way she had stepped their friendship up several gears in only a few weeks. Gwen had barely noticed it was happening.

Maybe it was generational, Connie being the product of a time when spontaneous plans were an exciting prospect, not a terrifying one. She wanted to call it "cultural," although she wasn't sure which culture, except that sometimes Connie seemed the most French of all the people Gwen had met who weren't actually French. Or maybe it was just her personality. Part of the intensity that made her vibrant and charismatic and good at life, as opposed to limp, washed-out dishrag people like Gwen. Either way, Connie always gave the impression of one who had never in her life pushed at a door marked "pull."

She had thought about returning the invite and asking Connie to hers, of course she had. But Gwen sensed that it wouldn't be enjoyable for either of them. Her, panicking in the kitchen that was also her lounge, spending three times her new weekly food budget to turn a piece of organic meat into chamois leather; Connie scandalized that she didn't own a garlic press or a lemon zester. One day she might be able to return the favor on an equal footing. But tonight they were eating beef stifado with Greek potatoes and talking about Connie's ex-husband again.

"He used to bite his toenails, for god's sake. It was a level of flexibility that always surprised me, and yet not one I ever benefitted from."

"My ex used to leave his in a little pile on the coffee table," said Gwen, keen to contribute. "Ex-fiancé," she added, though she had never used the word when she had one. "Not husband."

Gwen hadn't mentioned Ryan since that first dinner, suspecting that Connie would leap on the information and use it to form one of her pet theories. Which she did now, of course, exclaiming: "Aha!" as though she had uncovered a great secret. "Managed to dodge the institution, did you? Well done! How do you get on now, you and him?"

"We don't," replied Gwen, helping herself to more potatoes from a hand-painted dish. They were roasted to a crisp, in a tangle of sweet onions, herbs, and feta. She thought about the time Ryan had asked for her mother's roast potato recipe in an attempt to be affable, and Marjorie had been forced to admit they were Aunt Bessie's.

"I haven't seen him since I ended things."

"What, not *once*?" Connie seemed genuinely shocked. "Not even a cheeky reprise for old time's sake? A little trip down memory lane?"

Gwen shook her head. She supposed this wasn't very French of her.

"Oh, well, *Gwen*, there you go! You need some"—Connie affected a Californian accent, as was mandatory for the word Gwen knew was coming—"*closure*. You need to see him. Clear the air, exorcize some demons."

The idea of Ryan as a demon—Ryan, a man so mild he'd let a colleague call him "Rylan" for three years and never corrected him—was comical. Ryan, who had held her as she sobbed, and fielded messages from friends who had heard, and discreetly explained to those who hadn't. Who had knelt on his bad knee with a nice enough ring, and winced as he got up to embrace her. It would have been so much easier if there had been anything about him to hate. It would have been so much easier if there had been anything about him, full stop.

"You'll feel much better afterwards. Trust me," said Connie. Maybe this was true?

By the time they'd sunk a bottle of Xinomavro and Gwen had recounted the story of their breakup and her subsequent wilderness years, she was convinced it was true. Connie was a highly convincing person.

"Sounds like it was a case of shit or get off the pot," Connie declared, topping up both their glasses with a lavish glug. She wagged a long finger at her, tipsily. "And when you got off the pot, you clenched up so tight that you could never go again."

Gwen found her appetite for sticky roast figs with mascarpone had mysteriously vanished, but she had to admit the diagnosis might be right.

"You don't regret it though, do you?"

"No," Gwen replied, and not just because this was the answer Connie wanted to hear.

It wasn't regret that tormented her with Ryan, because at least regret was a feeling you could sink your teeth into. No, it was something more slippery than that: the infernal purgatory of not knowing whether things would have turned out better or worse. Whether sticking would have been better than twisting, after all. And knowing that you can never know, not now. Not for certain.

"You should message him right now! Ask him for a drink. Say you have unfinished business." Connie pushed her phone into her hand as though it were a slumber party dare, and Gwen watched herself opening a blank message and scrolling obediently through her contacts to "R." Was she going to do this, right now?

"The truth will set you free!" shouted Connie, drumming her hands on the table in anticipation.

The screen had become blurry, and Gwen realized with some surprise that she was crying. Or at least, her eyes were streaming, though it felt less a show of emotion than an allergic reaction to the whole conversation. She dropped the phone. She was not going to do this right now.

"Sorry," Gwen said, flapping a useless hand about in front of her eyes, then knocked her glass over. Wine began to seep into the table, and her silent tears turned to great, heaving sobs of frustration. Her hostess fetched a kitchen roll from the counter and passed it to her, calmly, watching her, head cocked to one side in rapt fascination.

"Sorry, oh god," Gwen said, lamely, dabbing at the spill with one hand while trying to blow her nose with the other. The red wine stain immediately looked glamorous, somehow adding to the patina of Connie's reclaimed wood. "Sorry, sorry—hgghhh—sorry."

After a few minutes she had stemmed the flow at both sources, but the pressure behind her eyes remained.

"You know your problem," Connie said eventually, lighting a cigarette, not bothering to open the French doors this time. "You're sorry for everything."

"I know. I'm sorry."

"It's not endearing, Gwen, it's annoying."

"Sorry," repeated Gwen.

"STOP IT, stop apologizing!" yelled Connie. She looked as though she wanted to shake her. "You walk around as though you feel guilty for being alive!"

"Well maybe I *do*," Gwen yelled back.

This was new. She hadn't snapped at Connie before. She hadn't snapped at anyone, for longer than she could remember. Connie looked startled for a second, then composed herself. She took another drag.

"And why the hell would you feel that?" she demanded, now

in full coaching mode. As though this were an improv exercise, breaking Gwen down to build her up again. "Give me one good reason."

Blood was pounding in Gwen's ears now. The room seemed to turn concave, lurching and slipping around her like the walls of a tunnel slide. Connie's eyes were the only constant, shrewd and narrowed behind their bifocals. Gwen took a deep breath, stopped scrambling for a safe foothold and let herself slide toward them.

"Because my brother died." She croaked the words out between gulps of air. "Seven years ago. Heart failure. Nineteen. I don't like to talk about it."

## 28

Connie let out the noise people always made. A soft, involuntary little "oh."

The noise contained the truth. The words that followed it—I'm so sorry how awful what a tragedy you poor thing if it isn't an insensitive question can I ask how—always felt scripted, she generally let them wash over her, nodded in the right places until the stream of sympathy ran dry. But the noise was the part that got her, every time.

Connie stubbed out her cigarette and started to speak, but Gwen wasn't quite done.

"Please, spare me your thoughts on counseling and support groups and talking my way through it and . . . and painting a fucking pot or something in his memory. I'm fine. It's fine. I don't need advice."

Connie reached across the table and gave her forearm a gentle squeeze. But when her voice came, it was brisk and assured as ever. "Actually, I wasn't going to say any of that. I was going to ask what his name was."

Gwen took another ragged breath. "Luke," she told her.

"Luke," Connie repeated. "So tell me about Luke."

# Cookbook

---

Despite the collective efforts of Edith Piaf and Robbie Williams, Gwen had many regrets.

Where Luke was concerned they were both minute in detail—words she'd chosen, fights she'd picked, a particular Cadbury's egg she'd stolen from his Easter hoard circa 2002—and vast in scale, regrets that spanned months and years, whole chapters of his truncated life that she wished she'd handled differently. It was hard to think about all of that regret without wanting to claw at her own skin.

For a while after he died she'd dabbled in self-harm, but only in amateurish ways that she didn't think counted. Walking for miles in the cold without a coat. Digging her nails into soft flesh until they drew blood. Taking baths so hot that her thighs would turn raw and her head would spin and she would have to stagger from the bathroom to her bed with brown spots swirling in front of her eyes.

She regretted not playing with him more when he was little. She regretted not phoning him more when he was older—or at all, if she was honest, but then what teenage boy wanted to have long phone calls with their dowdy older sister? She regretted the time he had wanted to visit her at university and she had said no, because you couldn't take an eight-year-old to a traffic-light party. She regretted the time he had wanted to visit her at university and she had said yes, and he had been scared at York Dungeons and bored at the Railway Museum and had eaten a pizza he didn't like and wanted to go home early.

She regretted not looking at him more. Was this an odd thing to think? She regretted not drinking in the details of him, not taking more time to catalog each of the places their cellular blueprints intersected and diverged. When he was a baby she would rejoice in the rare moments she had alone to look at him, without their mother hovering and fussing. She would sneak into his room when he napped and trace a finger along his cheeks—hers—his chin—not hers—his eyes—hers, but prettier—and his tiny snub nose—not hers, yet, but the trademark Grundle beak would emerge when he hit puberty and then she would laugh at it, at the fact that genetics come for us all.

These days Gwen saw traces of Luke's face in her own, which was the wrong way round. As though she was aging toward him, somehow, or *for* him, his youthful features becoming crumpled over time.

She regretted every critical word she'd ever spoken to him, and yet she also regretted not lecturing him more. She regretted not stopping him from running, which made no sense, because why would she ever have stopped him from running? Fit young men don't drop down dead, except when they do. She regretted not signing him up for Cardiac Risk in the Young screenings. When she went for her own, at her mother's insistence, and it showed no problems or abnormalities whatsoever, she regretted that too.

She regretted not being there when it happened. But more so, she regretted not being there on all the other days, when it didn't happen. She regretted not going home the weekend before, although there was no reason she would have. She regretted the fact she never went home without a specific reason, back then, and still didn't.

She regretted the days that she *was* there, after it happened, for being useless and pathetic and surplus to requirements. For not being able to fulfill her role as the elder sibling and lead by example, keeping her head while all about her were losing theirs. For not being able to tell her parents that they were wrong and it was all a mistake. For not being able to bring him back.

She had brought Ryan back instead, and he had behaved impeccably, which made everything worse. "*Shut up!*" she had wanted to scream each time he opened his mouth to say something appropriate, respectful, and helpful. As though he might be speaking over her brother. "*Shut up! We can't hear Luke.*"

Ryan and Luke had gotten on well; surprisingly well considering their age gap. Ryan had been fond of him in a way that fell somewhere between friend and nephew, relishing the excuse to feel young and cool and carefree while buying all the drinks. Luke had liked him back, despite his brown hiking trainers. "You can marry this one if you like," he had said to her once, more or less the only time they had ever had any kind of discourse around her love life. She'd appreciated the way he said "this one," as though there might have been hordes of men before Ryan.

When they'd got engaged, it wasn't her parents or her friends she'd wanted to tell. It was Luke.

She regretted not writing her own eulogy for the funeral, instead reading a poem that her mother had found and which Luke would probably have hated. She regretted being calm enough to read the poem, voice steady, when everyone else was strangled by tears. She regretted feeling hungry at the wake, when surely grief was meant to be the thief of appetite, eating an egg sandwich from the buffet and then being so worried she smelled of egg afterward that she couldn't bring herself to speak to anyone. None of the boys, who had looked gangling and pained in their borrowed suits, or the young women, wild-haired and Ophelia-esque and beautiful in their grief. She'd watched them all from the corner instead, wondering which he had loved.

She regretted not meeting the person—they never knew who—that had taped a wilting bunch of carnations to the lamppost on the street where he'd died, with a felt-tipped message: *for Luke*. Marjorie had ripped them off and thrown them in the bin. Gwen regretted letting her do that.

She regretted the last birthday present she'd ever bought him, a student cookbook, even though it was exactly what he'd asked for. *101 Stupidly Easy Student Meals*. She should have ignored the request and bought him something lavish, something ridiculous, something far too expensive instead. She could have taken the time to find a present that said "you are known, and you are loved." But she hadn't. She regretted it all.

## 29

Gwen told Connie about Luke.

First, she told her what had happened. And then, as Connie listened, suddenly the very model of sympathetic restraint, she told her a little of how it had felt.

"I couldn't understand why it wasn't on the evening news," said Gwen. Connie nodded, as though this made sense.

But it was true. In those first few days, the urge to sit and wail with grief hadn't been as strong, somehow, as the urge to run into restaurants and leap onto moving trains and to picket television studios, waving her arms and insisting that they all stop, stop what they were doing right now. She would see people laughing and smiling in the street and feel momentarily alarmed that she knew something these people did not. Had they not heard? Should she tell them? Then, as her brain clunked painfully into gear, the panic would be replaced by a calm, cold fury. Anger that they didn't care, and that they didn't have to care.

People had come to the house—not lots, but some—and she would watch them from the window as they left, looking out for the barely perceptible moment that their shoulders dropped and their pace relaxed as they shrugged off the posture of grief as easily as a coat on a warm spring day.

"I started to hate the words: *thinking of you,*" she told Connie. "I still do. They mean nothing. Worse than nothing, in fact—

the idea of everyone sitting around thinking of you. It made me feel . . . vulnerable. Everybody is thinking of you but nobody is *talking to* you, in case they fuck it up and say the wrong thing. In case you don't want to be disturbed."

Really though, thought Gwen, she had been the one with the power to disturb. She was the one who could end a party, sour a sunny day, smash a conversation to pieces with the sledgehammer she must now carry, awkwardly, everywhere, always. A sudden death is an act of emotional violence, and for months and years afterward, every part of Gwen had reverberated from the impact.

"The British are useless at dealing with death; it is one of the great failings of our culture," said Connie.

Gwen agreed. "The things people would say. One of the condolence cards read 'At least you were lucky enough to have him for the time you did,' and I just . . . I couldn't get over the gall of it. To write that word! Lucky." It felt good to rant, good to finally curse those good intentions with the fury they didn't deserve. "Other people would hold forth about all the things Luke must be thinking and feeling, how he would want us to be strong. As if they knew. As if anyone knew!"

"Twats!" pronounced Connie, with relish. She was apparently confident she'd never make the same mistake.

"Some even told us Luke was watching us all from some other realm," Gwen went on, "like the way we used to send him to bed on Christmas Eve and then look up an hour later to see his little eye pushed up against the gap in the living room doorframe." Her voice thickened on the end of this sentence, and she gulped the tears down with more wine.

"*Ugh*," scoffed Connie, patting her arm with one hand and refilling her glass with the other.

It wasn't that Gwen didn't believe in heaven, so much as she couldn't picture him there. She didn't know enough about him—this person who was closer, chemically, to her, than to anybody else in the world. She didn't know what his heaven would look like, or what he'd want to do all day there. She didn't know what song he'd listen to if he could only choose one for all eternity. She knew his favorite food was marshmallow, ever since he learned to make s'mores on a Scouts camping trip—but the idea of Luke bouncing around a cloudy nirvana eating fistfuls of pillowy pink marshmallows was too twee to entertain. So she didn't.

"I read books and listened to podcasts about grief and I felt jealous—actually *jealous*—of the people who had warning," she admitted to Connie. "People who had time. Last words and special holidays and funny moments to treasure afterwards. We had none of that."

Although sometimes she would try, inwardly cringing, to imagine what they would have done if they had known in advance. Disneyland? Days at the zoo?

"But you must have happy memories to look back on!" insisted Connie, and Gwen tried to explain. That their twelve-year age gap meant that her role in his life had always felt more like that of an absentee parent than a real sibling.

"I was too much older to be a fun companion for him,"—even in his teens, he never considered her cool enough to be a source of rebellious camaraderie or contraband booze—"but not old enough to be of any real help or support to my parents. Mum was so anxious about his safety and happiness all the time, which meant I wasn't allowed to look after him alone very often. Or at all, really."

Marjorie never quite used the words "second chance" or "this time round," but their implication was felt in every affectionate head stroke, every expensive hobby indulged, and every fussy whim catered for. For all she was a pragmatic woman not given over to flights of mysticism, Luke was the precise size of her capacity for faith. It was clear she felt she had been given an eleventh-hour encore, another shot at the big cash prize, another go on the potter's wheel just as her last creation had begun to harden in an imperfect form. She was not about to waste it.

But Marjorie was self-conscious at being an older mother, Gwen could tell, and thrown by how much everything had changed in the intervening decade. She made up for this insecurity by being sanctimonious at the school gates, issuing unsolicited advice among the younger parents with the imperious air of One Who Has Done It All Before.

Gwen realized with a jolt that her mother had been the same age when Luke was born as Gwen was now.

"You poor thing," said Connie, which felt strange. Gwen was used to garnering sympathy since Luke's death, but not for anything that happened before it.

Despite his status as the golden child, the miracle baby, she had never really been jealous of Luke. Or at least, not in a way she was aware of. Not while he was alive. As he grew older and the pressure cooker of Marjorie's love was turned up a notch, year by year, Gwen was mostly glad to be out of the way. After twelve years of intense only-childdom, it had been at once both freeing and upsetting to suddenly find herself outside of her mother's primary orbit.

For a while after Luke was born, her father had taken her on bike rides, just the two of them, every Sunday. Standing as she was, on the cusp of adolescence, it had been a couple of years too late for candid father-daughter bonding over Breakaway bars and lukewarm lemonade. Gwen had tried to summon the gung-ho energy of the ponytailed girls in her teen books who were always making peace with newly divorced dads who called them "champ." But since her parents were not divorced and there was nothing technically for her to make peace *with*, and since Derek Grundle's paternal ambitions did not extend to having views on the varying snoggability of East 17 or the shaving vs. depilatory cream debate, the conversation had usually been stilted.

Mostly they relayed the plots of sitcom episodes to each other. *Keeping Up Appearances*, *Two Point Four Children*, *The Brittas Empire*. Then he would ask for an update on each of her school subjects in turn ("Fine. Boring. Rock formations. *Of Mice and Men*."), followed by an inquiry about her friends, phrased in an only marginally more delicate way than ". . . do you have any yet?" By this point the Breakaways would be finished and one or the other of them could say—with legitimacy—"Best get back, Mum will be waiting."

"What about your father?" asked Connie, pouring out the last dribble of their second bottle. "Did he feel left out too, do you think?"

"I don't know," replied Gwen. "Maybe."

It had never occurred to her to ask her father questions in return. If she was honest, it still didn't.

Now, she didn't think of her grief as a hole or a missing limb, so much as a broken bone that had begun to heal before it had been properly set. She could almost feel it, as she crumpled herself into another taxi home from Connie's house and gingerly leaned back against the headrest. She was complete, just perpetually askew.

There was no word to describe it, being a person who had lost a sibling, or a person who had lost a child. To lose a spouse made you a widow or widower, to lose your parents made you an orphan. But Gwen and her parents existed in an unlabeled state, with no claim on a new identity—only broken versions of their old selves to climb back inside and make the best of.

Sometimes she forgot to feel sad, the way she sometimes forgot to drink water or worry about terrorists on the Tube. Sometimes she felt it wasn't his absence that hurt so much as the fact of his very existence. That it would be easier, if they could only manage to forget that he had ever been alive. She knew this was the exact opposite of the thing you were supposed to feel.

Part of the pain of sibling bereavement was supposed to be the loss of shared history, of the person who remembers all the same things you do. But there was so much time on either side of their siblinghood and so much they hadn't shared. To have lived twelve years without Luke, then nineteen with him, then another seven without, meant that her life was a clean fifty-fifty split. And they had only lived six years together under one roof before she'd left home. Six years was nothing.

Gwen hated the maths but she couldn't help doing it. She forced herself through the sums now, in the taxi, her head swimmy as the street lights blurred to two solid streaks of light.

She had now lived to double his age. And next year, her Luke-less years would outweigh the years in which he'd been alive. It wasn't the kind of milestone she could vocalize to anybody, or commemorate on social media with a long, rambling caption—but it felt significant, privately, to her. She was scared of what might happen when she crossed that threshold, yet sometimes she found herself willing the months to pass more quickly. To dilute the pain with time, and wine, seemed as good a plan as any.

# Hardback

---

It isn't the book she had wanted to write.

She had wanted to write something raw, spare, brutal, and profound—the kind the critics call "unflinching." But she is starting to suspect the book she has written is, in fact, a shameless flincher. Riddled with flinch. Extremely flinchy.

Certainly readers seem to be cowering away from it. Although, as her agent explained over lunches and her friends reaffirmed over cocktails and patient, late-night voice notes, it is far better to have a small band of actively engaged fans than a toothless horde of lukewarm book groupers and people who go to WHSmiths for the giant Dairy Milks.

Unless you want to make money, obviously. Then the opposite is true.

Sophie has never hungered for money so much as approval. Which is why she forces herself to read online reviews late at night while eating Biscoff spread from the jar. A spoonful of sugar to help the medicine go down. It's why she sulks at the announcement of shortlists for prizes that her book isn't even eligible for, and why she trawls charity shops looking for copies of her novel, never fully knowing if she is hoping to find it, or hoping she won't.

If it isn't there, and it rarely is, then she takes this as powerful confirmation of her meager sales. Spread so thinly across the nation's bookshelves is her book that she could walk into a hundred charity shops and never see it. She pictures her work as a homeopathic drop in a vast, churning ocean of literature. Probably nobody is donating it to the shops because nobody has bothered to read it yet. Probably the cover looked too flinchy.

But if it *is* there—and she has now learned to identify its spine at twenty paces from the doorway, or even sometimes the street outside—she feels personally affronted. That her book has made such a shallow thumbprint of an impression on its reader that they've felt able to pass it on again so quickly, and not even to friends or family, but to strangers. (Although it's also true that "I loved it so much I passed it around all my friends and family!" are words that kick a broke author right in the spleen.) It hurts to know that she spent four years of bar shifts and soul-mangling tutoring jobs writing the thing, but her readers don't feel the need to sit with it. Either metaphorically, or literally, on a small table next to their sofa.

Then there's the price tag, which varies wildly between charities and neighborhoods. She can't help herself comparing it to the price of the other books too, wondering what criteria they used. In one shop it was marked at £1.50 when all the other hardbacks were £3, and when Sophie casually inquired why, the expressionless man behind the till had said: "Gunk." She had taken this as a savage critical review and was almost on the verge of tears until he pointed to a jammy smear on the jacket, half-obscuring the cover quote. Gunk.

She supposes all this will get easier as time passes. In a few months, maybe—a reasonable time, she tells herself, in which to have read the book, been deeply moved, let it percolate, gone back to reread their favorite parts, left a glowing online review and then, only then, slipped it in the donations bag, safe in the knowledge that it would stay with you in heart and mind forever. Maybe then she'll see her book in charity shops and feel nothing but pride. She looks forward to the day.

For now, she is slyly turning it to face outward on the shelves, repositioning it next to Barbara Kingsolver and Arundhati Roy. She travels with a small packet of wet wipes in her handbag, just in case.

# 30

"Let's get you a job."

It was a quiet Thursday morning, made quieter by Silent Harvey being on steaming duty while St. Michael lay on the backroom sofa beneath a large beach hat, staving off a migraine. The threat of the migraine loomed, somehow, over the whole shop. Even the contestants on Ken Bruce's *PopMaster* were doing badly.

Harvey was working at a snail's pace through a rack of shirts, steaming with the precision of an Edwardian butler, paying particular attention to the small sections of fabric between the buttons. Connie was wrestling with an inflatable pool float shaped like the turd emoji, a task that threatened even Connie's eternal poise.

The shop bore the evidence of fads and micro crazes from across many decades. But while sixties and seventies knick-knacks were genuinely desirable and eighties and nineties items had become collectible kitsch, it was mostly newer ephemera that flooded the back room and clogged up the shelves. Cinema-style light boxes. Mugs with mustaches on them. Giant hairclips encrusted with plastic pearls. Fairy lights shaped like cacti, adult coloring books, plastic flower crowns, cushions shaped like alpacas, salt and pepper shakers shaped like pugs, gin-scented lip balms and gin-scented bath bombs and gin-scented candles and *Hey Sexy Lady: The Gangnam Style Workout*. Ring holders shaped like tattooed hands and flowerpots shaped like breasts and more ring holders decorated with signs of the zodiac. Rose gold everything. Decorative boxes of matches and pastel-colored A4 prints that said "But first: cronuts." *I Can Has Cheezburger: The Annual*. Finger skateboards and Pikachu onesies and wire head-massagers and velvet sleep masks and makeup bags shaped like slices of watermelon and miniature washing lines to hang up Polaroid photos and unicorn yoga mats and phone cases painted with tiny, freeform vulvas and countless other souvenirs from times too recent to have acquired any nostalgic value but not recent enough to have retained any monetary value, either.

Gwen felt a twinge of melancholy whenever she sold one of these things, though it was hard to say why. If a person had space in their life and heart for an inflatable drinks holder shaped like an avocado, who was she to deny them?

Connie was less open-minded. More than once now, Gwen had watched her lean across the counter, place a hand on top of a customer's hand as though sharing a profound secret, and tell them: "You don't need this crap." What Connie expected to happen after this was unclear. What did happen was that the customer usually bought the crap anyway, scowling.

Today, Gwen was counting jigsaw pieces. The first time Lise had asked Gwen to do this she had laughed, believing it to be a joke. Now, she scrabbled to write "352" on the nearest Post-it note before looking up at Connie.

"Let's get you a job," Connie said again, successfully propping the turd against a floor lamp and turning to face her. She said it the same way she said "let's get you a taxi" and "I'm buying you a gin." She said it the same way, Gwen was beginning to realize, that Connie said most things. With an air of unshakable authority and the confidence she would be obeyed.

Still, there was no denying she needed a job. It had been almost nine weeks now (Gwen preferred to count in weeks, this seeming less terrifying than "more than two months"), and her money was dwindling fast. Gwen was questioning how a person got to her age without a nice pot of savings tucked away for a rainy day. Or rather, how they got to her age *with* one. How did they manage to keep the hungry Pac-Man of modern life from nibbling it all away as quickly as it arrived?

Nobody could call her lifestyle extravagant. It felt like a stretch to even call it a "lifestyle." Yet all month, every month, her money was eaten away in unforgiving chunks. Not just rent and utilities, but her phone, her phone insurance, her travelcard, her home contents insurance, her streaming services, her contact lens plan, her prescriptions, several media paywalls signed up to for the purpose of reading one particular article and then maintained out of guilt for the ailing future of journalism ever since, and the donation to a donkey sanctuary that she had been making every month for the past four years.

She started the donkey donations because the man with the clipboard had made eye contact with her during a weak moment outside Pret. He had spoken so earnestly, almost tearfully, about the donkeys that Gwen had signed over her bank details then and there, wishing she could feel that passionately about anything, ever. She hoped to buy a bit of his integrity by proxy.

A week later she had seen the same man with his clipboard again, this time in a T-shirt for Hodgkins lymphoma, and felt oddly hoodwinked. She had tried to cancel the direct debit, but when the person on the phone at the donkey charity asked why, "missold passion by a man who also cares about blood cancer" didn't feel like a strong enough reason. By the end of the call she had upped her monthly donation by five pounds.

"Don't go putting ideas into her head," called St. Michael, from the back room, the hat still over his face. "Nobody needs a job."

"*You* have one," retorted Connie.

"Yes, and look what it does to me," he groaned, his muffled voice almost godlike from within its straw dome. "Don't do it, Gwen, horrible things. Commuting. Meetings. No free biscuits."

He was wrong about the biscuits but had a point about the

commute. Recently she had stopped renewing her travelcard and started using contactless instead, which made economic sense now that her only regular journey was a twelve-minute walk to the charity shop. But it was shameful to admit that her world had shrunk to the breadth of a couple of postcodes. Gwen feared it was a slippery slope, that what started with giving up her travelcard might end in her getting rid of her microwave and refusing to complete the next census. She thought of Marjorie's second cousin, who made her own yogurt in the airing cupboard. She thought of the soft-spoken man who came into the shop every few weeks and bought travel guides to far-flung destinations but never seemed to acquire a tan.

"The trouble is," she told Michael, "I do occasionally need to buy things."

Gwen was aware that the upside of being a single, child-free woman in her late thirties was supposed to be a certain amount of financial buoyancy. She knew she was supposed to be the lavish friend who sent designer candles and always paid for dinner; the person who gently taunted everyone by going on solo tours of Greek islands while they stayed home and panicked about nursery fees. She was meant to cultivate an aura of expensive self-maintenance, to have regular facials and artisan hand soap and a weekly fresh pasta subscription box.

But ever since her mother taught her, at a tender age, that the "check balance" button was something to be feared ("No!" she had yelled once, slapping Gwen's small hand away from the ATM and reflexively leaping to cover the screen as though it featured a pornographic tableau. "You must *never* press that button, do you hear me?"), money had been a source of tension. Not one that was discussed openly within the family, but a tension Gwen carried privately and silently inside her, panicking any time a significant outlay came along—new school shoes, a new car exhaust, the annual week at Pontins, Luke's hobbies and sports equipment and school trips—and interpreting every tut at a price tag, every quiet word behind the closed kitchen door as a sign of their imminent slide into destitution.

Now she looked back and understood that they had been fine. Not *comfy,* perhaps, but comfortable enough, like a pair of jeans that pinched only slightly in the crotch. She knew now that off-brand trainers and caravan holidays were not markers of poverty. But still, this didn't mean she could go to her parents as a thirty-eight-year-old woman and start asking for handouts from their pension pots, because she was too lazy and useless and generous to donkeys to maintain her own life.

No.

"I know!" exclaimed Connie, as though the thought had only just occurred to her and hadn't been the whole reason for starting the conversation. "I'm going to put you in touch with a brilliant friend of mine, Saskia. She has a start-up!"

A muffled snort of disdain came from the back room. Connie ignored it, busily tapping out a text with her glasses perched on the end of her nose. Gwen made a few noises of protest, but she ignored those too.

"Don't ask me *what* she's starting up, I always go to the loo at the first mention of venture capital. But she'll sort you out with something, god knows she owes me a few favors. Say you'll meet up with her? For me?"

Gwen meekly agreed. The world of street fundraising could use Connie.

# Scarf

There are a hundred different ways to wear a scarf. Which makes it all the more of a shame that charity shops are so full of them, these wafting scraps of not-quite-clothing that never lived up to their potential.

There are a hundred ways to wear a scarf, although most people's repertoire doesn't extend beyond the obvious. Around the neck, that's the classic. Around the neck twice, or thrice if you're daring. The old loop-the-loop, the twist-and-tuck, the waterfall, the croissant. The Rupert the Bear, The Doctor, the Katniss Everdeen, the Lenny Kravitz. The art teacher and the erstwhile indie fan. The "I own an Audrey Hepburn wall decal." At least five different incarnations of David Bowie.

As a cravat, as a tie, as a toga. As an ineffectual neck brace. The Keith Richards, and the Richard the Third. The Fred from *Scooby-Doo*.

As a symbol of religious devotion. As a way to keep your hair smooth at night. As a feminist statement, a political scapegoat, or a natty bandana for those to whom "culture" means drinkable yogurt.

As a belt. As a sarong. As a sleep aid on an airplane. As a very small top, to flaunt the fact that you do not need a bra. As a lead for a small dog. As a sling, for a small baby. As a protective shield for those who get heat stroke at the literal drop of a hat.

As a concealment device for hickies, or regrettable tattoos. As a way to let Mr. DeMille know you are ready for your close-up. In a bow at the neck, like a lovely present or a bad prime minister. As a small knapsack, containing sandwiches, tied around a stick.

As a bandage. As a beach towel. As bunting for a happy occasion. As a sexual accessory for those too busy or embarrassed to buy special tape off the internet. As a gift for those who believe Emma Thompson's character in *Love Actually* was making a fuss about nothing. As a piece of art, spread behind glass.

As a way to spruce up student accommodation and let people know you've *traveled*. As a way to say "I'm practical, but adorable" while doing DIY. As a "cover-up" at a wedding when your bastard boyfriend won't give you his jacket. As a prop for a rhythmic gymnastics routine, or the beginning of a promising career in stage magic. As an integral part of pin the tail on the donkey. As a means to mop up vomit on the bus.

As a fancy-dress pirate. As a fancy-dress nun. As Dame Jenni Murray, or a Celtic warrior queen. As dressing for a snowman. As dressing for a wound. As something to breathe into, when the person beside you had mackerel for lunch.

As a way to protect your modesty, should you lose all your clothes while swimming in a lake. As a cunning ploy, left behind as a reason for a love interest to get in touch. As a classy way to wipe tears away when they abandon you on a train platform.

As a fancy-dress Frida Kahlo. As a fancy-dress Scottish Widow. As an actual Scottish widow. As a picnic rug.

As a pledge of allegiance to a football team, or a Hogwarts house, or the Queen. As a superhero's cape. As a comfort blanket. As a throw for the sofa you spilled hummus on and know you will never have cleaned. As a makeshift curtain that will stay taped to your window for three years. As giftwrap. As food wrap. Tied pointedly around an arm, or pointlessly to the strap of a handbag.

As a speedy cause of death in an open-topped motorcar. As a way to signal surrender to an advancing army. As a face mask in the viral war you don't even know is coming yet.

Dramatically. Elegantly. Enthusiastically. Self-consciously, fearing it might be *a bit much*. Treacherously. Flirtatiously. Apologetically. Mysteriously. Casually. Cozily. Posily. Disposedly. Like you're miles outside of your comfort zone, or like you've worn one every damn day of your life.

There are a hundred different ways to wear a scarf—and yet up they pile, like gauzy spaghetti, clinging to the very fringes of usefulness, knowing that at any minute they will be wound into a ball, shoved into a tote bag and sent away. For being diaphanous and superfluous, for taking up too much space.

But they'll earn their keep if you let them; will wiggle into the cracks in your life and wait for when you need them most. *Give scarves a chance*, Michael would implore his customers as they passed by the chest that sat in the corner of the shop. A few blessed regulars would make a beeline for the box, plunging their arms into the lucky dip of chiffon and tassels and buying the most unlikely spoils. But for the most part, scarves were the writhing infestation he could never quite keep on top of.

Michael never bought them himself, of course. He wasn't a scarf person.

**31**

"Excuse me?"

The woman in front of Gwen was agitated, shifting slightly from one foot to the other. She craned her neck to look around the shop while Gwen gave the customer in front his change.

People were often agitated in here, and in a cruel streak of malice she found their urgency only made her want to move more slowly.

It was often the people who had nowhere to be that moved fastest, she'd noticed. The ones her mother called "poor souls" or "people with problems," as she discreetly crossed the road in case their problems were infectious. You saw them coming, charging down the pavement at double speed, swinging their rigid arms in military parody. They would stride purposefully up and down the length of the shop, eyes darting between the racks, picking up objects at random before charging out again.

Sometimes they stole something, sometimes they didn't. Sometimes they would ask to take things for free, which should have been better but felt worse. Because then it became a judgment call. Then, she would have to watch one of the store managers listen to the plea, watch them pretending not to scan for track marks and slurred words, clothes that looked too clean or a tone that sounded too cheerful. Too entitled. Not quite desperate enough. Drawing the arbitrary line between Charity with a capital *c* and just plain old charity, while the irony throbbed through the room like a disco beat.

Michael was reliably inconsistent. Gwen had seen him give away whole outfits on some occasions, merrily tossing in a bonus scarf and a pair of leather driving gloves "to really set off that jumper." But on other days he would issue a clipped apology and sweep the asker out of the door like crumbs, muttering, "We are not the Chancers and Scoundrels Outfitters' Society," or some pompous variation, while other customers listened, aghast. Lise usually let them take whatever they wanted.

But this woman was agitated for different reasons.

"My mother thinks she might have donated something by accident," she explained. "A clock. Big thing, gold? It's been in the family for years, used to be my grandad's. Worth a bit. A lot, between you and me. She says she might have brought it in here, but honestly who knows." The woman leaned in and lowered her voice to a stage whisper. "She's not all there, I'm afraid. For-gets things."

Then, louder again, "Don't you, Mum? Forget things?"

Only now did Gwen notice an older woman, hovering behind. She had the same anxious expression as the younger face but in deeper relief, like a pencil tracing. The older woman nodded, attempted a wan smile. Despite the muggy June heat outside, she was wearing a purplish coat, zipped up to the neck, quilted and embroidered with small flowers over the pockets. Gwen recog-nized it as having been on the shop's racks a few weeks before.

"I do," said the woman, with an apologetic shake of her head. "I get things wrong. Or so's I'm told."

"I haven't seen one I'm afra—" Gwen began, but the woman went on, wide-eyed, as though pressed to explain herself.

"It's all my silly fault, I didn't mean to . . . it was my dad's you see, he loved that clock, used to say it brought the sunshine. I wanted to get it back to him for his birthday, but I—I got confused, I don't know—put it in with my Henry's clothes, you know, Henry's old pullovers? Still good but he doesn't like green, never has, daft sod, and yet I keep on buying them for him don't I!" she clucked, fondly. "So I buy them here then I only end up bringing them back here, have for years, but I wasn't supposed to bring the clock—the clock was Dad's and I look after it now so the men can't . . . the men won't . . . it's worth a bob, did you know? *Japy Frères,* it's a very good make. French! From before the war. Oh and so beautiful, it is, absolutely beautiful—gold, shaped like the sun, far too posh for me really, but I'd never sell it of course, it ought to be on the wall, needs to stay on the wall or he'll be so . . ." The woman's voice had become high and wavery now, spiked with panic, and she fumbled in her handbag to produce a small coin purse. "I'm sorry, I know it's for the charity, I do feel rotten. I'll gladly buy it back if you've not priced it too high, although of course you'd be within your right, it's worth a bundle and I know it's all for charity, but please—oh please . . ."

She trailed off at this, her hands trembling around the purse, and looked urgently around the shop as though the clock might be being sold from under her as they spoke. Gwen felt her own heart pounding.

"Have you seen a clock?" she asked in the back room.

"I tend to use my phone for that these days," replied St. Michael, who was carefully coloring with felt-tip pens on an A4 piece of paper that read *We No Longer Accept Bedding or Bathroom Items* in extravagant swirls. Michael prided himself on the shop's handmade signage. Head Office had long since stopped bothering to send official branded materials.

Brian was in his favorite spot, poised over the CCTV monitor. He looked at the clock on the wall above Gwen's head, and said, helpfully, "Two forty-five."

"No, no—a big, gold clock? Has anyone seen one? A woman is saying she donated it by accident."

At this, Michael looked up and said, "Nicholas, didn't I hear you had a big clock?"

Brian snorted. Gwen made a noise like a strangled seal.

She hadn't noticed him in the room. Besides the notification (who did their postcoital admin on *LinkedIn*?) she hadn't seen or spoken to Nicholas since waving him off in the small hours of last Saturday morning. She had been reliably assured by the schedule that their paths wouldn't cross all week—and yet here he was, sitting on the floor in a pile of coats, studiously wet-wiping a gravy boat.

Nicholas cleared his throat, in a great show of phlegmy theatrics. "Uhhhughgh." This went on for some time. "Harrghh ahaggh. Ahem."

Then, finally, once the others had lost interest and gone back to their activities, he said: "No? I mean, uh, well—there *was* a clock."

"A big gold one?" asked Gwen. "Donated a couple of days ago?"

"Like, medium-sized, I'd say? And I suppose you could call it gold-*toned*, although it was really more of a . . . uh, gilded bronze. Just gold leaf, overlaid on wood—"

"Do you have it?" Gwen cut him off, keen for the exchange to be over.

More throat-clearing. "No, not as such," Nicholas replied.

"What does that mean?"

"Obviously it means I don't have it, Gwen."

"But you did have it?"

"It . . . passed briefly through my possession, sure. I sourced it, and now it's found a new home with a client. It was a very desirable piece. American, I'd guess. Mid-century modern, circa roughly 1955 was my estima—"

"You *sourced* it? By which you mean . . . what, you wrote £2.99 on the price tag and then bought it yourself?"

"Obviously it wasn't like, *valuable* or anything," he held up his hands in protest. "Not without expert market positioning."

"Well, according to the woman's daughter, it's very valuable. Financially and sentimentally." She lowered her voice, conscious that the customers were only a few feet away and the door was ajar. "I think you need to give it back."

"No can do on that score I'm afraid, sorry, Gwen."

"Nicholas. She has dementia, from the sounds of it. She's quite upset."

"Sure, totally. Obviously that's super tough." He was nodding like a politician at a constituency surgery. "But I'm afraid it's going to be tricky to do anything about it at this stage, you know?"

"No, I don't know," she hissed. "We're a mental health charity. I can't go back out there and tell her whoops, sorry, our resident Del Boy has snagged your family heirloom for personal profit."

Nicholas's face clouded at this. He stood up.

"Look, Gwen. Obviously it's a real shame the lady made a mistake, I feel for her. But it's quite literally out of my hands. If I still had it, I swear, I'd happily sell it back to her."

"You mean *give* it back to her?"

"Obviously, that's what I said, I'd happily get it back to her. But maybe it's, like, the circle of life? The clock has found a new home now. Somewhere with great spirit, somewhere really sympathetic to its history."

She could feel furious tears begin to prickle at the corners of her eyes. Gwen considered it one of the great unfairnesses of her life, that she always cried when she was angry, which made her look weak, and rarely when she was sad, which made her look cold and uncaring. She narrowed her eyes at him, willing her ducts closed.

"Where?"

"I can't tell you, Gwen, client confidentiality."

"For *fuck's sake* Nicholas"—at this, St. Michael and Brian both looked up again—"*WHERE?*"

He swallowed, and shrugged. "The Boar and Balls on High Holborn."

"Right." She turned on her heel and stormed back into the shop, a move that would have been more effective if she hadn't clipped her shoulder painfully on a rack of clothes hangers as she did so.

The daughter and her mother were waiting. One looked impatient, the other apologetic. "I'm afraid . . ." Gwen began, but the truth was just too unbelievable.

She began to construct the lie—snapped up this morning, no way to trace the customer, huge apologies, what a terrible shame—but something stopped her. The woman in the purple coat wasn't even very old, she realized, looking at her more closely. Not much older than her own mother. She had a similar expression of perpetual half-worry, the same nervous flutter around the eyelids. But where Marjorie's face tended to be clouded with a kind of preemptive displeasure, forever on the lookout for something to be vexed by, this woman merely looked exhausted by life. She smiled hopefully at Gwen, a gummy smile. Her daughter drummed her long nails on the counter.

"I'm afraid we think it may have been sent to one of our other stores," she told them. "But we're hopeful we should be able to get it back for you. Could you leave your contact details and we'll get in touch as soon as we find out more?"

They did so, the daughter watching closely over her mother's shoulder as she noted her name and telephone number. *Janet McAffery*, the woman wrote in a shaky cursive. "That's your maiden name, Mum," the daughter pointed out, making a grab for the pen. But Janet snatched it away. "The clock knows me as a McAffery," she replied, as though this was obvious. The daughter opened her mouth to say something else, then clearly thought better of it.

They gave their thanks and left the shop together, the daughter striding ahead and Janet McAffery shuffling behind.

*

At the end of the shift, Nicholas dropped a paper napkin onto the counter in front of her. *Forgive me x*, it said, in blobby ink.

Gwen picked it up and blew her nose into it, in front of him, as she left the shop. For the first time in a very long time, she felt almost assertive. The effect was diminished when she got home and discovered she had ink smeared across her nose, but only slightly.

# Pickle Forks

There were four of them, in a creamy cardboard box flecked with age spots. "Pickle forks" said the little felt-tipped sign in front of them on the shelf. It had an air of exasperation, that sign, as though one too many flummoxed customers had been to the till to inquire what they *were*. But Tim liked to think he'd have known even without the sign. Tim was into pickling now.

Previously it had been fermenting. Kefir, kombucha, kimchi, kvass. But the level of nurture and maintenance required was too much, on par with having a medium-sized family pet. All the burping and feeding and maintenance of the scoby (his symbiotic culture of bacteria and yeast had been christened "Scoby Doo," a move that struck Tim as depressingly unoriginal even as he was doing it) was endless. He needed a hobby with a greater reward-to-effort ratio.

Before fermenting it had been sourdough, which had ended when he lost his starter, Clint Yeastwood, in the breakup. Tim had spent hours finessing his craft, experimenting with hydration levels and posting crumb shots to Instagram. Competing with other dough bros over the size of his rise and the gape of his holes.

Before that, it had been curing his own salmon—the fumes from his improvised smokehouse in the utility room might not have been to everyone's taste, but she'd enjoyed the results and couldn't pretend she hadn't—and before that, building a wood-fired pizza oven out of reclaimed bricks. Before that, homebrew. Before that, latte art.

Before that, ketamine. Before that, rolling his own sushi with a little bamboo mat.

But now, pickles. He had started with the entry-level stuff: cucumber, onion, beetroot, the withered old carrots that knocked around his crisper drawer. But quickly he began to branch out, pickling cauliflower florets, watermelon rind, grapes, even herbs. He started to see the world as a series of would-be, could-be pickles, eyeing the produce in his local corner shop as if through a pair of vinegar goggles. Could he pickle tomatoes? Bananas? Cheese? Was there any food that wasn't enhanced by a little time and a lot of tang?

The whole thing was reminiscent of the time his family had bought their first toaster, and ten-year-old Tim had eaten nothing but toast-based meals—beans on toast, tuna on toast, shepherd's pie on toast, Mars Bar on toast—for a solid month. Eventually, severe constipation (a very solid month) had forced his mother to take him to the GP, and the toast had been rationed to breakfast time only. But Tim still liked to commit to a project wholeheartedly. It was the main reason the breakup had bothered him so much.

Now the top two shelves of his fridge were entirely given over to pickle jars of varying size and vintage, and the act of making food to accompany his pickles was interesting him less and less compared to the pickling process itself. He was going through a packet of antacids every few days, and his fingers smelled perpetually of vinegar and cloves—something his last Hinge date had actually remarked upon. At the time he had hoped she might not have meant it in a negative way, but now three days had passed without a message so he was forced to conclude she must have.

Still, at least this was one aspect he could work on. Because now, he didn't just have pickles. He had pickle forks.

## 32

*A chat* was how Connie's friend had phrased it in the email. Let's meet for a chat! ok? Fab.

Like many superiors Gwen had worked with over the years, Saskia seemed to communicate as though niceties and punctuation were a sign of weakness and excess spare time. She messaged in brusque staccato sentences that rarely contained all the necessary info, leaping between platforms and channels at random. HI Gwyn still on for tmrw, an anonymous text asked at 11 p.m. last night. Running late b there in 10 announced an unknown number in her WhatsApp. She was mildly surprised to see Saskia walk into the café at all.

The woman who walked in was elegantly rumpled in the same way as Connie but about ten years younger, with an expensive-looking ash-blond blow-dry streaked with purposeful gray. She was wearing flared jeans, white cowboy boots and a Motörhead T-shirt with a tiny, embellished waistcoat and an oversized blazer on top. Gwen tugged at her dress, feeling painfully provincial.

"Saskia? Gwen. Lovely to meet you."

She stuck her hand out to shake, but Saskia seized her by the shoulders and pulled her in for a double-cheek kiss. Gwen's hand ended up briefly inside Saskia's blazer, where it met with a warm, silken lining. It felt nice to be Saskia. She retracted it quickly.

"Hi hiii, so glad we could do this," Saskia continued to look at her phone as she settled herself in her chair and removed her jacket, then placed it facedown on the table and flipped her gaze up to Gwen as though a meter had started. "Connie's told me amazing things."

*Amazing things.*

"Some of them true, I hope!" replied Gwen, and Saskia gave a husky laugh.

"Connie *only* speaks the truth. Shall we get coffee? Or . . . wine?" She was looking around her now, seeming to expect a waiter to appear in what was clearly a chain coffee shop. Behind the counter, a blue-haired barista was watching videos on their phone.

"Coffee is fine for me, thanks," said Gwen, in case this was a test. Though wine could as easily be the pass as the fail.

"Fab. And cake? Let's get cake, shall we? Yes."

Gwen's lower intestine had performed its usual nervous pyrotechnics in the café toilet about fifteen minutes earlier, but she sensed that refusing cake would be a foolish move. Not just for the job, but possibly for feminism. She chose carrot and pistachio loaf, feeling this to be the most businesslike option on offer. Saskia looked mildly disdainful and asked for a brownie.

Provisions secured—Saskia had sent Gwen to the counter with her debit card, giving things a distinct "treat day with Auntie" air that didn't exactly help matters—they embarked on small talk. Saskia was effusive, scatty, and lavishly indiscreet. Gwen was tense, on the lookout for the moment at which "chat" might suddenly give way to interview. It felt a little like riding a log flume, bracing herself for the drop.

But after nearly an hour of cruising in the shallows, Saskia was displaying no signs of suddenly asking her to rustle up a presentation deck. They'd talked about where each of them was from ("Us Home Counties evacuees have to stick together!" said Saskia, with no apparent trace of irony); places they had lived ("I thought about moving to Bristol, once," said Gwen. "But I didn't."); how each of them knew Connie, wasn't Connie great, didn't you want to *be* Connie when you grew up; Saskia's husband's book group ("It's an all-male group but they only read female authors"); the perils of running a Southwold Airbnb remotely; and everything that was wrong with vegan cheese. "Like Blu-tack dipped in Wotsit dust," said Gwen, at which Saskia snorted approval.

Just as Gwen was wondering if Connie had set her up on an interview not for a job but for a high-end swingers' community, Saskia said: "So. Let me tell you about Fred."

"Is Fred your partner?" Gwen asked. "Or . . . pet?"

Saskia squinted at her. "Fred is the *company*," she replied. Then she began hooting with laughter. "So yes, in a way!"

"I'm so sorry!" blustered Gwen. "Connie never actually said. Is it an acronym?"

"No, no no," said Saskia. "Just Fred. But it's all lowercase."

"Ah," Gwen said, as though this explained it. "Lovely."

"So Gwen, what you'll be doing," said Saskia—hang on, *was that it? was she hired?*—"is providing a kind of semi-creative, semi-logistical, semi . . . managerial lead support role. We're at a really exciting point, about to start our first round of investment, and so I need someone really *on it* in the office while I'm running around fluttering my lashes at the money men. Someone who can take charge and bring their own vision to the mix. Who doesn't need to be babysat, you know?"

"Sure, absolutely," said Gwen, wishing she had paid for her own coffee.

"But I know you must have your fingers in a hundred pies! So I was thinking we could keep it really flexible at first," Saskia went on. "See how much you want to pick up, let you fit it in around other projects."

"Mm-hmm," said Gwen, nodding as though she might have other projects.

"I'd set you up in our office space, of course," Saskia said. "I think it really helps in those early days to be in the same place, don't you think? Throw ideas around, see what sticks. We're looking at expanding to bigger premises soon, but of course that all hinges on the funds!"

"Of course," echoed Gwen. "So where is Fred"—*was it possible to pronounce things in lowercase?*—"based right now?"

"Gospel Oak," said Saskia. "That wouldn't be too much of a trek, would it?"

No, she insisted, it wouldn't. Saskia continued, but Gwen wasn't listening, because images of a very different kind of working life were forming in her mind. A life where she would gad about the rarefied perimeters of Zone Two like a graceful swan, never having to venture into the murk of the city proper. She would flit between the well-preserved older women of Hampstead, with their taut cheekbones and dewy, pickled appearance. She could walk up to the Heath on her lunch hour, maybe swim in the ladies' pond before work. That was a thing people did, wasn't it? Ponds.

Gwen pictured herself taking meetings at pavement cafés, with reeds in her hair and a baguette sticking out of her handbag. Perhaps this was the reward she deserved, after seven years of strip lights and carpet tiles and festering doughnut platters, of "chemistry sessions" with men who walked around the office in their socks. This could be the pivotal meeting she looked back on a decade down the line, as the point at which she gathered up the straggling ends of her life and started to weave a beautiful new future.

"I'll send you the decks over," Saskia was saying now. "What would be really great is if you could work up a few ideas by Thursday so that I have something to show Giles"—*who was Giles?*—"and come into the office on Friday to chat them through. Then we can get you going on the other digital properties next week."

Digital properties. She had digital properties now. And an office. And a Giles. Gwen nodded, made affirmative noises, gathered up a few stray cake crumbs with the pad of a finger.

"Does that work with your other commitments?" asked Saskia.

She thought about her other commitments. She pictured Brenda and Harvey wearing Bluetooth headsets, wiping down piles of old James Pattersons around a long, glass conference table. Asha tapping out an impatient email to ask for her take on the latest conspiracy theory about a fake celebrity baby. Customers in suits and bowler hats, leaving crisp packets in the shoe display, and mystery smears on the changing room mirror.

"Sure," she said. "That should be fine."

Saskia smiled broadly, bearing a glamorous gap in her two front teeth. "Great, great. Wonderful."

It was only afterward, as Gwen watched Saskia leave and then walked back to the counter to buy a brownie of her own, that she realized she had no idea what the company did. Or made. Or was.

In an act of blithe optimism, she typed "fred" into Google. It didn't help.

# Disposable Camera

Finn was an artist. Finn was an artist in the same way all his friends were artists, which is to say that he believed he had something vital and urgent to communicate with the world but hadn't figured out what it was yet.

He had dabbled in various mediums—clay, tapestry, tie-dye, TikTok—but was yet to settle on the form that expressed his truest self, and would also fit into the room in a Clapton houseshare that he unofficially sublet from an Aussie drag queen. Barbie Q Prawn was rarely there at night but had strong feelings about vegetable dyes near her lace-front wigs.

Finn had no qualms about monetizing his work in progress, because everyone knew the idea that art should be given away for free was a neoliberal scam. As a result, his friends bought a lot of his work and he was obliged to buy quite a lot of theirs back. This meant that he had begun to lose track of which things he'd actually created and which had been merely acquired.

"It's an interesting thought though, isn't it?" he'd said to Li recently. "By recognizing the value of a work and giving it a platform, am I not in some ways its true creator?"

"No," she'd replied. "It's my painting because I painted it. Look," she said, nudging the canvas with the tip of her clog, triggering a small shower of glitter. "It has my name on it, next to the fallopian tubes."

When Finn found the disposable camera, he was thrilled at it as an object in its own right. Look at it, all plasticky and gray! A relic from a time when photography was only for special occasions—an optional add-on, rather than the metric by which the ups and downs of everyday life were measured.

Although Brenda pointed out that you could still buy disposable cameras—they sold them in the chemist, next to the insect repellent and travel sickness bands—Finn bought this one for its authenticity. For the faded Fujifilm logo and the small warning label on the side that read "Keep cool."

At first he intended to take it to parties and capture his friends through a medium most befitting their cycling shorts and bucket hats. But he was even more delighted when he discovered that the film inside was already full. Or rather, when Brenda showed him the little window with the number—"27," so weirdly arbitrary and yet maybe somehow symbolic?—in the same way she had taught him about chip and pin on his very first shift, when he had asked a confused older customer to "just tap when you're ready, please." Finn and Brenda were good friends.

The idea of this little plastic box having contained someone else's memories for the past twenty years was thrillingly romantic to Finn, who had a fatalistic streak that had been cultivated by a recent fling with an amateur shaman, and a voyeuristic streak that had been cultivated by a single father who dated widely and didn't believe in locked doors. Maybe this would be his art?

"Reminds me, I once gave my camera to a bloke on holiday who looked exactly like Steven Seagal" said Brenda, as she rung it through the till for him. "And when we got the photos back, instead of Roy and I at the Parthenon, they were entirely of his— Hello, love, the gray sweatshirt was it? On my way."

By the time Finn took the camera to the chemist, he had hyped up its contents to an unhelpful degree. He imagined scandal, murder, impossibly beautiful people doing dastardly deeds—or else quietly romantic scenes of nothing, the kind that made it into galleries and centerfolds in the *Guardian*. Gas stations in remote locales that could just as easily be the US or the USSR. Boxy old cars speeding down sepia-tinged highways and glass-eyed children clutching teddy bears on dirt-track roads.

He was disappointed, then, when the photos revealed a series of normal-eyed children, clutching Slush Puppies in a water park.

There were individual portraits (one child turning his eyelids inside out while bearing his lower teeth at the camera) and group shots (the same child, clawing at a small girl's hair while she screamed). There were still lifes, too: a portion of chips with ketchup and mayonnaise; a yellow Teletubby toy, half-buried in sand; and a pair of feet, striped brown and white with tan lines, waving aloft against a background of cloudy gray sky. The feet were almost interesting, Finn decided, imagining the caption he could spin along the lines of "conceptions of selfhood in a pre-smartphone era."

Then he flipped to the penultimate photo and was confronted by a blurry image of what seemed to be a naked arse, half-obscured by bushes, its owner entangled with a woman holding a Bacardi Breezer at arm's length like a grenade. It was beautiful, exquisite in its grubbiness.

Finn took in the period detail—the hair gel, the chainmail halter top, the cargo trousers in a heap around a pair of Reebok Classics—and decided to put this one in a frame. Barbie Q would love it. Possibly Brenda would too.

## 33

Gwen was stressed. After some extensive digital potholing, she had managed to locate Saskia on Facebook, LinkedIn, and as an active member of an interior design message board called "Farrow & Ballers NW3." But clarity on fred (*fredd? frhed?*) was not forthcoming.

If the job required special technical knowledge that Gwen didn't have, surely it would have come up by now. Saskia had seen her CV. She knew that Gwen's career path was a gentle meander from temp receptionist work, slowly up through the ranks at a media monitoring agency and then on to a consultancy that specialized in public awareness campaigns for local councils ("She tells people when to put their bins out," Marjorie had explained to a neighbor) before getting her job at Invigorate. Which meant she could probably rule out any need for a working knowledge of the endocrine system or, say, an HGV licence.

But even assuming fred was just another breed of ambiguous content marketing enterprise—which it might not be!—Gwen wasn't sure if that was a job she wanted to do anymore. If she ever had. For Saskia to assume Gwen would simply hop aboard without so much as a cursory waft of a mission statement was, in hindsight, rude.

Ruder still was the fact that no deck had materialized, twenty-four hours later, and she was about to write the whole thing off as a caffeinated mirage when an email arrived at midnight.

Deets 4 you! xS it said. Gwen had always admired people cool enough to put the kiss before their initial.

Attached to the email were several documents—a set of branding guidelines featuring Pantone references for various shades of putty and taupe; a Tone of Voice document which took pains to explain that fred was "witty but warm, friendly but authoritative, colloquial but not over-casual," and a one-pager headed "who is fred?" Gwen sent up a silent prayer as she opened it.

> fred is a brand-new experience, it read. fred is not one-size-fits-all. fred is for all the people you are. fred is for your yesterday, your today, and your tomorrow.

"Fucksake," breathed Gwen.

> fred is storytelling for people who don't have time for stories. fred is a new type of family. fred is the friend you wish you'd made, and the lover you should never have let get away.

Gwen dug her fingernails into her thigh.

> fred is rooted in nature, but optimized by science. fred is committed to radical transparency. fred is not afraid to cause a stir.

Gwen bit down hard on her knuckle.

> fred is an app

An app! Of course it was an app!

.... but not as you know it.

Just as she was on the verge of hurling her laptop at the wall, she noticed a URL at the bottom of the page. This led her to a holding page—sit tight, fred is coming—which was linked to an Instagram account—six taupe-toned tiles, each containing a fragment of the word "*fred*"—and a Twitter page, consisting of identical tweets to TV presenters and podcast hosts reading Hi @name, we'd love to tell you more about fred.

"Tell ME more about fred," Gwen begged the universe. She stared at a blank document until gray shapes started to dance before her eyes. She wrote three generic paragraphs about achieving cut-through in an oversaturated digital landscape, then put them in size-14 font. She read a long article about a woman in Wisconsin who had become a millionaire by selling her used cleansing wipes to men on the internet. She went to bed.

In the morning she woke to find another email from Saskia, sent at 5:47 a.m.

It read: forgot to attach brief, soz ! xS

# Vase

It was the kind of object you'd notice in a room, and therefore the kind you'd notice missing.

About thirty centimeters high in curvaceous clay, painted in vivid, splashy colors, with a chorus of fat tulips dancing around its swollen middle. A vase so decorative that it mostly sat empty, because it seemed to make a mockery of any real flowers placed within it.

For years it had been assumed to be a Clarice Cliff, until Lucinda's mother had taken it along to the *Antiques Roadshow* at Bramber Castle and been told, at some considerable dent to her pride, in front of Fiona Bruce and the Sunday night viewing public, that it wasn't.

"An admirer, no doubt!" the ceramics expert had said, trying to soften the blow, while her mother scowled at him the way she did when the dogs brought in a dead bird. "And it's such a good impression that it hardly matters!"

The vase had sat, for as long as she could remember, on her grandmother's mantelpiece, between a wedding photo of her parents—long since divorced of course, but hers had never been a family to let the truth get in the way of good optics—and a carriage clock, presented to her grandfather on his retirement from the Legal & General. The clock was supposedly valuable, although Lucinda had privately always thought it looked like the kind they gave away free with the premium life insurance policies. Maybe they'd had it blessed by June Whitfield.

The vase didn't strictly go with the rest of the room, in that it was bold and cheerful and the rest of the room looked like pursed lips in interior design form. Everything in shades of fawn, a prim antimacassar on the back of each armchair and a cut-glass apple on the side table where the remote control should be.

Once, when she couldn't have been older than four, Lucinda had vomited behind the settee on Easter Sunday. A sticky brown torrent of half-chewed Cadbury's, quickly diluted by floods of tears. She remembered the shouts and she remembered the smack—just one, delivered outside the back door, a *thwack* that seemed to reverberate around the entire cul-de-sac, so that the shame reached her before the pain did.

She remembered her mother, white-lipped with fury on the drive home, and she remembered the brand-new carpet on their next visit, fawn with small pink roses, which nobody mentioned despite the unmistakable smell of plasticky underlay that hung in the air. She'd been relieved not to have to confront the ghost of her crime, scrubbed into submission by her grandparents' cleaning lady—but also hurt, once she discovered that they would rather rip everything out and start again than let the house bear the mark of her existence. Their adopted grandchild.

Not long after this, the stealing began. Small, inconsequential things at first—stock cubes from the box in the pantry, leaflets from the rack at the post office, tampons from her mother's dressing table drawer, which looked like giant versions of the caramel finger in the Quality Street tin but turned out to be nothing more exciting than teddy bear stuffing come loose. Then bigger things, relishing the fizz of adrenaline with each tiny new trophy. Change from the pot her father kept in his study. A brand-new tortoiseshell hairclip from a classmate after PE. Nail polishes, freed with a sly twist of hand from the front of magazines in the newsagent.

She kept them all in a shoebox under her bed, only taking them out to look at as a special treat, in her lowest moments, or when the shouting and crashing from downstairs became too much. For a long time she kept her prizes small, rationalizing to herself that as long as everything she took could be safely contained in one box, then so could the guilt.

In her teens the objects became bigger but the thefts more sporadic, more targeted. She used them not so much to gain something as to release something, a choking, pent-up something, the way her friends sometimes took razor blades to their thighs. A wallet from the favorite teacher who humiliated her during a dorm inspection. A bracelet from the stiff-haired woman who threaded a predatory finger through her father's belt loops at the parents' weekend. Lipsticks from the village chemist where they refused to sell her condoms. Chanel earrings from the drunk cousin who cornered her at the golden wedding party, touched her hair, and asked if it was time for her to "go find her real family."

Nowadays she did it so rarely that it shocked her each time the impulse returned. Sometimes it was the first way she knew she was angry—a telltale twitch that arrived in her fingers, where other people might feel tears spring to their eyes.

Last night, when she'd heard vile, muttered words about her escape the kitchen (her grandmother was deaf now, though she refused to admit it), she had sat perfectly still and balled them into fists until her knuckles turned white, listening to the tick of the carriage clock for a few seconds before giving herself over to the urge.

This morning, after she had wrapped it carefully in newspaper, placed it at the bottom of a carrier bag and deposited it calmly on the charity shop counter—"A few bits of old junk for you!"—her hands had trembled for an hour. She pulled the frayed cuffs of her sweatshirt down over them now, as her mother appeared in the doorway.

"Lucinda," she asked sharply, holding one hand over the landline that nobody else ever called on. "Do you have any idea where Grandma's vase is? The Clari— the colorful one, from the mantelpiece."

Lucinda furrowed her brow in mock recollection, then replied, "Vase? Nope. No idea."

Her mother held her eye for a second, just long enough to let the understanding pass between them.

She was lying. But it was such a good impression, it hardly mattered.

## 34

The office address wasn't, as she had assumed, a neat little Hampstead loft space nestled above an estate agents and a branch of JoJo Maman Bébé, but a house. Or at least, it looked like a house. A white sugar cube of modernist real estate, perched at the end of a Victorian terrace.

Saskia opened the door with her phone lodged between shoulder and ear, mouthing, "Hi, hiii," at Gwen in an apologetic grimace. She was wearing—improbably, given that it was twenty-seven degrees Celsius outside—a pair of leather trousers and a voluminous white poet's blouse. A neon baseball cap and pair of chunky, crayon-bright trainers didn't so much complete the look as give the impression of Lord Byron turned into a Pez dispenser.

Once through the door, Gwen had it confirmed that what looked like a house from the outside was very definitely a house on the inside. A vast bunch of hydrangeas sat on a table in the parqueted hallway, which stretched to a gleaming white glass-roofed kitchen beyond. Perhaps the office was nearby, and they were meeting here before walking there? Perhaps Gwen had accidentally interviewed for a job as Saskia's new nanny.

While Saskia continued her phone call with a flurry of *yeah yes yep yuh-huhs*, Gwen looked at herself in a big, round mirror. Her fringe was flicking in two separate directions and she couldn't tell where her heat sweats ended and her nervous sweats began. She was very aware of the smell of her own bra.

Saskia finally hung up and turned to greet her. "Hello! Sorry! Welcome to the madhouse!" Gwen looked around for signs of madness but couldn't see anything beyond an unwashed coffee mug and a copy of *Elle Decoration*, slightly askew.

"So glad you're here," Saskia continued. "There's just, *argh,* so much to do, it'll be amazing to have another pair of hands to share the load. Coffee? Wine?"

It was 10 a.m. Gwen wondered if the wine thing was a nervous tic. She asked for a glass of water, and Saskia decanted some from a Brita jug into a very small tumbler. Gwen drank it in two gulps and was left clutching the empty glass as Saskia led her out, confusingly, into the garden.

"And here . . . is the office," announced Saskia with a "ta-da" flourish, gesturing toward a modest shepherd's hut at the bottom of the garden, painted in attractive duck-egg blue.

"The . . . ? Oh! Oh, right. I see," said Gwen, because suddenly she did see. Suddenly a lot of things made sense.

"Of course I'm in and out all day, so you'll have the space to yourself a lot," said Saskia, leading her to the hut and kicking open the door, which stuck a little in the frame. Gwen followed her in. "Space" was an interesting choice of word. Inside the hut smelled strongly, if not unpleasantly, of bark chippings. There were two desks, positioned at right angles, two expensive-looking wheelie chairs with flexible lumbar support, a Dyson fan, a few tins of paint and a huge plastic sack with a label on it reading *Premium Luxury Mulch.*

"Of course it's a bit rough around the edges, but so much nicer than a horrible soulless corporate fish tank, isn't it?" said Saskia. Gwen was struck with sudden longing for her horrible soulless corporate fish tank. At Invigorate she may have been contractually obliged to keep her desk clear, but at least nobody ever tried to store mulch underneath it. Saskia appeared to take Gwen's silence as awestruck delight, and she went on.

"The Wi-Fi is a bit spotty out here, but if you're struggling you can always nip into the snug to send emails and things. Graham won't mind. And you're welcome to use the Nespresso whenever you like, as long as Magdalena isn't cleaning it, and of course I'll keep the snack trough fully stocked." Here she indicated a small wicker Fortnum & Mason hamper on the desk, containing a pouch of Cadbury Miniature Heroes and a multipack of Popchips. "Got to keep my worker bee fueled!"

At that moment, a middle-aged man in a gray tank top, combat shorts, and Timberland boots appeared beyond the window wielding a chainsaw. *Ah,* thought Gwen, calmly. *This is how I die.*

"Is that Graham?" she asked, as the man continued to the far side of the garden and began mauling a tree.

"Graham? What, where?" Saskia jumped slightly. "Oh! No, that's Olek. The garden man."

Olek the Garden Man sounded like a kid's TV show. What with the heat of the shepherd's hut and chocolate fumes wafting up from the snack trough, Gwen wondered if she was on the edge of a dissociative episode. *Gwen in the Shed. Gwen the Busy Worker Bee.* A ghoulish vision loomed into view of herself as a slack-jawed marionette, perched on Saskia's leathery knee. She felt faint.

"Shall we go through the deck?" Saskia was asking now, sitting on one of the ergonomic chairs and swiveling a little impatiently. Gwen sat down next to her—in the confines of the office-hut, their knees were almost touching—and opened her laptop. She was having flashbacks to an ill-fated appearance in the Pontins Junior Talent Jamboree thirty years earlier. She wondered if freestyling a three-minute disco routine to Belinda Carlisle's "Leave a Light On" could save her now.

Gwen stammered something about her ideas being rough—

*more pre-ideas, really, idea-ettes, speculative musings*—and killed a few seconds resizing the text and adjusting the angle of her laptop screen. Eventually she could stall no more, so she handed it over and watched Saskia reading, scrolling, murmuring words to herself softly as she went. *"Activation . . . Cross-pollination . . . Influencer outreach program . . ."*

Amazingly, Saskia seemed satisfied. "Great. Great. Giles will make much more sense of all this than me, I'm sure, but it looks like you've made a really solid start." Had she? Gwen wondered if she was really far cleverer than she imagined, or if everyone else was just more stupid.

She was about to ask who Giles was when Saskia announced: "Right, I've got to head. Sorry, manic day! But you can stay here, get settled in, man the phones."

"There are phones?" Gwen asked, turning to scan the shed for a switchboard or a bank of jangling rotary dials, and losing control of her chair. Saskia looked at her the way Eliza May Fletcher used to.

"No no, just an expression! Ha! Although actually, if you wouldn't mind keeping an ear out for the Amazon man, I'd appreciate it. And I'll send over a few little jobs for you to be going on with."

Then she disappeared. It was unclear whether she'd gone out, or was just skulking inside the house on more pressing domestic business. Gwen sat for a while, fanning her neck and questioning her life choices. At one point, Olek met her eye through the window and gave her a sympathetic little shrug.

After twenty minutes or so, a text arrived.

> So Gwyn what would be really great is if you
> can find some ©-free imagery we can use on
> the website—something that fits the fred visual
> guidelines and doesn't look like stock photos but
> also crucially is free ok ?? You're a lifesaver! xS

This was one of the jobs they had used to give interns at Invigorate. There had been a customary panic every time reception called to say a new intern had arrived, people scrabbling around to produce entry-level tasks that seemed proper enough to constitute "work experience" but which wouldn't take longer to explain than it would to simply do it themselves. They had called it "shit-scraping."

The interns were usually either sixth-formers from the local academy school or the nephews and nieces of agency board members. All were identifiable as such by their shoes; the former wore smart lace-ups and loafers, the latter pairs of artfully grubby Gucci trainers. When she saw them sitting at their desks after 6 p.m., the panic in their bright young eyes lit up by the glow of a laptop screen as they strained to complete whatever nonsense job they'd been given, Gwen had often felt the urge to confess. She wanted to lean over and whisper, "Psst . . . nobody cares!"

But to do so would have shattered the illusion and set the whole professional ecosystem crumbling. And then what? Instead, she would call them "a lifesaver" and send them home.

Now here she was, a lifesaver herself. In a shed, on an as-yet-unconfirmed salary for an as-yet-indefinable company, scraping what felt, very suspiciously, like shit. Or at least premium luxury mulch.

Slowly, half-expecting to change her mind at any minute, Gwen put her laptop back in her bag, stood up and left the shed. She waved a cautious goodbye to Olek as she crossed the garden and let herself quietly out of a side gate.

Then she ran.

# Tie

"I'm the first part in the play!" he said, bounding out of the gates with his PE bag trailing on the tarmac behind him.

"Do you mean the main part?" Greg asked.

"No, the first part! Roxy Robinson. I get killed right at the beginning."

"Killed? Straight away?"

"Well, splurged," explained Louie, patiently. "We shoot each other with squirty cream, Dad, not guns."

"Right," said Greg.

"Because we're only children, we can't have guns."

"Got it."

Louie had lines in the play at least—three of them, though they were mainly the word "boss." Still, he and Greg had fun perfecting the gangster accent—"*bawwwse*"—and discussing the way Roxy's chin might wobble in fear as he met his messy demise.

"I'll have to do some very good acting, won't I, Dad?" said Louie.

"Sure," agreed Greg.

"Because the thing is," Louie went on, "I actually really *like* squirty cream."

When it came to costume, Greg was reluctant to spend money on anything that was going to be seen for all of two minutes and then discarded on the floor of a Portakabin. Especially because *Bugsy Malone* had been chosen, surely at least in part, so the kids could wear their parents' too-big clothes and look adorable, without any tension between the families who could afford proper costumes and those who couldn't. Even the small contingent of the PTA who'd been complaining about the hypersexualization of Tallulah, and the group who had objected to the lack of non-dairy alternative splurge (there was a substantial overlap) couldn't fail to admit the whole thing would be cute.

Greg didn't know about this, however, because Greg didn't go to the meetings. Greg hadn't put his name down for walking bus duty and Greg never contributed to the WhatsApp group. He didn't know which of the children in the class had a nut allergy, or how to comb most effectively for nit eggs, or that in their bitchier moments, Gabriella and Shappi referred to him as a BMP. Bare Minimum Parent. Although they had also both admitted, after he made a rare appearance at Milo Pevensie's swimageddon birthday party in a pair of trunks, that given the chance, they both *would*.

Not having any suitable ties in his own wardrobe—just an old knitted number from his mod days, and a moth-eaten paisley cravat—Greg took Louie to the charity shop near his school to source something. Which was how Roxy Robinson acquired a polyester navy-blue tie for £2.40, and how Greg saw Michael again for the first time in eleven years. Still looking a little too bright for his dingy surroundings, the way he once had in the all-night builders' café.

This kind of thing, Greg told himself, was how the helicopter parents got punished.

## 35

Gwen ran until she reached the end of Saskia's street, at which point her fitness levels overrode her adrenaline levels and she was forced to stop and walk. She tried not to picture her heart hammering wildly, perilously, against her rib cage, like one of those punch-ball balloons at a funfair.

Gwen had always believed that in situations of grave danger—a fire, say, or a zombie apocalypse—she would be able to tap into a kind of special Herculean strength reserve that would see her to safety. She was sad to discover this to be untrue. But for a few seconds at least, before her lungs filled with slime and her limbs began to scream in protest, it had felt kind of wonderful.

When had she last run anywhere? The memory of a cursed all-agency HIIT class loomed up, of Gwen being forced to do team-bonding ass crunches with a squad of junior account execs in skin-toned cycling shorts. But running for the hell of it? Running for the sake of running? Not since her twenties. Not since—and now it seemed blindingly obvious, her stomach plummeting as though she had stepped off a curb without realizing—not since Luke.

Now she walked, panting, until she reached the nearest parade of shops and found a café. That way, she rationalized, if she bumped into Saskia she would have a plausible cover story.

Being 11:05 a.m., the café was nearly empty. "Welcome! What

can I get you?" asked the man behind the counter before she'd had a chance to look at the menu. Gwen hated this. Flustered, she ordered a sandwich she didn't want and ate it resentfully on a bench.

As she chewed, she thought about the sandwich she wished she'd bought instead—concentrating so hard on the flavors and textures of the other sandwich that it turned the one in her mouth to sawdust and glue. Of the many thousands of meals she had eaten over the course of her life, Gwen would estimate that only 5 to 10 percent had caused her no regret at all. Around 20 percent were sources of such remorse that they had the power to ruin a whole evening, or holiday. The rest remained a nagging source of annoyance for anywhere up to two hours.

An ambulance was parked on the other side of the street, paramedics and rubberneckers huddled around an immobile figure on the pavement. Meanwhile, on a patch of grass no more than twenty feet away, a boot camp exercise group did star jumps. "One more! And another!" yelled their leader, and everything about their healthful vigor seemed obnoxious in the context.

Gwen averted her eyes from both groups, looking up at the sky instead. The moon was out in broad daylight, which was never not unnerving. A thin, watery trace of moon, looking almost sheepish as if to say, "I'm not supposed to be here."

"Neither am I," replied Gwen.

After the sandwich was finished, she took out her phone and tapped out an email to Saskia, explaining that she was very flattered to have been offered the job but sadly on second thoughts she didn't think that it *would* work with her other projects after all. Such a shame! She hit "Send" and held her breath as it whooshed from her outbox, not even bothering to go into Sent Items and read it back for tone and typos. She put her phone on airplane mode and immediately felt better.

On her way to the station, Gwen stopped at an ice cream van. It was a second-tier van that only seemed to stock off-brand ice creams ("Big Choc" instead of Magnums, "Brill" instead of Fabs), so in a fit of nostalgia she bought a lemonade lolly. It made her blissfully happy for as long as she was eating it, then thirsty and sticky afterward.

Arriving home, buzzing slightly on sugar and liberation, she found Heather from downstairs in the hallway, sorting post. "Hi, Heather!" she heard herself say.

"Hi, ah, Gwen," Heather replied, with a hint of a question mark, and Gwen was glad to be able to smile in confirmation that this was indeed her name. They exchanged banalities—*wasn't it hot, so hot, too hot, although now they'd said that of course it would rain*—and Heather said she hoped the kids hadn't made a lot of noise last night, and Gwen was pleased to reassure her that they hadn't (they had).

"That looks like something nice," said Heather, handing her a few pieces of post and pointing out the thick silver envelope on top. "Looks like an invite."

Gwen opened it there and then, feeling she owed Heather an answer. It *was* an invite, to the wedding of a university friend. Nell, someone Gwen had once been fairly close to, but had last seen across the room at a Christmas party the previous year, mouthing, "How are you? Catch you in a bit!" over an argument about the cancellation and subsequent reinstallation of "Baby It's Cold Outside." They hadn't caught each other in a bit. The wedding was next month.

"Ooh, a wedding! Jealous!" sighed Heather, and Gwen looked at her to see if she was joking. "Since the kids, we never get to dance anymore," she went on. "Used to love it! Now I'm lucky if he spins me round the kitchen. Anyway, you have fun."

Heather turned to go, and on impulse Gwen called to her. "I can babysit!"

Her neighbor looked taken aback.

"I mean, I could—if you ever needed someone. You know, give you a night out some time?" Gwen was panicking as she even suggested it. Could she remember the children's names, if pressed? *Something beginning with J?*

But Heather smiled, and said thank you. She'd bear that in mind.

# Tie

---

It wasn't the first time Michael had encountered an old flame in the shop—far from it—but it was the first time he'd needed to restrain a seven-year-old while it happened.

Michael was good with children, which surprised people. Kids responded well to his casual indifference, becoming needier for his approval the longer he pretended they didn't exist. So did the flames, although that was harder to keep up.

For a second he thought it was the sight of this man that had winded him. This man who looked so much like Greg, standing by Michael's tie rack. But then he looked down and realized it was in fact the small boy, who also looked like Greg, and who had just collided at high speed with his torso.

"Louie!" shouted the man, and Michael was irrationally wounded at this man who looked like Greg calling some child's name, some *stranger's* name, before his own. But then Michael looked at the boy who looked like Greg, who had dusted himself off and gone to wipe his snotty fingers over the sunglasses display, and he saw Greg's chin and Greg's nose and Greg's determined cowlick in his hair, and he understood. There was no longer only one Greg in the world, but multiples, and all had the power to hurt him.

"Careful now," Michael said to the boy in his dolorous Black Country accent. "There was a straight razor in that cabinet yesterday and we're not insured for parental neglect."

Greg smoothed his own determined cowlick—he had kept his hair, then, although the shade was now more salt, less pepper—and focused on Michael.

"All right, mate," he said softly, and chuckled. His voice held just a hint of the same inflection. "Fancy seeing you here."

"So you're back then, are you?" asked Michael. He was aiming for nonchalant but had gone in too strong. He knew his lips were twitching at the corners.

"Back from where?" asked Greg, frowning. "I haven't been anywhere." But the small, squirming figure between them looked like a souvenir from places Michael had certainly never traveled.

"Louie here is going to be in a play," Greg explained, clapping his son slightly too hard on the shoulders.

"*Bugsy Malone*!" yelled the child.

"That isn't a play, Louie, it's a *musical*," said Michael. "I hope your dad isn't coaching you. He thinks *Moulin Rouge* is about a Chinese warrior princess."

Using the word "dad" was a small leap, but he thought it would be less painful to assume than to ask and have it confirmed. The boy gawped at him. "How do you know my dad?" he asked. Nope, still painful.

"We were at school together," Greg answered quickly.

"Technically we weren't," Michael addressed the boy directly. "He was conjugating Latin verbs at the grammar, I was having my head flushed at the comp up the road."

"Well, we were at school *next to* each other," Greg conceded. "But you were always the brainy one." Michael didn't disagree.

"We kept being friends when we were grown-ups, too," Greg told Louie. "Although he was always a much better friend than me." He kept the same singsong tone, though Michael could feel the making of A Speech begin to color the air. "I was sometimes very . . . silly." But Louie had already lost interest in this personal history. He was now smearing up the valuables cabinet, which housed a Sega Megadrive, a dusty gift set of Clarins miniatures, a diamond ring in a small velvet box, and a Perspex brooch shaped like a glittery clam.

Greg turned back to face him. "I didn't know this was your gig now, Mickey!" he said, brightly.

He did, actually. Michael had told him about the shop the last time they had seen each other—2008, an awkward 5 p.m. catch-up in Soho that had been too late for coffee, too early for dinner, too bitter for booze, and too strained for any other substance to feel like a good idea. At that point, Michael hadn't been long out of the facility—he'd liked to call it this, *the facility*, with an eyebrow wiggle, in the hope people might assume he'd been drying out alongside a Libertine rather than sharing malted milks with a suicidal carpet fitter called Tony—and he'd applied for the job as a temporary stopgap, grateful there was no humiliating uniform and little chance of seeing anyone he knew.

Greg had laughed at the idea of him working in a charity shop, back then. Michael had laughed at the idea of Greg's third wife.

But Greg always got forgetful when he was anxious, it was a trademark of his. Exams at school had been hopeless, his stint as a new wave frontman even more so. The time they'd been hauled up in the magistrates' court he had genuinely got his own date of birth wrong. And the first time they'd kissed, around the back of The Rialto after a Fine Young Cannibals gig, it had seemingly slipped his mind for a full eighteen months afterward.

Greg was looking around now, his face unreadable. "Quite a place you've got here."

Most days, in his irascible way, Michael was exceedingly proud of the shop. He dressed it and primped it, protected it from the sullying forces of the customers. Entered it—so far fruitlessly—into awards with the Charity Retail Association. His passionate defense of "second chance saloons" was a party trick that had led more than one friend of a friend from the old Primrose Hill dinner party circuit to pitch up in rubber gloves for a shift or two, basking in the experience as though it were a detoxifying mud wrap for the soul.

But from Greg, who wore every second chance he was given like it was personal haute couture, the words were wounding. Michael wanted to scoop up the whole building and tuck it inside his jacket, away from judgment or ridicule.

"Thank you, Gregory," he said lightly. "Now I've met your baby, I suppose it's nice for you to meet mine."

"Are there more?" asked Greg.

"Oh, a whole brood! One in Kilburn, one in Golders Green. One in Streatham, one in Elephant and Castle."

Michael looked over at the child, who was now wearing a white blouson shirt with medieval sleeves, striking a pose in the full-length mirror. He looked like a tiny New Romantic. He looked like a tiny teenage Greg.

"Are there more?" asked Michael.

Greg laughed and shook his head. "Just Louie." His voice moved into a childish register as he turned to the boy and caught him in a mock-headlock, rubbing his knuckles over his brown hair. "But he's more than enough, aren't you L-man?"

Louie nodded, gravely. "I'm an armful," he told Michael. "It's like a handful, only more."

Michael nodded back. He sold Louie the tie at a 20 percent discount, which was unheard of on St. Michael's watch. Customers had found bloodstains before and not been offered more than ten.

"Give Mickey the money," Greg instructed, making eye contact with Michael as Louie tapped his father's card against the reader with the ease of the modern-day infant. "Tell him we'll come back and say hello again soon."

"You just told him!" giggled Louie, rolling his eyes.

"But I think he'll believe it more, coming from you," said Greg. Not meeting his eye this time.

"Break a leg with Bugsy," Michael told the boy, solemnly. "I'll look out for the review in *The Stage*."

"Good to see you, mate," said Greg, clapping a matey hand on Michael's arm and giving it a hard squeeze. The counter between them meant he had to reach slightly too far for this to look natural. "Nice to know you're here."

That was the trouble with working in retail, mused Michael after they'd left; it made you a sitting target. People always knew where to find you, if they wanted to.

Meanwhile, you—you ended up on edge forever. Tuned to the vibrations of every door swing, core aching from the effort of looking poised all day behind a plate-glass window. Sifting through the fallout of other people's past lives and failed relationships, all the time wondering if and when they'd walk in. Hoping that they wouldn't, and praying that they would.

## 36

Some volunteers made it their mission to entangle themselves in the lives of as many customers as possible. Finn was the worst for it, or the best, depending on your perspective. Barely a shift passed without at least two or three people popping in to update him on a relationship drama, a birthday gift, a dodgy mole.

"Oh *hey!*" he greeted every customer, indiscriminately, as though he shared an intimate personal history with them that only manners prevented him from discussing over the counter. He greeted Gwen this way. She secretly loved it.

There were customers that intrigued her too, from time to time. Like the woman who had donated a dress—a bright, floral midi—and apologized, darkly, for the aroma of burnt sage. Or the woman who had asked to know, in a high, quivery voice, why a certain book was priced so much lower than the others. "Is there a system? A set of criteria, or . . . ?"

After she'd left without the book in question, St. Michael had given Gwen a rare conspiratorial smirk and flipped to the back of the dust jacket. There she was, in pristine monochrome, hair swept unnaturally over one shoulder, lips parted in mock-naïveté. Gwen had started to laugh but Michael had taken a Sharpie and marked the book up an extra 50p.

"If it helps her." He had shrugged, slipping it back onto the shelf.

But generally, Gwen preferred anonymity. She liked to be a

sentient piece of furniture, observing the shop from stage left without feeling obliged to join in the action. Which made it all the more jarring, then, to see Suze walk in through the door one Sunday morning.

She looked extremely normal, was Gwen's first thought. Not the glossy "weekend lifestyle" version of Suze that lived in her head these days, in immaculately cut jeans and expensive trainers, sourdough under one arm and peonies under the other. She simply looked Suze-like. But seeing her in the shop still seemed surreal, like a human actor starring alongside cartoons.

"Oh *hey*!" said Finn.

"Hiya!" Suze greeted him brightly. Gwen hovered, wondering if hugging the customers was on St. Michael's list of verboten behaviors. But Suze pulled her into a one-armed embrace.

"Why are you here?" Gwen asked into her hair.

"I'm going for brunch at that new place in the railway arches." Gwen didn't know there was a new place in the railway arches. "I walked past and thought 'Hang on, that might be Gwen's shop,' and I peered in to see if you were here, and here you are."

"Here I am!" she echoed, fighting the urge to ask who Suze was having brunch with, and why it wasn't her.

"I'm Finn," said Finn, leaning over to shake her hand. "Have the potato hash, it's unreal."

"Was already planning to!" Suze told him. "Can't eat anywhere without looking a menu up in advance, obviously."

"Obviously," he grinned at her.

"I'm no amateur," she replied, her cheeks flushing in a way Gwen hadn't seen for years.

"Oh, I can tell." Finn actually winked.

"Where's Paul?" Gwen asked, crashing in like a bucket of iced water and immediately feeling bad about it.

Suze grimaced. "Golfing. In Wanstead. My husband is one hundred and three."

If anything, Finn looked happier at this revelation.

Connie emerged now with her arms full of skirts, just in time to hear Suze ask the inevitable.

"How's the job hunt going?" She mouthed the words "job hunt," delicately, as though it might be offensive to Gwen's new colleagues to suggest she wouldn't want to volunteer here forever.

"Oh, I've found her one!" announced Connie, striding up and throwing her arm around Gwen's shoulder in a way that was neither comfortable or normal. "With a friend who has a start-up. All sorted!"

"Oh. Nice!" replied Suze, looking amused, while Gwen stammered something vague about it only being a trial, let's not count our chickens, it might not work out. Suze and Connie both told her not to be so negative. Finn asked if Suze was on Instagram.

Suze left shortly afterward, having done a cursory circuit of the shop, picking up a few items out of politeness but ultimately buying nothing. They hugged again, Gwen squeezing her harder than usual in a way she hoped would say everything she couldn't.

"Have you seen the place up the road with the clothes all hanging on wires?" Suze asked as she left. "You should do that here."

Gwen said she'd pass the suggestion along.

# Jeans

---

The not-quite-jeans will be bought as "emergency trousers" by a woman who has sat down in a warm pile of pigeon shit, left by a pigeon who appears to be having about as bad a day as she is.

"It's lucky!" her friend will say, which everyone knows is the kind of crap only said to make you feel better about your misery, like "sickness means the baby is healthy!" or "nits only like clean hair!"

And anyway, the luck must be bestowed upon you from above. It doesn't count if you sit in it.

She will grab the almost-jeans in a huff because she is due at work in ten minutes and they are the only trousers in the charity shop in her size that don't have pseudo-graffiti down the sides or a diamanté affirmation across the arse. They will be unexpectedly comfortable—something about the roomy knees?—and to her surprise she will end up wearing them again. And again and again after that.

She will be wearing them on the day she finds herself sitting back on the same bench, long since washed clean by rain, taking the phone call she has been waiting for, hoping for, for months. So maybe pigeon shit is lucky after all.

## 37

Gwen had been on the reserve list, that much was obvious.

To receive a wedding invite at only a month's notice might, in other circumstances, have been the action of a cool, spontaneous couple throwing together a chill, last-minute celebration. But this was Neil and Nell, the kind of couple who sent out "new address" cards featuring multiple professional photos of their marble-topped kitchen island. Nell and Neil, who had met while leafleting for the Liberal Democrats in 2015 and been so smitten that even the embarrassment of having near-identical names couldn't keep them apart.

Besides, Gwen remembered seeing an engagement shoot—the pair of them flinging autumn leaves in the air before a soft-focus lens—at least eight months ago. She was definitely on the reserve list.

She was offered a plus-one with the invite, however, which softened the blow of being a seat filler slash matrimonial Tetris piece, but came with its own anxiety.

The idea of taking somebody from the shop crossed her mind. Connie would be the obvious choice, although Gwen didn't trust her not to spend the whole day talking loudly about the futility of marriage and the ubiquity of goat's cheese tartlets. Asha would be a safer bet. Since she'd returned to the shop they had worked several shifts together, Asha seeming a little more like her old self each time.

Although, Gwen realized, she had never really known Asha's "old" self at all—and she might not, once she felt well enough to take her old self back to work. Outside the context of the shop, would she want to hang out? Gwen cringed at the words "hang out," even as they formed within her own brain. The nine-year age gap between her and Asha seemed more important, somehow, than the twenty-five years between herself and Connie. As though the under-thirties existed in their own special biosphere, and must be protected at all costs from people who didn't understand NFTs or what constituted a "cute top." Maybe she could take her for lunches? But the notion of "taking" Asha, with her City salary and her quickfire curiosity and her rich, throaty laugh, anywhere, felt absurd.

"Why don't you just not go?" asked Asha, when Gwen told her about the wedding.

Oddly this hadn't occurred to her. Though it would have been easy enough to invent an excuse on a month's notice, she found she was grimly determined to see the thing through. She had a mission. She had a dress, even. A metallic thing, bought for last year's Invigorate Christmas party under the brief "urban space-walk realness."

"No, wait—take him!" Asha flicked her head toward the books section, where a regular customer, a tall man with glasses, was studying the back of a Jeffrey Eugenides.

"Sure, sure," deadpanned Gwen. "Do you think he's chicken or salmon?"

"I'm serious, he always looks at you." Asha's stage whisper was louder than her normal voice. "And I see him looking around for you when you're not in."

"Piss off."

"He does! I thought you knew. We call him Mr. Gwen. Sir Gwen and the Green Shirt."

"No you don't."

"Fine, we don't. But the looking part is true, I swear."

Gwen looked at him now, more closely. He was probably early forties, she'd guess, with thick, wavy hair that was graying at the temples, tortoiseshell-rimmed glasses and a green checked shirt undone over a white T-shirt. He could be a lower-rung graphic designer, or a moderately stylish accountant. Although if he were the latter, she reasoned, then he probably wouldn't be browsing in a charity shop on a Tuesday afternoon. In the time they'd been discussing and appraising him, the man had continued examining the back of the book—or pretending to—and now it occurred to Gwen that he must either be a very slow reader or fully aware that they were staring at him. She prodded Asha and they both turned away in unison, stifling giggles. She felt about fourteen.

After another couple of minutes, during which they busied themselves with some fake tidying and he presumably memorized the book's ISBN number, the man walked up to the counter.

"Just this please," he said, placing the book down.

Everyone said "Just this please." They either said it apologetically, as though they felt guilty not to be buying more, or defensively, as though they feared she might try to upsell them a tea set. Since noticing it, Gwen had tried to stop saying "Just this please" in other shops, but it turned out it was physically impossible.

She looked at the price sticker on the back—£2.50—even though she knew this already. All the paperbacks were £2.50 unless they were battered Penguin Classics (£3) or had irremovable gunk on the cover (£1.50). As the man stood there, Gwen noticed herself trying to tap the numbers into the till in a sassy, assertive way. Head cocked to one side, little finger oddly erect. Her usual rote patter—hiyaa that'll be two fifty then please fab just tap your card when you're ready great thanks here's the receipt for you have a lovely day—came out nervous and stilted. She reached the "receipt" part before the receipt had actually appeared, and was forced to point at it, tragically, as it chugged its way out of the machine.

The man thanked her, cheerfully, neutrally, and left.

Asha stepped forward from the doorway where she had watched the whole encounter, and laid a sympathetic hand on Gwen's arm.

"Why don't you just not go?" she suggested again.

"That was your fault," said Gwen, as they watched his green shirt retreat up the road.

Suze and Paul were going, of course.

Oh brilliant, you're coming!!! Suze texted back—Gwen was so pleased to have an excuse to make contact that the fact of being an understudy was already beginning to sting less—followed by a string of opinions on the dress code, plans to share an Uber back from Greenwich, and thoughts on how to interpret the exhortation: *No gifts please! But if you absolutely insist, we'd love a little something from our West Elm wish list.*

Only after a day and a half of halting but jolly back-and-forth did Suze drop the bombshell.

> By the way—just checking you know Ryan is
> going? He and Neil still play football or something x

The kiss was the only hint here that Suze was tiptoeing around her emotions, although Gwen was grateful for it. Of course she didn't know. Where else did Suze expect her to have got this information? Still, she understood it might be less stressful for Suze to kid herself that Gwen still spent time with all their mutual friends independently of her, and just never happened to mention it.

> Oh! she messaged back. I didn't.

Suze began typing. Gwen wrote more, quickly, before a reply appeared, and hit send.

> But I guess that makes sense. Thanks for
> the heads-up!

*Typing.*

> I'll be fine. Fiiiiine.

*Typing.* She could feel Suze drafting and deleting. Gwen hurriedly wrote more.

> I've been thinking it might actually be time to get
> back in touch. See if he wants to have coffee or
> something. You know, clear the air. Exorcize some
> demons. Be a grown-up.

The typing stopped. Gwen paused. It started again. Finally, the message appeared.

> I think that's a really good idea x

## 38

She put it off for a week. But in the end, it was almost easy.

His number was still the same, Ryan not being a person who invited the kind of life chaos that necessitated a number-change in this day and age. And so was Gwen's, meaning the hardest part of the process was seeing their last conversation appear in the window above her message. It was a polite exchange about an end of tenancy cleaning fee. Surely other exes would have drunken reminiscences, passive-aggressive digs, a midnight "hey" left dangling like a rogue plastic bag in a tree? Connie was right. It was odd to have made such a clean break. The clean break was its own kind of mess.

She kept the message brief and straight to the point, but tried to make it breezy enough so as not to suggest a terminal diagnosis or secret love child waiting in the wings. She didn't mention the wedding, to maintain the illusion that she was reaching out entirely off her own bat. As though perhaps six years had passed in a whirlwind of professional success and erotic adventure, and only now was she finding time to catch her breath and wonder what had become of that man she almost married.

> Just wondering how you were, and if you'd like to
> have a drink some time? If that's not too weird! It'd
> be good to catch up.

A solid text. *A good decision.*

He replied thirty minutes later with a sorry for the delay!, which was default Ryan. He seemed unsurprised and unflustered, smoothly suggesting dinner instead of a drink, which wasn't default Ryan at all. Or hadn't been.

They sent a few messages back and forth to find a date and make arrangements, his self-conscious references to "bedtime" and "nursery pickup" confirming in broad daylight what she already knew from her late-night online fact-finding missions. The not-so-secret love child. Gwen was irritated, but grateful he didn't feel the need to announce it outright. Ryan was at least still a person who knew that the correct answer to "how are you?" was "good, thanks" and not a video clip of his progeny singing "Itsy Bitsy Spider."

"I'm having dinner with my ex next week," she told Connie the next day, with some pride.

"Why the hell would you want to do that?" asked Connie. "Are you a masochist?"

Gwen had the familiar sensation of being on a fairground waltzer, trying to keep her head facing in the right direction.

"Oh, you know," she cleared her throat, affected an ironic little laugh. "Clear the air. Achieve some sort of . . . ah, *closure?*" She did the accent, hoping to remind Connie this had all been her idea. But it came out sounding Swedish.

"Well," snorted Connie. "Good luck to you, Gwen. In my experience, if you try too hard to slam a door, it swings back and hits you in the face."

"She's right," chipped in Gloria, from behind a handbag display. "That's how my sister-in-law got her new nose."

# Plant Pot

They had a silent war over the placement of a potted plant on the living room shelf. He would move it to one side of the television, she would move it back to the other. This had been going on for six years now and neither of them had ever mentioned it.

Depending on how things were between the two of them at any given time, the pot might stay in one place for a week or two, or for only a matter of hours. Once she had punctuated an especially bitter argument by picking it up—for a moment he thought she might throw it at his head—and then slamming it back down in the right spot. Or the wrong spot, depending whose side you were on. But otherwise the pot was never mentioned, though the plant in it—a peace lily, of all things, sent by a family friend to mark the first anniversary with an insufferable message about "green shoots" and "new beginnings"—was watered regularly, its soil fed, its curling brown tips occasionally remarked upon.

Marjorie and Derek weren't strictly houseplant people. Their generation preferred its greenery in the garden, where it belonged. But peace lilies couldn't survive a British winter, and now they had been saddled with an emotionally laden plant to keep alive at all costs. On one side of the TV, or the other.

They never progressed to separate bedrooms, each of them privately believing that to sleep without the reassuring weight of the other in the bed would be worse than any temporary relief the distance might grant. But they did begin eating separately, Marjorie making herself endless rounds of eggs on toast or sad platefuls of Ryvita with cottage cheese and tomatoes before Derek got home. He began buying frozen ready meals on the way back from work, "to save her the bother." Sometimes, without warning, she would change tack and spend the whole afternoon cooking a big meal— then as Derek walked through the door at 6 p.m. clutching his boxed biryani, she would look from it to him and say, tersely, "I see you've sorted yourself out." And he didn't know how to tell her that he hadn't, he hadn't at all.

Eventually, things had thawed. Mellowed. They hadn't practiced radical forgiveness or "fallen back in love," so much as they had just forgotten, very gradually, over a series of months and years, to keep on punishing each other. Lost the taste for it. Run out of energy. They were more practiced at the life they'd lived before, after all. Below the pain, the muscle memory for fond words, affectionate squeezes and gentle, spousal harassment remained.

Retirement had helped too, although Marjorie had dug her heels in. First she dug her heels in over Derek leaving the logistics firm he'd worked at for thirty-five years ("You'll be under my feet all day! I have things to do, you know.") and then she dug her heels in over stepping back from her own part-time position in the office of a local community college ("What will I *do* with myself all day?"). But finally, confronted with the reality of each other at close-range, they found it was easier to fall back into their old habits than to continue living like housemates, cautiously stepping around each other's grief as though it were an inconsiderate pile of dirty washing. Gradually, they began to eat together again. Derek even began to cook, and in a maddening twist turned out to be better at it than Marjorie ever had been.

Still though, the plant went back and forth, back and forth. It had grown, but not much. By rights it should have been repotted several times by now, but somehow even that felt too risky. The friend who had sent it had never visited to check on her bequest; was unlikely to, now, as she'd moved to Northumberland and hadn't even sent a card the last three Christmases. But they kept up the watering, the feeding, the checking and the passive-aggressive relocation, because now it was all part of the routine. The branch their mishappen lives had grown back around.

And anyway, what if the friend turned up unannounced one day and asked to see it? What would they say? "Whoops, sorry, we let the death plant for our dead son die too?"

No.

So the plant went on—not thriving, but surviving. As did they.

## 39

A woman called "Thank you!" to the bus driver, and after she got off she banged on the glass near the front of the bus and mouthed it again through the window—"THANK. YOU."—just to ensure the point was made.

Gwen always wanted to thank the driver. She could see that it was objectively a nice thing to do. But it felt painfully attention-seeking to yell her thanks down the length of a bus when nobody else had done it, and so she rarely did. Sometimes she wondered if other people didn't because *she* hadn't. And if, in turn, more people didn't because *they* didn't, and if really that was everything that was wrong with the world.

Today, traffic was everything that was wrong with the world. Gwen was running late, because she had spent an extra fifteen minutes trying to coax her fringe into a convex rather than concave arrangement. Getting the bus had been a stupid call. She'd thought it would feel cooler and calmer than the Tube, that it would be nicer to look out of the window. Now she was suffering the torment of the bus's constipated passage through Haringey, her senses heightened by stress. The vibration of the engine buzzed through her bones, and loosened her bowels. The little huffs and *tsks* of fellow passengers twanged at her nerves, and the bus kept lurching forward and stopping suddenly in a way that seemed designed to drive her slowly mad. Lurching and stopping, lurching and stopping. Hope and disappointment, over and over.

A few seats away, a man sneezed violently into his elbow. Gwen felt the same about blessing a stranger's sneezes as she did about thanking the bus driver.

Should she message to say she was running late? Or would that look neurotic if she managed to get there on time after all? Perhaps Ryan would expect her to be late, assuming she might want to make a dramatic entrance. But he'd only assume that if he'd entirely forgotten who she was. Gwen was the kind of person who hated being late—not so much out of consideration for whoever she was meeting, but because she hated having to immediately interact with people when she arrived anywhere, preferring first to go to the toilet and spend a few minutes checking her appearance for smears, food stains, wayward hair behavior, and any other source of embarrassment that might have sprung up on the journey. Ryan would remember that about her. Surely.

The bus was moving again now. A man on the back row was blasting music from his phone. But instead of the usual grime or EDM, he was playing "Father Figure" by George Michael at full volume. This gave the journey along Green Lanes a sweeping, cinematic air and Gwen enjoyed it, feeling briefly united with her fellow passengers, forgiving them for their huffing and tutting. Then she remembered that Ryan was now a father, something she was going to have to ask him about and look interested in. She clenched.

Was the song actually about fatherhood, though, or was this like all the years she'd spent thinking Ace of Base's "All That She Wants" was about a woman who actually wanted another baby? The song ended before she could listen more closely and figure it out.

As it happened, she made it to the restaurant (Mexican, a chain pretending not to be a chain) with two minutes to spare. Ryan was late instead. Gwen's gut was back on the lurching bus again as she watched him walk in and consult with the host on the door, giving the name, waiting patiently to be walked to their allocated table by a server, rather than just looking around the room and spotting her the way that most people would. Ryan had always had a great respect for systems and order. As such, Gwen's first interaction with her former fiancé after six years of estrangement came with a smiling chaperone, asking if they'd like to "kick things off" with chips and a dip selection.

"Hey there," said Ryan, sitting down without making any move to touch her.

"Hello yourself," she said back, a little too brightly to be natural.

"Yes, please," they told the waiter.

Ryan had grown a beard, which was jarring at first although not unexpected. It would have been more unusual for a man of his generation and situation not to have grown a beard. And as they spoke, halting and formal at first, Gwen found she was grateful to only have half of his face to interact with.

He looked older—tireder, a few deep furrows in his forehead and the beginnings of some squirrelly pouches below his eyes—and fatter—just a little, a softening of his frame that evoked not hedonism and hard drinking so much as contentment and finishing up fishfinger teas. There was a smear of toothpaste visible around his mouth, which was either the result of a special brushing for her benefit, or had been there all day. Either way, she tried not to look at it.

Gwen sat up a little straighter in her chair and sipped the margarita she had ordered on a whim, and which she had regretted as soon as Ryan asked to see the selection of zero percent lagers. Her hand shook a little each time she reached for the glass. She tried to look serene through a mouthful of salt.

They filled the first part of the meal exchanging updates on people they knew. Which is to say that Gwen would dredge her brain for some crumb to offer him—"Omar got a new job and moved to Amsterdam"; "Polly had a load of grief with a dental abscess"; "Suze and Paul are having their bathroom done"—and Ryan would say that he knew, he'd seen it on social media, and Gwen would say "oh." In however illusory a way, he seemed to be more in touch with her friends than she was.

She asked after his family, and he filled her in on more of the same: on job moves and babies and house renovations and health scares, on old parental quirks now amplified by retirement. Ryan asked after Marjorie and Derek, and Gwen said, "Oh, you know—same old, same old!" which didn't feel sufficient.

"Dad isn't an eighth Māori after all," she added, and Ryan said he was sorry to hear that.

After this they both fell quiet, making small appreciative noises as they set to work on separate selections of food. Sharing small plates had seemed too intimate when they were ordering, but now they looked like two business associates dining together for the sake of an expense account. Ryan made a familiar snuffling sound, and Gwen knew he was enjoying the irrigative effect of hot sauce on his sinuses. She hated that she knew this. But then he smiled at her kindly, almost encouragingly, across the silence and she had no choice but to step in and fill it.

"So, I wanted to . . . well," she hesitated. "I asked to see you today because I thought it might be good if I—That is to say, if we . . . ah. You know."

"Achieved some closure?" He didn't do an accent.

"Um, sure. That."

"Oh, cool. I thought maybe you'd found my goalkeeper gloves," Ryan joked. *Was* he joking?

"No, I—sorry, they never materialized in the end," she told him. She pictured the long-gone bin bag of his things, of the shin pads and flip-flops and the beard butter, which he would actually be able to use now. "I did look for them, I swear! But anyway, that wasn't—like I said, I thought it might be good, helpful, if we . . . talked."

"Great." He steepled his fingers like a psychiatrist and waited. She forced herself to go on.

"I . . . I wanted to say . . . well, sorry." It felt like she was swallowing her own epiglottis. "I'm sorry for ending things the way I did. I'm sorry I cut you out of my life. You were very good to me, and you didn't deserve it, and I wanted you to know that I have felt like shit ever since."

She didn't say, "I have felt like shit about it." Just, like shit.

Ryan nodded, and sniffed, and nodded again.

"I really thought I was doing the right thing, the kindest thing, at the time," she went on. "But I handled it badly, and . . . I'm sorry."

She could hear Connie in her head, counting apologies. Gwen vowed that there would be no more sorries now.

"What do you, er, think?" she asked, but Ryan had just shoveled in a large mouthful of nachos. She sat patiently, listening as his chewing noises grew softer and wetter. Eventually he swallowed, and said: "I think it was the bravest thing you've ever done."

She hadn't been expecting this.

"Brave?"

"Oh yeah," he said casually, chasing a blob of guacamole around his plate with a tortilla chip. "It must have been terrifying for you. Especially in the wake of everything else."

It had been. She still remembered Marjorie's anguished sobs down the phone—"not Ryan too!"—which was a bizarre thing to say, especially since she'd barely treated her future son-in-law with more warmth or affection than she had the undertakers. When they'd announced the engagement, her mother hadn't sounded delighted so much as tolerant, relieved to have a go-to conversation point that had nothing to do with clearing Luke's things, writing thank-you notes or phoning the council about a commemorative bench. Her father, though, had been touchingly pleased. He'd already written his speech, he told her, by the time they'd broken up.

"What happened was, after Luke died"—Ryan said this casually too, as though he were recapping a sitcom plot; Gwen flinched a little at the name—"everything felt like we were pedaling uphill. Everything was so much harder, and everything I did for you was wrong. And *I* felt like shit about that, because I was meant to be the person who magically knew what you needed and how to support you."

Gwen nodded now. She recalled the way, in those weeks and months afterward, she hadn't felt sad so much as raw. Flayed. Every nerve ending exposed, as though she were wearing her organs outside of her skin. She hadn't felt like a person so much as an embryo: formless, pre-life. A cluster of helpless cells, squirming in jelly. When Ryan asked her to marry him, even while she heard her own voice saying yes, her thoughts had said: "I am not old enough, I am not authorized to make this decision." Surely he knew that? Surely it was obvious? *Where was the person in charge?*

Ryan went on: "It was like—I didn't just have to be a good boyfriend anymore, I also had to be a grief counselor, and a personal assistant, and this calming, cheering, eternally stabilizing presence without any emotions of my own. I had to work extra hard to make you even the tiniest bit happy. But"—here came the plot twist—"I was happy to do that, Gwen, I wanted to do that. For you. For us."

Telling people they were engaged had felt like announcing that something had happened to her, at random. Like an extreme weather event, or petty crime. A few people had looked concerned. She'd seen it flickering behind the smiles; as though they wanted to stage an intervention but didn't know how.

But most people cooed and squealed and said what lovely, *lovely* news—with emphasis on the second "lovely," an extra helping for poor old her. "Finally, some good news!" they said, as though this frilly doily of a decision could blanket all the pain that went before it. Paper covers rock. Wedding trumps death.

She started to speak, but Ryan cut across her. "No, seriously, let me say my bit. Because I've thought a lot about it over the years and I really want you to know that I didn't ask you to marry me because I felt like I had to. To make up for your brother dying. Did you know that? I worried, afterward, that you thought I had.

Maybe everyone did. But I would have done it anyway, you know. I was happy to do it. Because I loved you and I was happy. And, well, you know. It's just what you do."

Gwen picked at a piece of congealed cheese, oozing from the side of a now-cold quesadilla. He had used the word "happy" so many times that it had started to sound less like a word and more like a noise—chirruping and inane.

He sat back now and let her reply, which she did slowly, the thoughts forming only as the words were leaving her mouth. "The thing is," she said, "you may not have proposed because you felt like you had to. But I think I said yes because I felt like I had to."

Admitting this out loud felt radical. She half-expected to look up and see an army of mutual friends and acquaintances marching through the door, pointing and yelling "a-ha!," asking for their engagement gifts back. But none came, and Ryan hadn't burst into tears or stabbed himself with a novelty corn holder. He didn't even look surprised. She carried on.

"You were my . . . continuity, I guess? Luke knew you. He liked you. He approved. You were something left over from the before times, something I could cling to. I think I felt I owed it to my parents, to give them something positive to focus on. And I think I felt I owed it to you, of course. For being all of those things you just said, and for sticking with me even when I know I must have been a nightmare. I said yes because I couldn't find the energy to say no. At the time."

She took a gulp of her drink, eyes watering as the acid hit the back of her throat.

"Also," she added, shrugging, "it's just what you do."

Ryan took all this in, nodding at her with an expression of tolerance and patience that she suspected was borne out of parenthood. He smiled again, almost beatifically, and suddenly his eye bags didn't look weary; they looked wise. So Ryan had achieved enlightenment, had he? Was that it?

"Of course," he said, after a little while. "I like to think there's another timeline in which we'd stayed together."

"Another . . . timeline?"

"Yeah. You know, quantum physics?"

"Oh. Sure. Quantum physics."

"On the other timeline, we stayed together and worked through your issues, together—"

"My issues," she repeated.

"Sorry, your *trauma*," he rephrased, earnestly.

"Right."

"—and we got married and we had kids and maybe we moved to Hitchin or wherever—"

"Hitchin?"

"—or wherever, and maybe it all worked out for us."

"Right."

"Or maybe it didn't. We'll never know."

"No."

Sometimes she did the maths with Ryan, too. If she had married him, they'd have celebrated their five-year anniversary by now. They could have, theoretically, two kids by now. They could be making stilted conversation across a restaurant table for entirely different reasons. Would that be better? Who knew.

Yet Ryan sounded completely comfortable with this. The infernal purgatory of not-knowing, the thing that had tormented Gwen for so long, was the very same thing that soothed him. Knowing the two of them might be nesting and spawning in a parallel universe apparently brought him joy.

"But it's okay," he went on, a coy grin creeping onto his face, "because on *this* timeline I met Clea. And then everything became, well . . ."

*Don't say it*, Gwen begged him silently.

". . . clear." Ryan gave an indulgent little chuckle and busied himself with a dripping taco. This was obviously a favorite line. *I can see Clea-ly, now that dithery bitch has gone.*

She wondered if they had discussed her beforehand. *How to be kind to the unhinged ex*. Had there been strategizing? Ryan was a person who liked to be properly briefed before all meetings. She sensed Clea was a person who would be happy to help with this. A person who was secure in herself, and generous to others, and who would never make him forty minutes late for a party because she was hurling clothes around the room and clawing at her own face. She didn't know whether to apologize some more, or tell him he was welcome.

In the end, she settled on telling him: "I'm glad." Which didn't, in the moment, feel so far from the truth.

On another timeline, perhaps she really was glad. On that other timeline, perhaps she would invite herself round for dinner at the Streatham semi-detached, coo over the child and tell Clea how much she loved her tablescape while her hosts had muttered conversations in the kitchen. On another, she might turn to her hostess during dessert and ask, pleasantly, "Tell me, do his legs still shake right before he comes?"

On yet another timeline, perhaps she would reach across the table and wipe away the drop of mole sauce that was hanging, seductively, off his beard. Perhaps she would lean in close and claim ownership of his rattling sinuses once more.

But on this timeline she was doing a good impression of gladness, and that was enough. She was eating black beans and sweet potatoes opposite the man she could have married, but didn't, and she could be finding it unbearable, but she wasn't. To lie back and kick through those lukewarm waters felt like victory in itself.

# Coat

---

Lise had been clean ("In both senses," she liked to say to disarm her Hinge dates) and employed for two years before she felt ready to part with the coat.

The coat she hated and resented and yet had washed tenderly by hand in the sink of her new flat, reluctant to leave for the laundrette in case she could never get back in again. *A fixed address.* The coat she had hung out to dry on the tiny brick balcony, from which she could see the Gherkin, the Shard, and Canary Wharf, a skyline of jagged objects from which she was protected by the boxy brown sprawl of Wood Green Mall. *A fixed address*, like the point at the center of a roundabout. Cling tight or you'll get flung off.

For the first week she'd been here she had slept in the coat. First out of force of habit, then out of some superstitious impulse that said the moment she took it off, relaxed and made herself at home, her home would be ripped out from under her. After that it had lived on the back of her front door like a shitty mauve talisman, a watchman, a *bogeyman* to remind her how ugly things could get. Who knew? If they'd given her a nicer coat, she might be back out there now.

Eventually though, she was ready. After she had scrubbed down the flat and put up curtains and grown dill in a terra-cotta pot and covered the sagging sofa with a scarf and painted the miserable, council-issue chairs in soft green chalk paint. After she had saved her call-center wages for a new mattress and a stovetop coffeepot and an extra heavy-duty chain on the door. After she had heard the news about Jakob and had not collapsed in on herself, had not allowed herself to be dragged back below the surface by grief but stayed rigid and upright in the sharp, bright daylight of her pain—only then did Lise feel ready to get rid of the coat.

On the day she donated it, she'd seen the advert for the Assistant Manager job taped to the counter. It was less an advert, to be honest, more a poster reading ARE YOU MANAGERIAL MATERIAL? next to a cut-out photo of Jürgen Klopp. Lise didn't believe in fate but she did believe in narrative, and this was a very good story. The shop had been her only constant for years. It was a place to go when she had nowhere to go. When even the least discerning cafés kicked her out, when even the libraries turned chilly and hostile, charity shops were a public right of way and this one a particular favorite.

She hadn't seen the old woman buy the coat, but she had seen her wearing it afterward, and had been glad. It looked warm. Too warm, really, for the weather—why did old people always dress as though they were oblivious to the weather? She supposed they and junkies had that in common.

It was still an ugly coat, Lise thought. But perhaps slightly less ugly than before.

**40**

All that week, Gwen had struggled to get Janet McAffery's face out of her head.

Janet's daughter had been back to the shop twice now, asking if there were any updates on the missing clock. Once she'd been alone; the other time she'd parked her mother outside on the pavement like a dog, where she could be seen in her purple anorak, smiling apologetically through the window. Both times Gwen had promised they were doing all they could to locate the clock, and at the time the lie had felt like enough of a gesture to sub in for genuine kindness. It didn't anymore.

Her dinner with Ryan had been unexpectedly galvanizing. She was brave, he had said. She was a person capable of big, decisive action. And now she felt compelled—almost duty-bound, in some strange way that wasn't entirely unconnected with having seen him naked—to take Nicholas's wrong and make it right.

Today was the third in a row of swampy, thirty-degree heat and she and Connie were finishing up an afternoon shift, taking it in turns to stand in front of the shop's sputtering aircon unit. Every twenty minutes or so, a person would come in asking if they had any fans. If Connie was on the counter she would reply, "Yes, I'm huge in Japan!"

If Gwen was on the counter, she would say, "Sorry, no."

Connie was in the middle of telling a story about seeing a teen-age boy on the bus that morning, wearing thick jogging bottoms and a hoodie with the hood pulled up—"Imagine!"—and having turned to him and said: "I'm sorry but aren't you frightfully hot in all that?," and that just when she thought he might knife her, he'd smiled and admitted that yes, he was, and they'd laughed together. Gwen wasn't convinced this had really happened.

She pictured the clock now, this clock she had never actually seen, sitting on the wall of some soulless City pub. *Instigate social occasions*, said a voice in the back of her head. It was blandly robotic, like a sat-nav.

"Connie," Gwen began. "You know the clock I told you about?"

"Clock? The one your boyfriend purloined for selfish gain?"

"Never call him that, please."

"If the bootscraper fits!" Connie dug a sharp elbow into her ribs.

"Anyway, yes, that clock—I was thinking of . . . ah, that is, would you like to come and . . . well, liberate it with me? Tonight?"

As friendly invitations went, it was a harder sell than the cinema—but she sensed that Connie would enjoy this kind of caper. Plus, she could use Connie's confidence and chutzpah; her effortless way of moving through the world would surely come in handy when it came to charming the pants off a suspicious publican. Maybe they could go for pasta afterward.

"Can't, sorry!" replied Connie. Oh. *You have missed your desti-nation.* "Sounds like a fool's errand, if you don't mind my saying, Gwen, and anyway I have Pilates."

"Sure, sure," Gwen replied. "No worries at all! You're probably right." She felt alarmingly as if she might cry again.

Then a voice behind them said: "I'll come." They turned and found Asha stood there, arms folded, face unreadable. She had been quiet and withdrawn again this afternoon, relegated to inspecting CDs for scratches in the back room while St. Michael made her cups of tea. Michael never made other people tea.

"There you go, take Ayesha!" said Connie. Asha didn't correct her. Gwen felt the window of time in which she should leap in and correct her on Asha's behalf slam closed, while she gawped like an idiot.

"You sure?" she asked Asha instead, as Connie bade them farewell and bustled out of the shop.

"Hundred percent!" Asha said. "Take Ayesha!" She smiled wryly. "I need an adventure. I'm going fucking mad at home. I mean, more so."

"Something to do, isn't it?" agreed Gwen. This was all it had ever taken to get Suze to agree to a plan. *Something to do.*

"So what's the idea?" Asha asked. "We go down there and explain that our pal Nearly Soulless Nick has swiped the clock from some confused old dear, and ask very nicely for it back?"

"Sure! Yes, totally," said Gwen. She paused. "And if that doesn't work, we just take it."

"Steal it?"

"Er. Yes?"

Asha narrowed her eyes coolly, and Gwen had a sudden vision of her in court wearing a barrister's wig. She knew this wasn't Asha's job, but it should be.

"Gwen, I'm not getting arrested. What the fuck."

"No! No, obviously not." Gwen forced a laugh, as if to suggest she had obviously—*obviously*—been joking. But inside she was mortified. Back in her houseshare days, they had often stolen from pubs. Pint glasses, mostly. Sometimes cutlery. Whole toilet rolls, when occasion demanded. Aside from the time Suze had opened her bag to a nightclub bouncer to reveal it clinking with contraband—he had winked her in anyway—they never got caught, and generally rationalized the habit away as a victimless crime. They were skint, the pubs were rich. It was an unofficial loyalty scheme.

They had grown out of the habit as they got older and could afford to buy sets of matching tumblers from Wilko, then from John Lewis, relapsing only when an especially handsome or noteworthy glass crossed their path. And then it could be justified as nostalgia: a little thrill to spice up their otherwise staid, law-abiding lives.

The last time had been a couple of winters ago. Gwen had been enamored with a neat little whisky glass in a pub with a roaring fire in Highgate, next to which she had sat for three hours watching Suze "do the rounds" of Paul's birthday drinks; stopping at each braying cluster of friends, colleagues, and Barbour-jacketed cousins to be charming and hilarious for ten minutes before moving smoothly on to the next. Gwen wondered where she had learned to do this. Eventually, Suze had plonked herself down next to her and rested her head on Gwen's shoulder.

"Met anybody nice?" she'd asked.

"This glass," Gwen had replied, holding it up for her friend to see how snugly it fitted into her cupped palm. "This glass is my new life partner."

"Strong, solid. Nice curves. Good prospects. I think you'll be very happy."

On the bus home, Gwen had found the glass wrapped up in napkins at the bottom of her bag.

> No idea, Suze had texted back the next day. Must have been elves! Obviously you belong together x

Gwen had tried to be touched by this, rather than offended.

And now here she was, offending Asha by being the kind of white woman who regarded petty crime as an indulgent treat. Gwen apologized, flustered and stammering. Asha raised her eyebrows and smirked.

"All right, Winona, calm down. I'm coming."

## 41

Gwen spotted the clock as soon as they walked in. On a far wall, it glowed against a ubiquitous shade of teal. It really was a lovely clock, as far as Gwen had ever had an opinion on a clock before. Far too good for the Boar and Balls—*the Bore and Bollocks*, Asha had christened it immediately—which had faux-vintage French soap adverts in cheap frames, and signs on the toilet doors that read "Chicks," "Chaps," and "Whevs."

The clock was surrounded by the usual array of self-conscious junk: several china plates in plate holders, a trio of ceramic flying geese, a neon sign that read "Seize the Yay!" in cursive script and a portrait of a young Elizabeth II wearing a graffiti trucker cap and gold chain, with pennies glued over her eyes. A card in the bottom right-hand corner of the frame read, alarmingly, "£860."

"State of this place," muttered Asha under her breath.

The room smelled of ripe bodies and industrial disinfectant. It was busy—more so than she'd been expecting for 6 p.m. on a Tuesday—and there was a cluster of women sitting around a low table in front of the wall with the clock on it. They were all passing their phones back and forth to each other, shrieking with laughter.

Asha and Gwen approached the bar, where a laminated sign read "Happy hour! Spritzes 2 for £12," and began the routine they had practiced on the way.

"What can I get you, ladies?" asked a barman with a gelled fringe.

"Hi there," Gwen began, her mouth suddenly dry, her lower back sweating. "We were just wondering about your . . . ah, lovely decor! Your owner must have a great eye."

The man looked baffled. "Er, thanks?" he replied, glancing up at the shelf where a pheasant in a glass case held court alongside a collection of old Nintendo game cartridges and a LEGO Millennium Falcon. "Head Office sent someone in and did it all last week. Before that we looked like a Premier Inn."

Gwen laughed at this, a little too hard to be natural. Asha jumped in.

"Do you see that clock on the far wall? We'd like to speak to you about that clock."

She was modulating her voice, Gwen noticed. It was a little higher, her vowels round and her consonants crisp. Gwen stood up straighter beside her, trying to match her lawyerly poise.

The barman looked at the clock, then back to the women. "What about it?"

"We're afraid it's been sold to you by mistake."

"Mistake?"

"Yes," Asha went on, her face grave. "Unfortunately the clock was wrongly given away to charity, whereby it fell into the possession of a third party who sold it on to you without permission or the necessary, ah, license."

"License?"

Asha nodded. "You see, charities being protected under different regulations from commercial businesses"—she waved an illustrative hand around the bar—"means that unfortunately the sale is rendered illegitimate and ownership of the clock reverts to the original proprietor."

"The original what?"

"Proprietor."

"Of the clock?"

"That's right."

He frowned, looking back and forth between the two of them.

Eventually he said: "Is this another one of those DesignMyNight treasure hunts? Are you on a hen?"

They strenuously refuted this accusation. Asha tried again, slightly less composed.

"We're here as representatives of the clock's owner—an elderly lady who is suffering significant distress at its absence. The sooner we can reunite her with her property, the better. Ideally without being forced to contact any higher, um, powers."

Gwen wondered if she meant the brewery chain, or the police. Or—God?

"Right," said the barman, after she had repeated several variations on the same word salad. "So let me get this straight. Someone sold us the clock but they shouldn't have, and now you need it back because an old lady is sad? That the gist?"

Asha opened her mouth as though about to say more, but she appeared to have run out of steam. She merely nodded.

"Nope, soz. I can't do that, it's more than my job's worth."

"Can't—or won't?" she goaded him.

"Honestly, nah, my boss would kill me."

"Your boss, could we speak to him please?"

The barman smirked unpleasantly at this. "*She's* not in today, sorry."

"Fuck," Asha replied, still in the same crisp, businesslike tone. The barman snorted with laughter and walked off to make a round of frothy cocktails for a group of LEGO-haired estate agents. Gwen turned to laugh it off with her, but Asha seemed to deflate before her eyes.

"Fuck," she repeated, exhaling heavily and refusing to look at Gwen. The bar was filling up now and they were being buffeted from all sides by happy-hour elbows.

"We could offer him a bribe?" Gwen suggested, without much conviction. "Slip him a twenty?"

"You carry cash?" asked Asha.

"Well, no."

"So what, we grease his palm with a card reader? Do him a cheeky Venmo?"

"Fine, forget it."

Asha clenched her fists against her eyelids and whimpered in frustration. "That was my fault. I fucked it."

"You didn't! You were amazing!" Gwen told her. "It was stupid. The whole thing was an extremely stupid idea." It was, she saw it now. Extremely stupid. A *heist*? She, Gwendoline Grundle (38F, scared of texting), a smooth-talking swindler? She suggested they stay for a drink, but Asha claimed her dignity wouldn't allow it.

"Let's get out of here," she said, "before he googles 'clock licences.' Or offers to lend me his copy of *Lean In*."

She was joking but she wasn't smiling. Gwen agreed, but her bladder didn't deal in dignity.

"I'll meet you outside," she told Asha, heading for the loos.

Did she know then that she was going to do it? For the sake of her own pride she never would have dared. But now Gwen had Asha's disappointed face in her head alongside Janet's, and the barman's turnip haircut alongside Nicholas's contemptuous sneer. Suddenly it wasn't the clock liberation plot that seemed absurd, but everyone else beyond it, everyone laughing and flirting in front of it, the gruesome masses with their fluoro drinks and their poreless faces and the seething injustice of the world at large. It was funny, really, thought Gwen, as she sat behind the saloon door in "Chicks" listening to a true crime podcast being piped in through invisible speakers, that she had held on for so long without turning to a life of crime.

Walking out of the toilets, everything was perfectly aligned. The barman had his back to the room, chopping limes in precarious fashion with one careful eye on his phone screen. Asha was safely outside. She saw her clear path to the door, presided over by a gilded flamingo and a windmill from a miniature golf course. She took a few sideways steps toward the clock, shimmying apologetically as she approached the group sitting in front of it. They barely glanced at her, and kept on talking.

*"So we glossed over the stripper,"* one of them was saying.

*"Would Dave not have been okay with it?"*

*"No I mean literally. With baby oil."*

"Oop," said Gwen, steadying herself on the arm of the sofa. "Sorry, just need to . . ."

She stood on tiptoe and stretched above them and lifted the clock off its hook in one clean motion. It was heavier than she expected it to be, and her wrist almost gave way as she balanced its jagged form upright in her fingertips. At that moment, the women looked up and saw her: stood on one leg in Superman pose, the sunburst hovering above their heads in her outstretched hand like a statue of Helios. One false move and she'd be responsible for a highly original maiming. Her blood went cold.

But they just said "oh, sorry!" for no reason in particular, and shuffled themselves a few inches to the right, allowing Gwen to lower the clock safely into her arms. How many women, she wondered in that second, would apologize to a thief for being in their way? Probably most.

Gwen thanked them calmly, shot a final glance at the barman, and set off for the door in the posture of an Olympic speed walker—hips and ankles working frenetically, upper body braced for collision. As she passed the bar, she turned away to hide the clock from view and weaved her way through the other punters—she loved the crowd now, wanted to buy each and every one of them a massive orange cocktail—until finally, finally, she was at the door, breeze on her face, delicious polluted High Holborn stretching before her like Xanadu.

"Fuck!" yelled Asha in delight as she spotted her tumble through the doorway with the clock.

"Run!" yelled Gwen.

42

In hindsight, the running was unnecessary. Nobody was chasing them, nor was likely to. But running felt appropriate in the moment, their feet thundering childishly along the pavement and "Lust for Life" playing—how embarrassing—in Gwen's head. It was her second flee in two weeks, she realized, and hoped this might qualify as a fledgling exercise regime.

Afterward they lay in the middle of Red Lion Square, wheezing with self-congratulatory laughter, the clock a conspicuous mound on the grass between them. They'd wrapped it in an old pashmina, one Gwen had worn to her graduation ball and kept in her life for reasons unclear. "Good thinking on bringing the blanket," Asha had said, and she hadn't corrected her.

After a while, they stopped laughing but stayed lying down, the tickle of ants in their hair and parched yellow grass scratching at their ankles. Around the edges of the park, office workers sat with their jackets off and their skirts hitched up to their thighs, drinking rosé and eating three-grain salads out of boxes, tilting their faces hungrily toward the sun. Snatches of conversation floated over, all of it banal. Gwen felt like a trespasser for being here at all. They all looked so young. She could sense it: the determination to create a bucolic moment and the mutual agreement that everyone pretend it was lovely. "Lovely," they would be saying, over and over until they believed it. Or until it genuinely did feel lovely.

"My office is right over there," said Asha, suddenly. She didn't point to indicate where, just kept her eyes closed and her hands behind her head. Gwen opened her mouth to say something similar, but Asha went on. "This is the closest I've made it in six months."

Gwen stayed quiet and let her continue. Asha's fingers were teasing and tearing up blades of grass as she spoke.

"Every time I've tried to come back, even on the weekends, I have this—I don't know, this kind of full-body reaction. Like all the blood drains out of my brain or something. Last time I ended up sat on the platform in Chancery Lane Tube for an hour and a half, I'm not even joking."

Gwen noticed she was holding her breath, as though one audible exhale might be enough to send Asha back into her shell.

"The whole time I was convinced someone from work was going to walk past and see me sat there, looking like shit. It was like one of those dreams where you need to run, but you can't, and you need to scream, but no sound comes out. I needed to get myself off this bench, but I just . . . couldn't. Every time I tried to stand up, my brain went 'nope.'"

She shook her head, slowly, her eyes still closed. Then added: "Luckily it was only six p.m. and they all work until at least nine, so I was safe."

A pause. "What did you do in the end?" asked Gwen.

"A Tube guy came over and asked if I was okay," said Asha. "I don't know if he was helping me so much as profiling me, but he got me some water and gave me a Jaffa Cake and then I started crying and couldn't stop. In the end they took my phone and called my mum."

"Oh god."

"Yeah. But she wasn't angry, she just came and collected me like

I was a lost umbrella. Apologized to the Tube guys about twelve times, kept thanking them on my behalf. Somehow got me on the train and all the way home in total silence, then put me to bed and made me a stew and never said anything else about it."

"Aw."

"It was only about a week later I remembered that my mum is terrified of the Tube. She hasn't been underground since 2001."

Then Asha was quiet again.

"I'm sorry," said Gwen, after a short while. "I wouldn't have made you come here if I'd known."

"I offered, you idiot," said Asha, which was true. "Anyway, it's good. Confront the ghosts! Get back on the horse."

"So this is a day of successes then," ventured Gwen.

"Oh, I'm incapable of enjoying success." Asha said this matter-of-factly, the way a person might say, "I can't digest cheese."

They fell silent again.

"Go on," Asha said after a little while. "I know you want to ask me questions, Gwen. You keep making little noises like you're about to say something and then stopping yourself."

"Okay," said Gwen, who hadn't realized she was. "Okay, I do have a question." She paused. "So are the ghosts . . . riding the horse? Or is the ghost a horse and you're riding *it*?"

Asha laughed a single, hooting laugh and grinned up at the sky, her eyes still closed. Her face in profile was beautiful and inscrutable.

"I'm Seabiscuit, baby."

Gwen was laughing too. "What does that mean?"

"An unlikely symbol of hope in the Great Depression."

They lay there, cackling, until the last of the post-work pic-nickers had packed up and gone off for their dates and dinner reservations, and only a clutch of men drinking tinnies on a bench remained. Gwen became aware of it, as the sun went behind a cloud and the heat of the past few hours began to cool on her skin: the unbearable sadness of having had a nice time, which sometimes begins creeping in even while the nice time is still being had.

"Come on, Robin Hood, let's go home," Asha said eventually.

The two of them sat in companionable silence on the Piccadilly line, Asha hugging the swaddled clock to her chest like a big mutant baby. As the train approached Russell Square, a family of tourists leaped up too early for their stop and one of them fell, impaling a khaki-clad buttock on one of the clock's many spikes. Gwen called "*Scusa! Pardon!*" after them as they limped onto the platform, while Asha quaked with laughter beside her.

"Well, that was fun," Asha said as they parted ways, standing stiffly opposite each other, the clock in the gap where a hug ought to be. "Proud of us, Team Justice."

Gwen's heart swelled a little with that old sense of camaraderie, the one she had used to feel when the agency won a big pitch. Only better, because this time the moral ends justified the madcap means.

The next day, she presented Janet McAffery with the clock on the doorstep of her small flat in a sixties council block. The woman looked at her blankly and said, entirely without thanks or ceremony, "Oh, the clock is back is it?," and just for a second, Gwen was seized with the urge to snatch it away again.

But then she looked past Janet into the living room, and saw the brighter patch on her faded floral wallpaper where the clock clearly belonged. Gwen hung it again for her, using a folding step stool with a vinyl top. It was satisfying to slot the clock into place and see it up there, glinting in the morning sun as though newly risen. She got carried away and opened the curtains without asking, flooding the room with light, but Janet squinted and asked her to please draw them again because she couldn't see the television. Gwen understood.

"It's still keeping the right time!" she told Janet, checking the clock against her phone.

"Oh yes," Janet had replied, not looking up from *Escape to the Country*. "Never goes wrong, that one." She gave a soft chuckle. "It's the rest of us what do that."

As Gwen stood there in the dimly lit room, she found she was tempted to pull up a chair and watch along with Janet—perhaps attempt to strike up a charming intergenerational friendship. "Really, *she* takes care of *me*!" she imagined herself telling people smugly at Suze's next dinner party. But then a carer bustled in and asked, pointedly, if Gwen would be staying long, so she made her excuses and slipped out.

"Bye then love, you look after those legs," Janet said. Which felt incongruous, but nice.

# Going-Out Top

"Going-out top" is the descriptor sent through to the factory, which Leakena assumes must be a clumsy translation, but is in fact the way the brand classifies the top on account of its smallness and silliness.

It's funny, ponders Leakena, the way less fabric is required for going out than for staying in. Not just in Phnom Penh, where heat shimmers off the streets and white backpackers acquire the appearance of steamed pork, flopping pinkly out of their hostels to exclaim at the humidity and retreat back inside—but in Britain too, where the going-out top is headed, to be bought by women apparently unbothered by their nation's sunless reputation. She worries for them, and hopes they wear coats on top.

Leakena's boss has been given eleven, maybe twelve days to get the top from the design to the shop floor: a circuitous journey, given that the top and its thousands of identical sisters will travel just shy of ten thousand kilometers to be sold within spitting distance of the drawing board they were born on. But logic can't fight a bottom line. Leakena works for eleven, maybe twelve hours, but she is paid for the number of tops she manages to sew, not the length of time it takes to sew them. Nor for the time she spends fainting, because the relentless heat and the chemical fumes conspire to smother her.

Leakena is attending beauty school in her spare time, with the small amount of money she does not send home to her parents. It is to be her route out.

Leakena may get out, but the top will not. The going-out top will journey those ten thousand kilometers but will never even make it to the shop floor; will sit in a crate in a warehouse for eleven, maybe twelve months, while outside the almighty conveyor belt of fashion chugs on, each new going-out top consigning this one to another night in. Week by week, stitch by stitch, beyond the gloom of the crate, in the warehouse, on the industrial estate, it is surpassed by brighter, shinier, sillier, going-outier tops, cast further into irrelevance by each one fresh and hot off the production line. Until, finally, it is called up and into the light.

Not to a nightclub, sadly, but sent straight to a charity shop where it will join the eternal dance of the deadstock—a generous donation of surplus product from a #caring company no longer allowed to torch their margins of error on the bonfire. But not before its tag is cut out to protect the brand from being tainted by association. The top is exclusive in its excess, after all.

There it will sit on a rack, next to floral blouses and roll-neck jumpers and a misspelled hen party T-shirt, for another two months—because, truly, it is a very silly top. People will flip past it, occasionally stroke an idle finger along it while thinking about their dinner. It will slip off its hanger and fall on the floor eleven, maybe twelve, times a week, waiting for Gwen (or Asha, or Brenda, or Lise) to pick it up and hang it back on. And when it becomes clear that still nobody is going to take the top out dancing, it will be relegated to a rag bag, a Cinderella in reverse, and cast off again, across oceans again—this time to Accra and a vast mountain range built from all the other clothes that nobody wanted. Clothes that nobody wanted to be their problem.

*Obroni waawu* they are called, "dead white man's clothes," though no living body ever even breathed within this top. Young women scale the mountain every day, farming the clothes as if they are crops, looking to spin their heavy bales into something consumable. If it is lucky, it will be plucked from the quivering hillside by another young woman, Nanyamka, who will carefully clean, repair and remake the silly top, adding panels of beautiful fabric where before there was only thin air. Like a fairy godmother she will give the top its best fighting chance, but still, nobody takes it out. It is one of a hundred thousand silly little tops, after all.

Eventually, having danced away from its fate for long enough, the top will be buried in the dark for good this time. This sadly thwarted going-out top, which never got its chance under disco lights—but did, at least, see the world.

## 43

Connie answered the door in her usual way, as though greeting a very late plumber. "Well come on then, come in! Food's almost ready."

She was wearing a dark linen jumpsuit, miraculously uncreased, and a pair of painterly clogs. There was—and Gwen squinted, to check she wasn't hallucinating—a pencil holding up her hair.

In the kitchen, intensely savory smoke was billowing from the pot on the hob and they had to shout to be heard over Neil Young played a fraction too loud.

"So, tell me!" Connie passed Gwen a glass of red, which she gulped at thirstily in lieu of water. Connie never served water unless you asked for it. "How's the job with Saskia?"

Gwen panicked. "Ah. I— well, actually, I turned it down," she told her. She was surprised this news hadn't made its way to Connie already. "I'm sorry. Thank you though! Really grateful for the introduction. But it wasn't . . . you know. I'm not sure it's . . . quite what I want to do."

Connie's eyes bugged a little at this, then she shrugged and turned back to the stove.

"Suit yourself!"

She lifted the lid of the Le Creuset and stirred it, frowning. Gwen felt obliged to say more.

"I mean, Saskia seems *great,* and I'm sure fred will go on to big things—"

"Fred who?" Connie asked, taking a tray of charred tenderstem broccoli from the oven and shaking it so vigorously that a few stalks flew overboard.

"It's . . . the company? The app start-up? Fred," Gwen repeated, and couldn't resist adding: "All lowercase."

Connie barked at this, and slammed the oven door. "It's called fred? Jesus wept."

"Anyway," Gwen went on. "I know she's your friend and I feel terrible about messing her around. I really hope it won't make anything awkward between the two of you."

"Saskia? Oh god, I hardly know her," replied Connie, waving a dismissive hand. "Just an acquaintance from around about the place, I forget how we even met. But I thought she'd be a good contact for *you,* Gwen. Get you out of whatever midlife"—Gwen flinched—"crisis you're clearly in the middle of."

Connie took the pot off the hob and carried it to the table, thudding it down heavily next to a vast, oiled focaccia. But it seemed the job discussion was still on the table too. "No no, I won't take it personally," she went on, brandishing a ladle. "I thought I was being helpful! But look, if you're not interested then that's entirely your decision."

Gwen spluttered in protest. She insisted that Connie *had* been helpful, thanked her again, apologized again, while Connie spoke over her.

"Oh no, don't worry about me—lord knows I'm not one to be oversensitive about these things. Ha! It's your life, Gwen, for god's sake, you have to make yourself happy."

Gwen continued spluttering, thanking, insisting. Connie looked satisfied for a moment, and took a sip of wine.

Then she added: "I only hope you'll be able to find something else, Gwen. After all, you know what the jobs market is like at the moment."

Gwen nodded. *Did she?* More to the point, did Connie?

They sat down to eat. But despite all the protestations on both sides, tension was filling the room like expanding foam. The cat made a rare appearance, stalking in from the hallway and settling itself on a chair between them like a referee. It occurred to Gwen, then, that she didn't actually know the cat's name. She didn't feel inclined to ask.

Seeing Connie sulk was unsettling. Gwen hadn't experienced anything that could accurately be described as a "falling-out" in two decades—not since a showdown over the headcount for their leavers' dance limousine, which had ended up with Suze and Gwen being dropped off in Derek's Mondeo as an act of public protest. Gwen had always been the peacekeeper; the holder of hands, beer, and earrings, never the person screaming bloody murder across the chip shop. Confrontation was a language she had never learned to speak, and yet she knew it by pitch and cadence. She knew to crane her neck when she walked past it in the street, to pause her channel scroll when it blasted out of a *Real Housewives* marathon on ITVBe. And she knew that when Connie said: "Suit yourself!," it meant she was now an unwilling participant in a one-sided grudge from which the only way out was through.

"You could retrain as a teacher, it isn't too late!" Connie offered now, not having been asked. "The money isn't as bad as everyone says, especially not if you're happy to work at the schools where the kids all have knives in their socks. But perhaps you'd find that too overwhelming."

"Mm," said Gwen. "Perhaps."

"My niece is something impressive in coding. Can you code?"

"Not exactly."

"Would you be willing to learn? Come on, Gwen, skills are the new currency."

Conversation limped on in this fashion for a while, with Connie suggesting other actions Gwen should take and Gwen making acquiescent noises. *Yes. Maybe. You're probably right. Honestly, I'd settle for the old currency.* A second helping of osso buco sat heavy in her stomach, and she felt swollen, sleepy, and stupid. She felt guilty too, as though accepting Connie's hospitality without also taking her advice made her a kind of confidence trickster. How many dinners equaled how many opportunities to dig a two-pronged fork into Gwen's life? At what point had they struck this deal?

"I'll be fine, Connie, honestly." She sat up straight and attempted a conversational landgrab. "Anyway, enough about me! How are *you*? What have you done this week?"

Her hostess ignored her, and asked:

"What would Liam say you should do?"

"Liam?" Gwen blinked at her.

Connie's lips were stained purple with Côte du Rhône, which combined with the darkening sky outside to lend her a kind of villainous glamour.

"Your brother." She was topping up their glasses again.

"Luke."

"That's the one." Connie snapped her fingers. "What would he say? I'm sure he'd want you to push yourself a little further, to achieve somethi—"

"Can we not bring my dead brother into everything?" Gwen asked. She tried to sound irreverent, to disguise the desperate note in her voice. She wasn't about to tell Connie that tomorrow was the anniversary. Tomorrow he would be in everything, and nothing.

"But he clearly *is* in everything, Gwen, that's the trouble!" Connie reached across the table and laid a hand on her forearm, squeezed it a little too hard. "You obviously have a lot of unresolved grief, and frankly I think it's stunting you. Didn't your parents put you in therapy afterwards?"

"Well," she said, "I was thirty-one. It wasn't really on them to put me anywhere."

"Even so! These things tear families apart if you're not careful. The only way to stop them defining you is to define *them*, to get them out in the open and work through them together."

"I'm sure you're right, but—"

"Have you tried running?" Connie interrupted. "Brilliant for the brain, you know."

Gwen did know. It wasn't a well-kept secret.

"I don't run," she replied flatly. Connie humphed.

"And have your parents dealt with their grief?"

She asked it the way one might ask if they'd bought a bungalow, or taken the bins out. *Dealt with*. Gwen started to try to explain, grasping for a way to describe the edgeless state in which her family had been suspended for so long. "The thing is," she began, "there's no word for a person who loses a sibling, or a parent who loses a child—"

"*Vilomah*," interrupted Connie.

"Pardon?"

"*Vilomah*. It's the word for a parent who has lost a child. It's Sanskrit."

"Oh," said Gwen, feeling stupid. "I didn't know."

"Not many people do," said Connie.

"Okay," said Gwen.

She paused. "Is there a word for a person who loses a sibling too?"

"I imagine so," said Connie, airily.

"Right. Well."

She had lost momentum now, and fell silent.

Connie had made dessert, as usual. A huge mixing bowl of chocolate olive oil ganache, laced with unidentified booze. Gwen ate it, as usual, spooning it into her mouth under Connie's cut-glass gaze. She winced as the sugar hit her back molars and twanged an exposed nerve. She had ignored another reminder text from the Lovely Smile Dental Clinic last week.

"Have some more," Connie pushed. Gwen's throat felt slick

with it. Her head ached with the sweetness. She didn't want any more, and said as much.

"God, you're no fun," huffed Connie, and ladled the rest of the bowl into the bin. As Gwen watched in disbelief, something inside her twisted and snapped.

"Now," Connie landed heavily back in her chair. "If you ask me—"

"I never asked you!"

The words ripped through the room before she was aware she'd decided to say them. Joan Armatrading had stopped playing on the stereo some time ago, and now the screams of two distant, rutting foxes punctured the silence.

Connie stared at her, nostrils flared. It felt to Gwen as though Connie was only seeing her, properly, for the first time. The cat stared too, in alarm.

"I was only trying to help," said Connie eventually, her voice flinty and wounded. "I worry."

Gwen felt suddenly cold, and incredibly tired. An unexpected longing ached in her now. For Marjorie. Marjorie, who *did* worry, who bought the wrong hand soap and read the wrong newspapers, who understood her perhaps no better than Connie, but whose failings were nonetheless woven into hers, whose hopes were knitted tightly through her own. Gwen wondered why she was sat here every week scrabbling for approval when she already had a mother to disappoint.

"I never asked you to help." She said it steadily this time. Firmly. "I never asked you to worry."

Connie said nothing, but stood up and began loading the dishwasher, clanking each piece of crockery into place and slamming the drawers shut with force.

"I think I'll head off now," said Gwen.

She picked up her bag and pulled on her jacket, struggling to stuff her arm into an inside-out sleeve. She needed the toilet but wasn't about to ruin her exit. Connie didn't see her out.

*

Back on the street, Gwen called an Uber. But instead of going home, she ordered it to take her to Victoria station. The driver asked no questions and she rested her cheek against the window, allowing her eyes to slide out of focus as the city whirled ink and neon beyond the glass.

Arriving after midnight to an echoing concourse, she found the last train had already gone. She'd known it would have, and wondered why she'd ignored this fact until now.

Gwen could make peace with ruining this exit, she decided, but not with losing her momentum again. So she pulled her jacket around her, tightly, and sat on a bench until morning.

# Puzzle Box

After she left, Connie cried for precisely seven minutes and then began clearing the room.

It should have been a familiar routine, given that Maddy had been coming and going for years now. She swung in and out of her parents' lives like a wrecking ball, staying for visits that were always either rude in their brevity—arriving at midnight, gone before breakfast—or rude in their protracted length, teasing them with weeks of wet towels on the floor and strange friends in the kitchen, before everything imploded and she vanished again.

But this time, words had been exchanged that surely no surprise house eviction or early morning flight from Stansted could blot out for the sake of convenience. This time there had been no screaming, no cathartic rush of loathing, no coughing it all up to feel better afterward. It had been quiet, controlled, as though Maddy were reading her speech from a script for an unseen director.

Words had floated before Connie, fashionable words, but she struggled to grasp how they related to her. *Toxic. Manipulative. Boundaries. Self-compassion.* This time, there was no "them," no "us," no fellow spurned parent to pull her out of her sulk. Connie was alone now, and the empty house whistled with her pain.

Maddy's phone number was no longer in use. Messages bounced back. Connie didn't even know where she was living. Pride had stopped her from asking, and she doubted she'd have got a straight answer anyhow. But a few weeks ago, Connie had bumped into an old acquaintance who had said, "I saw your Madeleine the other day, she looks so much like you now doesn't she? Must be lovely to have her back. And so wonderful about the baby!"

And Connie had had to stand there and suffer the humiliation of agreeing that yes, it was lovely, and yes, wonderful news, and yes, wasn't she just the spit (Maddy would hate this, preferring to believe she had inherited her father's genetic code wholesale). She had to smile benignly, then make excuses to leave the conversation before her maternal failure was exposed in the cruel chill of M&S Simply Food. She caught herself trying to walk away like a good mother, however a good mother might walk.

Anyway, all this suggested that Maddy might have stayed local, and this haunted Connie. Knowing that her daughter was rejecting her and resenting her in Bogotá, Belgrade, Margate—that was one thing. But knowing she was potentially rejecting her and resenting her from within the same postcode was somehow both better and worse.

Connie couldn't help looking for clues everywhere she went, in case Maddy was leaving her some kind of trail. The half-drunk coffee on the next table over, was that her dark lipstick mark? The flyer pinned to the deli noticeboard advertising a TEFL teacher "with limitless patience and intuitive wellness experience," was that her bid for stable employment? She found herself adopting certain poses, making certain decisions, going about her days in a conspicuously cheerful and casual way. All in case Maddy was watching.

Volunteering at the charity shop was a way for Connie to get herself out of the house, but also to anchor herself in one place—to make it more likely that their paths would cross sooner or later. It was a reversal of the wisdom she had dispensed years before, always telling her daughter to stay in one spot if she ever got lost. *I'll come to you. Don't go wandering off all the time. Stay still, and I'll find you eventually. I promise. I promise.*

The shop was supposed to be little more than a soothing back-drop. A place to be now that she had nowhere to be. *Better to do something than nothing.* But as the weeks had passed, Maddy hadn't found her—ridiculous hope, she was probably pregnant up a tree in Tbilisi or something—and now Connie was pitching up for more and more shifts out of sheer superstition, convinced that the one day she didn't work would be the day her daughter would walk through the door.

In the meantime she busied herself sprucing up everything else around her, as she saw fit. Everything from the way the paperbacks were arranged on the shelf to the way poor, lost Gwen organized her life. And which was the more thankless task?

It was while initiating a full overhaul of the bric-a-brac section one Tuesday in mid-August that Connie found the puzzle box.

Smooth, pale wood, covered on all four sides with complex geo-metric marquetry. A few small chips in a couple of places, which only made it look more desirable and less like something that could be bought from Flying Tiger for £5.99.

Was it the same box? It was hard to tell. It's not like only one had been made in the world, after all, and it was a long time since she'd last seen it.

But if it were the box, then what if it were here on purpose? What if there was some clue from Maddy hidden in the middle? An apology, or confession? Or—and this seemed more likely—some further, definitive, rejection? Either way, curiosity gnawed at Con-nie like heartburn. She shook it, smelled it, held it up to her ear. Slid a couple of the inlaid panels out of place, and jabbed helplessly at the squares of bare wood they revealed.

She thought about her daughter as a gangling child in the play-ground, clutching the box that may or may not have been this one. Truth was, she'd only tried the Malteser trick once and none of the other children had been interested. It might have been the very last time Maddy had ever taken her mother's advice.

She banged the box against the side of the counter in frustration. St. Michael poked his head out from the back room and raised an eyebrow.

The problem was, Connie didn't know how to solve the puzzle herself. She never had.

## 44

Gwen ate an egg sandwich on the train as an act of defiance.

She chewed slowly, taking her time, putting it down between bites and looking around so that if anybody met her eye she could look right back at them with an expression that said, "Yes, I am eating an egg sandwich." No one did.

The station had felt like a film set that night, curiously small and intimate without the expansive lens of a thousand other people's onward journeys. Faded Union Jack flags hung from the roof above the concourse, left over from the last burst of government-issue patriotism—the Jubilee, or was it the Olympics?—and their presence fed Gwen's mood for melodrama. If it wasn't for the neon signs above shuttered branches of Wetherspoons and Paperchase, she could have believed she was waiting to see if her soldier sweetheart would return from Normandy.

She had slept upright against a pillar for seven minutes total, which it turned out was still long enough to give her a crick in her neck, and had woken, confused and hungry, to the unmistakable scent of the twenty-first-century railway station: organic bath bombs mingling with reheated pasties, diesel fumes, and takeaway soup. She'd shuffled about Victoria for an hour in a daze, weighing up breakfast options and prodding at testers in Boots. Gwen had always enjoyed stations. She liked their liminal state, in which everyone was either chasing time or killing it, and every spare minute became recreational by default. They were similar to charity shops, in that way. A hinterland between real life and home.

Now she was charging onward at alarming speed, trying to focus on her sandwich and not her destination.

When more people got on at Clapham Junction and Sutton, she saw a few sniff the air and walk up the aisle in the opposite direction. This pleased her. It felt good to create a kind of repellent force field through the sheer force of obstinacy and egg mayonnaise. She had a sudden vision of herself aged eighty-five in a beret and fingerless gloves, eating a rotisserie chicken with her hands on the back row of the 141. Dunking a drumstick into an open jar of mustard in a string shopping bag and waving it at misbehaving schoolchildren.

Gwen shook a few crumbs out of her hair and smiled at the thought.

## 45

"There is no promotion."

She began blurting it out as her mother's wavy form appeared behind the glass-paneled porch door. But by the time Marjorie had opened it and registered her daughter standing on the doorstep at 8:30 a.m. on a Saturday morning, the words had been lost and the whole cathartic moment had to be repeated. This somewhat diminished its impact.

Her mother did, at least, shout "Gwendoline!" in a way that was gratifying. She followed it up with a sharp, "What are you doing here?," but at least she hadn't mistaken her only living child for the man who came to read the gas meter.

"There is no promotion, Mum."

She said it again, more slowly. "I've been made redundant. A while ago. I'm sorry." Out of the corner of her eye, she became aware of Alison Nextdoor pulling up in her Yaris. But the words were already pouring forth, sounding more pathetic than they had in her head. "I've spent all summer unemployed, and nobody wants to hire me, or maybe they would but I've been working in a charity shop for free instead of actually looking for a job, because I don't know what I want to do and I don't know what I'm fit for and I hate everything and I have no leads and no prospects and no energy and sometimes on the days in between I don't even shower, and I know I'm very lucky to have food and a roof over my head and I have no right to feel like this when actual people have actual problems but I am somehow thirty-fucking-eight and I have driven my own life into a ditch and I have no idea what to do about any of it. And I'm sorry to dump all this on you but I missed you and I needed to tell you because you're my mum and then I slept on a bench in the station and I'm sorry and I . . . I . . ." Tears had arrived now, hot and furious, her nose streaming and her cheeks stinging with self-pity. "I . . . I wanted you to know."

"Right! Well." Marjorie was flustered. She had also spotted Alison, who had now started to unload her Morrisons shop in an exaggeratedly natural way.

She put an arm around Gwen, not a hug so much as a means to steer her wailing daughter into the house—but even so, the touch was almost more than she could bear. Her mother smelled of her signature scent, a blend of Elizabeth Arden and Cillit Bang Active Foam. Gwen crumpled against her, while Alison examined an invisible scratch on the hood of her car.

"You slept on a *bench*?" Marjorie hissed as they navigated the doorstep.

"Sitting up," Gwen told her, between gulps.

"Right. Well," she repeated. "Let's get you inside."

# Shoes

---

There was sick in her hair again.

She could smell it but she couldn't find it. Mhairi raked her hands through her curls, trying to locate the source of the scent—lactic, cloying, oddly sweet—but she couldn't find a clump to pick out with her fingers.

Perhaps if she looked in the mirror? But then that would mean opening her eyes, and god knows when she might have the luxury of closing them again. It would also mean getting up off the bathroom floor, which currently felt so impossible it was almost hilarious. A superhuman feat of strength.

Never mind. Maybe there wasn't sick in her hair at all, maybe the smell just radiated from her pores now. *Eau de Bébé. Newborn by Givenchy.* Or maybe it had taken up residence in her nostrils, the way they said police officers could never un-smell a dead body. Was she comparing motherhood to homicide again? Apparently so.

Mhairi opened her eyes. Her mother-in-law had taken the baby half an hour ago, in a grand performance that involved lines like "The Cavalry is here!" and "Super Nana to the rescue!," which she had clearly rehearsed on the journey up, or perhaps borrowed from one of the grandparent message boards that she had started frequenting at least five years before Mhairi finally got pregnant.

"Now, you can take a nice shower"—an order, not a suggestion—"and tackle that washing pile in peace!" As though this were a precious gift. "And if you could be a dear and rustle me up a bit of lunch that would be lovely, the sandwiches at East Croydon looked shocking."

Getting them both out of the house had been a forty-minute endeavor, and now Mhairi was lying on the bathroom floor. She had been here since they left.

She heard a soft scuffling by her ear, and looked over to see a woodlouse trundling across the tiles next to her head. It looked like a happy existence. When she was a kid, she had once taken a woodlouse by both ends and pulled it apart, watching as the long, white rope of its insides came out in one clean motion. It had been immensely satisfying. She didn't remember feeling guilty about it.

Now here she was, her own insides pulled apart from top to bottom, trapped and squirming under glass. Now, she felt guilty.

Mhairi got up. She hauled herself off the floor, avoiding the mirror, and padded through the flat to the bedroom, picking her way over a trail of toys and wipes and towels and pads and crumby plates and rogue socks and tiny, soiled onesies. Although she knew she should get into bed and sleep—screw the washing, sod the shower, be a dear and stick lunch up your hole, Genevieve—she found that she didn't want to. Her body ached for it, but her brain was already sick of this topsy-turvy underwater life, the daytime sleeping and nocturnal warfare, sick of keeping antisocial business hours while the rest of the world cooed and told her she was a "champ" and a "hero" and a "warrior" for managing to put her legs in the right pant holes while they all went out for brunch.

So Mhairi went out. Not for brunch—although, she could?—but to the first place she could see that looked bright and clean and had music playing loud enough to nourish her. Donna Summer was singing "Love to Love You Baby." It felt like sarcasm in the circumstances, but still. She drank it down and let it pulse through her veins.

Mhairi stroked a hand along the rails, feeling the different fabrics, not really looking—*were her eyes open? Just*—but feeling.

What was this place? A shop. A charity shop. Okay, yes. She could be here, smelling of sick. They couldn't kick her out. Charity shops were made for people who smelled of sick. They couldn't send her home to do the washing and sterilize bottles and make her mother-in-law a fucking frittata. Perhaps she could stay here until they closed, or forever.

*When you're laying so close to me*

Mhairi was singing along now, she realized, though at first she thought the sound was coming from somewhere else. That high, animal wail. Not so different from the deep, guttural howls she'd let out during labor, which had also sounded as though they'd come from a different place altogether. The song was supposed to be sexy, she knew, but right now it sounded like a cry of frustration. Frustration at being trapped in a body at all. Bodies brought nothing but trouble.

*There's no place I'd rather you be*

She wondered where the woodlouse was now. Maybe miles away.

Mhairi carried on singing, willing herself to up, up, up and out of her body in a cloud of glitter and space dust. Behind the counter, an old lady was laughing with a beautiful boy in a bucket hat. They didn't care if she hadn't showered. They'd let her stay.

*You put me in such an awful spin*

Then she saw the shoes. They seemed to be lit by their own spotlight, or maybe that was just reflected off a sequinned jacket in the window. Seeing them was like recognizing an old friend in a crowd, out of context, and wondering for a minute if they were in fact a famous person and you'd never really known them at all.

The shoes were white, with crisscross straps—a different kind of bondage, which she'd enjoyed, once upon a time. She longed to kick off her Birkenstocks and strap herself in. And so she did: slowly, fumbling with the buckles and swearing as loose hair fell forward into her eyes. Below her gray jogging bottoms they looked perfect in their absurdity.

Mhairi did a few salsa moves, wobbling slightly into a coat rack. *Still got it*. She twirled in front of the mirror in the far corner of the shop, milking every beat of the music, somehow tuning out the phone that was ringing, ringing, ringing in her pocket while Donna sung on.

*Soothe my mind and set me free, set me free*

Buying these shoes would be absolutely the least practical, most pointless thing she could do right now, Mhairi knew. Donna knew.

And so she did.

## 46

Gwen had reverted to a quasi-adolescent state within ten minutes inside her parents' house, which had to be a new record.

She stood in the kitchen, blowing her nose and looking on helplessly while her mother spooned Kenco granules into a mug and tidied up around her, clucking with the air of one who has been asked to entertain foreign dignitaries on ten minutes' notice.

Nobody sat down. This was learned behavior in the Grundle household, where no meal passed without Marjorie leaping up half a dozen times to fetch things, wipe things, switch things off, add garnishes, remove bones, apologize, scold. Watching her from a seated position was enough to make a person guilty. Better to be on your feet already than jostled out of comfortable repose.

So, standing right there before them both, Gwen repeated her outpouring for Derek's benefit. Or she attempted to, while her mother interrupted.

"But surely they can't—"

"How ever will you—"

"Why on earth didn't—"

"Of course, charity shops are all more expensive than normal shops now."

Gwen took the bait at this last one. "They're not, Mum."

"Well," said Marjorie. "I saw a Per Una skirt for twenty pounds in the Air Ambulance the other week, barely cheaper than new!"

"Maybe it *was* new," said Gwen. "Did it have the tags on?"

"I didn't look. But people don't go to charity shops to pay twenty pounds for a skirt, not here they don't. Maybe in London—"

"London, where the skirts are lined with gold," said Gwen.

"I'm *only saying*—"

"Gwen," her father interrupted. They both turned to look at him. "You could have told us, you know."

But when she heard him say it, she realized she really couldn't have told them, not until now. The words would have choked her. The last time she'd really told them anything had been six years ago, telling them she'd left Ryan, and then she'd thrown up afterward. Not from the fact itself but from the trauma of the telling. The telling made it real, nonrefundable, and being the person with "some news!" instead of the recipient wasn't any easier on Gwen's constitution.

"I know," she said, her voice still thick with leftover tears.

"I don't understand why you didn't," her mother bristled. "All that lying about the promotion. We could have helped!" Even Marjorie didn't look convinced as she said this. "You should have told us," she repeated, weakly.

"I'm sorry," said Gwen. "I'm sorry I didn't tell you. It was only a few months, I didn't want to worry you."

The phrase sounded trite, given she'd now delivered three months' worth of worry in a concentrated dose by turning up sobbing on their doorstep. "Or I suppose, if I didn't tell you then it was easier to pretend it wasn't happening. I didn't feel I should tell you until I had a new job, or at least a plan. Until I was a little bit more . . . together."

Gwen took a swig of coffee, from a mug she didn't recognize. It tasted faintly of washing-up liquid.

"Anyway, I've told you now. So."

"Indeed," said her father. "Consider us told."

They all stood and sipped their drinks. Derek hummed, softly, under his breath. *Dum de dum de da.* Marjorie looked out of the window and toward the patio, where a fat-bellied pigeon was sloshing around in the bird bath.

"You do have savings, don't you?" she asked suddenly, her attention snapping back to the room as though on a length of elastic.

"Yes, I have savings," Gwen lied. She half-willed her mother to ask more, to demand bank statements as evidence—but it seemed to be all the reassurance she needed.

"So you won't need to move home?"

This stung. Even though Gwen could more easily imagine herself moving full-time into Saskia's shed then she could willingly relocating to Dorking, there was panic in her mother's voice and it hurt.

"No, no, don't worry, I won't be imposing on you."

Relief flashed across Marjorie's face, before she registered the sarcasm. "Of course," she added, blustering now, "if you needed to, I'm sure we could—"

"Yes, yes of course we could," her father joined in, glancing worriedly at his wife and then at the ceiling above his head.

"If we'd only had some warning—"

"Give us a bit of time to—"

Gwen looked between the pair of them, squinting for the thing that wasn't being said. It had been the defining pose of her youth, forever analyzing her parents for hints of unpaid bills and untold problems, mysteries she needed to solve, secrets she was too young to be let in on but too old to blithely ignore.

"What is it?" she asked, beginning to feel frantic again.

Derek looked at his wife and placed a tentative hand on her shoulder. Something passed between them then, an understanding that Gwen stood completely outside of. She felt a stab of loneliness. Right there in her childhood kitchen, with its faded tea towels and TK Maxx table mats, her parents posed before her like a piece of Regency portraiture, she was somehow more alone than she had ever been.

"Nothing! It's nothing." Marjorie snatched up Gwen's near-empty mug and began attacking it with a scouring pad. Outside, the pigeon was air-drying its undercarriage by strutting along the top of the fence. "Now, if nobody minds, I have a lot of dead-heading to do."

With no further apology, she opened the back door and left.

Gwen followed her.

In the garden, she watched as her mother knelt at the edge of the lawn and began snipping, briskly, through the browning remains of the summer. She kept up a running commentary as she did so, remarking on each plant's progress or lack thereof. The pests it had battled, overcome, or succumbed. Praising the survivors, admonishing the weak.

The little garden must have looked sensational a few weeks ago, Gwen realized. She wished she had seen it. This realization annoyed her, and annoyance spurred her forward.

"Mum, why are you so horrified by the idea of me moving back here?"

"What? I'm not! Don't be silly, I never said—"

"You looked relieved, it was all over your face."

"That's just my face, Gwendoline."

"No, it isn't. Your resting face is the opposite of relief."

"Well, that's very rude."

Marjorie snapped at a brittle stem. Her features were flattened now into a self-conscious posture of calm, but a familiar twitch pulsed in her mother's left eyelid. It was the same twitch she had learned to fear as a child, the warning light that signaled enough was enough. Yet, surrounded by uprooted weeds and clumps of soil, Gwen found that all she could do was keep digging.

"Look, I'm hardly saying I would *want* to move back here. Of course I wouldn't. But it seems like most parents, if their adult child was suddenly unemployed and living alone in one of the world's most expensive cities, might at least *suggest* it? At least *pretend* to want to welcome them back into the bosom of the family home and, I don't know . . ." her voice caught, shamefully, on the end of the sentence, "look after them, for a while?"

"But we just said, we'd be happy to have you back here if you needed to! Very happy! You've caught us off guard with all this, that's all." Then: "Pinch that calendula down to the bud, please."

Gwen began to choke on another rising tide of emotion in her throat.

"I'm sorry, should I have briefed you beforehand? Penciled in an appointment for my life to fall apart at a more convenient time, one that doesn't clash with the horticultural calendar?"

"Not the rudbeckia." Marjorie slapped her hand away as she reached for a crisping yellow daisy. "The birds love the seeds."

"*Christ*, Mum, is that all I get? Plants?"

Marjorie looked genuinely affronted at this, and confused. "Well," she said, turning back to the rhododendron. "I'm sorry to bore you."

For a while, neither of them said anything. They continued to work alongside each other, Marjorie pruning with tenderness and precision, cupping each aged bud in her hand before snipping it, while Gwen yanked indiscriminately at anything that wasn't green or pink.

It had begun to drizzle, in the apologetic way of summer rain, dampening the earth beneath their knees and teasing both women's hair into the same thick carpet of curls that had gotten Marjorie teased at school for looking like David Essex, and Gwen for looking like King Charles II. Her mother seemed determined not to acknowledge the rain, or the hair, nor the fact that her daughter was crying now. Hot, furious tears.

Gwen's knees began to give up before the rest of her did. Eventually she creaked to her feet and sought ineffective shelter under an apple tree with a gnarled trunk. She wiped her nose on her sleeve, feeling twelve again.

"Are you and Dad hiding something?"

"Don't be ridiculous!" Marjorie scoffed, a little too quickly. "What would we ever have to hide?"

Gwen thought about this, looking back up toward the house. In the top right, a dark square sat like a black eye amid the pebbledash. Drawn curtains.

"Look I'm sorry you're having a difficult time, it's a real shame," Marjorie added. "But there's no need to get worked up about it. Not out here, please."

"For fuck's sake, Mum, there's nobody here! Or are you scared we're going to end up in the parish newsletter?"

Marjorie winced at the expletive but the pruning continued, each tinny *snip*, *snip* goading Gwen until she couldn't take it any longer.

"ARGGHHH!"

She surprised herself with the volume of the roar, deep and guttural, sending the pigeon skyward like a feathery flare. It felt good, but it wasn't enough. Gwen looked around impotently for something to throw or something to slam. This was why people shouldn't argue in gardens.

She settled for kicking the apple tree, which made no visible impact on the trunk but badly hurt her big toe. Her mother pursed her lips and looked away, embarrassed, the way she would if she saw a stranger making a spectacle of themselves in the street. Gwen screamed again, wretchedly this time.

"Owwwwwwwaghhh!"

From nowhere a memory surfaced of Marjorie, young and energetic in jeans, getting down on the floor of Asda and beating her fists and kicking her feet alongside a tiny, beetroot-faced Gwen in front of an audience of horrified shoppers, until her daughter was stunned into silence and the tantrum subsided. Marjorie had once given as good as she got, where public displays of emotion were concerned. But not now.

Now, she continued pruning as her thirty-eight-year-old daughter turned and limped back into the house, slamming the back door as a final attempt at fireworks. The uPVC frame granted nothing so much as a deflated *pfffftdd*.

Inside, the living room door was ajar and she could see her father watching the racing on TV, feet up and a packet of chocolate fingers on a side table. Gwen stormed past and headed upstairs, ostensibly to the toilet though mainly for the childish pleasure of tramping muddy smears up the clean carpet.

But by the time she reached the top, a different sense of urgency was driving her forward. Or was it backward?

Gwen stopped, breathless, on the landing, in the spot she never usually let herself pause. She reached out a hand and ran it along the flaking paintwork. Before she could talk herself out of it, she pushed open Luke's bedroom door and stepped inside.

## 47

The room was still exactly as he'd left it, which meant disgusting. The air was stale and thick with dust, mingling with another kind of pungency, riper and keener, like the bottom of an animal's cage. It was a shock after the lemon-fresh surface wipes and Glade plug-ins of her mother's jurisdiction. Gwen inhaled, deeply.

As her eyes adjusted to the dimness, piles and stacks of his possessions emerged. Heaps of muddled clothes, mountains of books and magazines and sports kit. The ash-preserved landscape of a life. Once she had been a sporadic visitor: tiptoeing in to wake him, hot-cheeked, from nap time; sneaking in to deliver his Christmas stocking; barging in to say that dinner was ready, his friends were here, his music was too loud, the bathroom floor was covered in towels again. She felt like a tourist now.

Gwen must have known, on some level, that they had never cleared it out. She certainly hadn't checked in recent years, preferring to walk quickly past his bedroom door, the same way she let her eyes slide quickly over the blank square in the calendar every August. By never asking, by returning home less and less frequently, she had allowed the whole room to fall into the void along with her unread messages and smear test reminders and the toaster for which she was never, sorry, going to leave an online review.

It dawned on her now that this might not be a personal failure but a genetic hand-me-down. Like parent, like child.

She stood there for a few minutes longer, afraid to disturb the heavy, dank peace. She feared alarms would go off, triggered by invisible lasers. Dogs would rush out and she would be forced back into the present day with pitchforks, handcuffs. But after a while she gingerly picked her way across the carpet, squinting, to the window.

Gwen tugged open the curtains, letting watery gray light flood the room. In the garden below, Marjorie was still hunched over a hardy perennial. She was soaking now. Soaking and sulking, her small frame fragile and bud-like in its bright pink anorak.

Just then, she looked up toward the house and straight at her daughter, silhouetted in the window. Both flinched a little as they made eye contact.

And then, Gwen did understand. She understood that she was needed here after all.

When Marjorie arrived on the landing and saw Gwen standing there in his bedroom, she made a small noise. More a hiccup than a word.

"You could have told me, you know."

"Yes, well," said her mother. Marjorie used these words as an all-purpose retort for any statement she didn't much care for. *Yes, well. I'm fully aware that my hair is on fire.* She stepped into the room now, with the same hesitance Gwen had, and looked around as though seeing it for the very first time.

"I would have helped. I *wanted* to help. You knew that."

"Ohh—pfft, well," Marjorie huffed a little. "We didn't want to make a big song and dance about it."

"There's a fairly broad spectrum," Gwen said—archly, breaking the vow she had made only seconds earlier to be patient and kind and mature with her mother this time—"between making a song and dance about something, and pretending it hasn't even happened."

"Nobody was pretending anything of the sort," replied her mother.

"Yes, Mum, you were." It was no use, her voice was becoming shrill again. "You never bloody shut up about the garden, and the neighbors, and the vandalism on the roundabout, and yet—and yet I'm not supposed to be offended that you never want to talk to me about anything that actually *matters*?"

Her mother's reply came, shriller than her own. "It wasn't *you*, Gwendoline. We didn't want to talk to *anyone* about it."

Gwen snorted in exasperation.

"It's the one thing, famously, that you're supposed to do. Talk about it! Grief 101."

"Well, what the hell would we have said?" Marjorie burst out. "None of our friends could relate; they all made ridiculous comparisons with their parents dying, or their aging husbands, or babies who weren't even born yet. Which is sad—of course it is, it's all very sad—but it isn't the *same*. I'm *sorry*," she insisted, as though defending herself against an invisible chorus of critics, "but it just isn't."

Gwen made a noise in reply, but the floodgates were open now. Her mother gesticulated wildly, whipping off her gardening gloves with a small shower of dirt. "Nobody knew how to talk to us. Nobody seemed to know who we *were* anymore. Lord, everyone says outliving your child is the worst thing that can possibly happen to you, but there's not even a proper word for it—"

"*Vilomah*," interrupted Gwen, without thinking.

"Pardon?" said her mother.

"It's the word for a parent who loses a child," she explained. "It's Sanskrit."

Marjorie set her mouth into a thin line. "Well, there's no *English* word for it! No word anyone we know would use."

Gwen agreed that this was true, and regretted saying anything.

Her mother went on, wild hair quivering with emphasis. "But you—well, you were out. Out of this house. Out of this town. Having your career, living your life, getting married and getting your promotions and doing your"—she grasped for an accurate detail from Gwen's abstract career—"your *presentations*. Your life still had so much potential. You had the chance to move on. You didn't have to stay here and think about it every day."

"I—What? Mum, come on." Gwen's voice came out strangled, a tearful whine she hadn't heard from herself since adolescence. "That's so unfair. None of that means I didn't think about it—about *him*—every day. Of course I did. Sometimes he was—*is*—*all* I can think about, sometimes I—"

"No," Marjorie interrupted, shaking her head violently. "No, that isn't what I meant. I meant that you—you were all we had left. You were everything. You still had your whole life to live, and we didn't want to . . . I don't know. *Infect you.*"

"Infect me?"

"I don't know! Drag you down with us. Taint you with our misery. Turn your life rotten and hopeless too."

She sunk down onto the bed as though exhausted by this admission, and began stroking the duvet cover with rough, knotted fingers. In the pause that followed there came the sound of next door's conservatory door opening, and both women looked toward the window in alarm.

Marjorie spoke again, more softly. "It seemed like the one good thing we could do, to give you your space. Let you go off and be happy."

"You thought I was happy?"

"We assumed you were happy!"

"That's because you never asked!" she cried.

"People don't go around *asking* other people if they're happy, Gwen."

Gwen agreed that this was also true.

She fell silent, turned and looked out of the window. After a while, she felt Marjorie get up and walk over to join her.

When her mother finally spoke, she said: "We planted that tree the year he was born. The apple tree."

Gwen remembered this, dimly. Derek trying to hold a kind of breaking ground ceremony. Luke eating a fistful of dirt and having it pried out of his mouth, clump by clump, by his panicked mother. Gwen, reading a *Point Horror* book and refusing her turn with the spade.

"Your father had some old-fashioned idea about children climbing trees. Wanted to build a treehouse for him when he was old enough."

"Well that's sexist," Gwen said. "I might have liked a treehouse too."

"He offered you one, when you were five," her mother replied, mildly. "You said you hated trees, and birds, and you thought the house would be full of spiders and it might fall down and crush you."

"Yes, well," said Gwen.

Marjorie tried again, her speech halting and precise as she tried to explain. "That first winter. After—after it happened. I couldn't bear to be inside too much. I felt like the walls were closing in on me. All the time. Suffocating."

Gwen knew this feeling. Although in her case, living within the solid, silent bounds of Ryan's love, it hadn't been the walls that felt claustrophobic.

Her mother went on, eyes fixed on the flowerbeds. "I used to go out there, every chance I got, all funny hours of the day and night, and plant things. Totally the wrong timings, of course, and the soil was half-frozen and I knew that I was throwing money away on bulbs that would probably never see the light of day—stupid really. But that cold air was like a . . . a slap, in a way. It woke me up every day. Forced me to breathe, and move, so I didn't just crawl into bed and sleep forever. And then when spring finally came after about a hundred years, and a few little shoots started poking their heads through, against the odds . . . well."

She cleared her throat a little and scrubbed at her face with the sleeve of her fleece, leaving a streak of soil across her forehead.

"Maybe it sounds like a silly cliché to you. But it felt like the only sign I had that the world was still turning."

Gwen nodded, although her mother was still looking down at the garden.

"Funny," murmured Marjorie. "I never see it from this angle. It's easier to see from up here what's missing."

"It doesn't sound like a cliché," Gwen said gently.

"I suppose I tell you about the garden because it helps me, and I thought it might help you too. And because you might want to know that a few things were still blooming and happening, back here. I didn't want you to think of home as a place of . . . well." Marjorie hesitated.

"Death," said Gwen.

"Yes," agreed her mother. "That."

Just then, the sound of gentle, nonsensical *doo-be-doo*ing beyond the door announced that Derek was on his way upstairs. In search of his family, or perhaps the toilet. Mother and daughter both looked back at the apple tree, which was solid and stately and gave the impression of always having been there, despite only being planted . . . when? Twenty-six years ago, Gwen calculated quickly. That wasn't nothing. More than a quarter of a century had passed quietly under its leaves.

"I don't think of it like that," she told Marjorie, as the door was nudged gently open and her father appeared in the doorway, looking bewildered, and promptly tripped over a discarded trainer. "I promise. I never have."

48

None of them mentioned the date; they didn't need to. If her parents had other plans for the rest of the day then they didn't mention those either. The conclusion was reached more or less wordlessly, seven years of indecision brought to a head in several seconds once they were all gathered there in Luke's bedroom. Together, the family began to sort.

It was a colossal effort at first. She could feel her parents bristling and resisting, just as her own body would rather be absolutely anywhere else. Marjorie visibly tensed as Gwen picked up the first item at random—a giant plastic cup, the kind filled with luminous slushies at theme parks and bowling alleys—and wiped off the dust with her hand. She felt jumpy, braced for each object she touched to trigger an avalanche either physical or emotional. The familiar things were painful to look at but the unfamiliar were worse, making her feel like she was rifling through a stranger's belongings. Guessing at their significance, or lack of.

She thought she could picture Luke with the giant cup. Perhaps? Clutching it after a summer excursion to Thorpe Park, bounding into the house from a friend's parent's car in a blaze of sugar and sweat and sunburn, quenched by a day spent having the kind of dangerous, overpriced fun that Marjorie would never sanction on her watch. But maybe it was a false memory, one she was willing into existence. And none of that explained why the cup was still here, or why it deserved to be. This piece of flimsy rubbish that would nonetheless live on for hundreds of years while her brother did not.

To her, it all belonged in a museum. Every old exercise book and festering trainer felt as though it weighed more than she did; every movement like wading through treacle. But they carried on, not quite methodically, skimming the most incongruous things off each pile, cherry-picking the items least likely to break them.

Gwen found a zippered wallet of CDs, which looked quaintly archaic even in the room of a boy who'd been dead for seven years. She flipped through its contents. Chart hip-hop and mainstream indie, interspersed with home-burned albums on plain silver CDs: relics from the last gasp of the analog age.

What was she expecting? A CD labeled *"For Gwen,"* filled with bittersweet tracks that perfectly captured the complex nature of their siblinghood? Well, there wasn't one. But there was a CD titled *Mike's Sick Mix* in royal blue marker pen.

She hadn't interacted with many of Luke's school friends, having not been around enough—or, she suspected, not hot enough—to warrant their attention. But she remembered Mike, who even as a frog-voiced thirteen-year-old had possessed a cocky, wheeler-dealer mentality and rarely visited the Grundle home without trying to sell her parents some crap or other. Dubious charity wristbands, pirated DVDs, a clock made of spoons for his Young Enterprise project. She took a chance and put Mike's Sick Mix on Luke's battered CD player, which had once belonged to her.

The sound of Black Eyed Peas' "My Humps" filled the room. *The object least likely to break her*—and yet.

A sob that had been ready and waiting in her throat now escaped as a snort instead. It was too ridiculous. She tried to smother further giggles in her sleeve but soon Gwen was bent double and wheezing, her parents watching in bewilderment as their daughter laughed, eyes streaming, clutching at a nearby chest of drawers for support—which promptly collapsed, spewing shards of MDF, odd socks and balled-up T-shirts across the floor, making her laugh harder. For an agonizing moment, she worried she had ruined everything and lost them again. But then they started laughing too, in their own way, Marjorie clucking and eye-rolling, Derek coughing out a few guilty guffaws. The CD stayed on, jarring and inappropriate and oddly perfect, sweeping them along on a wave of obnoxious late-noughties chart hits. They carried on gamely; sorting, folding, packing, bopping slightly in time to the beat.

Oddly, her mother was the most ruthless of the three of them. Every time Gwen held up an old item for her appraisal—a trucker cap, a BlackBerry phone case, a fistful of plastic lanyard bracelets—she would wrinkle her nose and say: "Get rid." She had picked up her pace now, sifting through the drawers in her jumble-sale mode, elbows going like a corn thresher, as though worried that if she allowed herself to slow down, she might crash.

"Lots of these tops are still perfectly good," announced Marjorie, her head muffled from within the wardrobe. She was holding up a checkerboard jumper with fraying thumb holes bored into its cuffs, a relic of Luke's short-lived emo phase. Gwen felt such a burst of love for her brother then, knowing how mortified he would be to see them standing there looking at it. Luke had hated it when she called his hoodies "tops."

"We can't throw them away, some are barely worn. They'll have to go to charity. You can take them back with you, Gwendoline. For your shop."

Gwen stopped herself from pointing out that this was nonsensical; that there were several charity shops within walking distance, and several hundred in the miles between here and north London. She stopped herself because she knew this was a gesture, of sorts. It was her mother's way of making peace with her reconfigured world, building a bridge between the child she had lost and the one who stood solidly before her.

"It isn't *my* shop" was all she said.

Derek was more sentimental. Several times Gwen noticed

her father hunched and immobile over some piece of childhood ephemera—a piggy bank from the Woolwich, an old FunFax organizer with inserts on magic tricks, snooker and "How to Draw Sharks"—and she had to put her hands over his, gently cajoling him back to the present. But it became easier as they settled into the motions. Lifting, dusting, placing into a reusable bag for life. And repeat.

Gwen remembered something Suze had used to say, every time they did a Tesco shop.

"Of course, 'bags for life' implies the existence of bags for death."

It had become less funny each time she said it ("I'm *recycling* the line!" "Well, don't.") but now it felt both profound and hilarious. Here they were, the bags for death. Ready and waiting to carry their cargo to the afterlife.

After Luke died, Suze had been supportively pragmatic, systematic, pushing her gently for small details and decisions. What food? Which flowers, and hymns? Do you have an appropriate bra? She asked the same questions a year later as Gwen's would-be maid of honor, nudging her listless friend gently but firmly into action. Each time Gwen wailed that she didn't know, she couldn't choose, Suze had shrugged and said, okay, we'll put a pin in it. Come back to it later.

She had said the same in the years that followed, each time Gwen had refused to get rid of the bin sack of Ryan's things. Your emotional baggage. Put a pin in it, come back to it later. As though it was that easy. Suze made life easy. Her patience and her constancy had carried Gwen through those early months, and now, as they quietly bundled the souvenirs of a truncated life into Marjorie's best reusable shoppers, she had the urge to call Suze and tell her all about it. To take the pin out now, and see what happened.

# Jumper

For the most part, Marjorie kept her memories of that day under netting. Carefully restrained, down in the murk. But from time to time, certain images would escape, rising straight to the surface with no warning. They would bob there in her subconscious, monstrous and grotesque, rotten from having been left for so long.

Seeing him there on the gurney, looking exactly the way he had when he slept in too late before school. Wanting to take him by the shoulders and shake him awake. To snatch the sheet off his body, to crouch down and scream into his pale, placid face that this wasn't a joke anymore. "Get up!" she had hissed at him, with such violent animation that Derek had put a reflexive arm across to restrain her. "Get up! Get up! Get up!"

The order had become a plea, had become a beg, had become distorted by heavy, rasping sobs of the kind Marjorie only ever produced when she was angry, not sad.

*Get up. Getupgetupgetup.*

*Get.*

*Up.*

"Sad" wasn't a word that held meaning for her in those first days, and months, even years. It rang hollow. Written down, it was like reading another language. She wasn't sad. She was furious. Furious at everything and furious at nobody; furious without an object or an outlet, which is the most painful kind. Anger coursed around her like a circuit with no break, cauterizing her from the inside out.

Sometimes she was afraid to touch people, in case she shocked them. In case it sparked.

Derek had been sad. While his wife blazed with rage and turned brittle, grief weighed upon him like wet sand. Grief, and something else: shame. He was embarrassed that this had happened, embarrassed at the fuss and the failure, embarrassed that this great crashing wave of misfortune had engulfed his family and not someone else's. He was deeply ashamed that he hadn't been able to save Luke, but more so that he hadn't resisted it harder, hadn't somehow appealed the decision, had given up the fight too soon. He was ashamed he hadn't leaped into the grave and persuaded them, whoever "they" were, to take him instead. Lying beneath a shroud of cool, damp earth would have felt entirely fitting; it was what he deserved.

Instead, Derek had to go on living in the daylight, blinking and squinting his way through who-knew-how-many more years. He didn't know how to accept that fortune, or live with that privilege. Didn't know how to tilt his face to the sun anymore. For that, he was ashamed.

Now, while his family were engrossed in their task, Derek quietly tucked his old jumper into one of the bags for life, beside a dog-eared student cookbook and a pair of paint-spattered speakers. He picked the bag up, and carried it downstairs to the hallway, where the afternoon's cloud had finally broken and a few golden beams were dappling the carpet. It was heavy, but for once he felt lighter.

## 49

Several hours had passed and Gwen was beginning to ache, both inwardly and outwardly from all the bending and lifting, when she spotted them inside an old nylon drawstring kit bag. She let out a low, hollow laugh.

They were still in good nick, as far as she could tell—orange and black neoprene and ridged latex, with Velcro wrist straps and puffy cartoon fingers. They could have been any old goalkeeper gloves, except she knew that they weren't. Because suddenly it came back to her, as though someone had blown a layer of dust from the memory. Ryan bringing them down for a visit, still in the early days of their relationship, "in case Luke fancies a kickabout"—and cringing even as she told him it was a nice idea. She remembered smiling gratefully at Luke as the two of them set off, obligingly, for the park around the corner while her mother shouted after them both to take jackets and Capri-Sun pouches from the pantry.

They had returned a good while later, pink-faced and damp-haired and buoyed with the triumph of having actually, seemingly, had a good time. "You hang onto them for now," Ryan had said as Luke handed back the gloves, because that was the kind of guy Ryan was, and he never played in London anyway.

Gwen smiled to herself, the gloves cheerful and innocuous in her hands. It was a nice memory, made nicer by the petty confirmation that she, after all, had been right.

# 50

In the evening, Derek made his Saturday spag bol and they ate it on lap trays in front of the TV, passing a tub of pre-grated Parmesan back and forth between them. It was good Bolognese, rich with wine and shimmering with oil, and Gwen tried not to feel angry that her father had waited sixty-seven years of his life to learn how to cook.

She asked for second helpings as a show of appreciation, but there weren't any. Because they hadn't been expecting her.

Even the question of her staying the night was an awkward one, her mother putting on a big show of making up the spare room for her—the room that had once been her own bedroom, with its *Smash Hits* posters and swagged curtains and dusty feather boa wound around the bed frame, and which was now painted magnolia and filled with tins of sweetcorn, an exercise bike and plastic storage boxes containing old copies of *Reader's Digest*. Gwen wondered at what point during the past twenty years she had crossed over the invisible threshold that meant she now had to ask politely to spend a night under her parents' roof. When did you become a guest in the house you once called home?

Gwen went to bed before they did, knowing that if she didn't she would be asked to "turn everything off, please"—a request that always left her so nervous about phantom house fires that she almost unplugged the fridge. Once or twice in later years she and

Luke had raced to see who would be the last one left downstairs, scrambling over each other and physically scrapping like the small children they'd never been together.

As she stood up and stretched, wondering whether to ambush her mother with a goodnight hug, Gwen noticed a plant on the side of the TV stand. A withered peace lily in a too-small glazed ceramic pot. Its leaves were all brown at the tips, its flowers entirely crisp.

"This looks half-dead," she said to her parents. "Does it need watering?"

They both looked up from the television.

"It doesn't get enough light on that side," said Marjorie hurriedly, at the same time as her husband protested, defensive, "It's always getting in the way of the screen."

They glanced at each other and her mother's expression changed, became almost mischievous. Without saying anything else, she took the plant from Gwen, walked into the hallway, emptied the whole thing into a waiting bin bag and placed the pot carefully in one of the boxes marked CHARITY SHOP.

"There," she said, dusting the soil off her hands and settling herself back on the sofa. Derek patted his wife on the knee. "Better."

# Slippers

It was Doug's first outing in seventeen days.

A wave of nausea hit him as he entered the shop, although it was hard to tell if that was panic or the scent of sugary vanilla that hung in the air from a nearby glass bottle full of sticks. He was disappointed to find not a single travel guide on the shelf, besides an old copy of *Lonely Planet Lisbon*: the same edition he had already, so he couldn't even compare updates to the text. But still, it was good to be out.

As he left, after completing his usual circuit—once around the shop, two minutes by the books as soon as the approach was clear, another circuit in the opposite direction, home—a pair of slippers caught his eye. White toweling, still in their plastic wrapper, with an embroidered insignia on the top of each mule reading *Grand Hotel Kempinski Vilnius*. Doug took a deep breath, circled back to the counter again, and bought them.

Two pounds fifty might be considered a lot by some, for an item that is famously free. But given he knew the precise cost of the cheapest room for a night at the Grand Hotel Kempinski Vilnius circa 2016, Doug thought it a pretty good deal.

## 51

Gwen woke with a jolt, from a dream in which she and will.i.am had been smuggling a brace of stuffed pheasants out of a pub, only to realize the birds were still alive, blowing their cover and showering them both with a confetti of feces. The sun was streaming onto her face from beneath a pair of gathered roman blinds, and she felt desiccated from the inside out. Her mouth was dry, her head woolly. It felt like a hangover, but she couldn't be hungover. Could she?

She stretched experimentally, to see what hurt. Her foot met with the radiator, confirming that she wasn't hungover but in fact at her parents' house, where the heating stayed on overnight as standard. Even in August. The events of the previous day reassembled themselves in her mind. Now, she knew what hurt.

It was only a little after 7 a.m., but Gwen could already hear squirrelly activity in the room next door. She groped for her phone.

Won't be able to make it in today I'm afraid, sorry! she messaged the shop's group chat. Ordinarily her gut would be churning with the stress of letting people down, but here among the *Reader's Digest*s, she was unusually calm. The shop felt far away, almost fictional. A lurid Oz peopled with characters that nobody here in Kansas would understand.

She did need to give a reason, though. "Family emergency"

would have fit the bill, except that the family emergency had happened seven years ago.

She could say she was ill. But then there would be follow-up questions, possibly a bootlegged prescription from Gloria. And of course she didn't technically *need* an excuse—volunteers canceled their shifts all the time, for the most spurious of reasons. Last week Finn had failed to turn up because he was having an emotional response to a Netflix documentary.

> Have had to go away for a few days unexpectedly,

she typed. Really sorry x

Within minutes, Asha messaged her separately. You all right?

Just sorting through some stuff with my parents, Gwen replied, as this was both literally and metaphorically true. Asha sent a thumbs-up emoji in reply. Gwen felt disappointed she didn't ask more.

After the strange festivity of yesterday, there was an odd Boxing Day-ish air to the morning. She felt half-compelled to rustle up a stuffing sandwich and climb under a blanket with the *Radio Times*. Instead, next door, she found Marjorie wearing yesterday's clothes and kneeling over a large plastic storage box. The room looked devastated but peaceful, washed clean by the morning light streaming through the newly open curtains. Kansas after the storm.

Her mother looked up and nodded at her—a simple "there you are" nod. And so Gwen knelt down beside her in her borrowed pajamas, and began to sort again. The job felt harder today for having been paused. She wondered if they'd been wrong to stop and go to bed. Then, looking around at the packed boxes and bags, more than a dozen of them now, she wondered if her mother even had.

"How are you doing?" Gwen asked, after a few minutes.

Marjorie ignored the question and began explaining her sorting system in the manner of Stealers Wheel. "Tops to the left of me, bottoms to the right. Sportswear on the ottoman—Yvonne's Laura might be able to take it for the asylum seekers."

"Are you okay, Mum?" she tried again.

"Me? Yes! Fine, fine. Just need to—"

She turned away and began scrubbing at a spot on his old desk, again and again, her knuckles turning white with exertion. Gwen knew without looking that it was the remnants of a long-faded football sticker.

"—this bloody thing, I told him—"

*Scrub. Scrub.* Crackling paint and splintering wood beneath her muttering.

"—never listened, that boy. Maybe white spirit—"

Suddenly it became too much. Gwen shuffled across the carpet and put her arms around her mother from behind, forcefully, pinning her elbows to her sides and quieting the frenetic scrape of the scouring pad. Marjorie struggled for a second and then Gwen felt her relent, becoming heavy within her embrace. She gripped more fiercely, as if to prevent her mother from sinking or slipping away.

When Marjorie finally spoke her voice was small and high, muffled against Gwen's arm.

"It was the right thing, you know. Not marrying him." Gwen relaxed her grip a little in surprise. "I don't think I ever said that to you, at the time, what with, you know, all the upset. But perhaps I should have. It was very . . . very . . ." she tailed off.

"Brave?" Gwen supplied, through a mouthful of hair.

"Yes," agreed her mother. "Very brave."

"Thank you," said Gwen. "That means a lot." She was surprised to realize that it did.

From the kitchen below came the croak of an elderly kettle and the traffic bulletin on Radio 2. They stayed in the hug for some time.

## 52

Her parents both hugged her goodbye, harder than usual, and Marjorie told Gwen her jacket was too flimsy.

"It's August!" said Gwen.

"*Late* August," her mother retorted, "which may as well be autumn." And even as she rolled her eyes, Gwen could feel the telltale cut of coolness in the air. Blackberries were visible in the brambled alleyway beside the house, which felt too early. But then it always did.

On the train back, she sat within a fortress of bags for life (for death) and watched as the Surrey Hills gave way to the thinly rolled edges of suburbia.

It had always been her tradition to cry on the train back from her parents' house. Back in the before times, when it had felt poetic to play Joanna Newsom through her headphones and press her cheek against the window and let her eyes brim with worry that she wasn't a good enough daughter. Reliving every sharp word and stroppy moment, reminding herself to cherish them now because one day they'd be gone. She had usually been over it by Worcester Park.

But since Luke had died, she hadn't indulged it. She had trained herself to block out everything that existed beyond the automatic doors, filling each of her sporadic journeys with podcasts and books and scrolling, scrolling, scrolling until her brain whirred blankly in time with the tracks. Now, Gwen gave herself permission to wallow again. She tentatively lowered herself into it, as though into a too-hot bath.

Mid-wallow, a message from Asha arrived.

> So I covered your shift this morning. Brian rugby-tackled a customer because he thought they were stealing a hat.

> He didn't.

> Right to the floor.

> Were they stealing a hat?

> Nope. Just . . . wearing a hat.

> Oh, Brian.

> It was a fugly hat, to be fair. I think we should be more insulted than they were.

Gwen sent a cry-laughing emoji, hoping Asha would forgive her for it. A pause, and then the reply:

> No pressure but when are you back?

It was nice to be asked.

> Today! On the train from Dorking Deepdene as we speak.

> As if that's a real place.

I promise you it is.

Shall I come and fetch you off the train yeah, carry
your bags?

Gwen smiled to herself. Please! she riffed back.
Hold up a small sign with my name on it. Maybe
wave a lacy handkerchief?

Asha sent a thumbs-up emoji, then nothing.

But when Gwen got off the train, there was Asha, sitting on the platform outside the sandwich kiosk beneath an obscene photo of a stuffed croissant exploding with molten cheese. She looked up, saw Gwen through the gaps between swaggering football fans and dithering tourists, and grinned.

"Came to meet you!"

"You . . . what?"

"I came. To meet. You." Asha enunciated as though to an idiot. "Like you wanted me to." She was already wrestling one of the many bags from Gwen's arms.

"I was joking! I thought we were joking! I didn't mean—"

Asha swatted a hand at her. "I know you were, you twat. But it sounded like you actually probably *did* need someone and I was sat on my arse at home, so." She shrugged, as though the thirty-minute Tube journey were a mere amble round the corner. "Ask and ye shall receive, Gwenneth."

Gwen swallowed down further protests, and threw her arms around Asha instead. "Thank you," she breathed into her shoulder.

She really did need help, as it happened. Two bags per hand was a lot to manage even without a suitcase, and the woven straps were already cutting into her wrists. Gwen let Asha take three of them from her, grateful she didn't look inside or—for once—ask any questions. Nor did Gwen protest when Asha led her out of the station and steered them not toward the entrance to the Tube, but into the nearest pub instead.

It was the trad kind of pub, with framed stock images of fish and chips on the walls and mercifully no neon or muskets. A clutch of tourists sipped delicately at foamy-headed pints, Harrods carrier bags around their feet.

Marjorie had taken her to Harrods once, when she was thirteen, and they'd argued the whole way up because Gwen had wanted to wear a tank top and Marjorie didn't think they'd be allowed in. In the end it had been fine, and they'd spent a jolly couple of hours, first trying to find the cheapest thing they could buy for the largest carrier bag, and then looking for the loos.

"So, some personal news," announced Asha, as soon as they were sitting down. Gwen's stomach performed its usual Pavlovian lurch at the words. "I'm going back to work. Next month. So you'd better soak up the best of me now, before I'm just a nocturnal husk of a human again."

"Oh! That's great!" said Gwen. Then, "*Is* it great?"

"It's fine. I think." Asha shrugged. "They're implementing a load of new HR policies, shorter hours, better support, new systems for reporting megalomaniac bosses, blah blah. We'll see. But they're letting me do four days a week for a while, so I'll still volunteer Saturday afternoons at the shop. You know, for kicks." She examined her cuticles, nonchalantly. "And because you'd miss me too much if I left."

Gwen agreed that she would.

"Anyway, there's my announcement. But how was your weekend?" asked Asha, mimicking hairdresser cadence. "Do anything nice?"

"It was . . . good, actually. In the end," said Gwen. "Cathartic."

"Yeah? Want to fill me in, or would you rather not?"

Gwen hesitated.

"If you don't want to, I'm going to tell you in minute detail about this date I went on last night with a guy who tried to sell me an eight-week course of motivational business seminars. It's a pretty spectacular story, so honestly I'm not bothered either way." Asha slurped at her own foamy-headed pint.

"Well, now I just want to hear that," said Gwen.

"We've got time for both," said Asha. "Or do you have hot Sunday-night plans?"

"*Antiques Roadshow*?"

Asha snorted.

"Okay," Gwen relented. "So."

It was the first time she'd ever said the words without holding her breath. Amid the strangeness of her surroundings, Asha's face open and encouraging and entirely without agenda, they slipped out easily. My. Brother. Died. She held them up in the stale, Sunday afternoon air and presented them as fact.

But Asha didn't give the usual response—I'm so sorry how awful what a tragedy you poor thing if it isn't an insensitive question can I ask . . .

Instead, she said: "Mine too."

Gwen took a second to register this.

"Wait, your . . . ?"

"Brother, yeah. Emmanuel. Leukemia. He was sixteen, I was twelve."

Gwen made the noise herself, then. The soft, involuntary little "oh."

And Asha laughed, gently, presumably at her stricken face. Gwen tried to rearrange her features to look less like someone who believed she had the monopoly on sibling bereavement, but her muscles seemed to be frozen.

"I know," said Asha, nodding as though her gawp spoke volumes. "Sucks."

Gwen agreed that it did.

"Anyway, I want you to finish your story," Asha went on, unfazed. "What's all this stuff? Why have you brought it back here?"

"Emotional baggage," explained Gwen. "His old things—for the shop. It's my mother's way of supporting me, I think."

"Fair enough," said Asha. "St. Michael will make you volunteer of the month when he sees all this."

"I didn't know we had volunteer of the month?" said Gwen.

"Oh we've always had it—it's just that most months he doesn't consider anybody worthy of winning."

"That makes sense."

"So, do you want to ask me about it?" Asha ran a finger methodically across the inside of a split-open crisp packet.

"About Emmanuel?" asked Gwen. "I'd love to, if you're comforta—"

"Oh—no," Asha shook her head. "I mean, you can, sure! I like talking about him. It's good, it helps. But I meant the motivational business guy."

"Oh! A hundred percent."

"Gwen, it was called 'Demand Your Destiny' and it was eight hundred quid."

"Oh god."

"He told me he knew I was going to sleep with him because he had *man-i-fested ittt*." She slapped her palm on the table in time with each syllable, eyes wide with gleeful horror.

"I'm so sorry. Thoughts and prayers."

"Thank you." Asha paused, looking sheepish. "I mean, I slept with him anyway."

"You WHAT?"

"He was hot, Gwen! It was very motivational for me."

They both spluttered with laughter as Asha made the case for the defense. "I didn't sign up for the course, so frankly I think that demonstrates excellent strength of character."

"Hey, I can't judge," said Gwen, keen to offer up some morsel of solidarity and realizing, for once, that she could. "I've not made the best decisions recently. In that . . . area."

Asha's eyes widened again.

"And what do you mean by that, young Gwen . . . nifer?" she wiggled her eyebrows suggestively.

"Gwendoline."

"Sure."

Despite the mood of unfettered honesty, Gwen found herself unable to look at Asha while she said it. So she smooshed her cheek against the gummy lacquer of the pub table and said, in a muffled voice: "Nicholas."

"Oh, I know about that," said Asha, ripping calmly into a fresh bag of Thai Sweet Chilli.

Gwen peered up through her fringe. "You *knew*?"

"Yep. 'Course." Gwen hauled herself upright.

"Did he tell you?"

"To be fair to him, no he did not."

"Who then?"

She half-expected Asha to say that she had sensed it, picked up on the vibes, had a feeling in her waters. But instead she said: "Connie."

"Oh." Gwen waited to feel shocked and furious, but she found she didn't have the energy. Instead she said: "That makes sense."

"She said she was concerned for you because of your poor decision making."

"I bet she did." They were both grinning again now.

"She said it in front of Nicholas, which was harsh."

Gwen sighed. "Sounds about right."

They stayed in the pub for several hours—first rinsing the Nicholas saga for every drop of comedic value, and then swapping stories about Emmanuel and Luke. The ways in which their brothers had often been pricks. And the ways in which, now more than ever, they were loved.

# Handbag

Sheena couldn't quite believe her luck. Sure, the bag was a bit scuffed and there was an oil stain on the lining—but the scuffs were nothing she couldn't buff out with a little shoe polish, and anyway, didn't that add to it? Made it look used, which made her look like someone who could afford to buy a posh bag and not keep it in a cupboard for best. It might just have been the talisman she needed for this new job, this new life, in which she paid her own way and nobody could call her a freeloader anymore. In which she was a *small business owner*. A small business owner with a large business handbag.

It was pricey, yes, for a charity shop, but then the Gel Lyfe handbook said you had to spend money to make money. Everyone said that, in fact, it was a common expression. And with the fancy bag, people would know they could take her seriously at the meetings. People would look up to her, and trust her when she explained that they, too, could liquify their solidified potential and join the pool of dedicated Gel Lyfe "gelievers."

It needed somebody trustworthy, somebody with a bit of something about them. Sheena knew that, because she had been skeptical at first too. It was a lot to spend on herbal gel, all in one go. It was a lot to spend on *anything* all in one go.

But when Maxine—Maxine was her Diamond Team Queen, having worked all the way up from lowly Flint level like herself, so inspiring—had arrived at the meeting in her aloe-green Maserati with the personalized license plate, and she had taken both of Sheena's hands in her own and looked into her eyes and said, "Doubt is the dam that holds back the reservoir of your potential," and Sheena had thought of her giant teenage sons and their slammed doors, the way they looked through her and past her and over her head, never in the eye unless they were asking for money again, and she imagined being able to present them with brand-new Yeezys and iPhones and Xboxes on Christmas morning, she had simply felt in her gut that spending the money was the right thing to do. The brave thing to do, Maxine had said.

"It is brave to make an investment in *you*, in your own future and your family's future," she had said, while her assistant passed out the Gelicious Booster Packs. "Cowards stay comfortable in the present. Winners take a leap into the future. Which are you going to be, a coward or a winner? A rock or a river?"

"A river!" they had all shouted. Then Maxine had explained that rocks were sometimes diamonds in disguise, and needed the pressure of the river to make them sparkle. This had seemed contradictory (was the river made of . . . gel?), but nobody challenged it.

So Sheena had taken her savings, borrowed a little more from her sister, spread the rest across a couple of credit cards, and invested in herself. In her future, and her family's future. It was all so exciting. The day the crate arrived (and alarmingly it was a crate, not a box, but it could double up as a coffee table until she started shifting units), she'd felt such a strange rush of what Maxine called "potential reverberations" that she'd had to go to bed for the afternoon. Apparently this was normal.

All she had to do was wait for her Gelevation Starter Pack, and then she could finally begin recruiting her team. And now she had the handbag! It was all coming together.

"This actually used to be my bag!" said the girl on the till when she took it up to pay—half in cash, half with the dregs of her overdraft. Sheena didn't know what to make of this. If the girl was in a position to donate expensive handbags then why was she working in a charity shop?

"It never suited me," the girl went on. "Or maybe I never suited it? But anyway, glad it's going to a good home. I hope it brings you loads of luck."

Sheena decided to take this as a good sign. She made a mental note to come back once she'd achieved full Geligibility and see if the girl was interested in joining her team.

## 53

By the time she next saw Nicholas, a week had passed since the gold clock had been returned to its owner.

If he was aware of what had happened then he showed no sign of it—but nor did he look at, speak to, or otherwise interact with Gwen, beyond necessities like passing her a rubber band when she asked for a rubber band, and not walking directly into her in the stockroom. It was hard to tell if this was because he was angry with her, or bored of her, or because he believed they had moved into some spicy new phase of their relationship where they fought and ignored each other, and eventually burst out and humped in the bubble-wrap pile.

To everyone else, he was still being Nicholas at his most Nicholas-esque—shelling pistachios as a snack, reading out choice extracts from *The Mindful Book of Gut Health*, dancing Gloria around in a little waltz when Andy Williams came on the radio—but Gwen was frozen out, persona non grata, not even worthy of the most basic attention. It was bliss.

She thought for a while about the advantages of having sex with somebody objectionable but not having to speak to them afterward. If she could guarantee the same outcome, how many more times might she have done it over the years? With the man from the organic shop who wore those rubber shoes with individual toes? With Gregor, the slick-haired security guard from her old office building, whose Kafkaesque qualities included scuttling sideways into the lift just as the doors were closing, and lying on his back doing yoga stretches behind the reception desk during quiet periods?

Maybe Terry, the man who came to fix and service her boiler, and who always spoke to her with thinly disguised contempt at her lack of boiler-based knowledge. Fuck it, maybe Jeremy? No, not Jeremy.

Maybe Jeremy?

It was during these reveries that Gwen felt a sharp tap on her shoulder and turned to see Janet McAffery's daughter standing there, a little out of breath, this time wearing a nurse's uniform and turquoise Crocs.

"I just wanted to say thank you for getting Mum's clock back," she said, loudly. "We're so grateful." She thrust a small box of Celebrations into Gwen's hands.

Gwen accepted the thanks as quietly and graciously as she could, sounding like a firefighter being interviewed on the news ("Oh, it's all part of the service!"). But when the woman left, she turned around, slowly, to see Nicholas standing exactly where she somehow knew he would be. Listening to the whole exchange. Watching her, after all.

He caught up with her as she left the shop, trying to fall coolly into step beside her but stumbling a little over his deck shoes as he swerved to avoid a bin.

"Hi, Nicholas."

"So, obviously, you stole the clock."

Gwen swallowed. "I—I wouldn't say *stole*."

"Seb at the Boar and Balls said someone swiped it straight off the wall during happy hour."

"Okay, yes, well."

"Obviously you had no right, Gwen."

"I'm not saying I—Janet, who it belonged to, she . . . look, this is ridiculous," she blustered. "I'm not apologizing, Nicholas, it was the right thing to do."

"It was a legitimate business transaction," he fired back. "You undermined my . . . my *business*, Gwen."

She took in his scowling face, his ears bright pink with indignation, the way he made "my business" sound like a toddler talking about their own poo, and she wanted to laugh. At the absurdity of the whole conversation, the rollicking sitcom farce that her life had apparently become.

"You don't have a business, Nicholas," she snapped. "You have an Etsy account."

Nicholas made a noise like a faulty extractor fan.

"I turned over a hundred grand last year."

This stopped her cold. Could that possibly be true?

A more secure woman might smooth things over. Ask him *how*, exactly, and what were his top tips for success, and was he looking to hire a tat-sourcing associate? Instead Gwen said: "Well, woop-de-do for you."

Nicholas absorbed this with a small smirk. Woop-de-do for him.

They walked on for a while. Gwen studiously maintained enough space between them on the pavement so there was no danger of their hands brushing. She had to trot at an awkward, syncopated pace to match his lolloping stride. Sensing that Nicholas would continue this way for hours if necessary, Gwen caved first.

"Fine, fuck, I'm sorry. I'm sorry I stole the clock."

He turned and looked at her, visibly triumphant. "Thank you," he said, with exaggerated grace. Then: "You promise you won't do it again?"

"Why would I need to do it again?" Gwen yelped, swerving to avoid a dachshund on a lead. "How many senile old women are you planning to swindle out of their family heirlooms?"

She saw Janet's face again as she said this. In profile, her eyes fixed on the television as the stately *tick, tick, tick* of the clock filled the small room once more. Heard the weary voice in which she had remarked, less to Gwen than to the world at large: "Sometimes, I wish the bloody thing would stop. Just to give us all a rest."

Gwen had understood this. *Stop all the clocks*. An aunt had read the poem at Luke's funeral, because nobody had worked out how to ask her not to. "That lovely one from the film!" she'd prefaced the offer, so it wasn't even as if she didn't know.

Nicholas was still talking. "On track for even more, this year," he was saying. "I'm, like, diversifying into escape rooms? Signed a big contract with a new escape complex in Vauxhall. So that's obviously pretty cool."

Then he said, "By the way, you're not supposed to say 'senile.' The correct phrase is 'living with dementia.'"

"Oh." Gwen stopped processing the words "escape complex."

"My uncle is living with it."

"Right. I'm—oh god, I'm sorry, Nicholas." Certainly she felt worse about this than the clock. "I didn't know. About the word, or—"

"It's fine, he's a wanker. He was before."

"Right."

They had walked, now, all the way back to her street. She waited for him to make some final comment and walk away, but he showed no sign of it and instead seemed to be turning left with her, toward her flat. She recognized now that he wasn't angry, possibly had never been angry, so much as he was imagining the pair of them as sexy verbal sparring partners: a kind of discount Katharine Hepburn and Spencer Tracy.

Gwen stopped in the middle of the pavement and turned to face him. She felt incredibly tired.

"What do you want?" she asked.

"I thought we should, obviously, you know. Clear the air. Talk things through a bit more."

"Things?"

Not for the first time, Gwen marveled at some people's determination to seek out uncomfortable conversations while others, the normal ones, fled from them as if from rampaging dinosaurs. Was it a class thing? A patriarchal thing? A product of too much structured reality TV, everyone incessantly taking each other aside in wine bars for *words*?

"We could have a drink at yours?"

"Why?"

"Well, it's closer than mine, but obviously if you wanted to—"

"No, why would you want to do that?" she asked.

"As in . . . how do you mean?"

Nicholas looked puzzled.

"Why do you want to have a drink with me?"

"I mean"—his voice became haughty now, though she could hear the quiver beneath it—"obviously, because I like you. Obviously."

"I know," said Gwen, because she did.

"Obviously I assumed you felt the same way," he said.

"Obviously."

"But you don't?"

This was torture. Why did people have to go around being honest with each other? Why couldn't everyone accept that polite society was built on a grand tradition of lies and evasion, of reading between the lines, beating about the bush and never having to hear the damning words out loud? How did you tell a person the truth to their face without immediately bursting into flames?

"Uh," she faltered. "Look, I wouldn't say that."

Gwen had begun to sweat beneath her fringe. She could feel it prickling between her eyebrows. She wondered how she could still worry about appearing unattractive to a person even in the middle of sexually rejecting them.

"What would you say, though?" He sounded genuinely curious, the way he had asking about her life story in the ramen restaurant. Perhaps he kept a file. *Notes for future rejections.*

"I was . . . making my mind up?" She focused very hard on his left ear. "Um. Experimenting."

She cringed as soon as she said it, and harder when he repeated it.

"Experimenting?" He raised an eyebrow, which had quite the opposite effect on her now. As though someone had put a silica gel sachet in her knickers.

"Well, you know . . . I was previously in a serious relationship, and so . . ."

"I thought you said that ended, like, four years ago?"

*Six.*

"Well technically, yes, but—"

"So I think you're a little past experimenting aren't you, Gwen?"

She inhaled sharply at this. To be fair, so did Nicholas, looking taken aback by his own cruelty.

"Uh—I mean—obviously, not *past it*, but, obviously, just . . ." he tailed off, and Gwen stayed silent, listening to him flail, watching for the precise moment when he would realize that they absolutely, categorically, wouldn't be having sex again.

There it was.

"I'm sorry," he said. "That was uncalled for. But obviously you're not into it, so obviously I'll stop making a fool of myself."

He cleared his throat and looked down at his shoes. "I liked you," he finished, lamely. Past tense this time.

"I know," she said softly, and forced herself to make eye contact. Nicholas blinked. "I'm sorry." She hoped he might gather his wounded pride into his satchel and leave, but he stayed where he was.

"I'm sorry, Nicholas," she went on, "for the way I've . . . ah, treated you. I handled it badly."

Not until she said this did she realize it might be true. It was jarring to discover that she still had the power to hurt someone in this way. That her affection was not, after all, an obsolete currency.

"I've just been . . . you know, trying to work out what I did wrong. If there are, like, actionable points, it would be helpful to know." He flushed and rubbed his hand briskly over the back of his neck, and she saw his vulnerability in that moment; had an unhelpful flashback to his vulnerability panting into her left ear. "Except the clock, obviously, although I still maintain I was well within my rights to—"

"I think," Gwen interrupted him, the self-knowledge dawning in real time. "I think perhaps I was so busy focusing on my own insecurities that I forgot that you also had feelings."

To her relief, Nicholas seemed to accept this.

"Ah, that's the thing." He said it helpfully, as though correcting her in a pub quiz. "I do."

"Yes," she agreed, and gave his arm a consolatory squeeze. "Obviously."

# Hat

---

It was a stupid amount of money to spend on a hat, said Poppy. Especially from a charity shop, where stuff was supposed to be cheap, and especially when you could get a million hats online, where stuff was even cheaper. Besides, nobody they knew wore a hat like this.

Nobody they knew wore a hat like this, and Skye told her that was the point. At least it was to Skye, for whom teen conformity was beginning to feel like an old-timey arcade game, swerving to avoid as many potholes as they could in the race toward an ever-retreating finish line.

It felt to Skye that every decision was now a trick question, every innocent choice a trapdoor that landed them in a box they never asked to be in. Good/bad. Girl/boy. Alt/main. Dark/light academia. VSCO/kidcore/cyber/low-fi/nu-preppy/old-world romantic. Geography or history. Activist or nihilist. Almond or oat. The fear of having no identity was in perpetual seesaw with the fear of being swallowed up and swept away by the wrong one. Skye liked to picture themselves as a master of balance and resistance, their core muscles holding fast against all these dueling forces of cool in the same way they did against gravity on their skateboard. It was exhilarating. Sometimes exhausting.

But the hat knew none of this. The hat seemed sure of itself, ostentatiously so, and this appealed to Skye as much as its silken lining, the fancy scripted logo on the label and the tiny feather tucked into its brim.

It fitted into no subculture Skye was aware of; seemed instead to hang above all that on a lofty hook of its own. Surculture, could it be called? Skye had a great uncle who had once taken them to an opera at the Coliseum and explained at length the difference between subtitles and surtitles, between tenor and alto, between actual misogyny and beautiful art that was simply Of a Different Time, my dear. Skye had fallen asleep halfway through the second act, fighting to keep their eyelids open as the music pressed upon them like a weighted blanket. They'd felt bad until they turned to see the great uncle was snoring softly, head slumped on his chest.

"But that's why we come, child," he'd said afterward. "It's the best nap in town."

The great uncle might have worn a hat like this, come to think of it. Except he was dead now.

Skye bought the hat with the money from their job as tea-maker and sweeper-upper in a local hair salon. It was a place where their core muscles were worked hard every weekend, both in bending over the sink and in turning down offers of free highlights, toning shampoo, and deep conditioning treatments from the various stylists who wanted to "sort out" Skye's hair. The hat might help deflect this kind of attention, Skye hoped. They were a hat person now.

It felt heavy and solid on Skye's head, and they liked that. It was perhaps half an inch too big, and they liked that too—room to grow, it felt like, although at fifteen they didn't know if their head could reasonably be expected to get any bigger. While it might look like a wild choice on their next non-uniform day, there was a permanence to the hat that felt reassuring. That, unlike the candy-hued rainbow freckles that Poppy painted on each morning, over the bridge of her nose and up toward her temples, it belonged to a tradition, not a trend, and that couldn't be washed away.

The law of the out-there fashion purchase, Skye already knew, is that it only goes one of two ways: either you wear the thing incessantly, wondering who you even *were* before it came along to complete you, or you feel like a giant idiot on its very first outing and never wear the thing again.

Skye was curious, as they stepped out of the shop and surveyed their jaunty new reflection in the window, to see which this would be.

## 54

Among Gwen's wider social circle, the first wave of second marriages was well underway. As a general rule these tended to have smaller dresses, smaller budgets, shorter guest lists, and fewer blackboards with adorable messages on them in chalk, though she was relieved to find that the booze allocation had stayed the same.

In the end she took no one, styling it out as a noble sacrifice for the sake of the catering budget. It seemed easier to remain untethered. And there were enough people she knew at the wedding, not just from university but in all the various, tenuous ways one knows people from across the years—partners of friends, work friends of friends, "home friends" of friends, friends of friends with the mutual friend having slipped out somewhere along the way. There was a lot of overlap with the crowd who had so earnestly invited her round to dinner at Suze and Paul's wedding five years earlier. Dinners that had mostly never happened. A sea of people who either never messaged, or whom she never messaged back.

"Gwen! Where have you *been*?" several demanded to know. This felt baffling to her, as she'd been the one more or less stationary for the past half decade, sat in one place like a lost child in a shopping center. But she knew what they meant. They meant: where had she been *digitally*? Optically? Where were her headlines, her milestones, her proudly trumpeted life announcements? Why had she allowed herself to fall so carelessly off their radar?

"Oh, you know," she replied each time. "Just . . . around."

She spotted Ryan early on across the ceremony hall, and braced herself for Clea and the child to loom into view, probably lit with sunbeam halos like a painting of the Madonna. But they didn't, and her stomach gurgled in relief. Ryan appeared to have come on his own, although he spent most of the wedding on his phone to compensate. She passed him a little later during the canapés, giving detailed instructions in a harried voice on the whereabouts of something called a "Bluey."

He gave her an eye-rolling, "my life, eh?" kind of gurn. There was goat's cheese in his beard. She walked on.

Having clung to Suze and Paul for most of the day so far, at dinner Gwen was cruelly wrenched away by the table plan. She found herself seated with strangers, a couple roughly her own age on one side and the groom's uncle on the other. The uncle had brought his own condiment sachets, which he produced from a ziplock bag tucked inside his suit pocket as the first course arrived. Gwen turned to the couple.

"So," she began, hoping a better question would present itself before the inevitable one left her mouth. It didn't. "What do you do?"

"I'm a photographer," the man replied, with considerable pride.

"Oh, cool!" said Gwen. "What have you been shooting recently?"

"Cornstarch," he replied, reaching for the wine.

"Is that . . . a band?"

"No," he said. "For Tesco. I do the 'serving suggestion' pictures for the packets."

In many ways this was more interesting to Gwen than a band would have been. And so she spent the next twenty minutes learning about the ins and outs of the packaging photography business. She learned which retailers used stock imagery and which shot their own; the tricks used to get the best steam rise on a jug of custard; the possible legal ramifications of a misrepresented garden pea or an overly Photoshopped sausage. The photographer seemed thrilled to have such an engaged audience. His girlfriend seemed equally grateful for the chance to look at her phone for twenty minutes.

Just as he was finally obliged to ask her what she did and she was going to be obliged to tell him, forks began clinking against glasses for the speeches. These were mercifully short and surprisingly creative, most of the more obvious material having been used up at the first weddings. The best man had spent £30 on an app for a reality star to wish the happy couple a wonderful life together. He looked delighted with himself until it became clear that the bride and groom didn't know who the reality star was.

Afterward came the awkward milling around portion of the day—"the perineum," Suze always called it—while the happy couple and their photographer tried to make the best of an overcast golden hour.

Gwen found she couldn't help but look at the room with her charity shop goggles on. She took in its parade of tiny pointless clutch bags and individual picture-clip table settings, wondering how much of this stuff would eventually end up in a bin bag for someone like her to sift through. And then how much of that stuff would end up in further bin bags, and further still, as all the items that had once seemed so vital (the picture clips were, she noticed now, inscribed with today's date and the happy couple's initials) became embroiled in a giant game of pass-the-parcel that ultimately ended up in the ground.

"I see donations everywhere," she'd whispered to Asha last week, in a Hayley Joel Osmond voice. St. Michael had overheard, and nodded approvingly.

"That happens," he'd said.

The generational skew of this wedding was different too: more friends, fewer doddery relatives being helped around the buffet table. Was this because familial guilt was weaker the second time round, or because there weren't many doddery relatives left? There were fewer pregnant friends to fetch soft drinks for this time too, more who were wild-eyed and giddy on the promise of a babysitter and a last-minute deal on Booking.com. Dave SickInBush was petitioning the DJ for "Born Slippy" and it was barely 8 p.m.

She felt a hand brush her arm and turned to find Ryan at her side. He air-kissed her hello, which felt excessive given they'd been skirting around each other in the same room for the past six hours. Ryan had never been an air-kisser, and clearly still wasn't.

"Can't stay much longer," he began, waggling his phone at her. "Need to get back to—"

"—yes, yep. Sure."

"But I just wanted to, you know. Check in. It's really good that you came, Gwen."

Perhaps she was imagining it, but Gwen thought she could feel a small crackle of attention surge around the room. Eyes flickered in their direction. Heads turned toward them, then quickly away again.

"Thanks. I—Er, it's great to be here," she replied, sounding like a gameshow contestant.

"And if you ever need anything, you know where I am," he said.

"Streatham," she replied, distractedly. More eyes, more craned necks and knowing glances. She and Ryan were apparently more compelling entertainment than the £30 reality star.

"Er, yeah. Exactly."

"Thank you," she said, because this seemed to be what he expected her to say. The bride and groom were looking over now. Gwen felt lightheaded. The familiar creep of pins and needles began to prickle up the nape of her neck.

"Anyway, it's . . . well, good to be in touch again. Good to see you doing so well.'

He squeezed her bare arm, then left his hand there for a second, his index finger briskly stroking her skin, back and forth, back and forth, in a gesture she imagined was meant to be comforting. Suze beamed encouragingly from the other side of the doughnut wall.

The room began spinning. It was hard to tell the eyes from the spotlights reflected off the disco ball.

"Excuse me," said Gwen. She yanked her arm away from him and bolted out of the room, letting the heavy door slam shut behind her. *Closure.*

## 55

The loos were a state. Gwen went from cubicle to cubicle—two brimming with mounds of paper, one murky with brown water—flushing them as she went, like a kind of benevolent toilet fairy.

Finally she settled on the last cubicle and sat there for a while after she was finished. She leaned her face against the cool tiles of the cubicle wall, feeling blood pulse around her brain in time with the bass line from the dancefloor (currently "Hey Ya" by Outkast). Her heart was lodged in her throat like a too-large chunk of potato, her stomach somewhere south of her feet.

People talked about panic attacks as though they were emotional—just a fit of intense worrying that could be driven off with calming, medicinal thoughts—but hers were always physical. She could feel her eyelids and elbows, her esophagus, her liver, all twanging, quickening, threatening some form of imminent disaster. Every organ in her body vying for attention while her brain sat above it all, powerless to stop them. She placed her palms against the wall too, and tried to exhale for four counts. The third caught on the lump in her throat and left her coughing and rasping for air.

Someone came into the toilets then, and Gwen tensed as they let themselves into the stall next to hers and commenced a noisy medley of peeing, nose-blowing, and sputtering flatulence. The person then proceeded to fix their makeup at the sink, humming a little to themselves as they did.

Gwen was grateful for her tiny bunker, the way she had been grateful for hundreds of toilet cubicles over the course of her life. They were small sanctuaries, each one a temporary safe house that granted blissful anonymity for as long as there was a locked door with nobody banging on it. London was filled with these former panic rooms. She could hear the ghost of her own ragged breathing in chain coffee shops and department store stairwells across the city.

If this were a film, somebody else would come into the room now and Gwen would be forced to overhear an unflattering conversation about herself. *"Did you see even Gwen got invited?" "I know, such a barrel-scrape." "I heard she gave up her job to work in a charity shop." "Oh my god, weird." "I know, right?" "Don't get trapped talking to her!" "Come and rescue me if I do?"* Then she would have the option of emerging from her cubicle and washing her hands in their mortified silence, possibly sashaying out to the opening bars of Aretha Franklin's "Respect."

But this wasn't a film, and slowly, eventually, boredom began to override her nervous system. The pins and needles in her face had subsided, the frantic bellows in her chest had slowed. She recognized the beginnings of her usual panic comedown—still shaky, woozy, nauseous, but comfortingly pedestrian compared to the wildly unpredictable symptoms that sent her soaring upward.

Gwen lifted her head off the tiles, experimentally, and found it bearable. She left the cubicle and treated herself to a fringe-wash and blow-dry beneath the hand dryer. Connie's words echoed in her head. *You never regret going out. Not really.*

Walking back into the venue, she couldn't see Ryan anywhere and was glad. But she spotted Paul in a corner, slumped a little, his bow tie half undone and his pocket square billowing loose like a nightclub magician. Suze was on the other side of the room, deep in conversation with the artist formerly known as Wazzo, who was now something high up in a humanitarian aid charity and made regular appearances on Radio 4.

Gwen traced Paul's eyeline onto the dance floor and found he wasn't looking at his wife, but at a couple dancing with a wobbly toddler in a pair of ear defenders. The child looked less charmed by this situation than everyone around him, but he seemed to understand his role, stamping his little bootied feet arrhythmically to "Groove Is in the Heart" while the wedding photographer leaped around trying to capture the magic.

In the absence of anyone else to talk to, Gwen fetched a pint of water from the bar and sat down next to Paul.

He turned to smile at her, glassily.

"Gwen! Where have you been?"

"Toilet," she told him, truthfully. This should be the answer she gave every time. Where had she been all her life? Toilet.

"All right, mate?" she asked, handing him the water. She had never called him "mate" before. Possibly no one had ever called Paul "mate" before.

"I'm very, very well thank you, I'm very . . . yes."

"Very yes?"

"Indeed."

They sat in companionable silence for a little while, watching the dance floor. The bridesmaids were trying to perform some kind of choreographed routine, growing stone-faced as the photographer ignored them and the bride kept rushing off to hug departing guests. Waiters were beginning to circulate with bacon rolls on silver trays.

"It's all bollocks you know, Gwen," said Paul. "All of this." He flapped his hand solemnly at the scene before them. She felt a light spray of spittle gently fleck her cheek.

"Is it?" she replied. "Which part, specifically?"

"All the stuff. The fuss. The performance."

This wasn't a groundbreaking opinion, but she let him continue.

"You get married—I mean, not *you*. Ah—*one* gets married.

And it's all lovely and promises and foreverandever amen, bish bash bosh, you know?"

"I think we've established that I do not know," said Gwen.

"No! Sorry, sorry." He felt to be on the verge of calling her "old gel." "But the point is, you get married and you think you're sorted. But you're not sorted, Gwen."

"Not me?"

"No not you! Well, not you—but not anyone, is what I mean. You're still two clueless idiots pinballing around the place, just in a slightly sturdier box than before."

This was surprisingly profound. He ruined the effect by belching loudly and jumping, startled, at the sound.

"But you and Suze have a lovely, sturdy box," she replied. Paul snorted. Then he shook his head in self-reproach, and looked very sad.

"We do, Gwen, we do. I am very lucky. I don't know how I got so very, very—*hic*—very lucky. But my darling wife and I have different ideas about things, it turns out. We differ on a couple of fundamental points."

Gwen felt that this had been obvious for years to anyone with eyes, but now didn't seem the time to point it out. Vulnerability from Paul was alarming. She was reminded of the time, many years ago, when she had accidentally walked in on Suze applying antibiotic cream to a boil on his arse.

"Every couple has their differences though!" she heard herself say. "That's what keeps things interesting, surely."

"Oh yes, yess yes," Paul agreed, attempting a clumsy wink. "Very interesting. Very . . . very lucky." He paused. "But this is one *fundamental* difference of opinion, Gwen." His gaze drifted back to the dance floor, where the toddler was now lying belly-down on the ground, pounding his fists and hammering his feet in a tantrum being drowned out, somewhat poetically, by Daft Punk's "Get Lucky."

"Anyway, I'm sure you know all about Suze's feelings on the matter."

She didn't know anything about Suze's feelings on the matter, but even to Paul in his current state it would hurt to admit this. Besides, she was beginning to guess. To Paul, she smiled what she hoped would read as a knowing-yet-sympathetic smile, glad of the insight while ashamed that this was how, finally, she had to glean it.

"I want to be a dad, Gwen, is that such a crime? Doessit make me a patriarch-ch-ichal dinosaur? I'd carry the ruddy fetus myself if I could!"

Inwardly, something unknotted itself in relief and she felt ashamed of that too. All those years that Gwen had spent guiltily fearing the specter of the ultrasound photo, tensed for the Big News rip tide that would drag her best friend even further away. All that time, Suze had been struggling with her own place among the have-nots. They could have talked about it. Why hadn't they talked about it?

She patted Paul's arm, and he let out a childish whine and dropped his big, posh head onto her shoulder. Unsure what else to do, she put a steadying arm around him and let him rest there, slumped like a bag of wet sand. Mercifully, Suze had just broken away from Wazzo to begin weaving her way across the room to-ward them both, mouthing apologies.

"Sorry, this yours?" asked Gwen as she approached.

"Never seen it before in my life," replied Suze. "You can keep him."

But then she sat down on the other side of her husband, placed a gentle hand on his thigh and said, "Hey there," with such ten-derness and intimacy that Gwen looked away out of politeness. Paul lifted himself off Gwen's shoulder and turned toward his wife, smiling sleepily.

"Shall we?" he asked her.

"Let's," she replied, hoisting him to his feet and blowing kisses to Gwen as they made their way toward the exit.

\*

After they left, Gwen sat for a few minutes watching the dance floor. It was at the sweet spot now, where everyone has drunk enough to leave taste and dignity at the door but not so much that anyone has lost their momentum, or their eyelashes. From experience she guessed that they had about two good songs left, three at a push.

She stood up, planning to leave. But then, she remembered Heather, longing for her night on the tiles. She thought of Asha too, and Brenda, and Finn—even Connie, whose exasperation still rang in Gwen's ears like a smoke alarm. Instead of slipping out quietly, she moved onto the dance floor and allowed herself to be swallowed up by the throng.

People beamed delightedly as they saw her appear in their midst between whirling arms and flying hair. They hugged her and high-fived her, held her by the shoulders, and breathed warm wine into her face.

"Gwen! Where have you *been*?"

Gwen said nothing this time, just smiled and shrugged. And danced, and danced, and danced.

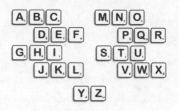

# Scrabble

The residents preferred the classic games, as a rule.

Or at least that was the party line among the care home staff, ever since a spirited game of Cards Against Humanity had resulted in several complaints from family members who feared their parent or relative had entered a dark new phase that even a *Daily Express* subscription couldn't account for.

No, classic games were best. Although "classic" in this case meant not so much the ancient and noble pastimes like chess, backgammon, mah-jongg—more those that evoked memories of Boxing Days wreathed in gaudy nostalgia and steeped in Blue Nun. Boggle, Cluedo, Monopoly, Battleships, Trivial Pursuit—*not* Twister, despite several residents' determination that it would make a diverting alternative to seniors' Pilates—and Scrabble.

Brenda had bought the Scrabble set from the charity shop where she volunteered when she wasn't at the home. The manager had told her repeatedly that she didn't need to wear the tabard as a personal visitor (this was the phrase she used, "*personal visitor*"), but Brenda insisted. "Not much in life makes me feel important anymore, Marian. Let me have a tabard."

"Besides," she had added, "it means I don't have to sit with the old lump if I don't want to."

Roy had been near enough nonverbal for over a year now, which for anyone would be hard. But for a person as chatty as Brenda it felt like an especially cruel joke. As though the universe was telling her: *hush, woman.*

She retaliated by talking even more. She would tell her stories, and his stories, and their stories, ostensibly to him but more often to anyone within earshot. Their travels, their adventures, their scrapes: all rubbed smooth by the years like beach pebbles. She narrated each time-worn episode with the commitment of a radio actor, accents and everything. Watching him all the time for a flicker of recognition, the ghost of a smile. Often she would embroider details or deliberately bungle facts in the hope that Roy might be moved to suddenly spring from his stupor and shout: "No! You're wrong!"

Brenda would play Scrabble with the other residents in much the same way, sitting next to him where he could get a clear view of her little tiles, spelling out the rudest words she could think of ("Fourteen points for 'titwank,' Royston, what do you think of that?") and taunting him by playing easy, short words when they both knew she could think of better ones with a little time and patience. Brenda had run out of time and patience.

Inevitably Gillian, a retired headteacher with dramatically lush eyebrows who had once made it to a series final on *Countdown*, would win the game.

"Enjoy the money, Gillian. Dear lord, Gillian, what a sad little life," Brenda would sometimes quip, before remembering that none of the residents knew that meme. She wished Finn were there, in those moments. Finn and Brenda had a kinship founded on mutual cultural education and a love of everyday melodrama. "Being extra," Finn called it. Brenda had often felt surplus to requirements in life and liked the idea of reframing this as a positive thing.

Once, after an especially tragic defeat, Brenda had upended the Scrabble board in mock-fury, tiles flying everywhere, a great, fake howl of anguish letting rip from her five-foot-one-inch frame—just for the sake of something to do. A few of the residents had tutted at the disturbance. One man, Kenneth, had cried: "Control your wife,

Roy!," to which Brenda had cheerily replied, "I'm not his wife, but good luck to her!" Most said nothing.

As she gathered the pieces up and packed the game away, she noticed writing on the bottom of the board. *Mark is a git and a bumhole, Rhyl '89*, it read, in a juvenile hand. Then, in much smaller letters, an addendum. *I hate Dad*.

She fished a small pencil out of the pocket on her tabard and added her own piece of graffiti while no one was looking. *B 4 R* in a wobbly heart with an arrow through it. Then, as an afterthought, *I hate Kenneth*.

# 56

Gwen was watching a woman across the shop, trying to work out if she was famous.

The woman had dyed, marmalade-colored hair in an angular bob that grazed her cheekbones, and a short fringe that reached halfway down her forehead. The overall effect was of somebody having scalped a twelve-year-old and perched their hair on an adult head instead.

*Who was she?* She wasn't low-key glamorous, like the disgraced breakfast newsreader who came in once a week to buy sunglasses—but she had that aura famous people have: a one-directional force field that says, "I mean something to you, but you mean nothing to me."

If she wasn't a celebrity then maybe she worked in a shop that Gwen shopped at? That had happened to Suze once, years ago—she'd gone up to a muss-haired man in winklepickers thinking he was a member of a B-list indie band, only to discover he worked in their local branch of Caffè Nero.

"I am actually in a band, as it happens," he'd said, and Suze had had to listen to a twenty-minute explainer on nu-prog as penance.

This woman wasn't in a band, Gwen was fairly sure, or if she was then her yellow rain mac and bike pannier backpack were doing a good job of disguising it. She didn't work in Caffè Nero either, but her face was so familiar that Gwen felt the urge to either wave hello or duck beneath the counter to hide. It was hard to say which until she worked out who she was.

Then the woman bumped into another customer and apologized with a soft Scouse accent, and suddenly Gwen did know who she was. She knew, and it was too late to duck and hide beneath the counter because the woman was walking toward her holding a gray hoodie, a heart-shaped ice cube tray, and a battered copy of *Shantaram*. Recognition was beginning to dawn on her face too.

"Hello!" said the woman, brightly, and Gwen could tell she was processing the incongruity of their surroundings, waiting for the penny to drop.

"Hello," she said back. Then, "Lorraine, isn't it? From New Roots? I think we worked together—er, briefly—at Invigorate?"

Whoomp, there it was.

"Yes! Yes of course," Lorraine cried cheerfully. She looked as though she was the one meeting a celebrity. "Gemma, wasn't it?"

"Gwen."

"Gwen! Of *course* it is, I'm so sorry. Useless with names. But I'm glad to bump into you, actually—"

Gwen began tapping the items through the till, glad of something to do while Lorraine began thanking her. "Gwen, we were incredibly grateful you piped up when you did about the, ah, financial discrepancies." Lorraine glanced from side to side and dropped her voice as she said this, as though one of the board directors might be lurking in the knitwear carousel.

Gwen made the requisite noises in reply. *Pssshht, pffft. It was the right thing to do. It was nothing.*

"No but honestly, it can't have been easy. I remember the way that man with the terrible mustache shot you daggers," Lorraine went on. "You saved us about eight grand in the end, once we moved to a new agency. Eight grand! That's a lot for an organization our size, Gwen, I can tell you."

Gwen nodded, and swallowed down the cold, queasy lump that appeared whenever she thought about money. Which was all the time now. Last week she had applied for an admin role at a "fintech accelerator lab" which turned out to be three twenty-two-year-olds working out of a branch of Joe & The Juice. She hadn't got a second interview.

"It's a shame though, because we were enjoying working with you!" Lorraine went on. "Not necessarily, uh, everyone at the agency—but *you*."

Gwen had enjoyed it too. Lorraine and her charity team had a kind of genuine enthusiasm that was less common in the hard-nosed razzle-dazzle of the Fast-Moving Consumer Goods market. She had, as far as she had been excited to work on anything in her later years at Invigorate—or on anything, ever—been excited to work with them and see the project realized. It had been a nice concept, launching a resource hub for parents and carers to find free outdoor school holiday activities. There had been extensive research about the benefits of time spent in nature, for developing minds. There had been smiling marrows and animated dancing trees.

"Anyway," said Lorraine, unzipping a small embroidered purse and extracting her bank card, "thank you so much, really, Gwen. And I hope you didn't end up in any trouble."

Only then did Lorraine seem to notice where they were, at midday on a Tuesday. Her words trailed off as she took in Gwen's volunteer lanyard, the shop counter that stood between the two of them like a beech-effect barricade. The phone-in debate that rumbled forth from the *Jeremy Vine Show,* on "woke culture ruining Britain's funfairs." She looked flustered.

"I mean, it didn't go over brilliantly," Gwen laughed, doing jazz hands.

"No!" Lorraine clasped a hand to her mouth. "They didn't sack you? For that?? Bastards!"

Gwen had decided she liked Lorraine, so she felt obliged to back-pedal a little. "Well, officially it was redundancy. Strategic restructuring, squeezed marketplace, etc., etc. Their outgoings were bigger than their incomings. So I became an outgoing too."

"They should have ripped off a few more clients, I guess," said Lorraine, and they both cackled. "God though, I'm so sorry, Gwen. Have you found anything else, or . . . ?"

Gwen didn't feel inclined to lie. "No," she said. "Nothing quite right. Not yet."

Out of the corner of her eye, she could see Brenda taping up another of St. Michael's signs. *Swimwear 30% off!* it read in blue felt-tip, over a poster of Hokusai's *The Great Wave off Kanagawa*.

"Except this," she added, loyally.

"WELL," said Lorraine, excited pink spots appearing in the middle of her cheeks, "as it happens . . . look, it hasn't been advertised as yet, and of course we'd need to interview you formally, but—we're actually looking to hire a Head of Marketing and Special Projects. Brand-new role, to keep tabs on everything from the inside so that we're not at the mercy of agencies and their markups. I don't suppose that would be in your wheelhouse, would it?"

Gwen suppressed another laugh at "wheelhouse," suddenly picturing Saskia alone in her woodshed. Okay Gwyn thx anyway, her email reply had read.

"I think it could be?" she told Lorraine.

"I'm sure it would be!" said Lorraine, with touching confidence. "It's more or less an internal version of the job you would have done for us anyway. Although I should tell you now, it's a slightly less glamorous setup than you might be used to. No treadmill desks or air hockey tables. Lots of meetings on allotments in the pissing rain."

"No hard seltzer on tap?" asked Gwen.

Lorraine shook her head. "There's a kettle. Is that a deal-breaker for you?"

Over her shoulder, Brenda and Silent Harvey were attempting to create a Back to School window display out of a couple of gray pullovers, a straw boater, a toy basketball hoop and a fountain pen. Their faces were earnest and childlike as they debated where exactly to place the pen.

Gwen thought for a second and said no. No, that would be fine.

## 57

The dentist's office was above a shop that sold mops, cat food, and small statues of dragons with LED bulbs in their eyes. It was accessed via a metal door with a sign taped to it that read "Lovely Smile." Without any other context, it gave the impression that a street harasser had left a placeholder while they went for lunch.

Gwen rang the doorbell to be buzzed in, and trudged her way up a dingy linoleum staircase.

She'd only been here once before, having registered as a patient back when she and Suze had moved into their penultimate flat together, above a Turkish restaurant—"Heartburn Hotel" they'd called it, for its proximity to the most generous servings of garlic sauce in the borough. Suze had become friendly with the woman who sat in the window, rolling out gözleme on a vast, round wooden board. For a while they had waved to her daily and enjoyed extra feta in their flatbreads, until the woman had seen Suze puking into a KFC bag during an especially rough hangover and their kinship had cooled. Suze always felt it wasn't the vomit that offended her, so much as the mass-produced fast food.

At the top of the stairs was another door buzzer, and beyond that a waiting room, bathed in the blue-white light that always made Gwen think of alien abductions.

"Hello!" she greeted the dental receptionist, half-expecting him to leap up and embrace her. *The prodigal patient.* "Can I book a check-up?" she asked, cheerily, determined to buoy herself on.

"So," he replied, already bored. "What you need to do is go on our website and click 'make an appointment.'" He jabbed a finger at a poster with a long Wix.com address written on it in felt tip.

"But I'm right here," said Gwen. She spread her arms, as though she were Liza Minelli emerging from a tinsel curtain.

"Uh-huh." He looked her up and down, to verify. "But all appointments need to go through our digital scheduling portal."

"Digital scheduling—"

"Portal, yeah. Do you have the app?"

"The—?"

"App, yeah."

"Right. No, sorry."

"You can download it through our website." He pointed to the poster again.

"So I can't just book a check-up here, right now, from you?" she asked.

"No, sorry." His expression hardened slightly.

"Even though you have a computer right there in front of you?"

"No, sorry."

Gwen stared at him, wondering if this was some kind of perseverance test—like staying on the line long enough to get a cheaper phone tariff. He stared back at her. Neither blinked.

As if on cue, her tooth throbbed.

"Fine," she said. "I'll sit down here and book the appointment on my phone."

"I'm afraid the seats are only for patients," he said. "It's policy."

Gwen wondered if people often tried to loiter in a first-floor dentist's waiting room, enough to necessitate this rule. Was it a popular teen hangout spot? Did people bring their laptops and try to order flat whites?

"But I *am* a patient."

"Not until you have an appointment," he said, a triumphant glint in his eye.

"Fine!" said Gwen. She attempted to huff out of the surgery but had to wait for him to buzz her back through the door. A woman in the waiting area tutted, although it wasn't clear at who.

Back outside, Gwen saw that her bus had just arrived at the bus stop about a hundred meters up the road. She launched into a sprint, surprising herself. But her footbed sandals kept slipping off and quickly she was reduced to a humiliating kind of lollop, managing to catch up with the bus only as the driver began to pull away. She thumped the glass to try and make him stop for her. And when he didn't, she thumped it again in frustration. A few passengers looked startled. A few more looked smug, because they were on the bus and she wasn't. Gwen thought of all the times she'd watched someone else have a strop on the curbside, and wondered if she had looked smug too.

An elderly man at the bus stop applauded as she slunk back to take a seat next to him. She pulled her phone out and ignored him, but he kept looking at her, chuckling and shaking his head a little.

After a few seconds he leaned over and said: "Three minutes! Only three minutes until the next one, it's okay." He pointed at the board. "There's always another bus."

Gwen was obliged to look up and smile sheepishly and say yes, yes, thank you. That was good to know.

# Vase

---

It was very Suze. This was the first thing she thought when she saw the vase, on the bric-a-brac shelf between a set of wireless headphones and an Edward and Sophie commemorative mug: *That's very Suze.*

Not current-Suze, perhaps, with her dried eucalyptus and matte charcoal everything, but original-flavor Suze, who craved color and kitsch and never met a piece of gaudy homeware she didn't adore. When they had first lived together, it was Gwen who'd had to beg Suze to stop bringing home tat from the markets every weekend— Camden, Spitalfields, Portobello; the holy trinity—because they were running out of surface space, and because one antique biscuit tin had turned out to still have antique biscuits in it.

"You have no soul, Gwenneth, that's your problem," she had bitched, scraping the blue-flecked remains of a custard cream into the bin with an ornate pickle knife.

It was a joke, but Gwen sometimes worried it was true. When her parents came to see their flat, Marjorie had run a finger along the dusty shelves and asked to have each curio explained to her ("This is a pair of candlesticks shaped like Pomeranians"; "This is a glass bowl we like because it is so ugly"), and Gwen had felt prickly and defensive, even though Suze had known her mother for a decade and loved playing up to her role as the zany best friend. If Gwen had no soul then it must be genetic.

This vase was a step up from the pieces Suze used to buy back then, but it had the same spirit, with its vivid, splashy florals and chubby, solid form. There was something expensive-looking about it that belied its £3.99 price sticker. And yet it wouldn't suit expensive flowers; they would clash with its man-made beauty.

Once, as teenagers, the two of them had spent a morning picking armfuls of cow parsley from the banks of the local disused railway line, thinking themselves geniuses to have discovered this bounty of free flora. They'd arranged it in pint glasses all around Gwen's bedroom, only for it to wilt and die within hours.

"You shouldn't pick cow parsley," Marjorie had scolded, as the white flowers withered on their drooping stems. "It's easily confused with poison hemlock."

But Suze had gathered up the remains and tucked them into her hair, defiant, until the smell of rank vegetation became unbearable.

Gwen bought the vase. She bought it thinking perhaps she would save it for Suze's birthday, which wasn't until November—but then the longer she sat with it, nagging at her from the shelf next to the TV, the greater the urge became to give it to her immediately, no reason, just because. She wanted to turn up on her doorstep and say, "Saw this and thought of you!," which was at least more socially acceptable than saying the true thing, the baldly exposing thing, which was:

"I think of you."

She bought the vase because it was the kind of gesture that TV had conditioned her to believe was key to winning back the loves of your life. And because it was, she realized now with some annoyance, exactly what Connie would tell her to do.

# 58

"Saw this and thought of you!"

Gwen thrust the gift bag at her—new, not a reuse, possibly the first time she'd actually bought one—and Suze took it, looking amused.

She probably should have given a little more preamble first. But attempting the spontaneous pop-in without any formal reason (who did she think she was, a sitcom character? A rural member of the clergy?) was agonizing, so she handed it over as soon as they were in Suze's hallway. Suze's immaculate hallway, with its regal dark green paint job and confusing, sculptural coat rack.

When Paul and Suze had moved into this house, Gwen had invited herself over "to help you unpack!," not realizing they had paid a company to do all that for them. She had bought a vast wedge of watermelon on the way over, feeling it to be a memory-making sort of summer treat—*"Remember that first night in the house, where we ate all the watermelon?"*—but Paul had looked at it obliquely, as though trying to work out if it were perhaps a *Dirty Dancing* reference he should pretend not to understand, and Suze had said: "Oh. I hate melon. But thank you."

Gwen had felt wretched for not knowing her best friend hated melon, or having forgotten if she had.

Now, Suze was opening the gift bag—Gwen was embarrassed to have written the little gold tag, in the hope that Suze might not answer the door and then she could stage a gift-and-run. Now she was lifting out the vase, looking equal parts suspicious and delighted.

"Mate! What the . . . ? Why have you . . . ? Aww. Aw, I love it. Look at that. Is it Clarice Cliff?"

Gwen busked it. "Sure! I mean, probably."

"Did you find it in your charity shop?"

"Yes. It just sung to me from the shelf," she said. "'I want to be with Suze.'"

"To the tune of *The Jungle Book*?"

"Exactly."

"Well, thank god you speak fluent Old Tat, because"—Suze put her cheek against it and nuzzled—"I love it." She looked at Gwen, eyes brimming a little. "Thanks so much, you lovely thing."

For a terrible second, Gwen wondered if that was it, if she was going to turn around, go home and wait by her phone for the next calendar-prescribed social invite. But then Suze said: "Tea?" and wandered into the kitchen as though this was normal. Which Gwen supposed it was.

At first they stuck to the mandatory script. *How's work? How's the shop? How's the house? How's the flat? How are your parents? How's Paul?*

Things stalled here until Suze, clearly at a loss, asked: "How's Weasel Boy?"

Gwen shuddered. "No idea. Hopefully bothering someone else's burrow."

Suze screeched at this. "Shame!"

"Shame on me."

"You're sure?" she asked. "He's not worth keeping on part-time?"

"Absolutely not. The fling has been flung."

"Flung and done?"

"Flung and . . . wrung."

"Methinks—"

"DON'T YOU LADY DOTH ME," howled Gwen, throwing a tea towel at her head.

If their friendship had been calcified—or as she pictured it now, crusted over with limescale—then a few fragments of something fell away in that moment. Suze cackled happily to herself as she squeezed out the tea bag, leaving a little trail of brown drips across the worktop and up the side of the food waste bin.

When they had lived together, Gwen had been the more fastidious one by a narrow margin. She wondered if Suze and Paul had a cleaner now, and decided they definitely did. Although she knew Suze would deny it if asked.

"So I saw Ryan," she said. It was a good enough segue. "Before the wedding, I mean. We had dinner."

"Shit, yes—tell me how it was," said Suze, pausing with an M&S Extremely Chocolatey biscuit halfway to her mouth.

Gwen told her how it was. She told her in minute detail, the way they used to, back when time wasn't a precious commodity. She combed through her memory of the encounter for everything of significance and plenty of irrelevance too—the beard, the baby, the uniquely unsettling experience of eating tacos with a person who once performed cunnilingus on you. When she got to Clea, Suze booed as if at a pantomime villain. Gwen appreciated this, even as she wondered whether Suze and Paul and Clea and Ryan ever secretly had drinks.

She told her about her apology speech, at which Suze grew serious and sympathetic. It was an expression rarely seen on Suze, and one that made Gwen oddly nostalgic for those days after the breakup, when Suze had moved her into their spare room. She had kept Gwen fed and watered like a houseplant, exposing her to indirect sunlight and airing the room as needed. They had watched Challenge TV and the Food Network from beneath a duvet on the sofa, chain-eating Marmite toast and cream of tomato soup, cosplaying a juvenile sick day. Then another, then another. It was the kind of tender post-heartbreak care plan that Gwen never felt she deserved, because she'd willingly broken her heart herself.

Paul had been mysteriously absent during most of this time, only coming home late at night with loaves of bread to replenish their stocks. Suze had taken a week of annual leave to look after her, Gwen only found out later. She had stayed with them, "temporarily," in her confused forest of boxes and bags and misappropriated possessions, for eight months.

"You didn't love him, you know."

Suze said it casually, playing with the fringed edge of a cushion.

"Didn't I?"

She shook her head and looked at Gwen. "Someone at a party asked you once what he was like, and all you said was 'tall.'"

"Is that so bad?"

"He's five nine, Gwen. He's not tall."

"Yes. Okay. Yes."

There was a pause, but a comfortable one this time. Then Suze gulped at her tea and said, still addressing the cushion: "I was jealous, if I'm honest."

"Jealous?"

"Yeah.'

"Of *me*?"

"Of . . . well. Now, look, obviously I love Paul . . ."

"Obviously," Gwen echoed.

"And I'm not saying for a minute that I regret anything."

"Of course not."

"But. It was like . . . suddenly it was like you were free. Like you'd ripped it all up and started again, just as everyone else was . . . I don't know. Putting their life in a frame. Lacquering it over with varnish. Getting all their twenty-something choices tattooed across their foreheads for eternity."

Suze always became grandiose and poetic when she felt defensive.

"*Is* that what was happening though? Forehead tattoos?"

"Shh. Point is, you could go anywhere and do anything."

"But I *didn't* go anywhere. Or do anything. I still don't."

"Don't be silly, of course you do."

"I really don't."

Suze looked at her, genuinely puzzled. "But . . . you take so long to message back sometimes—which is fine, obviously! Totally fine—but I always assumed it was because you were busy? Doing stuff. With other people."

Gwen hooted. "What people?"

"I don't know! Work people? I was slightly bitter about it."

"Suze." Gwen spoke slowly, trying to make her understand. "I don't have other people. I didn't do anything. I sat in my underwear and watched *Countryfile* because I was too scared to ask my friends if they wanted to go to the pub."

Suze scrunched up her face, processing this information. "Well, that's ridiculous."

"Yes, it was," agreed Gwen. "Is."

"I would have gone to the pub with you! I would have sat in my underwear with you, if you'd asked! But you didn't."

"Nor did you."

"That's true. Fine, hang on."

Suze was unzipping her jeans, and reaching for the remote.

"Not *now*."

"Why not now? Now is better than never."

In the end her trousers stayed on, but a bottle of gin came out. Suze's measures had always been generous to the point of sadistic, and there was something Proustian about the taste—so reminiscent of their first "adult" drinking sessions, having graduated to G&Ts from Lambrini and warm Strongbow in plastic bottles—that made Gwen feel instantly younger and bolder, less faded around the edges.

"So I had some deep chat with Paul at the wedding," she said, testing the water.

"About cryptocurrency?"

"About babies."

"Oh. 'Course." Suze laughed drily. "He's obsessed."

"Paul wants one?" Gwen asked, although she knew the answer.

"Paul wants several. A bunch. A whole brood."

An image flashed across Gwen's mind, a vignetted portrait of four strapping adolescents in cricket sweaters. Paul and Suze at parents' evening. Paul and Suze playing catch on the beach in St. Ives. Paul and Suze sweet-talking the police officer who wrote up young Arlo for selling weed to the other boys at Sea Cadets. Paul and Suze, gray-haired and crinkle-eyed, wiping away tears as the youngest one graduated with a First in Influencer Management from Durham. Something twisted and squirmed in her gut.

"But I don't," Suze went on. She faltered on the final word, as though it might be the first time she'd said it out loud.

Gwen made an effort to keep her expression neutral. It felt like coaxing a squirrel to eat from the palm of her hand. Suze had more in common with Asha than Connie, she realized now.

"Not at all?"

Suze shrugged. "Nope. I seem to be missing the gene." She paused, then added: "Or, fuck it, who knows, maybe I have the same gene as everyone else but I'm just better at overriding it with common sense."

Gwen laughed, softly, but said no more. They both turned to the TV, which was on mute. On the Food Network, a red-headed woman was making something called "seven-layer cheeseburger dip." They watched her pour pre-grated cheese onto a platter, and arrange it like potpourri.

Then Suze said: "I know what you're thinking."

"That two different colors of cheese don't count as two layers of dip?"

"That I should have told him before I married him."

"Oh." Gwen turned to look at her. "I wasn't. I don't."

"I wasn't sure about it then," said Suze. "I thought the instinct would kick in at some point. But all I know is, the closer we get to forty, instead of panicking about the decline of my fruitful years, I've been doing the opposite. Willing the years on. Wishing they'd go faster, get me across that biological finishing line so I can finally turn around and go 'Whoops! Too late. Shall we get a dog instead?'"

There was so much Gwen wanted to say in reply. She wanted to say that she understood exactly, even though she couldn't, and that she felt the same, even though she didn't. She wanted to say that she knew exactly the kind of parent Suze would be—a brilliant one—but that knowing so resolutely that she didn't want to be one was an intrinsic part of her brilliance, and so perhaps one thing couldn't exist without the other.

She wanted to tell her how often she got the urge to pull her phone out of her pocket and message Suze anything, anything at all, a blank text like a blank cheque for her to cash as she desired. Most of all she wanted to say thank you for the admission. She wanted to post a line of emoji hearts beneath her friend's face and applaud. *Thank you for sharing xx*.

Instead she said, "You hate dogs."

"I know," sighed Suze. "But I'd have to give him something."

They turned back to the TV and watched for a few more minutes, as the red-headed lady silently browned mince and doused shredded lettuce in caster sugar.

"So, Paul—he's . . . okay with this?" asked Gwen.

"He's okay," said Suze. Then she scrunched her face into a grimace and shook her head. "No, that's a lie. He is . . . resigned. Most of the time."

Gwen nodded.

"Then, y'know, another ultrasound appears in a group chat or he gets to jog a fat infant on his knee at a barbecue, or he watches *Field of Dreams* on ITV3 and it breaks him all over again."

Suze's own voice caught on this sentence, and she let out a long, shaky exhale.

"I feel shitty about it, the whole thing. But what can you do? You can't have a baby you don't want out of shittiness."

"No," agreed Gwen. "They're supposed to provide the shit, as I understand it."

Suze snorted at this. Then she buried her face in her hands and groaned. A deep, animal howl that sounded like it came from someone else entirely. "Maybe he's right, maybe we should just have one anyway," she muttered through her fingers. "Maybe I will regret it if we don't. Everyone says it's this transformative thing that nobody can possibly understand until they experience it, so how can I possibly understand I don't *want* to experience it?"

It was necessary, Gwen knew in that moment, for both things to be true at once. It needed to be true that love for one's child was a uniquely magical, unknowable, stupefying thing that made all the pain and poo and sacrifice worth it. She'd seen it in the eyes of enough exhausted parents to know: they needed it to be true. They needed that payoff in order to continue the human race.

But at the same time, it needed to be true that a life without children could be every ounce as rewarding, every bit as fulfilling, every bit as *meaningful* as one with. If this reproductive doublethink was ever exposed, society might crumble.

She thought about the phase, shortly after Luke had died, when she and Ryan had stopped using contraception without ever discussing it. No conversation, just wordlessly carrying on where the condom interlude would previously have been. It was hard to know if this was the result of caring less about future consequences or some innate need to juxtapose "death" with "fertility" like a GCSE set text, but after a few weeks Gwen had panicked and told him to stop being so reckless, that it was the last thing she needed. As though the call was all his, and the consequences all hers. After that they had stopped doing it at all.

On another timeline, she might have a five-year-old now. She might be telling Suze that this uniquely magical, unknowable, stupefying thing had been born out of the rubble and muck of that terrible time in her life, and that Suze couldn't understand unless she did it, and that everyone was right.

As it was, she just stroked her hair and said: "Fuck everyone."

Suze repeated it after her in a murmur, *fuckeveryone*, as though saying *amen*. Then she asked: "Do you want one? Am I allowed to ask that? I never know if I'm allowed to ask."

"Yes," Gwen replied, simply. "And yes." She couldn't be bothered to couch it in a hundred caveats. "I think so. If I still can."

Suze nodded, then after a beat she asked, deadpan: "Want to have one with Paul?"

"Ideal!"

"A handy solution for everyone!"

For a few moments they grinned at each other, perhaps both imagining a world in which they were the kind of people who could actually pull off such a scheme.

"But," Gwen said, "it'd be a lot of ad—"

"A LOT of admin," Suze joined in before she could finish, both of them dissolving into laughter. "You're right. Never mind. Sorry, Paul. Forever bound to the stone-hearted hag who lured him into marriage under false pretenses."

"You don't actually feel like that," Gwen protested.

Suze looked her in the eye and smiled weakly. "No, you're right," she said. "I actually don't."

"Good," said Gwen. Then: "I'm sorry."

Suze frowned. "For . . . ?"

"For not knowing about any of this."

"How would you have known? I never told you."

"But I never asked."

"Ach, you've had your own stuff going on."

"Not enough of it, let's be honest," said Gwen. "I have had essentially nothing going on, for . . . well, ages now. I should have made more effort. I just . . . I don't know. Couldn't."

Suze shrugged. "So what? You've had a fallow period. Like Glastonbury."

"Glastonbury doesn't have a six-year fallow period, Suze."

"Well," she said, considering this. "You've been through more than the grass has."

It got dark outside. The TV remained mute. The cheeseburger dip had been silently demolished by plaid-shirted actors at a silent potluck supper, and several generations of grillmaster and cupcake monarch had been silently crowned since. Meanwhile they had circled back—noisily, haltingly, tangentially—through all their previous catch-up topics and dug deeper this time. Work. Home. Family. Suze's exploitative boss and Gwen's professional misadventures. Connie's manipulative dinners and Suze's father's melanoma.

On hearing about Gwen's trip home, Suze became a little misty-eyed. "That's great," she kept saying. "Well done. All of you. Really, really great. Give them my love."

Eventually, more to stem this flow of praise than anything else, Gwen asked, "Where's Paul?"

Suze looked sheepish. "Gone for dinner on his own. I texted him hours ago and told him not to come home."

"Because I was here?!"

"Not like that! I wanted you to myself for once. Selfishly. I always have to share you with a group." She glanced from side to side, as if checking for spies. "And honestly, Gee, I think he's embarrassed after whatever he said to you at the wedding."

Gwen didn't know Paul got embarrassed.

"I didn't know Paul got embarrassed."

Suze hooted at this. "He wouldn't care with most people. But he knows you're the person he needs to stay on the right side of. Custodian of my heart."

"Aw" was all Gwen could say in reply.

As she left, they hugged hard but made no reference to anything being different now. There were no hollow promises to "do this more often" or spurious, half-formed plans for future dinners and weekends away, and Gwen was glad of that. Vocalizing the thing would have killed it, somehow. Like green shoots, wilting under laboratory lighting. Like the cow parsley.

"Oh, wait, Gwendy!"

Suze darted back into the lounge and picked up a solid gray lump of concrete—another vase, one too ostentatiously tall and thin to be of any use holding flowers. She made a show of slipping it carefully into the gift bag, within the nest of crinkled polka-dot tissue paper, and replacing it with the new vase, which clashed beautifully with everything else on the shelf. Paul, she felt sure, would have opinions.

"Wedding present," she explained. "Always hated it. It looks like a penis they chiseled off Mount Rushmore."

Suze held out the bag. "Be a love and drop it off at your shop?"

Gwen promised she would.

When she reached the shop it was closed, as she knew it would be by this time, but she found herself reluctant to take the vase home. It was heavy, her hand hurt, and she was craving a cheeseburger (no sugar) from the all-purpose takeaway on the corner to mop up the gin. So instead she committed the cardinal sin of charity retail and left it outside the shop. Still in the gift bag, tag still attached. Perhaps someone else would claim it first, she reasoned.

When she arrived in the morning for her shift, autumn rain was lashing the pavement and the usual mound of dumped donations outside the shop was sodden. Children's picture books growing wrinkled and mushy, sweatshirts turning gray in the deluge. But Suze's vase was gone.

# Umbrella

Umbrellas were among the most mysterious items donated to the shop—because who willingly lets go of a functional umbrella? Has any living person ever uttered the words: "I have too many working umbrellas, I must edit my collection"? Or, "There is such a thing as simply *too dry*"?

Even if you found an umbrella on the bus, you would keep it. Such treasures are our due reward for life on public transport. They're fair compensation for all the left-behind jackets and paperback books and empty Tupperware containers never seen again. When you leave behind an umbrella by accident, you comfort yourself with the knowledge that whoever finds it will keep it and use it, and it will be quid pro quo for all the umbrellas that they themselves have lost. You tell yourself that you'll be repaid with someone else's umbrella in turn.

But if you knew that the person who found your umbrella was already so rich in umbrellas, so *lousy* with expandable water shields that they think, "Huh, I'll just hand this in to a charity shop, let them take the burden!"—wouldn't you feel affronted, in a way? Imagine having your life that together. Or, perhaps, caring that little about rain.

"I don't really care about rain," announced Brian in the back room that soggy September morning.

He would, Gwen told him, if he had a fringe.

## 59

"Well these are looking great," said the dentist, a cheerful northern woman in a hijab who looked about her own age. Gwen mumbled surprise through a mouthful of fingers.

"No problems at all that I can see!" the dentist continued. She sounded genuinely delighted. "You've clearly been taking excellent care of them."

Gwen thought of the dusty box of floss which had sat untouched since the time she'd used it to attempt an unsuccessful home eyebrow-threading. She thought of all the mornings she'd forgotten to brush them, because once you have a second breakfast and a third coffee it's nearly 11 a.m., which is nearly lunchtime so what's even the point? She thought of marmalade on toast and chocolate Hobnobs and all of Connie's puddings, of Magnums and doughnuts and sticky toffee sauce, pooling on a spoon.

"I try," she demurred, through the fingers.

"Any pain?" asked the dentist. Reluctantly, Gwen told her about the throbbing. X-rays were taken, Gwen picturing the morbid outline of her own skull as she bit down on the plastic plate. But the dentist insisted there was nothing there to see. Her teeth were all fine.

"Probably just a little oversensitivity," she said. Gwen agreed that it probably was.

*

Afterward she sat in a coffee shop up the road, tearing strips off a cinnamon bun and rolling them into doughy pellets before popping them into her mouth. She was pleasantly jittery from sugar and caffeine and the rush of admin successfully completed. She longed to bump into someone she knew, right now, so that they could ask what she was up to and she could say, "Oh, just been to the dentist."

The woman next to her was editing a selfie. It was one she'd clearly just taken, as her clothes and hair were identical, the bare brick wall of the café visible in the background. Gwen looked away, embarrassed for her, but the woman didn't seem to care.

On another timeline, maybe Gwen would have taken a selfie too—baring her great-looking teeth to the world, preserving this tiniest and silliest of victories.

But before she could lift her phone to attempt it, the screen turned black and "MUM" flashed up on it, with a little photo of Marjorie squinting in a National Trust car park.

"What's wrong?" Gwen answered, heart hammering.

"Nothing!" said her mother, already aggrieved. "Can't a mother phone her daughter? Hello to you too."

"Oh. No, of course—only I wish you'd open with 'everything's fine!'" She waited for her nervous system to settle itself. "But hello. Hi! Um. How are you both?"

"We're very well thank you," her mother replied, in the manner of one practicing a foreign language. "It's been a nice week down here, less muggy than it was. Of course the delphiniums are on the out now, but the dahlias are still going strong. Yvonne and Barry were here the other day and we ate on the patio! Only quiche, but your father put sultanas in the salad."

Gwen murmured approval.

"And how are you?" asked Marjorie. "How is th . . . the thing-ummy . . . ?"

Gwen guessed silently, as she waited for her mother to locate the right word. *Shop? Flat? Climate crisis?*

". . . tooth?" she finished, finally. "I hope you've been to the dentist."

Gwen told her that she had, and gave her the good news. Her mother wondered if the dentist might be negligent. Gwen reassured her that she had seemed very thorough. Her mother said: "Well you don't want them too thorough, they'll charge you for things you don't even need doing." They went on pleasantly in this manner for a while.

"Any news on the . . . ah—" Marjorie stopped herself, then simply said. "Any other news?"

Gwen told her about the job interview at New Roots. Against every fatalistic impulse that warned her to keep it to herself, not to count her proverbial chickens, she filled her mother in on all the details—even painting herself as something of a heroic whistleblower in regards to the rate card slip-up. Daringly, she allowed herself to sound pleased.

"Horticulture, Mum! I might need to pick your brain about plants."

Surely her mother couldn't fail to be pleased, too, by this uncanny veer into her world?

"Well," sniffed Marjorie, after a pause. "You'll need a warmer coat."

# Scarf

---

Greg came back when Michael was least prepared for it.

Not, as hoped, when he was poised at the counter with his pen hovering wryly above the crossword, nor laughing warmly with a regular customer, nor being thanked by someone from Head Office for smashing the quarterly sales target. Which, in fairness, he never had. No, Greg came back when the shop was empty and Michael was wearing a pair of rubber gloves, scrubbing an unidentified stain from a Halloween costume for the forthcoming window display. Earlier that week, Finn had tipped him off that the Kindness Hub was erecting an eight-foot likeness of Audrey II from *The Little Shop of Horrors*, made by local schoolchildren using discarded iPads and single-use plastic waste. St. Michael had been in a state of rancor ever since.

It was after closing time, the sky beginning to darken outside—but on slow days he occasionally left the "open" sign up for a while longer, giving those who had missed out earlier in the day a bonus chance to shop. *Second chance saloons.* Never say he wasn't a forgiving man.

Greg was unaccompanied this time, hands buried deep in the pockets of his peacoat. Michael saw him coming, just in time to look down and pretend he hadn't, to listen to his heavy tread across the carpet, feeling every atom rearrange itself in the room. But regrettably not in time to take the rubber gloves off.

"What's that?" Greg asked, stepping around the counter to stand next to Michael, cocking his head to inspect the offending item. He smelled of cool air and spearmint over warm Golden Virginia.

"Sexy pumpkin," replied Michael, still scrubbing.

"The costume or the stain?" said Greg.

"Customers on the other side of the yellow line, please," replied Michael, curtly.

But there was only so long he could daub at the orange tutu with a wet sponge, and when he finally looked up, Greg was grinning at him.

"All right, Mickey," he said. "I need a new scarf."

"Ah," said Michael. "I'm afraid we only have old scarves."

Greg kept smiling. "They'll do too," he said lightly. "Sometimes old things are worth revisiting, don't you think?"

Michael had no quick reply to this. His tongue was a dead weight, almost choking him as a tide of something unexpected but distantly familiar rose from that bitter gut of his. Hope.

He coughed a little, turned wordlessly and led Greg to the back corner of the shop where the trunk of scarves sat: his box of strays and lovable runts, all crying out for new homes. Greg looked down at the box, as though expecting the scarves to fly out and begin an aerial display for his pleasure.

"Another school play?" asked Michael, affecting composure. "*The Snowman*, this time? *Doctor Zhivago*?"

"Nope," replied Greg. "I was just cold. And you always did have the best taste."

"I won't be flattered into another discount," Michael warned, as Greg trailed a fingertip lightly up his sleeve. "I'm a man of integrity these days."

Greg was suddenly solemn, an ambiguous look in his eyes.

"Oh, mate," he said. "You always were."

## 60

The evening before the interview—officially an interview this time, not a chat, which was reassuring—Gwen laid out her clothes. Laying out clothes the night before was the kind of women's magazine tip she'd had stashed in the back of her brain for decades now, along with "taking a look from desk to dance floor" and using half a lemon to exfoliate her elbows. Seeing her two-dimensional future self lying there on her bed was oddly emotional.

She tried on the generic smart-casual blazer she wore whenever she needed to feel "pulled together," which was ironic seeing as it didn't button across her tits. Gwen slipped a hand into the pockets and found a piece of notebook paper folded neatly into a square.

1. *Find something to do*
2. *Instigate social occasions*
3. *Call Mum and Dad*
4. *Go to the dentist*
5. *Get rid of it*

There was a brownish smear on the bottom of the page. She thought wistfully of Lutterworth's best sticky toffee pudding, wondering if it would taste as good now.

In the interest of procrastination, she sat down with a pen and ticked off every item on the list with a flourish. Then she added one more and ticked that off too, cringing a little as she did so.

*6. Get a life*

The TED Talk on Better Goal-Setting to Harness Your Untapped Productivity Superpower wouldn't endorse this one either, but Connie might.

Gwen threw the note away, then took the rubbish out for good measure.

The next morning she woke exactly ten minutes before her alarm went off, the way she always had in the days before redundancy scrambled her circadian rhythm. For once, she got dressed and ate breakfast without Netflix on or a podcast playing. No need to drown out the silence with somebody else's news.

Outside the figures on the street looked like a Lowry painting, their bodies bent toward the Tube station as though drawn by magnetic force. Gwen tilted her face as she walked past the Tesco Metro, waiting for the cold blast of croissant-scented air that made being up this early feel worth it. None came. She considered doubling back to try again.

She was forty-five minutes early to allow for natural, political, and gastrointestinal disasters—and yet she still felt antsy on entering the Tube station, fighting the impulse to tsk and huff behind a man who took too long to swipe himself through the barriers. How long did it take for metropolitan impatience to work its way out of your system? Five months and one week, wasn't it?

On the walls of the station, local council posters urged people to remember to go to the doctor. Cartoon adults clutched themselves in anguish, above the words *Have you had stomach pain for more than three weeks? Call your GP!*—as though cancer were a compensation they may be entitled to claim.

Gwen was beginning to feel reassured by the idea that other people needed to be nagged into this basic level of personal maintenance, when suddenly she heard a loud yelp. She looked up just in time to see a woman on the next escalator lose her footing and fall forward, limbs windmilling madly, her face a picture of pure terror. For several days afterward Gwen would see this expression every time she closed her eyes, frozen like a souvenir theme park keyring. She felt the gust of air as the woman tumbled past—or perhaps she imagined this, but she definitely heard the dull thud as she landed.

For one agonizing second, all was silent. The woman had disappeared from view and those behind her were in a frieze of horror-struck poses: arms outstretched, eyes covered, gripping the handrail, reaching for their phones. Then came the scream. A scream that Gwen recognized as containing more shock than physical pain—followed by "fuck fuck fuck fuck," which was reassuring.

Thumping down the last few steps of her own escalator, Gwen turned to find the woman in a heap at the bottom, several tote bags spilling their contents—mostly books and bananas—across the gridded metal, all of which were now being swept into the end of the escalator as a pile-up of commuters formed behind her. Not stopping to think, Gwen slammed her hand against the red emergency button. She felt a rush of power as the thing slowed to a halt.

"Are you okay?" she asked the woman, who, instead of scrambling out of harm's way, had tipped her head back against the metal wall of the escalator and closed her eyes. She looked oddly serene.

"I am okay," the woman breathed after a second, sounding unsure. People were stepping over her now, barely missing a beat as they navigated the commuter roadkill. Some craned their necks back as they walked away, clearly relieved to find someone else—Gwen, apparently—taking care of the situation so that they didn't have to.

Gwen scrabbled around for the woman's belongings, sweeping books and bananas and napkins and a hairbrush back into the tote bags while the woman clambered slowly to her feet. She wasn't wearing heels, Gwen noted. She was wearing sensible hiking sandals with Velcro straps.

"Thank you, thank you so much," she said, her voice heavily accented with what sounded like Spanish. She took her bags back from Gwen, and smiled weakly, a smile Gwen recognized, a smile she understood entirely. It was the kind that says: "I am humiliated, please go away now."

So Gwen went away, reluctantly, passing two harried-looking members of underground staff as she did. "I think she's okay," she told them, and the woman limped on toward the platform, swatting her hands at the world in general and saying, "I am okay! I am okay," although she could just as easily not have been. One of the attendants followed after her, feebly waving a first aid kit.

Gwen turned back to see the other Tube attendant shrug and flick a button to activate the escalator again, and a new stream of people began to descend, adjusting smoothly from solid ground to moving metal. And so life went on.

That evening, back at home, Gwen pulled on a racer-back top, faded and worn soft through washing. *South Downs Half Marathon 2009*, it read in cracked yellow and green script on the front. Luke's. Liberated from the bag of sportswear Marjorie deemed too scruffy for the charity shop, it was Gwen's now, along with several more of his T-shirts. She fished a very old pair of trainers, curled up at heel and toe like aged prawns, from the bottom of the wardrobe and put them on, bouncing experimentally on the balls of her feet. She took her keys but left her phone on the kitchen table.

Back on the street, the sun was setting and it felt strange but nice to be out in the world without a tote bag weighing her down. Gwen stretched an arm over her head a few times, looking around to see if anyone was watching.

And then, just for a little while, she ran.

# Goalkeeper Gloves

They sit on a shelf now, in the small area of the shop St. Michael has vaguely designated for "sporting pursuits," next to a toy dartboard, a heavy-duty bike lock, and that game where you fling fuzzy balls at a Velcro-covered hat.

Michael will pass them by while looking for gifts to win over Louie, the small boy with the determined cowlick who is now suddenly, determinedly, in his life.

Michael will reject the goalkeeper gloves not because he hates football—his lifelong loyalty to West Bromwich Albion is another seeming incongruity he enjoys dropping into conversation at parties—but because inevitably he'd end up being the one in goal, and Michael has had enough surprises crashing into his solar plexus for one year.

Eventually the gloves will be bought by a teenage girl, Ruby, who recently joined her school team in the girls' football gold rush brought about by England's success in the 2019 FIFA Women's World Cup. At fourteen, Ruby is already five foot ten and she likes the idea of taking her height and making it an asset; of framing herself with goalposts rather than the relentless demands of her phone camera.

She likes the idea that, instead of gamely absorbing every comment and joke and pointed glance that her peers throw her way, for once she'll be allowed to hurl something back.

## 61

She had just left the shop the next day when Lorraine phoned to offer her the job.

"I don't have a garden" was the first thing Gwen said, before thanking her. "I don't even have a balcony."

"All the more reason!" said Lorraine, unfazed. "You'll understand just how transformative access to outside space can be."

Gwen thought about her airless flat. When she'd viewed it, the sun had been setting in lavish pink streaks across the sky, and she had been so taken with the view from the living room window that at the time it had felt like all the outside space she needed. She thought of the window box Marjorie had brought her on that first and only visit, pre-planted with seeds that Gwen hadn't thought to ask the names of.

They had flowered, suddenly, lavishly, a couple of months later. Gwen had woken up to find them one morning, looming up like fancy strangers and making the whole view of the street look different. She had taken endless photos of the nameless blooms, swaying and dancing in the sunlight behind her cereal bowl. She'd never posted the photos, or sent them to anyone. Had she told her mother the flowers had come out? She couldn't remember. But the photos had stayed on her phone and in the years since she had occasionally found herself scrolling back to them.

Yes, she agreed with Lorraine. She would understand.

Not wanting to go home yet, Gwen walked for a while in the opposite direction, slightly dazed. The sun burned through the cloud that had been hovering all day and it felt almost trite in its symbolism. She rolled her eyes at the sky, and sweated a little into her blazer.

It was 5 p.m. on a Friday, and the surprise summer encore had visited a holidayish air upon the early October streets. Post-work drinkers swarmed outside pubs. School kids in uniforms shrieked and clutched at each other, scattering chips. In lieu of gardens and balconies, people sat on flat sections of roof and dangled their legs over window ledges. A family group in a front garden looked as though they'd been bidding goodbye for several hours, but kept on thinking of one last thing to say.

As she walked, she left Suze a voicenote. A new medium for the two of them and one that gave Gwen performance anxiety, but still, it felt intimate to carry her friend's voice around in her pocket. "Guess who's no longer funemployed?" she trilled, hoping it came off as ironic. Then: "By the way, did I tell you I stole a clock from a pub?"

Next she sent a message to her parents—Marjorie had relented and agreed to a WhatsApp group, which was now filled with blurry photos of Michaelmas daisies—and gave them only the top line news, as bait. Plans were in place to mark Luke's birthday next month with a hilltop walk and a takeaway. If they wanted to know more before then, they'd have to call for it.

On a roll now, she thought, *Why not?* and sent a message to the charity shop group chat.

> Got a new job! At last!

It landed with a silent thud beneath a three-day-old message from Lise asking if people could please stop leaving mugs of coffee directly beneath the counter because they were posing a "flopping hazard."

She stared at the screen for a few seconds, considered deleting it, then added a postscript.

PS. I'll still do Saturday afternoons.

After a further agonizing wait, replies began trickling in. They ranged from the excessive to the bemused. "YES GWEN!" from Asha. "Clever lady!" from Gloria. "Great news gwen all best brian," from Brian. A couple of polite, unpunctuated "congratulations" from people she'd never met, and whom she suspected had dropped off the shop schedule some time ago but hadn't worked up the courage to leave the group chat yet. A startling four exclamation marks from Silent Harvey. A single heart emoji confirming that Harp really was called Harp. A slightly proprietary "Atta girl!" from Connie. Even Nicholas sent a gracious row of applause. It should all have been mortifying, but oddly it wasn't.

St. Michael—he listed his own name as "St. Michael" on WhatsApp, an interesting detail—sent the longest reply. Excellent news Gwen, and thrilled to hear we won't be losing your peerless customer service skills entirely. xM

She wondered if everyone did this, promising to keep up shifts at the shop out of guilt? Probably. She wondered if she might live to regret it, and how soon, and concluded that if she ever had enough going on that she needed to claim her Saturday afternoons back, it would be a cause for celebration in itself.

Walking head-down along the street was becoming treacherous now, so she stopped and ducked into a doorway, leaning against the wall and allowing herself to revel in the news for a minute. At first she'd felt pure relief, but now there was something else—optimism?—creeping in around the edges. She began tapping out more messages.

Hey! So lovely to see you at the wedding. Let's have coffee soon? Would love to hear more about the kitchen renovations.

Hi Gemma! Was lovely to see you a few weeks back. Shall we actually have that drink? See if the Claires are free?

Hi! I enjoyed the sex we had in 2016. Fancy coming to the cinema with me tomorrow?

Hey Connie, I owe you a dinner. How do you feel about blue maize tacos with pickled plums and apple butter?

She sent only the first one. But seeing the others lined up there, teetering on the diving board's edge, felt exhilarating. Progress.

Hope ur doing sumthing nice 2 celebrate, messaged Brenda then, and Gwen watched herself reply: Going for a nice dinner!

Gwen checked her banking app. A nice, cheap dinner.

# Ring

---

"Would you fancy it?" asked Trish, the way she had asked if she wanted a cup of tea ten minutes earlier. Breezy, noncommittal. Except this *was* committal, this was as committal as it got.

"Marriage?" Bridie blinked at her.

"Yes."

"Marriage-marriage?"

"That's the one." Trish went back to her book.

"You and me?"

Trish idly turned a page and ruffled the dog's head, while Bridie stood, frozen, a forkful of cold leftover crumble halfway to her mouth.

"We'd be the main players, yes."

"But . . . but we always said we never would," she said. "Not again."

"We've said a lot of things," replied Trish. She looked up at her now, flinty gray eyes as steady as ever. No immediate signs of delusion or derangement. But she wasn't messing around, either; Bridie understood that much.

"We said forever and ever to the boys and look how that turned out," she went on. "You can hardly be surprised that I'm a flake on this score too."

It had started out as a private joke, calling their ex-husbands "the boys," but at some point it had stopped being ironic and become a convenient shorthand. The older they got, the more fitting it seemed—viewing those years as if through a rearview mirror as they sped away from the scene. The boys were preserved in their memories, never to grow old.

Meanwhile Bridie had softened and relaxed with each passing year in a way she liked to think of as poetically autumnal, sagging and sweetening and collapsing into her surroundings like an over-ripe plum. Trish had become smaller and harder and crinkled with age, like a crisp packet left in an oven.

But not, it seemed, harder on the inside. Twenty-six years was apparently what it had taken to fill her with sap.

Bridie carried on looking at her, appraising. "Why?" she asked. "And if you say 'why not?,' I will smash this bowl on the floor so help me God."

"Because . . ." Trish sighed and closed her book, annoyed. Trish always wore her emotions as though they itched. "Because I want to do it now, before we *have* to do it because one of us is dying or something and it becomes just another dreary piece of admin. Because I have spent twenty-six years sharing you with other people, never quite believing you're mine, and now I finally do believe it and I want to show off about it for god's sake. I want a bureaucratic pat on the back to commemorate the fact."

Bridie nodded, painfully slowly, the way she always did to show she was listening.

"Because," Trish went on, quieter now, "because all that time you were caring for Trevor, I used to think marriage was a straitjacket and I hated it. I hated mine and I hated yours even more. But then I realized something the other day. I realized you didn't do it because you were married to him. You did it because you're . . . well, because you're *you*. And I might have hated my marriage and hated your marriage, but actually I don't think I'd hate *ours*. In fact I think I'd like it a lot, and I'm thoroughly pissed off that it's taken me so long to think of it. And I've asked your children, and my children, and they ran the gamut from highly enthusiastic to completely nonplussed about the whole idea and I thought: well. Well, if we've got them on side, and all our parents are dead, and the dog sitter has some availability on Tuesday afternoons, well then"—there was a small wobble in her voice here and Bridie noticed now, with some alarm, that Trish was nervous—"well then, and I'm sorry, I *am* going to say it. Why not?"

Bridie was silent.

"Also, I love you," Trish added. "I should have said that first."

She sat back, seemingly exhausted, opened her book again and carried on reading. The dog was looking from one of them to the other like a tennis spectator, an expectant tongue lolling from the side of his mouth.

"Well," Bridie said, finally. "If you're sure all our parents are dead."

"Quite sure, I checked."

"Your mother will turn in her grave."

"She could use the exercise."

"Well then. Well." Bridie felt lightheaded. As though her heart was trying to burst from her mouth. She swallowed it down. "Okay, I suppose. Yes. Fine. Let's."

Trish smiled. A halo of late afternoon light creeping in between the blinds made her look positively saintly, just for a second.

"I'll be wanting a ring," Bridie called over her shoulder, turning back into the kitchen.

"Oh, I know that," replied Trish. There was a small pause, a rifling noise from the hall cupboard, then she walked up behind Bridie at the sink and wrapped her arms around her. In one hand there was a small leather box, open just enough to reveal the emerald-cut diamond glinting inside. "Don't worry," she muttered into her neck. "Charity shop. It was cheap."

On a Tuesday at three p.m., five weeks later, they made their non-committal commitment at the local registry office: a handsome art deco building with stone columns in the front and a sign saying HARINGEY COUNCIL AIR QUALITY ACTION PLAN: HAVE YOUR SAY.

It rained. Bridie was disappointed but Trish said she preferred it. The children took endless photos on their iPhones of the brides, huddled together with their hoods up, molting petals from their small bouquets across the steps, telling everyone to stop being ridiculous and beaming, just beaming at each other. They looked younger, somehow, than they ever had.

Afterward they all went to the pub.

"Which pub?" Eleanor had asked, and her mother had yelled, "Any pub! THE pub. I don't bloody know. In our day you didn't look up the menu on sodding Tripadvisor a month beforehand, you just rolled into the nearest establishment with pumps and stools and a few bags of KP nuts!"

So Eleanor and Bridie had quietly conferred and found a small, recently refurbished backstreet boozer with charcoal painted walls, and thick-cut chips among its selection of Venetian small plates. It was almost empty given the day, the time, and the weather, which made it feel like theirs. And so when somebody plugged a phone into the pub's sound system and put on Van Morrison's "Sweet Thing," Trish forgot to protest and roll her eyes and instead she took her new wife, her old wife, her new-old wife in her arms and held her close and spun her around, and again and again until they were dizzy and clutching each other to stay upright, and laughing, laughing the whole time.

Above them, on a mahogany shelf, a pair of stuffed otters looked on.

## 62

Instead of falling into her usual tortured pilgrimage from restaurant to restaurant, becoming more frantic and more exacting with each menu she looked at (Ryan had called it "the hanger games," which was quite a good joke for him at the time), Gwen settled happily on the first local option that presented itself. A ramen place. A new, and mercifully unfamiliar one.

Being barely 6 p.m., the restaurant was half-empty and she secured a table by the large open window, out of which she could stick her head like a dog.

*A good decision.*

As she waited for her food, Gwen watched people outside. A car roared past with its windows down, blasting Christian worship music at an antisocial volume. A smartly dressed woman at the bus stop ate chickpeas with a plastic spork, straight from the can. A huge teddy bear straddled a wall, its head drooping ghoulishly, next to a stick blender and a pink dressing gown. *Free please take*, read the invisible sign that nobody needed to post.

Gwen mentally steamed these items. Wiped them down, priced them up. She wondered if anybody was watching her, and if so, what they were thinking. She felt briefly embarrassed for thinking the thought.

Back inside the restaurant, somebody *was* watching her. On a table across the room, he'd just finished paying his bill (she felt gratified, and at the same time slightly judgmental, at the evidence of someone having dinner even earlier than her) and now he appeared in sharp relief against the backdrop of the restaurant, as though her eyes were suddenly in portrait mode.

For a second she wondered if he were a celebrity, or another former client with an awkward shared history. Did he work in a shop?

No, Gwen realized, he didn't work in a shop—she did.

He was wearing the same green checked shirt but he looked different today, his hair wet (had he recently showered?) and slicked into a side parting like a First World War soldier. He reminded her of a portly Clark Kent. He was smiling at her now, as he pocketed his receipt and gathered up his things to leave. Phone, wallet, paperback copy of a Jeffrey Eugenides. Reflexively, Gwen smiled back as she slurped, hitting herself in the chin with a dangling udon. She was still dabbing oily broth off her face when he arrived at her table.

"Hello," he said, waving the book up and down as though it were a sock puppet.

"You're actually reading it!" she said in reply.

He looked amused. "Shouldn't I be?"

"No—yes! I mean, it's only that people often buy books from us just for the sake of it," she said.

"Do they?"

"Or, you know, they buy them because they like to kill time in the shop."

"I do like to kill time in your shop, to be fair."

"Well, it's a special place."

"It is."

They both nodded, a little reverently, as though the charity shop were perhaps a tumbledown chateau they'd shared one hazy summer in the Dordogne.

He cleared his throat. "I always think I should volunteer, actually."

"Everyone thinks they should volunteer," she told him. "Just like everyone thinks they should give blood, and everyone thinks they should become a mentor for disadvantaged teens."

"Do you give blood?" he asked her.

"No," she admitted.

"I do," he said, triumphant. "Although mainly for the biscuits."

"Well there you are then. We're even."

He grinned. "Are you trying to put me off your shop?" She liked the way he kept calling it "hers."

"Not at all," Gwen assured him, although she had been and wasn't sure why. "Actually they'll be needing someone new, because I got a job today." Why was she telling him this?

"Oh! Well. Congratulations," he said. "Will you be celebrating tonight?"

"I am celebrating," she gestured to her noodles, to her flight of chubby dumplings, to the jug of water she'd begged for when the waitress had only brought over a thimble-sized glass. "This is how I celebrate."

He smiled, and said: "Good for you." She studied him for signs of pity or sarcasm, and found none.

Because she struggled to sit in front of food for longer than two minutes without eating it, Gwen pincered a dumpling with her chopsticks while the man watched, still smiling. Delicately avoiding his eye, she bit into it. This seemed to jolt him into action, as though someone had dropped a coin into a slot. He cleared his throat again, fumbled for the book beneath his arm, and said: "Anyway, I won't disturb you—enjoy your dinner. The pickles are excellent, by the way."

Gwen tried to reply through a mouthful of steaming prawn and chive, but the filling was so hot that all she could do was grimace and wave. The man took several steps toward the door, then doubled back and arrived in front of her table again.

"Will you be back at the shop at all, or is that you gone forever?"

"Saturday afternoons," she told him, finally managing to swallow.

"Saturday afternoons," he repeated. "Nice." He gave her a little thumbs up and immediately looked horrified with himself, which she enjoyed.

Then he did leave, and Gwen watched him walk halfway along the street before he crossed over and doubled back on himself in the opposite direction. She watched his back retreating and shrinking until it disappeared into the squirming mass of bodies near the Tube station. Then she shifted her attention back to her noodles, which were now the ideal temperature. Iridescent bubbles of fat danced on the surface of the broth, and the yolk of her egg was bright orange and perfectly jammy. There were crispy fried onions too, and the unorthodox but not unwelcome addition of charred Brussels sprouts. Gwen felt grateful, as she chewed and slurped, that nobody else was here to talk to her, or distract her. Not just now.

Tomorrow there would be hours to fill, people to reply to—she steeled herself at the thought—and hypotheticals to worry over while she waited for Monday, and the next Monday, and for every solid Monday after that. But for now, the only admin she had to complete was eating this meal and rolling herself home afterward, both tasks comfortably within her grasp and which she was confident of performing to the highest standard.

In that moment, Gwen was glad she existed. It could have been the weather, the job, the vague but persistent feeling that she did have people who might rally round her, if she needed it, after all. But it wasn't any of those things, she concluded, holding her last dumpling up to glisten in the evening light before shoveling it into her mouth.

No. It was the dinner that did it.

# Acknowledgments

I first invented Gwendoline Grundle in 2009, during the long summer of unemployment that followed university. I say "invented"—I wrote her name down in a notebook and did nothing more about it for a decade. So thank you, firstly, to Gwen, for waiting patiently until I got my act together.

Thank you as always to my agent, Jemima Forrester, for being a tireless champion, wise counsel, and an advocate for lunches that feature three different types of cheese. I'm so glad you teased those early chapters out of me when I was content to spend lockdown regrowing leek stumps on my windowsill.

Massive thanks to my UK editor, Molly Crawford, for believing in this book from the start and guiding it so skillfully across the finish line. I'm so grateful for your beautiful mind spreadsheet—and your beautiful mind. Thank you to Sarah Jeffcoate, Jessica Barratt, and Sara-Jade Virtue at Simon & Schuster for your passion and enthusiasm, and to Gill Richardson, Maddie Allen, and Heather Hogan for all your hard work getting the book onto shelves and into hands.

I'm thrilled *The Second Chance Store* has found a home beyond the British Isles. Huge thanks to Alice Howe and the translation team at David Higham Associates; to Michelle Brower and the team at Trellis; and to my lovely international editors, Lucia Macro, Dinah Fischer, and Maria Xilouri, and their teams for making Gwen feel so welcome overseas. Thank you to Asanté Simons for all your help, and to Justine Gardner and Jeanie Lee for so skillfully translating all my Brit speak into something that makes sense across the pond.

Special thanks to all my precious early readers—Daisy, Amy, Dan, Hannah, Rose, Mum—for braving my angst, steering me in the right direction, and reassuring me that *The Second Chance Store* was a proper book after all. Thank you to my parents; to the OG chazza fiends; and to my brothers and the rest of the Bravos, Cliftons, and Brennans for all their love and support. Thanks to all my brilliant friends for cheering me on and for shutting me up when necessary. I promise none of your partners are Paul.

To Matt, who was responsible for the two best plot twists in Gwen's life and for many more than that in mine, thank you for everything.

Finally, thank you to all the staff and volunteers at Shop from Crisis, Finsbury Park, past and present, who helped inspire this story—in spirit, though not (I swear) in specifics. The hours I've spent behind the counter over the past five years have helped keep me functional.

Charity shops and thrift stores are special places, and they do so much vital work to raise funds, keep stuff out of landfills, and fill gaps in public services. But these days they're overwhelmed with more than they can sell. Please support your local stores, and that means shopping in them as well as donating to them. No used dildos, please.